EXODUS

V Plague Book Thirteen

DIRK PATTON

Dirk Patton

Text Copyright © 2017 by Dirk Patton
Copyright © 2017 by Dirk Patton

All Rights Reserved

This book, or any portion thereof, may not be reproduced or used in any manner whatsoever without the express written permission of the copyright holder or publisher, except for the use of brief quotations in a critical book review.

Published by Voodoo Dog Publishing, LLC
2824 N Power Road
Suite #113-256
Mesa, AZ 85215

Printed in the United States of America
First Printing, 2017
ISBN-13: 978-1541138940
ISBN-10: 1541138945

This is a work of fiction. Names, characters, businesses, brands, places, events and incidents are either the products of the author's imagination or used in a fictitious manner. Any resemblance to actual persons, living or dead, or actual events is purely coincidental.

Table of Contents

Also by Dirk Patton 6
Author's Note 8
1 11
2 20
3 29
4 36
5 43
6 52
7 61
8 71
9 79
10 87
11 98
12 107
13 115
14 128
15 140
16 150
17 158

18	165
19	173
20	179
21	187
22	193
23	199
24	205
25	213
26	221
27	229
28	236
29	245
30	256
31	261
32	269
33	278
34	286
35	301
36	310
37	316
38	326
39	339

Exodus

40	347
41	356
42	364
43	373
44	381
45	394
46	402
47	412
48	419
49	429
50	439
51	445
52	454
53	466

Also by Dirk Patton

The V Plague Series

Unleashed: V Plague Book 1

Crucifixion: V Plague Book 2

Rolling Thunder: V Plague Book 3

Red Hammer: V Plague Book 4

Transmission: V Plague Book 5

Rules Of Engagement: A John Chase Short Story

Days Of Perdition: V Plague Book 6

Indestructible: V Plague Book 7

Recovery: V Plague Book 8

Precipice: V Plague Book 9

Anvil: V Plague Book 10

Merciless: V Plague Book 11

Fulcrum: V Plague Book 12

Hunter's Rain: A John Chase Novella

Exodus: V Plague Book 13

Other Titles

36: A Novel

The Void: A 36 Novel

Author's Note

Thank you for purchasing Exodus, Book 13 in the V Plague series. If you haven't read the first twelve books, you need to stop reading now and pick them up, otherwise you will be utterly lost as this book is intended to continue the story in a serialized format. I intentionally did nothing to explain comments and events that reference books 1 through 12. Regardless, you have my heartfelt thanks for reading my work, and I hope you're enjoying the adventure as much as I am. As always, a good review on Amazon is greatly appreciated.

I get frequent emails from people who haven't served and are confused by the different military ranks used in my books. Don't blame me, blame the Navy. They just had to be different! To all you squids out there, I'm only kidding. But, to try and help the readers who are a little lost, here's the basics of what you need to know. I won't even try to touch enlisted ranks as each service has their own naming convention, and the confusion is mainly coming with the officer ranks.

In the Army, Marine Corps and Air Force, officer ranks are consistent. A Captain is a Captain, a Major is a Major, and so on. But, in the Navy, a Captain is equivalent to a Colonel in the other services. A Commander is a Lieutenant Colonel, a Lieutenant Commander is a Major, a Lieutenant is a Captain, a Lieutenant JG is a First Lieutenant and an Ensign is a

Second Lieutenant. So, when reading about a character who holds rank in the military, it is important to know what service they are in.

Let's compare two of the characters you will recognize, Marine Captain Black (Admiral Packard's head of security) and Navy Captain West (Admiral Packard's senior aide). Captain Black is very junior in rank to Captain West. If they were both in the Marines, it would be a Captain compared to a Colonel. If in the Navy, a Lieutenant compared to a Captain. Got it?

Also, the Captain of a ship in the Navy does not necessarily have that rank, and typically won't, though there are notable exceptions such as an aircraft carrier. An officer in command of a ship or submarine may well only have the rank of Commander, but is referred to as Captain when aboard that vessel. Clear as mud? If you want to know more, well... there's this wonderful thing called Google. Or find a friendly sailor and buy them a drink in exchange for an education.

You can always correspond with me via email at dirk@dirkpatton.com and find me on the internet at www.dirkpatton.com and follow me on Twitter @DirkPatton and if you're on Facebook, please like my page at www.facebook.com/FearThePlague .

Thanks again for reading!

Dirk Patton 2017

Dirk Patton

Life it seems, will fade away

Drifting further every day

Getting lost within myself

Nothing matters no one else

I have lost the will to live

Simply nothing more to give

There is nothing more for me

Need the end to set me free

Things are not what they used to be

Missing one inside of me

Metallica – *Fade To Black*

EXODUS

1

Retired Brigadier General Anna Thompson wanted to see the sun. To feel something other than cold, smooth concrete beneath her feet. But most of all, she wanted the caress of a breeze on her skin. Of everything about living beneath the Nevada desert, that's what she missed the most. To be able to take a deep breath that didn't have the metallic taste of the atmosphere scrubbers. But, it wasn't time yet.

With a sigh, she climbed out of bed and padded into a cramped bathroom. Relieving herself, she pulled the nightgown over her head then whipped her long hair into a tight bun before stepping into a narrow shower stall. Quickly washing her body, she closed the valve well before it would have begun beeping a thirty second countdown to shut off.

Water was a precious commodity, not to be wasted, despite the facility having its own well in addition to a state of the art reclamation plant. Once, in the first few days of her being in residence, she'd washed her hair and made the mistake of not having thoroughly rinsed it clean of shampoo before the system shut down her shower. It had taken over half of her daily allotment of drinking water to finish the job. She hadn't been happy, but the rules were the rules, and she wasn't one to violate them for her own comfort.

Exodus

Toweling off, she stepped in front of the vanity mirror and shook her thick hair loose. It tumbled down her back, framing a face that could have graced glossy fashion magazines when she was younger. Not that she was old, she reminded herself, but once a woman reaches a certain age...

With a derisive snort, she stepped back for a better inspection of her nude body in the mirror and was happy with what she saw. Forty might be behind her, but everything was still smooth and firm. Well, maybe not *quite* as smooth and firm as when she'd been a cadet at West Point, but even under her critical eye, she knew she could still turn the head of any man she wanted.

That thought creased her face with a frown of sorrow and pain. She didn't want to turn the head of any man. She wanted her husband. Wanted to see his face, hear his voice, feel his strong arms around her body. Just one more time. But, that would never happen. He had failed to arrive after the attacks that had devastated the United States.

Anna had been raised an Army brat. Her father was a Chief Warrant Officer that flew combat helicopters. Growing up during the Cold War, she and her mother had followed as the military rotated him through seemingly every posting on the planet. Born in Germany, in a US Air Force hospital, she had been twelve before ever setting foot in America.

Dirk Patton

The Soviet Union eventually fell, and without the threat of Russian armor pouring into Western Europe, the US military began downsizing. No longer needing massive fleets of attack helicopters, and the pilots to fly them, her father retired and moved his small family to Alabama. Having read the writing on the wall, he knew that America would continue to need the unique capabilities of combat helicopters, despite what the politicians were saying to the public.

A year after retiring, he had founded an aviation consulting company and soon had the US Army as his biggest client. He did well, his business growing by leaps and bounds as Washington realized the drawdown of forces had been too severe. In the Army, he had been a faceless pilot, but now he was rubbing elbows with Generals on a regular basis. It was these contacts that had paved the way for Anna to be accepted into the US Military Academy in West Point, New York.

Not that she wasn't more than qualified. Athletically and academically, she'd been an over achiever since she began elementary school. She was driven and had rarely failed to accomplish any goal she set for herself. While her resume more than qualified her for admittance to the Academy, often it mattered more who one knew. And her father's contacts opened the door for her.

Graduating near the top of her class, she began her Army career in the Quartermaster Corps. She would have preferred to be almost anything other than

Exodus

what she referred to in private as a shopkeeper, but opportunities for female officers were limited. Working hard, she advanced, and through sheer persistence, eventually wound up with the infantry. Not leading fighting men, but taking charge of the logistics and materiel command for first a division, then for the entire First Army.

As much of her job involved ensuring that all the soldiers in the First Army were properly equipped, she followed her command structure to Iraq. It was there that she'd met Sean, her future husband. A retired Army Ranger Colonel, he was working for a private military contractor (PMC).

It was love at first sight for Anna. He was everything she'd ever thought a man should be, but had so rarely found. In short, he was perfect. At least for her. She'd made sure to catch his eye, and after a brief, yet intense, romance, they married. Happier than she'd ever been, Anna was preparing to leave for her honeymoon when word came that her father had passed away of a sudden heart attack.

Sean flew to Alabama with her for support as she dealt with the small army of lawyers who were responsible for the disposition of her father's business. Her mother had passed several years earlier, and she was the sole heir to the company, which had never been taken public. She now owned one hundred percent of an aviation consulting firm, and had little idea what it really did.

Sitting down with the legal team, she was shocked to learn that the business employed well over one hundred people and had annual revenues in excess of six hundred million dollars. Her father had always been very close-mouthed about his company, even though they were close and talked often. Whenever she asked how work was going, he'd offer up a generic answer that was more of a non-answer, then turn the subject back to her career.

Taking boxes of files with them after the first meeting, Sean and Anna retreated to her father's sprawling estate. While she wandered around, looking at photos and memorabilia that were spread throughout the home, Sean began digging through the papers. Needing time to process her loss, she wound up on the porch with a mug of coffee. That's where Sean found her, several thick files in hand. Sitting down next to his wife, he began flipping through them as he told her what he'd discovered.

The US Army wasn't Thompson Aviation Consulting's only client. There was also a fat contract with the CIA. Well, not that it said Central Intelligence Agency in plain English, but he recognized the shell company that had been used by the government. There was no doubt about who was really paying the bills.

And it could only be called a *consulting* contract if one closed his eyes and let his imagination run wild. Attack aircraft were being flown on behalf of the Agency. In addition to helicopters, Anna's father had been providing military trained, retired combat pilots.

Exodus

He was cashing in on the explosion of PMCs who were being paid to fill roles which the US Government couldn't, or wouldn't.

They spent several days becoming familiar with all the company's contracts. Had meeting after meeting with the lawyers. Talked to all the senior executives who were handling the day to day operations in the absence of her father. And they spent even more time trying to figure out what to do.

Five days after they arrived in Alabama, they received an unexpected visitor. A man who identified himself as a contractor liaison for the US Government showed up at the door, asking to speak with them. While Sean entertained their guest, Anna made several calls to verify he was who he said he was.

The company lawyers knew of him by name but had never met him face to face. Apparently, all in-person negotiations had occurred solely with her father. Not one to accept the easy answer, Anna began working her contacts within the Army. It took some effort, and finding the right person, but she eventually received confirmation that the man sitting with her husband was a high-level CIA officer.

Joining them after she finished the calls, she wasn't surprised to hear the two men discussing a military operation in Somalia from several years ago. From a time when Sean was still on active duty with the Army. Their conversation ended when she walked in, and never one to mince words, she told the man she knew who he worked for and bluntly asked why he was sitting in their living room.

The man smiled and nodded, having fully expected to be vetted. Deferring to his hostess's request, he had dropped any pretense for his visit and gotten to the meat of the issue. Thompson Aviation was an integral part of several extremely sensitive agency operations around the globe, and there was concern that with the passing of her father, those same operations could be at risk. He was there to ensure that, despite the transition in ownership, it would be business as usual.

He spoke for several minutes, initially appealing to their patriotism and sense of duty. Neither were impressed, nor were they offended. This was just how things worked with the government. Anna had cut him off before he could complete his spiel. She had no intention of resigning her commission in the Army to run a company that had become a CIA front. A company with which she'd never been involved.

She also argued that she knew nothing about running combat operations. The man had nodded and smiled before looking pointedly at Sean. It had taken Anna a moment to grasp his meaning, then she quickly ended the meeting and sent their guest on his way.

They stayed up late that night, talking about their options. Despite being married to a man who earned his paycheck from a PMC, Anna had reservations about the whole idea of what she thought

Exodus

of as mercenaries operating at the behest of the US Government. She was afraid to utter that word to Sean. Didn't know how he would take it.

Falling asleep, she could feel some distance between them that hadn't been there. Sean had made it clear that he would be happy to take over the company if she wasn't interested. Told her he was ready to leave the fighting in the field to younger men. She didn't like the idea of being half a world apart, even though she would much rather have him sitting in a board room in Alabama than operating in a combat zone in Iraq or Afghanistan.

Early the next morning her Army issue cell phone rang. It was Lieutenant General Olber, Commander of the First Army. Jumping out of bed, Anna ran into an adjacent bedroom, heart in her throat. Three star Generals didn't call Lieutenant Colonels. Not unless something was seriously wrong.

General Olber's voice was tight, and he was obviously unhappy. Due to budget constraints, certain commands were being consolidated in a cost savings measure. As a result, the Army was no longer in need of Anna's service. Paperwork to initiate her immediate retirement was being messengered to Alabama and her personal possessions that were in Iraq had already been boxed and placed in transit to her.

2

General Olber had ended the call quickly, not even affording her the opportunity to ask any questions. In shock, and trying to control her anger, Anna had called everyone within her chain of command. None of her former superiors would take her call. In frustration, she'd flung the phone across the room, nearly striking Sean in the face as he walked through the door.

"What happened?" He asked, keeping his distance from the enraged woman.

"The Army just fired me!"

She began pacing, and he quickly snatched the damaged phone off the carpet before she could pick it up and throw it again.

"What? They can't just fire you without cause. It doesn't work that way!"

"I know that, Sean," she shouted. "It's forced retirement. The goddamn paperwork is already on the way!"

He stood there for a beat, looking at her and thinking.

"Fucking Christians In Action," he mumbled, shaking his head.

"What?" She cried, whirling on him with fire in her eyes. "You think the CIA did this? That asshole from last night?"

Sean shrugged.

"That would be my guess. Twelve hours after the fucker was sitting here smiling at us, this happens? Did your CO give a reason?"

"Some bullshit about budget cuts," she said, dropping onto a bed and putting her face in her hands. "And it wasn't my CO. It was General Olber."

"Personally?" Sean asked in surprise.

Anna nodded, looking up. Her eyes were damp, anger threatening to seize control of her emotions.

"There's no way a three star calls you with this news! Not if it's because of something you did. He's pissed, but this came from over his head. Him calling you, personally, was his way of apologizing and showing respect."

"What do I do?" Anna cried, jumping back to her feet.

"What can you do? The Commander of the First Army just called you. I'll bet you anything that if he could do anything about it, he would. That means this is coming out of Washington. Probably SECDEF. Someone from Langley called him and he made it happen. There is no fighting this."

Sean stepped closer and tried to pull Anna into his arms, but she was having none of it.

"What the hell is wrong with you?" She cried, pushing him away. "You just give up? Or is it because you think this means you'll get what you want? My father's company!"

Anna immediately regretted her words, but it was too late. Sean's face changed to surprise, then quickly went blank as he slammed the door on his emotions. Calmly, he placed the phone on the bed and left the room. She wanted to run after him, to apologize and beg for forgiveness, but didn't trust herself to not say something else equally as offensive.

Minutes later she heard the front door open and close, then their rental car started. Rushing to the window, she watched as Sean drove down the winding driveway, disappearing beyond a thick stand of trees.

Anna's emotions finally got the best of her. Between the death of her father, the sudden loss of her career and now her husband walking out because of something she'd said in anger, it was all too much. With a sob, she threw herself onto the bed and buried her face in the pillows.

Close to an hour later, Anna raised her head when the doorbell rang. Thinking Sean had come back and was locked out, she leapt to her feet and raced down the broad, curving staircase. But when she yanked the front door open, it wasn't her husband.

Instead, a perfectly turned out Army Sergeant Major, wearing a Class A uniform, stood at rigid attention.

"Ma'am," he greeted her.

It took Anna a moment to gather herself, having expected to see Sean.

"Sergeant Major Hennessey," she said after a longer than proper amount of time had passed. "What are you doing here?"

Her eyes flicked across his uniform blouse, briefly pausing on the ribbon that designated him as a Medal of Honor recipient. He'd earned that medal by fighting single-handedly through over twenty Al-Qaeda soldiers to rescue the crew and passengers of a downed Black Hawk helicopter. General Olber had been Colonel Olber at the time, and if not for the man standing in front of her, would not have survived that day.

"Ma'am, I boarded a transport at Ayn al-Asad Airbase nearly twelve hours ago on orders of General Olber. He pulled some strings and had me flown directly into Fort Rucker, just down the road. And, personally, I think that Air Force pilot broke some speed records."

"I'm forgetting my manners, Sergeant Major. Please, come in. I'll make some coffee."

"Thank you, ma'am," he said, stepping across the threshold. "But, if you don't mind, I'll decline the coffee. I have a return flight waiting at Rucker."

Anna gently closed the door and faced him, eyes coming to rest on the large brown envelope tightly clasped beneath his left arm. There was also a garment bag slung over his shoulder which she assumed had held his Class A during the grueling flight from the other side of the world.

"So, you're the messenger," she said, still looking at the envelope. "Kind of overkill to tell someone they're fired, don't you think?"

Sergeant Major Hennessey extended the envelope, and after a long pause, Anna took it from his hand. He surprised her when he also extended the garment bag.

"This is yours, ma'am," he said.

"Don't know why you bothered to bring me a uniform," she groused. "I won't be needing one again."

"The General thought you might like to wear it when you deliver the paperwork to BUPERS at Rucker."

He was referring to the Army's Bureau of Personnel and held the bag out, waiting, chrome hanger hooked over one finger. Anna finally took it and tossed it onto a table in the foyer.

Exodus

"I've also got a message for you from the General," he said. "A message he couldn't put in writing or say over the phone. If you understand my meaning, ma'am."

Interest piqued, Anna stared at her visitor intently, then nodded her head.

"I understand, Sergeant Major. Go ahead."

"Ma'am. The General wants you to know that this was above his pay grade. He regrets that he had no input or latitude in this matter. He also wanted me to convey to you that despite your position, you had come to his attention, and he feels you are one of the brightest and best officers he has seen in a very long time."

The man paused, and Anna couldn't help the lump of regret that was forming in her throat. Regret for having doubted the General and even more for having treated Sean the way she had.

"Thank you, Master Sergeant. And please deliver my thanks to the General."

She started to reach for the door knob, but stopped when he spoke again.

"Ma'am, there's one more thing. The General wants you to know that it's in your best interest to cooperate with the individual who visited you. This person, and the organization he works for, has a history of solving problems in a very permanent manner."

Anna was taken aback, staring with her mouth hanging open as her mind whirled.

"What does that mean?" She blurted, though she was quite sure she got the meaning.

"I'm sorry ma'am. I'm just delivering a message. I'm not privy to the details behind it."

He turned and reached for the door, stopping when Anna put her hand on his arm.

"Sergeant Major, you're privy to every detail. Don't bullshit me! What does the General know? Is there more to my father's death than what I've been told?"

Hennessey turned to face her, stepping close and looking directly into her eyes.

"Ma'am," he said in a mumble. "The message is exactly what I relayed to you. Anything beyond that would simply be assumptions that are best not discussed. Do you understand?"

They stood unmoving for close to a minute, eyes locked. Finally, Anna nodded her head and stepped back, removing her hand from Hennessey's arm.

Exodus

"Thank you for making the trip personally, Sergeant Major. And thank the General for me. Tell him I've received his message, loud and clear."

"Yes, ma'am."

The Sergeant Major let himself out, gently closing the door. Anna remained frozen in the foyer, staring at nothing as she thought about the ominous warning she'd just received. The envelope in her hand was forgotten as she imagined what might have really happened to her father.

She'd been very surprised when told he had died of a massive coronary. He had always been very healthy and worked hard to stay fit, especially as he aged. Also, he still flew, which meant regular physicals by an FAA approved physician to maintain his pilot's license. It didn't make sense that nothing had been picked up that could have caused a fatal heart attack.

Had her father gotten in too deep with the spooks? Seen or heard something he shouldn't have? Or decided he didn't like being in business with them and tried to end the relationship? Had they killed him so he could be replaced with someone more malleable? The thought chilled her to the core, but it also angered her.

She jumped in surprise when the door opened, a frightened gasp escaping her mouth before she realized it was Sean. He stood there staring at her, a box of donuts and two cups of Starbucks coffee in his hands.

Exodus

3

"Did you read this?"

Sean looked up from across the table. The donut box and empty Starbucks cups were between them. To Anna's great relief, he'd forgiven her without a second thought, dismissing her unfairly harsh comment. He hadn't been leaving in anger, just removing himself from the emotion of the moment before either of them said something that couldn't be taken back.

"What?" She asked, looking up from a scattering of crumbs that seemed to be commanding her full attention.

"Your retirement paperwork."

He pushed the detritus of their meal aside and placed a thick sheaf of bound papers in front of her. The first two-thirds of the stack was folded over, and he tapped a spot on the exposed page.

"I don't care to look at it," Anna said, reaching out to clean up the empty containers on the table.

"Yes, you do," Sean said, sharply tapping the paper.

With a sigh, Anna pushed her thick hair off her face and leaned forward to look at the bulleted section he was pointing out. She read it, then paused in confusion. Grabbing the document off the table, she reread the section several times before raising her eyes to see her husband grinning at her.

"This can't be right," she breathed. "This just doesn't happen!"

"It is right, and it did happen," Sean smiled back. "At least it will. As soon as you sign and deliver this to BUPERS."

Anna looked back at the page, slowly shaking her head.

"General Olber can't do this. He doesn't have the authority."

"Turn the page."

She did, getting another shock when she saw the signatures that approved the orders.

"This isn't possible."

She still couldn't believe what she was seeing.

"Well, that's SECDEF's signature," Sean said. "And while I'm not sure how the whole legality thing works without the President's signature, I'm willing to bet it's legit, and you've got some people who are looking out for you."

Anna flipped back a page and reread for the sixth time. Then a seventh. Turning forward, she looked at the crisp signature and date stamp.

Exodus

"I'm a Brigadier General," she whispered in amazement.

"You will be, for all of one minute, then you'll be retired," Sean said.

"But why? What the hell's the point?"

"Honey, just think about it. This whole thing stinks of Langley. The message the SarMajor delivered basically said as much. It also told you to watch your ass and don't make waves. But, if General Olber knows anything about you, he knows you aren't one to go along to get along. So, somehow, he managed to convince SECDEF to give you the one thing that's almost guaranteed to keep you safe."

"I'm not getting it. What the hell are you talking about?"

Anna was growing frustrated. The events of the past several hours had upset her, and she wasn't thinking analytically. Despite her emotional state, she was thankful Sean was with her and able to look at the situation calmly.

"You're about to become a retired one star. It doesn't matter whether you ever served in that capacity, you will forever be General Thompson. General Thompson! Think about what that does for just a moment.

"Instant credibility in political and military circles, as well as immediate respect within the civilian world. You've just inherited a multi-million dollar PMC business. Would you rather walk into a meeting as Anna, daughter of the founder and an officer of some forgotten rank in the Army, or as *General* Thompson, President and CEO?

"And, let's not forget that ominous warning from General Olber. I know you're already wondering if the CIA had your father killed. And the very fact that it's a possibility should worry you. It does me. But, as a retired General, you're much harder to touch."

"I don't understand," Anna said, calming as she thought about what Sean was saying.

"If the CIA felt you weren't playing ball, and decided it was time for you to go, do you think they'd hesitate to go after a retired Lieutenant Colonel? But, now, they've got to consider the repercussions of going after a retired *General*! Consider that for a moment.

"I know you don't operate in this world, but I do. There's an unwritten rule that anyone above the rank of Colonel is off limits. At least when it comes to permanent solutions. They might dig up something to disgrace you, but if physical harm were to come your way, or even something that appears to be natural causes, the Army is going to take a very close look at the circumstances. A closer look than the CIA would be comfortable with. General Olber has sent them a very strong, yet subtle, message. They may have gotten their way, but not with impunity."

Exodus

Anna stared at him, comprehension slowly dawning.

"You've got friends in high places," Sean said, reaching across the table and taking her hand. "A three star doesn't put a Sergeant Major on a flight around half the planet to hand deliver paperwork and a personal message unless he's trying to make a point. FedEx could've done the same job for a whole hell of a lot less."

He squeezed her hand, and after a moment she smiled and squeezed back.

"Did you check the uniform he brought?" Sean asked.

Anna's eyes opened wider in surprise. She'd forgotten all about the garment bag she'd tossed carelessly to the side. Jumping to her feet, she rushed to the foyer and snatched it up, whipping the zipper down and pulling the heavy, protective plastic to the side.

A Class A uniform was inside, but the only thing Anna could look at was the gleaming star on each epaulet. Sean came up behind her and circled his arms around her waist, hugging her gently.

"You're going to outrank me," he whispered in her ear, giving it a nuzzle.

"As it should be," she said, turning and giving him a kiss.

The emotions of the morning fueled their passion, and soon clothing was being shed as they stumbled into the living room and fell onto the closest sofa. Two hours later, freshly showered and wearing her new uniform, Anna descended the stairs. Sean was standing in the foyer, waiting, and as she approached he snapped to attention and executed a parade ground perfect salute, despite trying to contain his smile.

"Cut it out," Anna grumbled.

"What's the matter?"

"I was thinking about my dad while I was getting ready," she said, turning to check her appearance in a mirror. "Wondering if I'm paranoid or if the CIA really had something to do with his death. I wish he hadn't been cremated. I'd have his body exhumed and reexamined."

"You're not paranoid," Sean said.

Anna, patting her hair into place, paused with her hands held on either side of her head and met his eyes in the mirror.

"I don't mean that I know something," Sean said quickly. "But, you're not paranoid if the possibility of something occurring is real. I think it might be a good idea to get a copy of the autopsy report."

Anna resumed fussing with her hair, turning to face her husband when she was satisfied.

"After BUPERS, let's go by the medical examiner's office," she said. "I'll go in uniform. We'll see if this star carries any weight in the civilian world."

Sean shook his head.

"I'll go," he said. "No reason to draw that kind of attention."

She thought about that for a moment before nodding.

"We've only got one car. How do you want to do this?"

"We've got two. I made a call while you were in the shower and Thompson Aviation promptly brought over a company vehicle for their new CEO. Didn't your dad have a car? The garage is empty."

"No," Anna said, chuckling. "Dad flew helicopters into combat, but he didn't like to drive. As soon as he started making enough money, he sold his car and hired a driver. He always said the odds were higher of dying in a vehicle accident than a chopper crash, but if he had to use a car it was safer in the back seat than behind the wheel."

Sean considered that for a moment, but kept his opinion to himself.

"I'll take the rental," he finally said, leaning forward to kiss his wife on the cheek.

4

When Anna arrived home, she was surprised to see Sean waiting for her in the courtyard. He was leaned against the front fender of their rental, arms crossed as he watched her approach. It wasn't until she stepped out of her vehicle that she noticed the pistol holstered at his hip.

"Let's take a walk," he said, pushing upright and taking her hand.

"What's…"

"Shhhhh," he interrupted her.

After looking around to make sure they were alone, Anna allowed him to lead her around the side of the house. A hundred yards away, an old barn squatted in a neatly mown field and Sean headed directly for it. The ground was soft from a recent rain, and she had to pause and remove her low-heeled uniform shoes which were sinking deep into the muck with each step.

In the barn, Sean closed the door behind them and walked to an ancient tractor parked in the middle of the open space. Reaching up, he pressed the starter button and the engine clattered to life with a roar and belch of blue smoke. Once it was settled into a noisy idle, he came to stand close to Anna. Even then, he had to raise his voice to be heard over the clattering racket of the old motor.

Exodus

"So, I don't think you're paranoid," he said. "We need to be careful what we say and where we say it."

"What happened?"

"I went to the medical examiner's office. Talked to a nice lady who helped me fill out a request and took my ten dollars for a copy of your dad's autopsy. Only problem was, when she went to print out the report, the file was corrupted."

"Corrupted? What do you mean, corrupted?"

"Exactly that. It wouldn't print. Wouldn't even open to view it on the computer. It's there, you can see the file name, but it's unusable."

"What are the odds of that?" Anna asked.

"I'm not a computer guy, so I've got no idea. But I did ask the lady how often that happens, and she said it never has before. She tried a couple of other reports that were created the same day, and they're just fine."

"The CIA!"

"Maybe. Maybe not. So, I asked her if I could speak with the examiner that performed the autopsy. Had to wait for a bit, but got in to see him. He claims he doesn't really remember it, even though it was only a few days ago. Said that means there wasn't anything suspicious, because he'd remember that. He was lying."

"How do you know that?"

"Because I never asked if there was anything suspicious. I just asked if he remembered performing the autopsy. Nothing else. He offered up the rest before I could ask another question. And, he's scared. He was nervous. I'm kind of surprised he even agreed to talk to me."

"Son of a bitch! I knew it!" Anna fumed.

"Hold on, that's not all," Sean said, placing a restraining hand on her shoulder. "I was followed, too."

The anger vanished from her face, replaced by fear.

"Followed? Are you sure?"

"Sure as I can be." Sean nodded emphatically. "Saw the same car twice on the way there. A lane over and a hundred yards back. Didn't think much of it until it was there again on my drive home. Stopped at a Home Depot and went in and wandered around for ten minutes, just to see. When I came back out and got on the road, there he was. Whoever it was is damn good. If I hadn't been trained on counter-surveillance, I don't think I would have spotted him."

"You think they're going to come after us?"

Anna was frightened, but also angry.

"I don't know, but I don't think so. At least not now. If I had to guess, I'd say they're just keeping an eye on us. You were probably followed today, too. And, it wouldn't surprise me to find out the house is bugged."

"What do we do?"

"That depends," Sean answered. "What do you want to do? Do you want your dad's company, or do you want to let the suits run it until you can sell and cash out?"

"I have to think about it," Anna said after a long pause. "What if we just walk away?"

"We can do whatever we want. I've got my retirement, and you've got a Brigadier General's pension. We don't have to worry about money. Say the word, and we can hit the road. Maybe get some property up in the woods somewhere and settle down. No more war zones or spooks or any of the other shit."

Anna looked into his eyes for nearly a minute before shaking her head.

"No! That's not us. We'd be bored out of our minds inside a week. Besides, if these fuckers killed my dad, I want justice. We're going to do exactly what they want. Lull them into thinking we're good little soldiers. Once they believe we're towing the line, we can start digging. Very carefully. We'll find something to nail them to the goddamn wall!"

Sean didn't answer, and Anna took his hand in hers.

"What? You want to run?"

"No," he said. "It's not that. I just hope you understand what you're getting into, climbing in bed with the CIA. These guys are good, especially in covering their tracks. We may never find the evidence you want, and by then it will be too late. We'll be so far in they'll never let us go. They will own us."

Anna released his hand and began pacing around the barn. The air was getting thick with the exhaust from the tractor, but neither of them was willing to shut down the engine. If the CIA was trying to listen in, there was no way their voices could be heard over the roaring clatter.

"I'm staying!" Anna finally declared with finality. "I'm sorry you got dragged into this. If you want out, I'll understand. This isn't how a marriage is supposed to start."

Tears sprang up in her eyes as she said the last. Sean smiled, shook his head and pulled her tight into his arms.

"You're not getting rid of me that easy," he said, grunting when she squeezed him hard enough to cause his back to pop in several places. "Now, let's get out of here before we asphyxiate ourselves. I need to make some phone calls."

"Thank you," she mumbled into his chest.

"By the way, are you OK with me hiring some new company employees? They don't come cheap, but they're worth every penny."

Anna stepped back and gave him a curious look.

"Trust me," he said.

After a moment, she nodded, then dried her eyes and reflexively tugged at her uniform to ensure it was hanging properly on her body. Sean shut the tractor down, the sudden absence of the harsh sound a physical relief. Hand in hand, they walked slowly back to the house, enjoying the fresh air after breathing exhaust fumes for so long. Rounding the corner into the courtyard, Sean paused and placed his hand on the butt of his pistol when they spotted a strange vehicle parked next to the rental car.

Looking around, no one was in sight, and he motioned for Anna to stay where she was. Drawing the weapon, he slowly advanced and checked each of the cars. They were empty. The sound of the front door opening snapped their heads around, and Sean aimed his pistol at the man who emerged through the front door.

"Dad?"

Sean forgot his training and took his attention off target to stare at his wife when she called out.

"Hi, Pumpkin."

The man smiled and nodded.

"Dad!"

Sean lowered the weapon as Anna raced forward into her father's arms.

"Well, come on inside," he called to Sean. "Swept the place while you two were playing with the farm equipment. There's no one listening."

5

"What the hell is going on?" Anna demanded.

She was seated across the kitchen table from her father. Sean had decided to slightly remove himself from the situation and had gone outside to use his phone. As far as he was concerned, the sudden appearance of the man they'd thought was dead didn't change anything.

"I faked it," her father said, shrugging his shoulders and giving her a lopsided grin. "Sorry, Pumpkin."

"Don't call me that!" Anna snapped.

"I'm sorry, Pump... Anna."

"You'd better start explaining," she said, eyes flashing with anger.

"It's a long story."

"I've got nowhere else to be," Anna said sarcastically. "Speaking of which, where the hell have you been?"

"Hotel in New Orleans under a false name," he said. "It really is a marvelous city. You and that young man out there should consider it for your honeymoon."

"We were going to New York, but instead we've been here because we thought you were dead. Now, enough bullshit, Dad! What the hell is going on?"

He paused and looked around when the door opened and Sean walked in. Standing, he extended his hand and smiled.

"My daughter really does have impeccable manners," he said, taking Sean's hand. "But she's a little distraught at the moment and neglected to introduce us. I'm Bill Thompson."

"Sean Thompson," Sean shook the proffered hand and moved away to lean against the kitchen counter.

"I must say, that has to be quite convenient," Bill grinned, resuming his seat. "Marrying a woman with the same last name. Saves a lot of mess, as long as she doesn't decide to hyphenate. Anna Thompson – Thompson. Does have a bit of a ring to it, don't you think?"

Anna slapped the table top so hard it sounded like a gunshot.

"Enough! This isn't charming, and it isn't funny! Start talking right now or I'm walking out that door, and you'll not see me again!"

Bill, still smiling, looked over at Sean as he pointed at his daughter.

Exodus

"She said the same thing when she was fifteen and her mother and I wouldn't let her go out with a boy we didn't like." He turned to face Anna. "What was his name, by the way? I always just thought of him as Mr. Foreskin."

"Dad. I swear to you; I've been through enough in the past week. I know you like to use thirty words when two will do the job, but I'm out of patience. I'm not kidding! I'm ready to leave if you're going to keep playing games."

"Settle down," he said, making a calming gesture with his hands. "You're just like your dear departed mother. Always right to business and no time to visit. OK, fine. I guess I can see why you're a little upset."

"A little?" Anna very nearly screamed.

Sean stepped forward and sat down next to her, taking her trembling hand.

"Bill, I think you'd better fill us in," he said in a low, patient voice.

"Right. Sorry. I do get carried away with the sound of my own voice sometimes. So, where to start?"

"How about answering a question," Sean spoke before Anna could explode again. "Are you hiding from the CIA?"

Bill looked at him for a beat before breaking into laughter.

"Oh, my goodness, is that what you two think? No, no, no. I work for the CIA. Have for years. Ever since I got out of the Army, for that matter. They're the ones that financed the start of my company."

"I don't understand," Sean said, risking a glance at Anna. For the moment, she seemed satisfied to let him ask the questions. "If you work for the CIA, why were you hiding? Why did you fake your death?"

"Because there's some of us that are worried about what's coming. We needed to do some things, and we needed the two of you here."

"What things?" Anna asked when it was apparent Bill was waiting for a prompt before he would continue.

"Russia's on the rise, again. So are the Chinese. And, there are elements within the CIA and DOD that are happy about that. They want nothing more than to see us return to the days of the Cold War. Unlimited funding, nearly unchecked power to run around the globe and do whatever they want. As long as it was couched in terms of being necessary to counter communist aggression, they pretty much got to do whatever they wanted.

"Get rid of a third world dictator and install a new leader that would let the Agency in? No problem. Withhold intelligence that could have stopped something horrible until it's too late? They have no qualms about it. As long as their end game is successful, and it usually is."

"What end game?" Sean asked.

"Why, money and power, of course! What else is there for men and women like this? They've determined the outcome of every US election for decades. Hell, Nixon was the last President that was actually elected by the people. Ever since, it's been someone that was weak and could be controlled to further their agenda, or was actually one of them.

"But, they're going too far. Getting in bed with the Russian mafia and the Chinese government. We don't know what they're planning, but it can't be good. Not for the American people."

"What are we talking about? A coup?" Anna asked, the earlier anger still simmering in her voice.

"No, no. Nothing so pedestrian. Besides, that's already happened. Just no one knows it. Not unless the media tells them, and the media isn't going to tell anyone anything that their masters don't want to get out."

"Then what?"

Bill took a deep breath and let out a low sigh.

"So, my company does a lot of clandestine work. We're kind of like Air America was in Vietnam, only we don't transport drugs. We take agents and spec ops forces in and out of places they aren't supposed to be. Places that the US Government would categorically deny we've ever been in. But, that's not all.

"Occasionally we are used to move cargo around inside the continental US. CONUS. Not long distances, mind you. Helicopters aren't made for that. But if you've got something that needs to go a couple of hundred miles without the risk of it being interdicted by the police or anyone on the ground... well, that's where we come in.

"So, about six months ago, we get this big job. Eight pieces of cargo, heavy cargo, that was to be picked up from this abandoned military bunker in the middle of Nowhere, Pennsylvania and flown into New York City. Now, this was kind of unusual."

"What was unusual?" Sean asked. "You said you move cargo around within our borders."

"Right. But never *into* a metropolitan area. Almost always from one hick, backwoods area to another. You know. Locations that are hardly a dot on the map, if even that. The kind of places the Pentagon and Langley like to use because there aren't any prying eyes in the neighborhood. A few times from a city out to the sticks, but never the other way around.

"So, this gets my antenna up and twitching, let me tell you. I'm already hearing rumors about some of the shit that's going on with Russia and China, then this. What the hell needs to be in New York that is so sensitive it can't go by truck? And, I start thinking about possibilities and don't care too much for the answers I'm coming up with."

"Which are?" Anna asked.

"Scary. Let's leave it at that for the moment. Well, I didn't like the idea of sending my boys out there to do something like this, so I decided to tag along. All our heavy lift birds were out of the country, but we had some Bell 407s that could do the job, so off we go with three of them.

"I gotta tell you, picking up that cargo in Pennsylvania was like something out of the movies. We landed and were immediately surrounded by heavily armed men. Pretty sure they were PMCs working for the Agency, but can't prove that. They wouldn't let us get out of the birds. Put blackout hoods over our heads so we couldn't see what was going on. Brought their own team out that fueled us while the cargo was loaded by more of them. We were just bus drivers.

"Well, they get us all loaded, and we're about to take off when three clean-cut young gentlemen come running up and get on board each chopper. Didn't need to see ID to know they were fresh off the Farm at Langley and were there to make sure we didn't mess with the cargo.

"So, we take off, and it's a little over an hour-and-a-half into New York. It was already arranged that we would land at three different heliports. The bird I was in went to downtown Manhattan. Landed at 0330. Raining like hell, but there's a dozen more of these armed PMCs waiting to greet us.

"They hooded us, got us unloaded, then all of them disappear into the night without so much as a wave. But, like I said, something about this whole job had bothered me from the very beginning, so I'd done a little prep work. Once we'd gotten back out of the city and joined up with the rest of our flight, I checked the instrument I'd hidden in the back. You know what a gamma sniffer is?"

Sean went still as a stone when the question was asked, as had Bill. Anna looked between them, concern on her face.

"What's a gamma sniffer?" She asked when neither man said anything.

"Detects gamma rays," Sean said without taking his eyes off Bill. "One of the signatures of a nuclear warhead."

Bill nodded slowly as Anna's mouth fell open in shock.

"You transported nuclear warheads into New York City?" She blurted.

"Possibly. Probably," Bill said, looking at her. "There are other things that emit gamma radiation, none of them good, but if I had to bet I'd say that cargo was eight nukes. Old, cold war era ones, too, because they were heavy as hell."

"Are you crazy?" She shouted. "What have you done? Did you call the FBI or Homeland Security?"

He just looked at her and shook his head.

"What the hell is wrong with you?" She was on her feet, leaning across the table. "You have to tell someone!"

"I tried," Bill said. "Now, sit down and quit all that shouting and I'll tell you the rest."

6

"Who did you go to?" Sean asked when Anna had calmed down and taken her seat.

"First thing is, I called the FBI. Didn't tell them anything on the phone, just said I was coming in with some potentially vital information. Had an appointment set with a specific agent. That was here in Alabama. Birmingham. Anyways, I showed up right on time and was taken into a conference room.

"Couple of guys in suits were waiting for me, but not the agent I had talked to on the phone. Seems he'd been suddenly reassigned right after my call. They weren't interested in asking why I was there, just informed me that my company and I were about to come under investigation for trading with foreign powers. That there was a very good chance I'd wind up in federal prison."

"What did you do?" Anna asked.

"Got the hell out of there as soon as they finished threatening me. Went back to my hotel and booked the next flight to Washington D.C. Was going to walk right into the Hoover building and tell my story. When I got to the airport and went to check in, the airline had no record of my reservation. Before I could do anything, the same two guys from the FBI office walked up, slapped cuffs on me and hustled me out of there. Thought for sure they were gonna kill me.

Exodus

"They took me back to my hotel room. Guy from the CIA I'd run across a couple times in the past was sitting there, waiting for me. Some smug asshole that likes Hawaiian shirts and straw hats. Calls himself Delker. Pretty sure he used to be an operator. Sure has the look. Anyway, the FBI thugs uncuff me and leave me there alone with him. Didn't know whether to kick his ass or run, but he shut me down with one sentence."

"What was that?" Sean asked.

"First words out of his mouth. And that's all it took," Bill lowered his eyes and stared at the table. "Stop what you're doing, or I'll kill your daughter."

The kitchen was silent for several long seconds, Bill finally looking back up at Anna.

"I wasn't going to risk that," he said. "Not for nothing. They can have New York, as long as they don't hurt my baby girl."

"Dad," Anna said but didn't continue.

"Don't 'Dad' me, young lady," he said. "You may be a grown woman, but you're still my pumpkin. Always will be. No way am I going to let them hurt you."

"What else did he say?" Sean asked, getting the conversation back on topic.

"Said that if he and I ever met again, he'd be delivering sad news about my little girl. Reminded me that Iraq is a very dangerous place, even in supposed secure areas, and that being an officer in the Army is an inherently dangerous occupation. That's how the smug cocksucker put it. *Inherently dangerous occupation.* Well, I got the message loud and clear."

"So you just gave up?" Anna asked, a note of disappointment in her voice.

"Don't use that tone with me, young lady! Your dear mother mastered it, and you don't hold a candle to her in that department. And, to answer your question, have you ever, in your life, known of me to give up? Where do you think you got that goddamn bullheaded, stubborn drive that put you at the top of your class at West Point?"

Anna nodded, keeping her mouth shut.

"It's taken almost a year to get to where we are today. I found people within the Agency that I could trust. Really knew I could trust. And there weren't very damn many of them. You met one the other day. And, there's a couple more, but that's it.

"You gotta remember. All these men have families, too. People they love and care about. There wasn't anything we could do. No one we could go to. There was no evidence. No proof. Just my word, which wouldn't be enough when push came to shove. So, we started prepping."

"Prepping. For what?" Anna asked.

Exodus

"Pumpkin, haven't you been listening? You don't sneak eight nukes into New York City unless there's a plan to use them. And when that day comes, what do you think's gonna happen to this country? Blow it up and what happens to the rest of us? Wall Street gone. The Federal Reserve. Thousands of major corporations are headquartered there.

"Let me tell you, if New York City were wiped off the map, this country would very quickly devolve into chaos like no one has imagined. So, we all got together and started making plans. If we can't stop this, and frankly I'm surprised every day when I wake up and it hasn't already happened, then we have to survive it.

"We've been building for close to a year in an abandoned silver mine out in the Nevada desert. Getting ready. Stocking it. And we finally finished a couple of weeks ago."

"How did you manage to keep all that work hidden from the government?" Sean asked.

"Wasn't easy. But, as far as we can tell, we succeeded. That whole thing right there is a longer story than you probably want to hear."

"Dad," Anna interrupted. "We've got to go tell your story. Someone will listen! I'm not going to run and hide in the desert while my country is attacked!"

Bill shook his head sadly after she finished speaking.

"Who we gonna tell, Anna? Who will listen to a man who faked his own death? I'm old. Easy to write off as a crank, especially without any proof. You think I'm happy about this? OK with it? Not by a long shot, missy! But, I'm also realistic. Making waves will only get you and your husband killed. I don't care about me, but I do care what happens to you."

"No!" Anna was back on her feet, eyes flashing. "I will NOT sit by and let this happen. There's got to be a way. I know some Generals that can get to SECDEF. That's only a step away from the Oval Office. Hell, Dad, I'm a General! Let's go to the media! We'll make such a stink that they won't dare touch us."

Sean was shaking his head and Anna whirled on him in anger.

"What?" She shouted.

"Your dad's right," he said. "Without proof, no one is going to listen. You'll be characterized as a bitter ex-Army officer who was forced to retire because she couldn't get along with her peers. Something along those lines. And your dad? Legally, he's a dead man. The press would have a field day with that one. And me? I'm a PMC. To most people, that's just another word for mercenary, and if we're being honest, that's what it comes down to."

"Then I'll call General Olber!"

Exodus

"No one else will take your calls, what makes you think he will? He sent a personal emissary to deliver a message. He's not only trying to help you, but he's also letting you know that he's done everything he can. You'll never be able to speak with him."

Anna stared at the two men for half a minute before spinning on her heel and marching out of the room. Seconds later, the front door slammed hard enough to rattle every dish in the kitchen cabinets. Sean started to get up to follow her, but Bill placed a hand on his arm.

"Let her cool down," he said. "She's a good woman, but has her mother's temper. Just needs to think it through and she'll be fine."

Sean sank back into his chair with a sigh.

"What about the gamma sniffer?" He asked. "We carried them all over the place in Iraq, looking for Saddam's WMDs. The one I used had a built-in GPS and logged everywhere it went. That would be proof."

"Stolen out of my house when I was in Birmingham," Bill said. "And, I'm sure there's no record of those flights having landed in New York."

"Anyone check?"

Bill shook his head.

"No. We didn't see much point. I know the way things work. They didn't have to worry about deleting records. There weren't any created in the first place. I didn't file any flight plans and never talked to an air controller. None of my boys did. We were ghosts in the night, and there's no way to prove a ghost paid a visit."

"Why did you fake your death?" Anna asked, surprising them. Neither had heard her come back in.

"To get you home," Bill answered. "And to take the heat off of you. If they think I'm dead, they'll believe they can control you, and you're no longer in danger."

"You were behind her forced retirement, weren't you?" Sean asked.

"Had to make sure you stayed, once you got here," Bill said, unable to meet Anna's glare.

"That was you?" Anna cried. "How could you? Do you know what you've done? If you'd just called, I'd have come home! You could have told me all this, and I'd still be in a position to do something. What were you thinking, Dad?"

Bill stared at his hands, unable to meet her accusing gaze.

"General Olber knows," he mumbled.

"What?" Anna whispered, stunned.

"He knows," Bill said, looking up. "I told him everything."

Exodus

"Then why isn't he doing something?" She shouted.

"He's trying, Pumpkin. He's trying. But this is happening way above his pay grade, and he doesn't have any proof. He has to be very careful what he does with the information."

"You keep saying you have no proof," Sean interrupted before Anna could continue. "How did you get him to believe you? Why would he trust you?"

"Back when I was a Chief Warrant Officer in the Army, there was a young, wet behind the ears, second lieutenant that wanted to be a helicopter pilot worse than anyone I've ever seen. Smart as a whip and determined as hell. Kind of like your wife, there. Well, I was working a rotation as an instructor when Lieutenant Olber was accepted into the training program.

"He was a rising star, that much was obvious. But, the man's got no sense of up and down, right or left. No depth perception. At least not the kind you need to fly. He aced the classroom work. First person to ever do that, and probably still the only one. But, he flew like a pregnant albatross. No matter how hard he worked, you can't overcome that kind of innate deficit.

"But, he was doing just good enough to not wash out of the program. Don't get me wrong, he'd never fly in combat or even combat support, but he might have been able to ferry birds from point A to B, or maybe perform maintenance test flights. Unfortunately, it never got that far.

"He and I were up on a training flight. Simple stuff. Take off, ascend to five hundred feet, hover, then land. Easy. Only it wasn't for him. He did fine getting us in the air and holding a hover, but came down way too fast. By the time I could take control, it was too late. We hit the tarmac in a belly flop that bent the airframe.

"My fault, really. I wasn't paying close enough attention, even though I knew he wasn't up to snuff. So, I told him to keep his mouth shut and resign from the program. Then, I lied and took the blame for the crash. You see, I was within a year of retirement and knew the black mark wouldn't hurt me. But, if it had gone into his record, well, he wouldn't be where he is today. Probably wouldn't even still be in the Army.

"So, you ask why he trusts me? I've never asked him for a thing in return until now. I could have paved the way for Anna, and he knows it, but I didn't. Everything she got, she earned on her own. He understands this. That's why."

7

"Aren't you worried about them coming after you, now that you've surfaced?" Sean asked.

Bill shook his head, stood up and walked over to a liquor cabinet. He bent to peer at the selection, finally picking a squat bottle of whiskey. Grabbing three glasses, he tilted his head at an exterior door.

"Let's continue this on the porch," he said.

"Sure that's a good idea?" Sean asked, pointing at the ceiling as he raised his eyebrows questioningly. "Easy to listen in from a UAV these days."

Bill chuckled and worked the knob with his elbow.

"Think I don't know all about drones, sonny? Got a microwave emitter on the roof. They don't hear shit I don't want them to hear."

With a nod, Sean stood to follow him outside, but Anna grabbed his hand and pulled him close.

"Sean, we've got to do something! Unless Dad's gone completely around the bend, there are eight nuclear warheads somewhere in New York City. We've got to tell someone who can mobilize the Nuclear Emergency Search Team."

"Honey, who do we tell? There's a three-star General, the commander of the entire First Army, that knows. You think he can't pick up the phone and talk to either SECDEF or the Chairman of the Joint Chiefs whenever he feels like it? Either of those two can get in to see the President with one phone call."

"Then the media. I agree with Dad that they're in the politicians' pockets, but there's got to be a reporter we can find that will listen!"

"Listen to what? A second-hand story without a shred of evidence to back it up? There's not a reporter that would be listened to that would take us seriously. Besides, you know as well as I do that since 9/11, New York is blanketed with radiation detectors. Why do you think they aren't screaming an alarm?"

Anna stared at him, obviously not having considered that little nugget.

"There are only two possible answers," Sean continued when she didn't say anything. "One; your dad is off his rocker, and this entire story is just that. A story. But, he seems perfectly lucid to me. I believe what he's saying, for what it's worth."

"What's the second possibility?" Anna asked, nodding in agreement with Sean's assessment of her father.

"There's someone out there with enough juice to have had the detectors shut down or ignored when they went into alarm. You think about that kind of power for a minute. Come up with a viable plan of action that has a reasonable chance of success, and I'm with you one hundred percent. But, until then, we can't tip our hand. If we do, we won't live long enough to try and stop this."

Sean held her eyes with his for several seconds before leaning close and gently kissing her.

"I want to do something, too, but it has to be the right thing at the right time. We'll get one shot at this. That's it. We can't go charging in without thinking this through. Now, let's go see what else your dad has to say, then we can start working on some ideas to stop these fuckers."

He gave her one of his lopsided smiles, and after a minute she took a deep breath and returned it, allowing him to lead her out onto a broad patio. Bill was waiting for them, reclined in a plush lounge chair with a glass of whiskey in his hand. He looked up as they walked out the door.

"You two decide I'm not some tin foil hat wearing, conspiracy theorist?"

"Something like that," Sean smiled.

He poured a finger of whiskey for himself and Anna, passed her one of the glasses and sat down facing Bill.

"So, you didn't answer me earlier," he began. "Aren't you worried about them coming after you?"

"They aren't looking for me, and as long as I don't do anything stupid, they won't know I'm still kicking."

"Would something stupid be like following me all over town this morning?" Sean asked. "I recognized the car in the courtyard."

Bill grinned and shrugged his shoulders.

"Didn't know you spotted me until you went into that Home Depot. Thought I was better than that."

"You're good, but my training's probably a little more current," Sean said, letting the old man off easy. "But, that still doesn't make me feel better. How are you confident there's not a CIA hit team on the way here right now?"

"Anything's possible, but I've got people in the right places to give me a heads up, and I haven't heard anything from them."

"Yet," Anna said.

"Yet," Bill echoed her comment.

"So, where do we go from here, Bill?" Sean asked.

"Nevada, of course. I already told you, the facility is ready. It's stocked and manned. Just waitin' for its General."

"You're not coming?" Anna asked, the whiskey glass in her hand still untouched.

Bill shook his head.

"Soon as I know you're safe, I've got my own plans. That's where you come in, young man."

"Me?" Sean asked in surprise. "What do you need from me?"

Bill drained his glass and made a production of pouring another two fingers of whiskey before answering.

"Despite my daughter's poor opinion of me," he began. "There is actually something I'm going to do that just might upset their apple cart."

"Dad, I didn't…"

Bill smiled and held up his hand to stop her.

"I know, Pumpkin. I was just poking you a little bit. So, as I was saying, I've got an idea. There's one person I know of who probably has all the details about where those warheads wound up and what the plan for them is. But, he presents some problems. It isn't going to be easy to get to him, and it's going to be even more difficult to get him to talk."

"Who are you talking about?" Sean asked, starting to get an idea of what Bill had in mind.

"That Agency prick, Delker. The one that threatened Anna's life. What I'm thinking is we scoop him up and squeeze him until we get the info. Once we've got some actionable intelligence, General Olber is on board with doing whatever needs to be done."

"What do you mean by that?" Anna asked in surprise.

"Doing what's necessary to stop this before New York starts glowing in the dark. He's got the men and resources. Sure, it's going to be dangerous as hell, but when the time comes, he's ready to do what needs doing."

"You're talking about the United States Army operating within our borders without Presidential or Congressional authorization! That can't happen!" Anna exclaimed.

"Can and will," Bill said, nodding.

"Why hasn't he gone to SECDEF and POTUS with this?" Sean asked, forestalling Anna's horror at the thought of what amounted to an armed insurrection by the military.

"You know they can be trusted?" Bill asked pointedly.

"You can't believe that!" Anna said.

Exodus

"Pumpkin," Bill answered patiently. "As we've already discussed, there's someone with one hell of a lot of juice behind this. They've managed to co-opt the CIA and the FBI. They're pulling strings like a puppet master. I'm not saying that the White House is involved, but at the moment they can't be ruled out. What we've got to worry about is getting the info we need for General Olber to take action. The rest will sort itself out, as long as we can get those nukes off the playing field."

"What do you need from me?" Sean asked before Anna could continue to protest.

"Muscle," Bill chuckled. "That's the one thing my friends and I don't have. "Trained, military muscle. Got pilots coming out of my ears, but no one that can go toe to toe when the time comes. Figure you know some guys that would be happy to help out. If they need to be paid, I've got plenty of money, so that's not a problem."

"You've thought this through pretty well, haven't you?" Sean asked, a note of admiration in his voice. "If I didn't know better, I'd think you had something to do with Anna and I meeting and falling in love."

Bill threw his head back and laughed.

"I'm good, young man, but I'm not that good! That was just a fortunate circumstance."

"So, we snatch this Delker character and get him to tell us what we need to know. That pretty much it?" Sean asked.

"In a nutshell, yes. One of my associates is keeping tabs on him, so we'll know right where to find him when the time comes."

"Sean," Anna said, drawing her husband's attention. "This is crazy. Kidnap a CIA officer? Then what? Torture him until he talks? There has to be another way!"

Sean didn't answer. Didn't know what to say to his wife. He didn't like the idea, even if there wasn't another one. But, she was right. Forcing someone to reveal information wasn't like it was in the movies. You didn't just hit them in the face a couple of times and cause all their secrets to come spilling out. It could take weeks, or even months if the subject was a true believer in their cause, and then you couldn't trust what they told you until it was independently verified.

"Bill, do you have any idea how much time we have?" Sean asked.

"None. We could have minutes, or it could be months. But, those warheads were delivered a year ago. Don't know what they're waiting for. That's one of the first things we need to find out."

Sean was nodding his head before Bill finished speaking.

Exodus

"I'm in," he said firmly.

"Sean! We need to discuss this!" Anna cried.

"I think that's my cue to step inside," Bill said, getting to his feet.

Sean met Anna's eyes, his heart breaking when he saw her tears.

"Black Hawk coming fast," Bill said.

His head was tilted to the side, eyes closed as he listened to a sound that hadn't registered with the two younger people. Anna leapt to her feet, fear on her face as she imagined a load of CIA killers bearing down on them.

"My men," Sean said calmly, glancing at his watch. "Right on time, too."

He looked up and met Anna's questioning glare.

"The call I made earlier." He shrugged. "Thought we could use some firepower around us."

"How did they get here so fast?" Anna asked.

"This team was in Georgia. They were getting ready to head back to Afghanistan, but I've got enough authority to shuffle schedules around, so I re-tasked them and sent a different one overseas."

Less than a minute later, an unmarked Black Hawk helicopter screamed over the roof and banked sharply to bleed off speed before settling onto the grassy field between the house and barn. The side door was already open and eight men wearing black tactical clothing with rifles slung down their backs jumped out. Sean stood and raised a hand in greeting.

"Better get your checkbook, Bill. These guys are the best, and they don't come cheap."

8

Sean left the porch to greet the men, leaving Anna standing next to her father.

"That there's what I was talking about," he said with a grin. "You do know your hubby is quite the badass, don't you Pumpkin?"

"Never heard a story from him, but I asked around. Probably don't know as much as you, but I know enough."

"Everything I could find out, he's a good man. Unless you're a bad guy," Bill said. "Then, all bets are off."

"Dad?"

"Yes, Pumpkin?"

"*Did* you have anything to do with us getting married?"

Bill didn't answer immediately. They stood there and watched as Sean approached each man, greeting him with a handshake and quick, rough hug. Once the pleasantries were out of the way, they gathered in a tight circle with Sean in the center, listening intently to what he had to say.

"Well? Did you?" Anna asked when Bill remained quiet.

"I might have pulled some strings to make sure you two bumped into each other. After that, nature took its course. Would have been sorely disappointed if you'd kept your nose in the air and not given him a chance."

"What the hell does that mean?" Anna asked, smiling despite herself.

"You're just like your mother. You have no idea how hard I had to work to get her to notice me. Then, it was next to impossible to get her to go out with me. She was always walking around like I wasn't worth her time. But, in the end, I wore her down."

Anna chuckled and shook her head.

"What?" Bill asked.

"Mom told me the story years ago, Dad. She fell in love with you at first sight. Decided right then and there she was going to marry you. But, she wanted you to work for it. She always said you appreciate something much more if you earn it."

"Your mother could be a bit of bitch."

Bill smiled and wiped away a tear that had formed as he thought about his wife.

"Where do you think I got it?" Anna asked, taking her father's hand in hers.

Exodus

They fell silent as Sean broke away from the group and led the men towards the patio. He joined them, the heavily armed soldiers forming a loose rank and watching. None of them failed to notice the Brigadier General, and there were a few raised eyebrows and murmured exchanges amongst them.

"Five hundred K. Each," Sean said, looking at Bill.

"They know what they're getting into?" He asked.

"They know. This will be retirement money for all of them. They've been doing this shit for a while."

"Do you have four and half million dollars, Dad?" Anna asked.

"Four," Sean interjected before Bill could answer. "I don't want your money."

Bill looked at his son-in-law and smiled before turning to stage whisper to Anna.

"Told you he was a keeper!"

Sean briefly looked away, but not before Anna could see him blush.

"And, yes, I've got the money," Bill continued. "I'd like to meet them before I start writing checks, if that's alright."

Sean nodded and moved out onto the grass, Bill following. Anna stayed where she was, suddenly very self-conscious about the uniform she was wearing. Starting with the man closest to him, Sean began the introductions.

They moved down the line, Bill pausing in front of the next to the last man. He frowned as he stared at the powerfully built soldier with bulging biceps and hair hanging below his shoulders.

"Something wrong, esse?" The man growled.

"Not at all," Bill said. "Forgive me. You just look familiar."

"Cause he looks like that ugly fucker from the vampire movie with George Clooney," a tall man who'd been introduced as Boogie called from down the line. "You know. That Machete dude. What's his name?"

"Danny Trejo," a former Navy SEAL introduced as Goose spoke up.

"Yeah, that's the one," Boogie said, smiling a toothy smile. "Ugliest son of a bitch I ever seen."

A chuckle rippled through the men and the man in front of Bill started to turn to face Boogie. Sean barked a command and they fell silent.

"Nitro," Sean continued with the introductions after glaring at the assembled men. "Retired Delta Force."

Exodus

"I apologize if I offended you," Bill said, shaking Nitro's hand. "But, your friend is correct. You bear an uncanny resemblance to the actor."

"Better looking than Robert Redford, too, you ass bandits," Nitro said to the group, frowning and flexing his giant arms.

The man was intimidating as hell, and Bill took an involuntary step back. Nitro grinned, his entire persona immediately changing.

"Sorry 'bout Boogie," he said. "He was a Marine. They don't know how to act in polite company."

"Semper Fi, motherfucker!" Boogie shouted as laughter broke out.

Shaking his head, Sean introduced Bill to the last man who'd remained quiet and still throughout the exchange.

"Poon-tang. Also retired Delta, and a world class sniper," Sean said.

"Why Poon-tang?" Bill asked as he shook the man's hand.

"Cause he'd fuck a snake if he could hold it still long enough!"

Boogie and Goose recited the line in perfect unison, both cracking up before they could finish speaking. Poon just met Bill's eyes and shrugged his shoulders. Bill stepped back and looked over the group, smiling. The banter ceased as it was time to get serious.

"Sean has filled you in on what we're going to do?" Bill asked in a voice loud enough for all to clearly hear.

Up and down the line, heads nodded in affirmation.

"Any reservations, now's the time to speak up," Bill continued. "This is no bullshit, and there's no walking away from this. Once we get our hands on the target, the clock will be ticking. There's every chance the enemy's schedule will get advanced when they learn he's missing. That means there's no time for sensitivity. We've got a job to do, and the faster we get the information we need, the better our odds are of success. Are you all on board?"

It was quiet for a moment, then Boogie stepped forward and looked at Sean.

"Did he just say *sensitivity*, boss?"

"I believe that was the word he used, yes."

Boogie turned and looked at his fellow warriors.

"Anyone know what the fuck that means?"

Several of the men made a production of looking at each other and shrugging their shoulders. Sean shook his head and turned to Bill.

"Sorry about bringing the B team," he said, sounding sincerely distressed. "There weren't any good operators available on short notice."

Bill threw his head back and laughed, clapping his hands together.

"I'm assuming each of you has an account you'd like your money transferred into. Correct?"

Each man dug into a pocket or pack, stepping forward individually and handing a slip of paper to Bill.

"It will be wired today," he said, sorting through the pile in his hand. "You should be able to verify payment tomorrow morning."

He turned and started towards the patio, pausing and turning back.

"And, gentlemen. Thank you."

With a smile on his face, Bill headed into the house to initiate the eight wire transfers. Sean stepped forward and gestured for Anna to join him. He introduced her to the men, receiving surprised looks from most of them.

"Tomorrow morning, Goose, Nitro, Monk and Bunny are going to Nevada with the General," Sean said, ignoring the look he received from Anna. "The rest of you will be with me. Questions?"

"Yeah, boss," Boogie called. "What's it like sleeping with a General? I mean, I know you know, but this one's a *woman*!"

Sean hung his head to hide a grin and turned away as the entire squad roared in laughter. He didn't see the surprised smile on Anna's face, but they did. She didn't realize it, but that exhibition of humor just cemented her relationship with the men.

Exodus

9

It was still dark the next morning when Sean and Anna stepped onto the back patio and, holding hands, began walking towards the idling Black Hawk. The four men who would accompany her to the facility in Nevada were already aboard, waiting for the General to join them. The couple moved slowly, neither wanting to be apart from the other.

That had been the heated topic of discussion, late into the previous evening. Anna had initially insisted that she wasn't going to leave. She argued that she could help, growing angry as Sean steadfastly refused. When she wouldn't give up, he'd had to resort to reminding her that she wasn't a warrior. Sure, she'd been an Army officer, but had never trained for, nor operated in, a combat role.

This was a true statement, and a logical argument, but Anna had been beyond the point of listening to reason. Instead, his comments only escalated their disagreement until she stormed out of their bedroom, leaving Sean seated on the side of the bed with his head in his hands. After giving her a few minutes to cool off, he'd followed, pausing at the bottom of the stairs when he heard her voice.

Anna had charged into the kitchen, surprising Nitro who was busily loading a plate down with what must have been half the food in the refrigerator.

Snorting her anger at all males, she had ignored him and headed for the back door.

"Know you don't wanna hear it, but he's right," Nitro said, not taking his attention off the interior of the fridge.

"What the hell would you know about it?" Anna snapped, reaching for the door handle.

"Nothin', I suppose," Nitro grumbled. "Just another meathead Delta trooper here."

His words stopped Anna in her tracks, and she turned to face him.

"I'm really sorry," she said. "That was unfair… I'm sorry. I don't remember your name."

"Pablo," he said, closing the refrigerator and taking a seat at the table with a huge platter of food. "But, only my mom calls me that. It's Nitro. Want some fried chicken?"

He grinned at her and pointed at several pieces that were nearly hidden beneath half a pound of sliced roast beef. Anna stood for a moment, then joined him at the table, grabbing a drumstick.

"I'm sorry, Nitro. I had no cause to snap at you like that."

"Mo prolem," he mumbled around a mouthful of food.

Exodus

Anna giggled and bit into the cold chicken.

"But, the boss is right," he said a moment later. "You got no business going where they're going. You'll be safe as a babe in its mother's arms with us in Nevada. Trust me."

He grinned and, out of habit, flexed his arms and bounced his pecs up and down.

"Just because I'm a woman doesn't mean I can't take care of myself!"

Anna was starting to get angry again.

"Got no argument from me," Nitro said. "You going to eat that?"

He pointed at the other drumstick, finger hovering a fraction of an inch above it.

"Yes," Anna said, batting his hand aside and grabbing the contested piece of chicken.

Nitro sat back and looked at her, his face splitting into a huge grin.

"Hell, General, I don't think I got the balls to say you can't do somethin' just cause you're a woman."

Anna bit into the fresh drumstick and shrugged.

"Then what's Sean's problem?"

"Gonna hit me if I say somethin' you don't like?" He asked.

"Maybe," Anna said, trying not to grin. "Just watch your step."

"Yes, ma'am," Nitro barked, then chuckled briefly before getting serious. "Look, General. It's like this. Those boys are goin to a dark fuckin place. I'm talkin' bout what they've gotta do once they get their hands on this CIA dickhead. It ain't gonna be pretty."

"I'm not some little girl that needs to be shielded," Anna protested.

"Ma'am, respectfully, you do. But not why you think."

"What then?" Anna asked, finally calm enough to listen.

Nitro munched thoughtfully on a fistful of roast beef, staring intently at her for a few seconds before speaking.

"You got any idea what it takes to get a professional intelligence officer to reveal information he doesn't want to give up?"

"I've heard some things. Read some reports," Anna said.

"Pffffttt!!" Nitro made a rude noise with his lips. "Ain't the same, General. Not even close. Imagine standing there and watching a man get broken down to a sniveling, groveling shell of his former self. Smelling his fear, his piss and shit. His blood. Hearing him scream in agony and beg for death. That's what I'm talkin' bout. You ready for that?"

Anna stared at him, the food in her hand forgotten as she tried to visualize the scene Nitro had just painted.

"I can deal with it," she finally said. "If that's what it takes to find those nukes."

Nitro slowly nodded his head and leaned forward.

"Can you deal with watching your husband do those things to another human being? Would you ever be able to look at him the same way again? Sure, if you go to Nevada, you'll know he was involved in extracting the info. But it won't be a movie playing in your head every time he touches you."

Anna sat and looked at the massive soldier for a long time, thinking about what he'd just said. He never broke eye contact with her, just stared back with a blank expression on his face.

"There's more to you than meets the eye, isn't there?" Anna said softly.

"General, if you weren't married to my boss, I'd show you how much more there is to me!"

Nitro grinned and looked away to let her know it was a joke. Anna smiled and pushed her chair back. Sweeping her crumbs from the table, she dropped the remnants of her snack into the garbage and paused to put her hand on Nitro's giant shoulder.

"I'm glad you're coming with me, Pablo."

Nitro nodded without looking up, and Anna disappeared out the back door onto the patio. A few seconds later he looked up when Sean stepped into the kitchen.

"Thanks," he said.

"No problem, boss. I'll bill you for my time. How much you think Dr. Phil makes?"

Sean grinned and tilted his head at the door.

"Who's on watch?"

"Poon's on the roof with his rifle. Boogie and Goose is huntin' in the woods. Makin' sure no one tries to sneak up on us."

Sean stood in place, looking at the door Anna had gone through. He wasn't worried about her. There wasn't anyone that could approach the house and harm her with the three men that were protecting the perimeter.

"Thinkin' bout tomorrow?" Nitro asked, leaning back and shoving the empty platter to the middle of the table.

"Yeah. This CIA fuck, Delker, is in…"

"Delker?" Nitro interrupted, fully capturing Sean's attention.

"Yeah. Why? Know him?"

"Maybe. If it's the same guy. You know how the spooks like to recycle names."

"Little older than us," Sean said, looking intently at Nitro. "Likes Hawaiian shirts and straw hats."

"Sure sounds like the same fuck stick," Nitro grumbled. "Did a job in Africa a few years back when the Congo was starting to go to shit. He tagged along. Was a royal prick. My team leader put a gun in his face before it was all over. Think he was about half a second away from pulling the trigger, too."

"What can you tell me about him?" Sean asked, taking a seat in the chair Anna had occupied.

"Nothin." Nitro shrugged. "He was a fuckin' ghost. We was puttin' down warlords, and he had a couple assets in-country that was feeding us intel. Oh, yeah. I remember that he was a SEAL before the Agency. Other than that, I don't know. Can't remember that he and I ever said one word to each other."

"Your team leader. Could he give me some intel on Delker?"

"Maybe. Dunno. That was a long time ago, and he's out, now. Got married and went all pussy. College, then took some fuckin' suit and tie job, last I heard. But, you know, that girl he married. She was Agency. She might know somethin'."

"Think they'd talk to me?" Sean asked.

"Probably. Never met her, but he was a good guy. If I vouched for you, don't see why he wouldn't tell you what he knows."

"Who was your team leader?"

"Chase. John Chase."

"Know how to get in touch with him?"

"No, but he's a civilian now. Shouldn't be that hard to find."

10

It was one of those afternoons. The kind when anything that can go wrong, will. I barely stopped myself from picking up the laptop, that had just spontaneously rebooted for the fifth time in two hours, and flinging it against the wall. With a sigh, I reclined in my chair and waited for Windows to finish doing whatever the hell it thought it was doing.

"Should have stayed in the goddamn Army," I grumbled under my breath.

"I've heard that a lot, lately."

I looked up to see my wife, Katie, standing in the doorway to my home office. She was dressed in a lightweight summer dress, purse over her shoulder. Must be shopping time.

"Tired of computers," I smiled, standing up and wrapping my arms around her.

She snuggled against me for a moment before stepping away and making a production of fanning herself.

"I know you're trying to save money, but it's hotter than hell in here. Turn the damn AC down!"

"You saw our electric bill last month," I said, taking a quick peek at the laptop. "You know how much ammo I could have bought for that?"

"Would ammo keep the house cooler?"

She stepped close and kissed me.

"Going for coffee with the girls. Want anything?"

"Depends on what you're offering," I said, reaching for her.

Katie laughed, nimbly dodged my clumsy grasp and dashed for the door.

"See you in a couple of hours," she called over her shoulder, then was gone.

"That's why I didn't stay in the Army," I said, smiling as I went back into my office and looked at the laptop screen.

The damn thing still wasn't ready, doing nothing other than showing a blank screen with a spinning cursor. Slamming the lid, I walked down the hall to the master bedroom.

I had to get on a plane to Atlanta the next morning, and owed my anal-retentive boss an activity report on two of our clients. I should have sat back down and dealt with my computer issues and cranked it out, but I wasn't in the mood. Besides, I had a four-hour flight ahead of me. Plenty of time to create the corporate drivel that was expected of me.

Exodus

Changing clothes, I got into my truck and drove to the gym. A hard workout would probably do wonders for my poor attitude. And, as usual, it did. A couple of hours later I pulled back into the garage at home, having to squeeze far to the left because of the way Katie parks her car.

I looked at the tiny little Mercedes and sighed. Normally, Katie drops me off at the terminal when I'm traveling, but our schedules didn't line up this time. And, because my truck was too tall to fit into the airport parking garage, I was going to have to shoehorn my big ass into the cramped roadster and drive myself.

"Figured that's where you were," Katie said when I walked into the house.

"Couldn't take the computer any longer," I smiled. "How was coffee?"

She followed me into the bath as I stripped off my sweat soaked clothes and cranked on the shower.

"Boring," she said with a shrug.

"Thought you liked having coffee with them," I said, stepping under the running water.

Katie leaned against the bathroom counter, watching me through the clear glass shower door.

"It's not that," she said. "I just get tired of hearing them complain about their husbands. Seems as if that's all they can do."

"Not everyone gets as lucky as you," I said, leaning in to rinse soap off my shaved head.

A moment later the water briefly turned scalding hot, like it does when someone flushes the adjacent toilet while the shower's running. With a yelp, I jumped back and nearly slipped and fell on my ass. Blinking soapy water out of my eyes, I peered at Katie who was in precisely the same pose she'd been in.

"Something wrong?" She asked innocently.

"Yuck it up, chuckles," I growled. "You'll get yours!"

"I'm counting on it!"

She smiled sweetly and left the bathroom.

Several hours later we were sitting on our patio, enjoying the relatively cooler evening air. The sun had been down for a couple of hours, but it was still over one hundred degrees. Well, that's Arizona for you.

My bag was already packed and in the trunk of the Mercedes, ready to go early the next morning. I was tired of traveling for work and had dragged my feet while I was getting everything ready to go. Well, to be completely truthful, I didn't mind the travel. It was the job. The money and benefits were good, there was no denying that, but the job was soul-sucking. At least for someone like me.

Exodus

I never liked being indoors or having to make polite conversation with people I didn't respect or even care about. And, I sure as hell didn't like never being able to get anything done without it having to be discussed, ad nauseam, by a committee. I should have stayed in the Army, I thought to myself with a snort.

"What's funny?" Katie asked.

We'd been taking frequent dips in the pool to stay cool, and as soon as the sun had gone down, the bathing suits had come off. Now, she lounged on a chair next to me, faint moonlight gleaming off her bare skin.

"Nothing," I said.

"Thinking about the trip tomorrow?"

"Yeah," I said. "Don't want to go."

"Don't want you to go."

"No choice," I said.

"Always a choice," Katie said, fluffing her damp hair so it would dry faster. "Just might not be the choice you think you want."

I looked sideways at her, drained the last of my second margarita and lit a cigarette.

"What does that mean?" I asked.

"Means that it's abundantly clear you're miserable. You hate your job. So, quit!"

I snorted, smoke shooting out of my nose.

"And do what? We've still got bills to pay, in case you hadn't noticed."

"Don't be an ass," Katie chided. "We can get by on far less. We did when you were in the Army. You make twenty times that now. So, we scale back. We've got savings. We sell the house and my car. Get some property out in the boonies and enjoy life again. You think I like it when you're gone? It sucks!"

"Can I get a dog?" I asked, not really believing she was serious.

"I'm not kidding," Katie said, turning in her chair to face me. "I've been thinking about this for a while. We need a change. Neither of us are happy."

"You are serious," I said, surprised.

"Totally. So, what do you think?"

"I think I need to think about it," I said. "That's a hell of a change you're talking about."

Katie shrugged her shoulders, then we both looked at the door into the house when the phone began ringing. It was our home phone, an actual landline. The only reason we even had it was if I needed to send a fax.

"Let it ring," Katie said. "No one has that number."

Exodus

The line didn't have voice mail, and the fax machine wasn't set up to answer, so the annoying bell just kept sounding. After what must have been twenty rings, it fell silent. Then, seconds later, started again.

"Oh, for Christ's sake!" Katie snapped, jumping to her feet and stomping into the house.

I chuckled, expecting a telemarketer was about to lose a sizable chunk of his or her ass. But when she walked back out she was holding the phone pressed tightly against a bare breast to cover the microphone. I frowned a question at her.

"For you," she said quietly. "Says his name is Nitro."

I sat there for a couple of seconds, memories flooding in. Extending my hand, I took the phone from Katie.

"Nitro?"

"Boss! How the hell are you?"

There was no doubt. This was the voice I remembered, barrio accent included.

"What the hell? Are you in town?"

"No, nothing like that. Listen, boss. I'm real sorry about this, but I need a favor. You know who I went to work for after Delta, right?"

"I heard rumors. Couple of guys were talking about it at Spider's funeral. By the way, where the fuck were you?"

Nitro was quiet for several seconds before continuing in a much more subdued voice.

"Sorry, boss. I was out of the country. Didn't find out until I got back, and that was a couple months after the fact."

I didn't say anything. Wasn't sure what to say, or what favor he could possibly want. I hadn't seen or talked to Nitro in a long time. We'd been as close as teammates can be. We were brothers. But that didn't mean we were the kind of friends that stayed in touch to talk about what was going on in our lives.

"So, 'bout why I called, boss. You remember our trip? The one where we spent a few weeks with the Aussies?"

"Yeah. I remember it like it was yesterday," I said.

"Well, this is about one of those guys that tagged along. Not the tall, thin one that could keep up with Poon on our runs, the other one. Know who I'm talking about?"

"Yes," I said, sitting forward and lighting another smoke.

Exodus

I knew exactly who he was talking about. A CIA agent that called himself Delker. He and I had come to blows, and as we were getting ready for extraction he'd made some threats against Katie that had resulted in me pointing a gun at his face.

"What's going on, Nitro? Should we be talking about this on the phone?"

I could tell Katie was intrigued, hanging on every word I said, but I ignored her for the moment.

"Got no choice," he said. "Man's up to something bad. Real bad, and we've got to do something about it. That's why I'm calling. My new boss is standing here next to me, and he's got some questions. We was hoping you'd be willing to talk to him."

"Hold on," I said, covering the mouthpiece on the phone with my hand before Nitro could answer.

"What?" Katie asked.

I started to speak, then changed my mind and led the way into the house. Our neighbors weren't close, but I didn't want to have this conversation in the open.

"Remember my trip to Africa? Right after we got married?"

Katie nodded.

"The CIA guy that went with us. Nitro's with a PMC. They've got a job that's got something to do with him, and his boss wants to ask me some questions."

"About what?" Katie asked, looking concerned.

"Nitro said he's into some bad shit and they've got to move quickly."

"If you talk about a serving Agency officer, and the CIA gets wind of it, you're going to be in a world of shit," she breathed.

"I don't even know what I could tell them," I said. "I don't know anything about the prick."

"Then tell them that and get the fuck off the phone!" Katie said.

I thought about it for a long moment, then raised the phone back to my ear.

"OK, Nitro. Put him on."

"Thanks, boss!"

"Don't thank me. I didn't say I was going to answer any of his questions."

There was a scuffling sound as the phone on that end was passed over, then a new voice sounded in my ear.

"Master Sergeant Chase, thank you for speaking with me."

Exodus

"Who am I speaking with?" I asked.

"My name is Sean Thompson. Retired Colonel, third battalion Rangers."

"You know the only reason we're speaking is because of Nitro? And even then, I'm not at all happy about having this conversation. It's dangerous for both of us."

"I understand and appreciate that, but the gentleman we're discussing is involved in something that is potentially catastrophic for our nation."

"I don't suppose you can tell me what that is?" I asked.

"Not on an open line, no."

I nodded my head, not surprised in the least.

"Ask your questions, Colonel. I'll answer if I can."

Katie gave me a look and shook her head, but didn't interrupt.

11

Sean kissed his wife goodbye, holding her tight against him. The Black Hawk pilot fed in throttle, the big rotor speeding up until it was creating a hurricane around them. It was his not so subtle way of saying it was time to go. With one last kiss, Anna broke away and dashed to the side door of the waiting helicopter. Nitro leaned out, hand extended, and helped her in. The aircraft immediately left the ground, Anna turning and waving to Sean. He stood in place, watching until she was out of sight.

"Ready, boss?"

Sean turned to see Boogie standing a couple of yards behind him. The other three members of his team waited on the patio with Bill. They all towered over the older man, heads bent as they listened with rapt attention. From the way he was using his hands, Sean was sure he was telling a story about flying a combat mission.

"Let's go."

The men picked up their gear and headed for the front courtyard where a Suburban that belonged to Thompson Aviation waited for them. Piling in, they drove a short distance to an uncontrolled airfield. A twin-engine Beechcraft gleamed in the moonlight, and Boogie brought them to a stop a few yards off its port wing.

Exodus

It only took a few minutes for Bill to complete his pre-flight walk around. While he did this, the men squeezed into the cramped cabin. Satisfied with the readiness of the aircraft, Bill got behind the controls and started the engines.

"How is it a helicopter pilot can fly a plane?" Boogie shouted from the back seat.

"Who said I could fly this thing?"

Bill grinned and shoved the throttles all the way to their stops. Engines roaring, the plane leapt forward, throwing all the passengers back in their seats. They raced down the smooth dirt strip, becoming airborne well before the end.

As the plane climbed, the men settled in for the trip. They were flying into another uncontrolled field in the Virginia countryside, then would drive to their target's home in Richmond. Vehicles were already waiting for them, as well as an empty warehouse in nearby Alexandria where they would take Delker for interrogation. All of this had been arranged through Sean's contacts in the PMC world.

The flight was less than three hours, Bill setting them onto the tarmac with a barely perceptible bump. By this time, Boogie had settled down, putting his war face on. The time for joking was over. They were going to work.

Dirk Patton

Transitioning from the plane to a pair of Suburbans, they were quickly on the road. It was early morning, beyond the worst of rush hour, but traffic was still heavy. As an operator called Billy the Kid, or just Kid, drove the lead vehicle, Sean brooded in the passenger seat.

He was not at all happy about what they were doing. Not the fact that they were going to kidnap and torture a CIA officer. That didn't particularly bother him. He was worried about the time crunch they were operating under. This wasn't a snatch and grab of some third world shithead. This was dramatically different.

They were operating in an American city, and the subject was a trained operator and intelligence officer. By definition, that made him a hard target. And, to make matters worse, if he or his team made one mistake, there were probably about a hundred neighbors who would pick up a phone and dial 9-1-1. Despite the importance of what they were doing, he wasn't going to start shooting at cops.

Monk, one of the operators who'd gone to Nevada with Anna, had pulled up digital maps and images of their target's home the previous evening. The team that was making the grab had spent several hours going over every detail as they put their plan together. All things considered, it appeared to be reasonably easy. At least on the surface.

Sean had confidence in his team. They were all very experienced. Knew what they were doing, and time and time again had shown their ability to improvise when a plan went to shit. Reassuring himself, he let out a sigh and stared through the windshield at the cars and trucks streaming into Richmond.

A few miles later, a phone rang, and Sean twisted around in his seat to see who had violated one of his standing orders. Bill winked at him as he retrieved a cheap, disposable cell from his shirt pocket.

"Burner," he said before answering it.

Sean nodded, unhappy, but keeping it to himself for the moment. He watched as Bill listened for a few seconds.

"Target's on the move," Bill said.

"Where?" Sean snapped, worried about the unexpected wrinkle.

"Northbound on 295."

"North or south of 64?" Kid asked, looking at the built-in navigation screen.

"South," Bill answered after relaying the question.

"Talk to me, Kid!" Sean barked.

"We're on 895," he answered, looking between the road and the screen as he talked. "Intersect with 295 in three miles."

"Bill, give me that," Sean said, twisting around and taking the phone.

He barked into the handset, looking at the navigation as he listened to an answer to his question. After a few more questions, he closed the phone and tossed it into a cup holder.

"Maintain your speed and merge onto 295 north. We should get on less than a mile behind him. Looking for a silver Chevy Malibu."

He recited the license plate and sat back in his seat.

"How we gonna do this, boss?" Kid asked, changing lanes to be ready for the exit ramp. "Whole different ball game than grabbing the guy while he's in his jammies."

"Acquire the target and follow. We try this on the freeway, we'll have cops crawling up our asses."

"Roger that," Kid said, checking the mirror to make sure Boogie was staying close.

"What if he's going to Langley?" Bill asked from behind.

"Fuck," Sean said.

He leaned sideways to look at the screen as Kid merged onto the ramp for northbound 295. It took some time for him to figure out how to use the system, and a little longer to gather the information he needed.

"Silver Malibu. Hundred yards, left lane," Kid said, drawing Sean's attention to the windshield.

"See the plate?" Sean asked.

"That's him," Poon said from the back seat.

Sean glanced over his shoulder. Poon was holding a small, sniper's spotting scope to his eye, watching the target vehicle.

"OK, Kid, stay with him. If he sees us, we're fucked."

"Like a ghost, Kemosabe," Kid said.

"What are we doing?" Bill asked. "If he gets to Langley, we can't touch him."

"Well aware of that, Bill," Sean said, more patiently than he felt. "If he gets on 95 North, that's probably where he's going. Let's just wait and see."

Bill wasn't pleased with the answer, but since he didn't have a better suggestion, he kept his mouth shut. They followed for several more miles in heavy traffic, Delker sticking to the left lane. As they approached the exit for the Richmond airport, the Malibu suddenly swerved across traffic, nearly sideswiping an eighteen-wheeler, then shot down the ramp. Kid, who had been hanging back in the middle lane, had no problem merging right and taking the same exit without any dramatics.

"Fuckin' airport," Sean breathed. "This is bad."

He didn't need to detail for anyone in the vehicle that airports had lots of security and even more video surveillance. Once Delker crossed the outer boundary, there would be no way they could take him without winding up on the evening news.

"Boogie," he called on the radio. "Get your ass up here and stop him. Make it seem like an accident. Don't alert him if you can help it."

"Copy," Boogie answered.

A moment later the second Suburban roared past on their left. They were on a busy, four-lane road and it sliced through traffic, quickly closing the distance to their target. Pulling alongside the Malibu, he began honking his horn and waving angrily at the driver directly in front of him.

"Smarter than he looks."

Bill had leaned forward between the front seats and was watching the performance with a smile on his face.

"Not really," Kid said with a grin.

"Stay sharp!" Sean barked, silencing both of them.

Exodus

Boogie's act was working. The car in front of him wasn't going any faster, and Delker reacted exactly the way he'd been trained. Avoid stupid and angry people so they don't draw attention to you. The Chevy's brake lights flared as he slowed, intending to give the enraged Suburban driver plenty of room to go around.

"Now!"

Sean shouted into the radio as the Malibu began to slow. With a savage yank of the wheel, Boogie rammed the side of the much heavier Suburban into the front fender of the target vehicle, sending it into a spin. It came to a bone jarring stop against a wooden utility pole and Kid wheeled them into a nearby parking lot so they were not immediately visible. Boogie slammed on the brakes, stopping on the edge of the road as half a dozen other motorists slowed to a halt.

"Go, go, go!"

Sean shouted into the radio as he and Poon leapt out of their vehicle. As they ran towards the disabled Malibu, Boogie and his passenger, Snakeshit, jumped out of their Suburban and staged a world-class drama. Each pointed at the damage to the SUV's bodywork and screamed at the other. Within seconds, blows were thrown, and they fell to the ground to roll around at the edge of the pavement.

There was not a single set of eyes in the area that wasn't glued to the fight, and no one saw Sean run up and yank the driver's door of the Malibu open. One of Chevy's safety features was that if the computer sensed a major impact, it unlocked all the doors so rescuers could easily gain access. He knew this and took full advantage.

Delker slowly looked around, bleeding from a nasty cut on his forehead. He was stunned, but training started to take over and he reached beneath his jacket for a weapon. Sean pinned his arm as Poon yanked the passenger door open, jumped in and jammed a spring-loaded syringe into their target's neck. Within three seconds, he slumped unconscious into Sean's waiting arms.

12

Several hours later, Sean walked into the small office where Bill was seated at a rickety folding table. Sweat beaded his brow, staining his collar and the underarms of his shirt, but it wasn't from exertion. It was from the stress of attempting to extract information from a man who didn't want to talk.

"Any progress?"

Bill watched as Sean poured water over his hands and wiped them clean with a small towel. It came away stained bright red.

"No," Sean said, shaking his head. "He's well trained, and whatever his organization has planned, he's a true believer. Not saying a word."

"Maybe I should talk to him," Bill said.

Sean gave him a non-committal look before shaking his head and drinking deeply from a bottle of water.

"Still all quiet out there?"

"Yes," Bill answered. "Poon moved to the roof of a different building so he had an unobstructed view of the approach road, but other than that the guys are hunkered down and keeping their eyes open."

"So, what are we going to do?" Bill asked, making a point of checking his watch.

"You're looking nervous, Bill. Something I need to know?"

"No." Bill looked away. "Just a bad feeling."

"Failsafe?" Sean asked, earning a surprised look.

Bill nodded.

"Don't look so damn surprised," Sean groused. "We left his car crashed on the side of the road. First thing the cops would have done is run the plate, and as soon as it hits a computer, alarm bells are going to start going off somewhere. They're looking for him by now. I've got no doubt."

Bill nodded again, his eyes slipping to the side.

"What?"

"That's not the part I'm worried about."

"Then what?" Sean asked, squaring his shoulders and putting his fists on his hips.

"If he's as important to this whole thing as I think he is, well, what if things get advanced once his co-conspirators realize he's been taken? Will they move up the timeline for whatever they're going to do with those warheads?"

Exodus

Sean stood silently, considering what Bill had said. After a long, quiet stretch, he checked his watch. 1837, Eastern Time.

"Sean," Bill said gently. "I think you'd better resort to the drug."

Sean tilted his head back and looked up at the dark ceiling, fifty feet above. The vacant warehouse was huge, part of a massive industrial park that had fallen on hard times when the economy tanked a few years ago. It had never come back from the financial abyss that had devastated the region. But, that was good for him. There was no one to hear Delker's screams.

"Brain damage," Sean said, looking back down at Bill. "I give him that drug, we've got sixty minutes, ninety at the most, before there's permanent brain damage."

"Is that any worse than what's already been done to him? What will be done?"

Sean snapped a look at his father-in-law, eyes flashing in anger.

"I did not mean that the way you took it," Bill said softly. "You are doing what must be done. What I meant, was, when we get the information, he can't be allowed to live. I know you know that. He wouldn't rest until all of us, Anna included, were in a grave. What does brain damage matter if we're going to put a bullet in his head when we're done with him?"

"Goddamn, Bill. That's some coldblooded shit," Boogie said as he walked up out of the shadows.

He raised his hands when he saw the look Sean gave him.

"Sorry, boss. Just a routine patrol. Guess I'll keep moving."

The man quickly departed, Sean watching his broad back as he disappeared into the gloom at the far end of the warehouse.

"He's right," Sean said when they were alone again. "That's pretty fucking coldblooded."

"Surprised?" Bill asked. "You shouldn't be. You don't know me. You know Anna, but she's more like her mother. She'd be horrified if she knew what I'd just suggested."

Sean stared at him then slowly nodded.

"She'd be even more horrified if she knew I agreed with you."

"So, break the drugs out, son! I can hear that goddamn nuclear clock ticking."

Decision made, Sean turned to a hard-sided case that had been left in the Suburban for him. Dialing in a seven-digit combination, he popped the lid open to reveal a pair of loaded syringes nestled in foam cutouts. Lifting them out, he hesitated when Bill's disposable phone began ringing.

Bill answered and listened for nearly a minute without saying anything. Finally, he thanked the caller and closed the handset, looking up at Sean with concern on his face.

"General Olber is dead."

"What?" Sean asked, not sure he'd heard correctly.

"General Olber is dead," Bill repeated.

"How?"

"Plane crash into the ocean. I called him just before we left Alabama. Gave him a heads up. He was on his way from the Middle East with the commanders he trusted."

"Coincidence?" Sean asked.

Bill snorted and shook his head.

"You don't believe that. Besides. When's the last time you heard of an Air Force transport going down? They just don't."

"So, we're on our own."

Bill stood and placed his hand on Sean's shoulder.

"Let's get on with it, son."

Sean nodded and led the way to the office that had become an inquisition chamber. Bill followed, and when the door opened he wrinkled his nose at the smell that rolled out to greet him. Human waste, sweat, fear and desperation. The odor of fresh blood was strong.

Stepping through the opening, he closed it behind him and nearly faltered in his step when he saw Delker. The man was on his back, strapped down to a battered steel desk that had been left behind by the previous occupants of the warehouse. All his clothing had been removed, leaving him to writhe naked in his own shit and blood.

Fingers were broken. Teeth were missing. One of his nipples had been sliced off and was lying in a puddle of some bodily fluid on the floor. But, the worst were his feet. The soles of each had been flayed open. His toes had been broken and slit, the flesh pulled back from the bone. Bill shuddered involuntarily as he stepped around a thick stream of blood that ran across the floor to pool against the wall.

"Shudv knawn wus you," Delker said through his shattered mouth when he saw Bill. "Gone fuck your dowter first. Ten keel er slow."

Without any hesitation, Sean jabbed the first syringe into Delker's hip and depressed the plunger.

Exodus

"Want wok," Delker said, trying to laugh but only succeeding in coughing. "Twained"

"Not against this," Sean said, stepping back and checking his watch. "I'll give you the second one in ten minutes, then we're off to see the wizard."

They stood in silence as Delker continued to rave at Bill, but it was short lived. Within minutes he calmed, awake, but seemingly drifting from thought to thought.

"Phase one," Sean said. "He's no longer feeling any pain."

"Then how's he awake?"

"It's not a painkiller. Somehow it disconnects his brain from his body. He can't feel anything."

Bill nodded and they fell quiet again, Sean frequently looking at his watch. When time was up, he stepped in and injected Delker with the second syringe.

"How long, now?" Bill asked.

"Five minutes," Sean said.

"Then what? Just ask him questions?"

"Yeah. But we've got to ask the right ones," Sean said. "He's awake, but his brain is in a… a… fuck, I can't remember what the docs called it. Anyway, he's kind of like a computer, now. If you know what to ask, you'll get your answer. But you only get what you ask.

Nothing gets volunteered. That's why I didn't start with this. It's better if you can get someone to just spill their guts. A whole lot more information comes out."

"How do you know when he's ready?"

Sean leaned over Delker and peered into his glassy eyes.

"Agent Delker, do you want to kill Bill Thompson?"

"Yeth," Delker answered in a dreamy voice.

"He'd answer that way if he was sober as a judge," Bill said.

Sean glanced at Bill then back down.

"Are you involved in the smuggling of nuclear warheads into New York City?"

"Yeth."

Sean and Bill exchanged glances and Sean nodded.

"Do you know where those warheads are right now?"

"No."

13

They spent half an hour trying to come up with a question that would give them even a hint of where the nukes were located. Try as they might, they achieved no success. Finally, Bill caught Sean's eye and tilted his head at the door.

"Could he be faking?" Bill asked when they were back on the warehouse floor.

"No. At least according to the guys that created this shit. I've never personally used it before, but I've seen it used a few times. Watched an interrogation team get info out of jihadists that they'd have taken to their graves otherwise. I really don't believe he knows their exact locations."

"That's it!"

Bill snapped his fingers and rushed back into the office.

"Delker," he said. "Which areas of New York are the warheads in?"

Slowly and methodically, the man rattled off eight separate geographic locations. Unfortunately, the most specific one was Central Park. Sean and Bill stared at each other, elated at their small degree of success.

"Where in Central Park?" Sean asked.

"I dun know."

"Where in the Bronx?" Bill asked.

"I dun know."

"Wait!" Sean held up his hand to stop Bill.

"Delker, are the bombs inside buildings?"

"No."

"Vehicles?"

"No."

"Shit," Sean breathed. "Where else could they be?"

Bill had been listening, thinking as Sean ran through his list of questions.

"Delker," he said, looking down into the man's empty eyes. "Are the bombs on the roofs of buildings?"

"Yeth."

"That makes sense!" Bill cried. "Not an airburst, like an inbound missile, but there are some tall buildings in NYC, and the altitude will magnify the destruction."

"Do you know which buildings?" Sean asked.

"No."

Exodus

"Fuck!" Sean spat, turning away.

"When are they set to detonate?" Bill asked, ignoring Sean.

"Juwy fouth."

The two men looked at each other in elation. It was June. There was plenty of time to find the warheads. Before they could congratulate each other, Bill frowned and turned back to Delker.

"Is there a failsafe built into your plans?"

"Yeth."

"Tell me what the failsafe is," Bill said softly.

"If any printhipal ith apprehended or expothed, the thimeline to dethonation ith advanthed and the Chinethe operation is triggered."

"Chinese?" Sean blurted. "What do the goddamn Chinese have…"

Bill cut him off with a raised hand.

"Delker. How is the timeline advanced? To when?"

"Twelf hours from confirmation that a printhipal ith mithing or hath been compromised."

"Delker, are you a principal?"

"Yeth."

"Oh, fuck me," Sean said, looking at his watch.

"When?" Bill asked.

"Three to four hours from now! Depends on how quickly they moved when we took him."

"Delker," Sean said. "How do we stop the failsafe?"

"It can'th be stopped."

"Who is in charge?" Bill asked.

"The Cabal."

"What's the Cabal?"

"Who I work for."

Bill and Sean exchanged glances.

"Delker. Don't you work for the CIA?" Sean asked.

"Yeth."

"Is the Cabal the CIA?"

"No."

"Who are they? Who is in charge of the Cabal?" Bill asked.

"The…. The…. The Cabal."

Exodus

"What's wrong?" Bill looked up at Sean who was checking his watch.

"We're running out of time. The brain damage is starting," he said, then leaned over their prisoner. "Delker. What are the Chinese going to do?"

The man stuttered briefly as he tried to speak.

"Delker. Concentrate. Tell me what the Chinese are going to do!"

"N-n-n-n---erf…" his voice trailed off and a thin stream of bloody froth ran out of the corner of his mouth.

"Nerf? What the hell is Nerf?" Bill asked.

"Delker!" Sean shouted. "What is Nerf?"

"G-g-g---g---assssssssss," he said, drool flooding out of his mouth as he hissed the word.

"Nerve gas?" Sean asked. "Delker! Nerve gas? Where?"

Delker never answered. His eyes lost all remaining focus, and his breathing began to slow.

"He's done," Sean said in frustration. "What the hell do we do now?"

Bill looked at him, horror and sadness on his face as he shook his head. Sean suddenly turned and raced out of the room. Reaching the table, he snatched up Bill's cell and quickly input a number from memory.

"Who you calling?" Bill asked.

"CEO of my company," Sean said, listening to the phone ring.

It was answered by one of the women who staffed their twenty-four-hour operations center, and Sean gave her the emergency code word that would get him immediately transferred to his boss's cell phone. While he was waiting, he explained to Bill.

"My boss is a big shot political donor. Maybe he can get through to someone that can do something. It's our only shot."

Bill nodded as the call was picked up.

"Colonel Thompson, what's the emergency?"

"Sir, I have highly credible intelligence that there are eight nuclear warheads in New York City that are timed to detonate sometime within the next four hours. They are located on the roofs of unknown buildings throughout the metropolitan area, and there's an additional device in Central Park."

"Whoa! Hold on. Now, what? Are you sure? Where'd you get this information?"

"From a rogue CIA officer. Sir, there's no time, and there's no one else I can call. A warning needs to be sounded immediately!"

Sean was nearly shouting into the phone at this point.

"Calm down, Colonel. You surely don't expect me to start making calls and bothering people over the word of one man, do you?"

"Sir, this is not a joke! The intel is solid. I obtained it with Wizard."

There was silence from the other end for a moment.

"Colonel, are you telling me that you used Wizard on an officer from the Central Intelligence Agency?"

The man's voice was low and frightened.

"Yes, sir. That's exactly what I'm telling you! The intel is good, sir. He just didn't know the precise locations of the devices. NEST can find them, but only if a warning gets to someone with enough authority to deploy them. Immediately!"

There was another stretch of silence as Sean's boss worked through the information he'd just been given.

"So help me, Colonel, if you're wrong..."

"Sir, I pray to God I'm wrong. But, if I'm not, there are millions of people that are about to die! Sir, please! Make the call."

"I'm on it," the man said, disconnecting without anything further.

"Well?" Bill asked as Sean closed the phone.

"He's going to make some calls."

"Can he get to the right people?"

"He donates to everyone," Sean said, shrugging. "Never met a politician he didn't buy, so probably. Unless…"

"Unless what?"

"What do you think Delker was talking about? The Cabal?"

"Son, there's been rumors of a shadow government since the time of Benjamin Franklin. Maybe there is, maybe there isn't. All we can do now is wait and see. And, why didn't you tell him about the nerve gas?"

"Tell him what?" Sean asked. "Three words. Chinese nerve gas. What the hell that means is anybody's guess at this point. The priority is the nukes. If NEST can find them and defuse them in time…"

Bill nodded slowly.

"What about our guest?" He finally asked, nodding at the office.

Sean turned and looked at the closed door.

"Wizard will finish the job in a couple of hours," he said. "He won't feel any more pain and the drug will cause his brain to shut down his nervous system. When that happens, his heart will stop."

"So, what now?"

"I need to fill the guys in, then we've got to clean this place up. No trace we were here. After that? Guess we head to Nevada to get Anna."

"If NEST can find them," Bill said.

"If NEST can find them," Sean agreed, nodding.

He went and found each of his men, taking his time to explain what he'd learned and what was happening. They took the information as well as could be expected. Except for Poon. His sister had just moved to New York to pursue her dream of being an actress on Broadway.

With amazingly steady hands, he pulled out his phone, powered it up and dialed her number. A moment later he gave the handset a quizzical look and tried again, without ever getting a ring from the other end.

"Phones are down," he said.

Sean pulled his personal phone out, replaced the battery he'd removed for the operation and tried to place a call. He didn't have any better results.

"Think the boss got through to someone and they shut down comms?" Poon asked.

"Not that fast," Sean said. "I can see them doing it, try to disrupt the bad guys, but not in half an hour. No way."

"Then what?"

"I don't know, Poon. But, I got a bad feeling."

"You and me both, brother."

Sean went to Boogie and Snakeshit and had them power up and try their phones, hoping it was just an issue with the carrier he and Poon used. But, it wasn't. They had no better results. His attempt with Bill's disposable cell yielded the same results.

"I'm going for a landline," Sean said after an hour of waiting. "Poon, you're with me. We'll get a message to your sister. Boogie and Snakeshit, get this place ready. Kid will take overwatch."

"How you want it done, boss?" Boogie asked.

"Take his teeth," he said, referring to Delker. "Don't need them getting an ID off dental records. Then get the place ready to burn. They can sift through the ashes."

Exodus

"Roger that," Boogie said, turning and heading for the office where Delker was strapped down.

Evening had passed into night by the time Sean and Poon climbed into a Suburban and headed out in search of a landline phone. It was hot and humid, and there were a lot of people still up and moving as they drove closer to D.C.

Sean had intended to find a payphone, but for something that during his childhood had been on nearly every street corner in America, he came up empty.

"Are you fucking kidding me?" He asked in frustration as they drove past another gas station without one.

"Everybody's got cells," Poon said, looking at a time and temperature display on a bank.

11:26 PM 93 degrees

"About fucking time!" Sean said when he spotted a phone bolted to the exterior wall of a liquor store.

Whipping into the lot, he jumped out and ran to it, snatching the handset off the cradle and lifting it to his ear. There was a dial tone. But, he didn't have any change. Dashing inside, he slapped a five-dollar bill onto the counter and got change from the bored clerk who either didn't notice, or didn't care, about the blood splatters on his shirt.

Poon was waiting at the phone and fed some of the quarters in before dialing his sister's cell. He listened for a moment then hung up in frustration. Fear etched his face as he turned to look at Sean.

"Out of service recording," he breathed.

Sean squeezed his shoulder, then put in some more quarters and dialed Anna's cell. He didn't have great hopes that it was working, but maybe the outage was limited to the east coast. After several seconds of silence, he received a message that the number was out of service. Slamming the switch with his hand, the phone clanked as it returned his change.

"Poon, what's Nitro's satellite phone number?"

Poon scrolled through the contacts on his iPhone. He found the right entry and recited it as Sean dialed. This time there was an even longer pause, then a ring. It went on for a long time and Sean was about to give up when Nitro growled a greeting into his ear.

"Thank God!" Sean exclaimed, relief flooding through him. "Is Anna with you?"

"Oh, hi boss. Yeah, she's right here. Hold on."

"Sean?"

"Anna! Did you make it? Are you safe?"

He had to stop himself from shouting.

Exodus

"Yes. We're here, and everything's fine. What's wrong?"

Sean and Poon both looked up as a light airplane passed overhead, flying way too low, especially this close to the nation's capital. It was a couple of blocks away, and as they watched, it swooped down and turned to fly over the next row of homes. Its pattern reminded Sean of a crop duster spraying a field.

"It's not good," Sean said. "Your dad was right. Everything he said was right. New York is…"

A brilliant flash lit the night from the area of downtown D.C. Both Poon and Sean, who were looking in that direction, were immediately blinded, each crying out in pain. Sean dropped the phone, his hands reflexively covering his face.

"Sean! Sean! What happened? Sean!"

He could hear Anna's voice, distant and tinny. Fumbling blindly, he tried desperately to find the phone so he could tell his wife that he loved her. He knew what had just blinded him. Knew it was close and that a wall of nuclear fire was about to engulf him. As his fingers found the braided steel cable and began following it to the handset, he, and everything around him was incinerated.

14

I startled awake, my entire body jerking briefly as if I'd been jolted with electricity. It was dark, wherever the hell I was, and a shuffling sound caused my heart rate to shoot up. There was an explosive sneeze from close by, then the noise of a vigorous shake. With a sigh, I relaxed. I knew those sounds. Dog.

A cold, wet nose wormed its way beneath my hand and I automatically rubbed his head. For several minutes, I was content to lay there and pet him. Probably because the brain wasn't functioning too well at the moment. Continuing to scratch the spot right behind his ear that turned him into a puddle of jelly, I tried to figure out what was going on.

A fast trip to Mexico to rescue a pilot who was adrift in the Sea of Cortez. Coming back into Arizona and boarding a helicopter for the final few hundred miles back to southern Nevada. I remembered making a side trip to my house on the outskirts of the Phoenix area. Well, what was left of it. It had burned, the rubble collapsing in and making it impossible for me to get to my safe. I had been unable to get any of the photos of Katie that were inside.

In a way, I suppose that may have been for the best. She was gone. Dead because of the plague the Russians had released upon the world. I knew enough about loss to realize that dwelling on the dead, refusing to let them go, wasn't healthy. As that thought passed through my mind, I grew angry with myself. What exactly was wrong with hanging on?

A doorknob rattled, heralding a blinding light that caused me to raise my hand to shield my eyes. Well, eye. For some reason, I couldn't see anything with my left one. A figure was briefly silhouetted in the opening, then the door closed and blessed darkness returned. For a moment. Then there was a soft click and a dim desk lamp came to life.

"You're awake!"

Rachel leaned over me and placed a cool hand on the side of my face. She was smiling and looked better rested than I'd seen her in quite some time.

"What happened? Where are we?" I asked, able to lower my hand in the absence of the bright light from the hallway. "What's wrong with my eye?"

She removed her hand and sat on the edge of the bed, hip pressed against me. Bed? I looked around, recognizing a medical suite. Dog, on the opposite side of the mattress, rested his chin on the sheets and stared at me.

"We're still at Area 51. Do you remember rescuing Igor and the girls? The gunfight with the militia?"

"I remember a boat," I said, looking away in thought. "Igor and I shooting at them. It's all kind of fuzzy. Like a dream."

She reached out and brushed her hand across my face again, then leaned close for a better look at my eye.

"A bullet struck your rifle. Tore it up and blasted shrapnel into you. I pulled thirteen pieces of metal out of your face, neck and shoulder. A large fragment of the round ricocheted and lodged in your head. Close to your eye. Very close."

"How close?" I asked, reaching for my face.

Rachel grabbed my hand, gently placing it onto my chest and keeping hers on top.

"It was embedded in the upper orbit, just beneath your eyebrow. Nearly tore your eyelid off. When I got to you, it was hanging by a thread."

"So my eyelid's fucked up?" I asked, hoping that was the extent of my injury.

"It was, and I sewed it back in place. But, there's a tiny fragment of the bullet that splintered off when it hit bone. It made it inside your skull and came to rest against the optic nerve. Pressing on it, actually. There's a CT machine in this place, and I got a good look."

I heard the words she was saying and didn't want to process them.

"What are you trying not to tell me? Can't you take it out?"

She shook her head.

"No. It's way too deep inside your skull, and this type of surgery would be incredibly delicate. I'm not a surgeon. Certainly not of that caliber. Maybe, if we can get you to Hawaii, there's one there, but this is far beyond anything I'm capable of.

"I was hoping that your eye would be OK when you woke up. There's some swelling, and you still might regain your sight when it goes down."

"You don't sound terribly confident about that," I said.

"I'm not. But, it's possible."

"So, I just have to wait? See what happens?"

She gave me another smile and squeezed my hand.

"Was that a joke?"

"What?" I asked.

"*See* what happens?"

I snorted and shook my head. It had just been an expression. Fortunately, Rachel wasn't going to let me start feeling sorry for myself. Not that I didn't have plenty of reasons. It would have been easy to go find a bottle and hide in a corner somewhere. And, if it wasn't for her and Dog, that might be what I'd have done. But it wasn't what I wanted to do.

"Hungry?" She asked.

"Starving," I said, the mention of food causing my stomach to grumble loudly.

"Good. You've been out for close to two days. You need to get your strength back. Get your ass up, and I'll find you some clothes."

She stood and whipped the heavy sheet off the bed, revealing that I was completely nude. I looked down at my battered body, noting several places that sported fresh stitches.

"You were a little beat up," Rachel said, rummaging through a tall cabinet. "Took a while to clean you up and find all the wounds that needed treatment."

I swung my feet around and sat on the edge of the bed. Dog grunted his displeasure at having my back turned to him. Nails clicking loudly, he came around and pushed against my leg for more attention. Rachel handed me a pair of hospital scrubs, leaning in and kissing me gently on the lips.

"I really wish you'd quit scaring me," she said. "You're not bulletproof, you know."

Exodus

After breaking the kiss, she kept her face inches from mine, looking intently at me.

"I'll try to remember that," I said, leaning forward and kissing her.

We stayed that way for a few seconds, then our lips parted and she stood with a smile on her face. It should have been awkward. Uncomfortable. But, it wasn't. I started to reach for her hand, but she stepped away and gave me a stern look.

"Cool your jets, hotrod," she laughed. "You need food and water. And you really need to brush your teeth before your try that again."

With a smile, I worked the scrub pants over my feet and scooted forward to stand so I could pull them up. I swayed dangerously, Rachel grabbing my arm to steady me. The dizziness passed almost immediately, and I tugged the bottoms over my hips. They were a couple of sizes too small and didn't need to be tied to stay up.

Rachel looked down at my feet and laughed. The pants were also too short, ending several inches above my ankles. And, the way they fit, they left little about my anatomy to the imagination.

"Really? You couldn't find a larger size?"

"This is it for scrubs," she said, trying not to keep laughing. "Want me to go find you a clean uniform?"

I shook my head as I pulled the top on. The fabric brushed across my damaged eye and I hissed when raw pain blossomed in my skull. Getting the shirt over my shoulders, I tugged it down by the hem. It ended a couple of inches above my waistband and hugged me like a speedo.

Rachel stared for a second, then had to turn away, laughter threatening to double her over. I glared at her and rolled my shoulders forward, trying to stretch the fabric that was binding so tightly. Instead, there was a ripping sound as it tore down the middle of my back.

For a moment, she paused, staring at me with wide eyes and a huge grin on her face, then she completely lost it. While she tumbled into a chair against the far wall, gales of laughter pouring out of her, I ripped the shirt the rest of the way and tore it free. Tossing it onto the bed, I ignored Rachel and headed for the door.

"Where are you going, looking like that?" She asked, holding her sides and trying to catch her breath.

"Find a uniform," I grumbled, trying to suppress a smile.

"Well, slow down a little," she said, hurrying to my side and bringing a rifle around to hang in front of her body. "We've been encountering the occasional female inside the facility."

Exodus

"Is there a breach?" I asked, forgetting about the pain in my head.

"Not that anyone can find," she said. "The best guess is they were trapped in here and are as lost in the maze as we are."

I nodded and made a mental note to talk to Johnson as soon as I could find him. Ducking into the quartermaster's area, I grabbed fresh clothing and a hygiene kit, then went into the latrine. Dog followed me, giving the place a thorough inspection while I peered at my battered face in the mirror. Rachel, who had promised to wait in the hall, cracked the door open within ten seconds.

"OK to come in?" She asked.

"Why not," I said. "Don't think you'll see anything you didn't get an eyeful of while you were cleaning me up."

She pushed through the door with a smirk and came to stand next to me. Together, we looked at my face in the mirror. Frankly, I was a little shocked. I've been in a lot of fights. Kicked some ass, and had mine kicked. But this was about the worst I could ever remember looking.

The flesh around my left eye was red and swollen. The eyelid was puffy where Rachel had reattached it, and drooped lazily. That whole area of my face was dramatically larger than the right side and made me look like an alien. Well, I was at Area 51. I'd fit right in.

"I've got some painkillers if it's hurting too bad," Rachel said, the mirth from earlier completely gone from her voice.

I shook my head, then regretted the movement as a lance of pain shot through my eye.

"I'm good," I said, looking down at the items I'd brought with me.

It was difficult trying to do things with only one functioning eye. Hardly impossible, but it was going to take some getting used to. And, how was I going to function in combat? I'd lost the peripheral vision for the left half of my body. About the only good news was that I'm right eye dominant, so aiming a weapon shouldn't be a problem. Hopefully.

I shaved my face, then Rachel helped with my head. There were too many nicks, bumps, bruises and stitches for me to do it on my own. Brushing my teeth, I shooed her and Dog out, used the facilities and stepped into a steaming shower.

The water cleared the last of the cobwebs and five minutes later I shut it off and walked around the privacy wall. Not surprisingly, Rachel was seated on a long bench, waiting for me.

"Really?"

Exodus

"Deal with it," she said, tossing me a clean pair of underwear.

I reached for them, missing the catch by several inches. Standing there, I looked down at my hand in surprise.

"Sorry," Rachel said. "I needed to make a point, and thought this would be a way to get you to listen."

"What point? That I can't catch underwear?"

"Don't be a jerk," she said, frowning at me. "The point is, your brain is used to having two functioning eyes. Stereoscopic vision. They work in tandem, allowing you good spatial perception. I'm sure you've already realized you don't have left peripheral vision, but you need to understand that you've lost more than that."

"Like what?" I asked, picking up the underwear and pulling it on.

"Like what just happened. Judging speed and location. You're also going to have difficulty estimating distance. Those are the big things that will be a problem for you in the short term."

"In the short term? You mean until my sight comes back?"

"Not exactly. What I mean is that it's going to take time for your brain to adjust to the loss of half of the visual input its always had. And, assuming the worst, even when that happens, you're still going to have a noticeable def..."

She stopped speaking and looked away.

"Noticeable what?"

She shook her head.

"Going to say deficit, weren't you?"

She nodded, looking up to meet my one good eye. I stood there for a long pause, pants in my hands. As much as I hated to hear what she was saying, I knew she was right. The loss of an eye would be an immediate medical retirement from any Special Forces unit. Maybe, if one was lucky, the military would find a desk job for the injured warrior, but most likely it would mean you were done. It was a huge disadvantage, and I knew that.

But, I also knew that in the world we lived in, retiring to a shitty apartment and collecting disability pay wasn't an option. Now, when there was a fight, you had to step up. It didn't matter what might be wrong with you. Not if you wanted to live. What I had to do was remember that I had a disadvantage. I had to find ways to compensate.

"I get it," I said.

Stepping into the pants, I pulled them up and sat on the bench next to her to lace a new pair of boots. She

Exodus

placed her hand lightly on my shoulder but didn't say anything else.

15

When we walked into the cafeteria, Irina looked up from a cup of coffee and smiled in surprise when she saw me. Jumping to her feet, she rushed across the room and gingerly wrapped her arms around me, planting a delicate kiss on the undamaged side of my face.

"I am so glad to see you," she said, stepping back but keeping her hands on my arms.

Before I could answer, Tiffany pushed between us and hugged me, burying her face against my chest. With what I was sure was an embarrassed grin, I hugged her back.

"OK, OK, let him sit down," Rachel said, steering me towards the closest table. "You two keep an eye on him while I get some food."

Irina and Tiffany sat across from me as Rachel disappeared into the kitchen. Across the room, a group of girls huddled around a table, watching us. I didn't see Chelsea.

"How's your eye? Looks like hell," Tiffany said, leaning forward for a better look.

"That's how it feels," I said.

"Can you see?" Irina asked.

"Sure," I said, trying another smile, then changed the subject. "Where is everyone?"

"Keeping watch," Irina said. "The militia has surrounded us."

"What?" I shoved the chair back and stood, apparently too fast, as my head swam and I had to put a hand out to steady myself.

"Sit your ass down!"

Rachel had come back with a plate of food as I'd gotten to my feet, coming to a stop and glaring at me.

"Igor has everything well in hand," Irina said. "We are secure. They cannot get in."

"What do they want?" I asked, still standing.

Rachel strode to the table and set the plate down, harder than necessary. Hands on her hips, she stared at me until I slowly sank back into my chair. After watching me a moment, she took the seat next to mine and slid the plate in front of me.

"What do they want?" I asked again.

"Blood," Irina said, shrugging as if it wasn't anything unusual. "They are upset over all of their people we have killed. The ones in the desert when you were on your way to Mexico, and there were quite a few that Igor killed while rescuing the girls."

I nodded slowly, using a fork to pick at the food Rachel had prepared.

"We're even," Tiffany said in a voice laced with venom.

I looked at her, not understanding. It had looked like Igor had successfully retrieved all the girls that had been taken. Had they been abused while being held captive?

"Caleb," she said after an awkward moment of silence.

I hadn't realized until that moment that her boyfriend hadn't been one of the people who'd piled into the boat.

"What happened?" I asked gently.

She didn't say anything, finally looking away with tears in her eyes.

"He was with Igor," Irina answered for her. "They got to where the girls were being held, but an alarm was raised on the way out. Igor was leading the group, and Caleb was watching the rear. He did not make it."

"I'm sorry," I said to Tiffany.

After a long minute, she sniffed and wiped her eyes, turning to look at me.

"I'm sorry, too," she said. "I know about your wife. We've all lost someone."

We sat there for a bit, simply looking at each other. Again, she'd reminded me that she may look like a kid, but she'd grown up. I reached across the table and squeezed her hand briefly before turning back to Irina.

"How many are out there?"

"Igor estimates more than three hundred. Master Chief Gonzales concurs."

"Has anyone talked to them?" I asked, taking a bite of the food.

"No. They broadcasted their demands over a loud speaker when they arrived. They are using radios to coordinate their movements. We can hear them, hear the basic codes they are using, but they refuse to respond to our calls."

"What about Hawaii? Any help coming?"

Irina shook her head before I even finished asking the question.

"There was a large engagement between American and Russian forces. Heavy losses on both sides. There are large elements of the Russian Air Force occupying bases on the west coast, and the Admiral does not have enough remaining planes to fight his way through. We are on our own."

"Fucking marvelous," I grumbled.

The news Irina was giving me had killed my appetite, but I forced myself to keep eating. The food didn't even taste good, but my body needed it.

"What else do I need to know?" I asked.

"Those are the highlights," Irina said. "We are trapped, but I am hopeful that they will grow tired and leave."

"Yeah, well, if they've got any idea of what this place is, and I'm betting they do, that ain't gonna happen." I pushed the empty plate away and stood up. "Where's Igor? Never mind. You'd better take me there so you can translate."

"Sure you're up to it?" Rachel asked, standing up next to me.

"I'm fine," I said, even though a headache was threatening to crush my skull like an empty beer can.

"You don't look like you are," Tiffany said, earning an appreciative glance from Rachel.

"Let's go," I said to Irina, ignoring the concerned expressions on all three of their faces.

With a sigh, Irina got to her feet and I followed her out into the hall, Rachel and Dog sticking close. We all got into one of the electric carts, Irina taking the wheel, and headed out with a squeal of tires on the smooth concrete floor. The first stop was the armory where I spent close to ten minutes outfitting myself with weapons. Then, a few minutes later, we parked adjacent to a steel door simply labeled as *Security*. The keypad that normally controlled access was missing, a tangle of wires dangling from the wall to the right of the jamb.

When I pushed through, Igor looked up from a massive control station. When he saw me, he leapt to his feet, smiled, and in very Russian fashion wrapped me in a hug and placed a kiss on my uninjured cheek. I appreciated his enthusiasm for my continued existence, but I really needed to have a chat with him about how men in America greet each other. I'm not big into hugs, and sure as hell don't think lips should ever enter the equation. But, despite my discomfort, I returned the hug and grinned at him as he stepped away. He rattled off something in Russian, and I looked to Irina for help.

"Igor says he is very happy to see you on your feet, even if your face does look like a plate of borscht," she translated.

"Bite me, asshole," I said after turning to face Igor.

He laughed before resuming his seat and scanning dozens of monitors that covered the wall to his front. Moving closer, I peered at them, reminded of how hard it was going to be to adjust to only one eye when I bumped into a chair. The damn thing was to my left, and I hadn't seen it. If it had been an infected, I'd have been lunch by now.

On several of the screens, I could see men in a variety of quasi-military clothing standing around pickups. All of them were heavily armed but appeared to be poorly trained, if at all. Instead of putting a man up in the bed of each truck to keep watch on their surroundings, they were all clustered near the tailgates, smoking and talking.

"How long have they been out there?" I asked.

"Showed up a few hours after the pilot brought you in."

I turned at the new voice to see Master Chief Gonzales standing in the open door.

"Sorry I missed you, sir," he said. "Didn't know you were up and I was in the head."

"This isn't a parade ground, Master Chief," I said, earning a painful grin from him. "So, what have the ass hats out there been doing?"

"After you left, we found out how to lock down the facility. One hell of an impressive setup. Blast doors and everything. Best guess is it's intended to protect in the event of a nuclear strike. Not a direct hit, mind you, but anything short of that probably ain't getting through. They've tried to force their way in a couple of times. Tried some C-4. Didn't get very far. One of the dumb bastards blew himself up."

Exodus

He chuckled as he said the last. I nodded my aching head in thought.

"When we were on our way south, we swung by Nellis. Were gonna pick up some heavier weapons, but they were there, raiding an armory. Can you think of anything they might have gotten their hands on that could be a problem?"

Gonzales was quiet for a moment before shaking his head.

"No, sir," he said. "Not man-portable, at least. Now, if they've got a pilot, I'll bet you there are some bunker busters at Nellis that could ruin our day."

"Speaking of pilots, where the hell is Commander Vance?"

"Sleeping."

Gonzales shrugged, somehow managing to convey his distaste for the man.

"He been behaving?" I asked.

"Sir?" The Master Chief asked, frowning.

"Never mind," I said, not feeling like going into an explanation. "Irina told me they broadcasted a message when they arrived. What did they say?"

"They want the men that killed their men, and they want the girls back. Said they'll starve us out if we don't give them up."

"Nothing else?" I asked.

"No, sir. I've tried to raise them on the radio several times, but they refuse to respond."

I turned back to the screens in thought. Watched as several separate groups of men stood around in the dark desert. Tried to figure out what they could be waiting for.

"How are we fixed for supplies, Master Chief?" I asked without taking my attention off the monitors.

"Sir, the facility is apparently on a well, or wells. Got all the water we need. Food? Hell, there's enough food in here to keep all of us going for years if need be."

"Power?"

"Seems stable, but we haven't been able to figure out where it's coming from."

I took a deep breath and quickly ran over everything in my mind that needed to be dealt with. And, probably didn't think of at least three or four important things.

"OK, go roust our pilot out of bed, and get him down here. I've got some questions for him." Gonzales started to turn away before I stopped him. "By the way, what's Johnson up to?"

"Still opening doors. He's convinced he'll find an alien ray gun or something that'll zap all those guys outside into dust."

"Has he found anything interesting?"

"Not really sure," Gonzales grinned. "Most of the shit he's found, well, none of us have a clue what it's supposed to do."

16

While I waited for the Master Chief to return with Vance, I sat down next to Igor. Irina and Rachel had taken off in the golf cart when I'd asked if they could find me some aspirin. My head was pounding like a Friday night frat party, and it was hard to think.

"Have you seen the General?" I asked.

"General?" Igor asked, turning to look at me.

I held cupped hands in front of my chest in the universal symbol for big boobs that he and Long had used when they'd seen her at Nellis. His face lit up in understanding, then he shook his head.

"Nyet. Too sorry," he said, copying me and grinning.

"Have you told Irina you love her?"

That question wiped the smile off his face, and he dropped his hands into his lap.

"Not right time," he said.

"There is no right time, my friend," I said, slapping him on the shoulder.

"You tell Rachel?" He shot back.

"Been a little busy," I grumbled.

"I, too," he said, happy to ride along on my excuse.

"*Me*," I said. "Me, too, not I, too. Got it?"

"Me, too," he said, nodding his head.

"Me, too, what?" Rachel asked from behind, causing me to jump.

I turned and held my hand out for the aspirin bottle she was holding.

"Just a little English lesson," I said.

"Uh huh."

She shook her head and rattled two tablets out of the bottle, handing them to me along with a bottle of water. I swallowed them as Vance walked through the door, rubbing sleep from his eyes.

"You look like hell," he said as he flopped into a chair.

Dog had been lying close to it. He didn't care much for Vance and showed his displeasure by grunting and moving closer to me.

"Whatever," I grumbled. "Didn't have the Master Chief wake you up to give me an assessment of my appearance."

He looked like he had something smart to say but wisely chose to keep his mouth shut. I wasn't in the mood.

"You've seen those yahoos out there?" I asked, hooking my thumb over my shoulder at the monitors.

He glanced in that direction before nodding.

"When we were on our way to get you, we stopped at Nellis and saw them raiding what I'm pretty sure was the small arms armory. Nothing in there that's going to be able to breach this place. But, what about a bomb?"

"You mean like air dropped ordnance? Like a JDAM?" He asked, instantly growing more alert.

"Yes."

"Well, sure. If they've got a pilot, and personnel with the knowledge to get it loaded onto an aircraft and armed. No reason they couldn't. They could probably even figure it out. The biggest stumbling block for them would be having someone who can fly one of those jets and actually hit his target."

I nodded at what he said, which paralleled what I'd been thinking, but it was nice to get confirmation from an expert.

"What about without an aircraft?" I asked.

Exodus

"You mean just roll the bomb up to the door and detonate?"

"Something like that," I said. "Possible?"

"Anything's possible," he said. "But you're getting into an area that would require an ordnance expert so they didn't blow themselves up trying to rig the damn thing."

"Which we can't count on them not having. Lot of former military was attracted to these militia groups before everything went to shit."

"Yeah," he said. "I saw some of those same reports. So, sure, I guess they could make that work if they had the right personnel. But, from what the Master Chief showed me after they locked down the facility, that's not going to punch through.

"Bunker busters don't work by detonating on the surface of something. They're designed to penetrate into rock or hardened concrete before exploding. The pressure wave is contained within the material and magnified. You know, kind of like a firecracker on your open palm, or in your closed fist. Which one's going to fuck you up?"

I nodded, acknowledging he was right.

"So, as long as they can't put a plane in the air, we shouldn't have anything to be worried about," I said.

"As far as I know," he said, shrugging. "And, even then, they need to know what they're doing to deliver the ordnance on target. We train on that kind of shit all the time. It's not hard, once you know what to do and how to do it, but the first time out of the gate, even with classroom instruction, it's harder than it looks."

I looked up at Rachel and Irina who had been listening intently. They looked back at me but didn't say anything.

"OK, let's hope they don't have some former fighter pilot in their ranks. So, what about that Buck Rogers airplane? Have a chance to look at it?"

"Yeah," he said, the enthusiasm obvious in his voice. "That thing's the cat's ass, but we aren't going anywhere in it."

"Why not?"

"Two of the command modules are missing from the main computer. Probably got pulled for a software update, or debugging, or who knows what. No way to know. Something like that isn't going to fly without everything working at a hundred percent."

"So, even if we get the militia out of the way, we've got nothing to fly out of here."

"I didn't say that," Vance said.

Exodus

"You found something else?" I asked, hope surging.

"Yeah, but nothing sexy. There's a C-130 in another hangar. Looks to be in good shape and the flight and maintenance logs show it's ready to go. Just needs fuel and a runway."

"What's the range?" I asked.

I was already thinking about how long it would take to get to Australia in a lumbering C-130.

"Maybe a couple thousand miles," Vance said. "And if you're wondering, that's not enough to get us to Hawaii."

"Seriously?"

"Yep," he said, nodding. "To make that hop, you've either gotta have an auxiliary tank, or a tanker waiting for you between here and there. Already looked for an aux tank, and there aren't any I can find."

"Are you forgetting the Russians that are still on the coast of California?" Rachel interrupted. "They aren't going to just let us fly over and wave."

"See!" Igor called, pulling all of our attention away from the conversation.

Swiveling the chair around, I rolled it forward to look at the monitor he was pointing at. One of the deuce and a half's I'd seen them loading at Nellis was approaching the facility. It was towing a long trailer with a massive cylinder loaded aboard.

The driver piloted the vehicle cautiously, swinging it around and stopping within a few feet of one of the exterior blast doors. A pickup had followed, and as soon as the deuce was in position, he hopped into it and they raced away.

"Fuck me, that's a MOAB! That can be a problem!"

Vance was the first to recognize what was being towed behind the truck.

"What's a MOAB?" Rachel asked.

"Mother Of All Bombs," I said, jumping to my feet.

The correct, official name of the bomb that had just been parked next to the armored entrance is Massive Ordnance Air Burst. But, Mother Of All Bombs just sounds so much more sinister. What it is, is one hell of a huge amount of high explosive. The equivalent of eleven tons of TNT, to be precise. It is one of the top two or three most powerful bombs in the world that does not contain a nuclear warhead, and has a blast radius of nearly a hundred and fifty meters. I wasn't at all confident that the facility's bomb shielding could withstand that kind of force.

"How far is that door from here?" I shouted, looking around the room.

Exodus

After a brief moment of silence, Irina repeated my question in rapid-fire Russian. Igor was already working a keyboard and a moment later looked up as another monitor displayed a schematic of the facility. I leaned closer, feeling a little better when it appeared we were at the opposite end of the installation.

"Where's Johnson?" I barked, satisfied that, for at least the moment, we were safe.

"Opening doors," Gonzales answered, lifting a radio to his mouth and shouting into it.

Before he received an answer, several of the monitors blanked out with no warning. An instant later, my ears popped from a pressure change, just like taking off or landing in an airplane. A bass rumble rolled through the room, dust drifting down from the ceiling, then the power went out, plunging us into impenetrable darkness.

17

There were frightened exclamations from Irina and Rachel, and probably me too, but I'm not going to admit it. A light clicked on and I looked around to see the Master Chief with his rifle up, the flashlight attached to the rail providing some illumination. Another one, attached to Irina's pistol, came to life an instant later. Dog, completely freaked out, was pressed tightly against Rachel, ears flattened against his skull. Everyone was trying to talk at once, and I raised my voice to silence them.

"They must have breached," I said. "Anyone else feel the pressure wave?"

"I did." Vance spoke from a dark corner.

"OK," I said. "Vance, Rachel and Irina, get back to where we left the girls. Take Dog. Any of you have a radio?"

"Here," Gonzales said, pulling a small handset from his pocket and pressing it into Vance's hand.

"Watch your asses, and don't engage the enemy if you have a choice," I ordered, pulling my new rifle around and making sure it was ready to go. "Once you've got them…"

I paused as I realized I didn't know the facility well enough to pick a rally point. Moving deeper underground would only succeed in getting all of us trapped if the militia had made it inside. We needed some place where we could make a stand, but also fall back or even exit into the desert if we had to.

"Master Chief?" I asked, looking at Gonzales.

He didn't need for me to explain what I needed from him.

"Level A hangar," he said without hesitation. "Remember where that is?"

He was looking at Irina who quickly nodded.

"Where's Chelsea and Nicole?" I asked, suddenly remembering that I hadn't seen those two women since I'd returned.

"With Johnson, wherever the hell that is," Gonzales growled.

He had developed a relationship with Nicole, and I could see the worry creasing his face. But, first things first.

"Go!" I barked at Vance.

He leapt to his feet and rushed out of the room, the girls and Dog close behind.

"First priority is to find out for sure if we've been breached," I said to Gonzales and Igor. "Then we'll look for our missing people. Master Chief, keep trying them on the radio."

Dirk Patton

We hustled into the corridor. I glanced to my left, seeing a dim glow that was rapidly receding into the distance. Irina's light aboard the electric cart. Turning right, I fell in behind Gonzales who seemed to know his way around. Igor tucked in behind me, and we set off at a trot.

Passing through several corridors, the Master Chief led us around a bend and pounded up a flight of stairs, taking them two at a time. I dragged a toe on one of the treads, nearly going down before catching myself at the last possible instant. It wasn't because I was clumsy, which I can be. It was a lack of depth perception due to only having one functioning eye. Cursing under my breath, I focused as best I could and pushed harder to catch up with the SEAL.

Several more minutes of running and we skidded to a halt. The corridor in front of us was completely blocked with rubble. Dust still hung in the air, reflecting the beam of Gonzales's light and making it look like something out of a Sci-Fi movie.

"How far away is the door where they parked the bomb?" I asked.

The Master Chief stared at the pile of debris for a moment before looking around to orient himself.

"At least a hundred yards," he said. "And I'm probably being conservative. But no way they're digging through that shit without having more of it come crashing down on top of them. Dumb motherfuckers used way too much bomb."

"Be glad they did," I said.

All of us jumped back as several chunks of concrete broke free from the damaged ceiling and crashed to the floor only feet in front of where we stood.

"Any luck raising Johnson?"

"No," Gonzales said, shaking his head.

He raised the radio to his mouth and tried again, but only received silence in response. Trying again with no success, he sighed and called Vance. It took a couple of attempts, but the pilot responded. Confirmation that the radios were working properly.

At my prompting, the Master Chief had him verify he'd found the girls. They were frightened but unharmed, and now they were on their way to the rally point Gonzales had given them.

"Any idea what part of the facility Johnson might have been in?" I asked.

Gonzales shrugged his shoulders and looked at Igor.

"Johnson. Did you see him on the monitors?"

"Nyet," Igor said.

There was an ominous creak that started up from the ceiling above us, and we quickly retreated fifty yards back down the corridor.

You've been stomping around for a few days now," I said to Gonzales. "How big is this place?"

"Big," he said. "It would take us days to search it, and that's if the power was on. With just flashlights? Probably a week. And that's without stopping to eat or sleep."

"Shit," I grumbled.

"Electric," Igor said.

"What?"

"Fix electric," he said, pointing at a light fixture mounted to the ceiling over our heads.

"Master Chief?" I prompted.

"Sir, we haven't looked that hard, but we haven't found where it's coming from. And anyway, wouldn't we be better off to spend the time searching?"

I thought about that for a couple of seconds before nodding.

"OK, call Vance and have him meet us here with all the girls. We're going to break up into search parties, but I want a couple of people keeping an eye on this corridor. Just because it's blocked here, well… we've got no idea how far the rubble extends on the other side. The militia might be able to clear it in a couple of hours, then we've got them crawling up our asses while we're running around looking for Johnson."

Gonzales nodded and put the call out, passing on my instructions to Vance.

"They're on the way," he said.

I held up a hand to silence him. Something was making a faint noise, and it sounded to be coming from within the pile of debris. Moving as quietly as possible, I slowly approached the blocked area. As I drew closer, I couldn't help but cast a nervous glance at the ceiling. If more chunks of concrete suddenly broke free, I'd have no warning before my brains were permanently scrambled.

Igor and Gonzales slowly trailed behind, coming closer as I slowed to a stop and closed my eyes. Whatever was making the noise was definitely within the rubble. There was no pattern or regularity to it, just an occasional scrape or bang. With a sinking feeling, I was pretty sure I knew what I was hearing.

"They're digging through," I said, opening my eyes.

"Da," Igor said.

"How the hell are they coming so fast?" Gonzales asked.

"Maybe not far as you think," Igor offered.

"Master Chief, that rally point you gave to Irina. We'll have access to the outside if we have to bug out?"

"Yes, sir. Doesn't mean they won't be waiting for us, but there are a couple of exits in addition to the big hangar door."

"Alright. Call Vance back and tell him to disregard. Get his ass to the rally point." Gonzales nodded and lifted the radio. "Igor, get to the armory. I saw some Willie Pete in there. Grab all you can."

Igor stared at me, incomprehension on his face, and I shook my head and smiled an apology.

"White phosphorous grenades. Incendiary. Fire. Got it?"

He grinned with understanding and dashed off to retrieve what I'd asked for.

"What you thinking?" Gonzales asked.

"Setting up a little welcome surprise for our guests," I said.

18

Admiral Packard lit another cigarette, knowing he didn't need it, but wanting it nonetheless. He was exhausted, unable to remember the last time he'd slept, and the nicotine helped him keep going. There was a muted cough from the direction the smoke was drifting, and he turned to look at his head of personal security, Marine Captain Charles Black. The man was scanning the surrounding area, pointedly ignoring the Admiral's scrutiny.

"Did you have something to say, Captain?" Packard asked, puffing away.

"Me, sir?" The Marine asked innocently.

"Knock off the act, Captain. You threw yourself between me and a Russian sniper's bullet. I think you've earned the right to speak your mind when I ask."

Black looked at the older man, obviously hesitating.

"Well, Captain?"

Black made another scan of the area, ensuring his men were alert and doing their jobs, then took a deep breath and met the Admiral's eyes.

"Concerned about your health, sir," he finally said.

"And that's exactly why you're here," Packard said.

"Not what I meant, sir. I mean… well… it's just that if something were to happen to you…"

"Goddamn it Marine, spit it out," Packard grumbled.

"You're smoking like a chimney, sir. You're existing on coffee and cigarettes. And, begging the Admiral's pardon, but that's bad for a man *my* age. That's all I was thinking, sir."

Black looked away, afraid to meet Packard's sharp gaze. He turned in surprise when the Admiral threw his head back and laughed.

"Captain, you sound exactly like my dear, departed wife! Please don't take offense to that, I'm not saying you're a woman, but you're worrying like a wife or a mother. This old body's tougher than it looks."

"Don't doubt that for a second, sir. I'm just concerned about what would happen if we lost you," Black responded.

"You lose me, there's Admiral Black. Any relation, by the way?"

"No, sir. Not that I know of."

Packard stared at the young officer as he smoked his cigarette down to the filter. Stripping the cherry onto the lush grass, he stood and shoved the butt into his pocket.

"I appreciate your concern, Captain. I really do. But I'm fine, and I plan to outlive that Russian bastard, Barinov. There's no way I'm going until I've seen him strung up by his old, shriveled balls!"

"Oorah, sir," Black said softly.

"Now, if there are no other concerns about my well-being, let's get back to the CIC," the Admiral said, a note of sarcasm in his voice.

Black allowed an uncharacteristic grin to show for a moment, then it disappeared as he raised his hand to his radio earpiece. He listened for a few seconds before turning to look to the north.

"Captain West coming to see you, sir," he said.

Packard looked in the same direction, seeing a small procession of Marines coming his way. He knew his aide would be in the middle of the group, shielded by their bodies. As they were still some distance away, he sat back down on the bench and pulled out a fresh cigarette. Before he lit it, he cut his eyes at the Marine, who was once again studiously ignoring him. With a sigh, he put the smoke back in its pack and in his pocket.

Nearly a minute later, the group arrived. The four Marines who had formed a protective bubble around Captain West peeled away, and he walked the final few yards to where Packard waited for him.

"Captain. What can I do for you?"

"Sir, I've just spent the past half hour speaking with a Dr. Hironata from the University. She has some information that you should hear."

Packard's eyebrows shot up in surprise. Of all the possible things his aide could have wanted to tell him, this one wasn't even on his radar.

"What would that be, Captain?"

"Sir, I think it's better if we have this conversation in your office," West said, holding the Admiral's gaze.

After a few moments, Packard sighed and got to his feet.

"Captain Black, looks like we're not going to the CIC."

"Yes, sir," Black said, broadcasting the new destination over a heavily encrypted radio to the security detail.

Several minutes later, the Admiral strode into his office, Captain West on his heels. Captain Black followed them in, immediately placing himself in front of the woman who was seated on the sofa. Two other Marines stepped through the door, positioning

Exodus

themselves on either side of her. Packard sighed, walked around his desk and dropped into the chair.

Black quickly searched the visitor's purse and leather folio case that held her laptop. When that was complete, he waved one of the Marines forward to run a metal detecting wand over her body. Satisfied, he waved his men out and faded into a corner, keeping a watchful eye on the woman.

"Dr. Hironata, my aide tells me I need to listen to what you have to say," the Admiral began. "I'm pressed for time, so please forgive me for dispensing with the pleasantries."

"Quite alright, Admiral," the woman answered, her voice soft and lilting with the faintest hint of an indeterminate accent. "I certainly understand, especially under the circumstances."

Packard nodded and waved for her to take one of the chairs in front of his desk. After sitting and adjusting her skirt, she folded her hands in her lap and stared intently at the Admiral.

"As I'm sure Captain West has told you, I'm from the University of Hawaii. But, I'm not a professor. I don't teach classes. I'm a researcher, working under a grant from the Society for Conservation Biology."

Packard shot a glance at Captain West. If this woman was here to read him the riot act about the damage to the environment caused by battles with the

Russians, he was going to bounce her out on her ear and have his aid swabbing toilets in the Marine barracks.

"It's not what you're thinking, Admiral," she interjected after seeing the look she was so familiar with. "It's far worse."

This got Packard's attention. Leaning forward, he rested his elbows on the desk and peered intently at his guest.

"You have my undivided attention, Doctor. Please continue."

"My work for the past four years has involved studying and cataloging the impacts of humans on the vast variety of biological ecosystems in the Pacific Rim. Twenty years ago, even ten, this would have involved painstaking efforts to physically visit every location and spend inordinate amounts of time documenting the health of each. Then, we would have to repeat the process after a pre-defined amount of time had passed, study the same markers, then compare them to the original. Highly inefficient, and incredibly expensive, to say the least. But, this was a new endeavor. The grant that funded it came from Trey Final."

"The Silicon Valley billionaire?" Packard asked in surprise.

"Yes. He is… was… very concerned about global warming and its effects on the planet. I mention him because he not only provided the cash, he also designed, built and provided highly sophisticated, unmanned monitoring stations that have been installed in every nation that would allow us access, which has been almost all of the Pacific Rim countries."

"What do these monitoring stations do?" The Admiral asked.

"The basics, of course. Environmental data, such as air temp, water temp if they're close to the ocean, rainfall, humidity, CO_2 levels, and so much more. But, Mr. Final took it a big step farther. Each station also houses multiple drones that routinely collect and analyze environmental samples within a five-hundred-meter radius.

"What that means is that there is a drone that digs into the soil, not unlike the rovers we sent to Mars. Another drone will obtain a physical sample of the surrounding vegetation. Part of the leaf from a tree, a blade of grass or a flower bloom. This allows us to see what damage, if any, is being done to the plant life. There is yet another drone that locates and captures insects for study. And, finally, the last drone performs a routine survey of animal life. No capture, only information about their presence."

"Doctor," Packard interrupted. "This is all very fascinating, but I must ask you to get to the point."

"I'm sorry," she said. "I needed to preface what I'm about to say. To dramatically shorten the discussion, the planet is dying. At least the part that I am monitoring."

There was a stunned silence in the room. After a moment, Packard looked at his aide.

"I've verified she is who she claims to be, and the existence of the project, sir," Captain West said.

"Excuse me?" Dr. Hironata blurted, clearly offended.

"Forgive us, Doctor," Packard said smoothly. "We may not be scientists, but we do know a little about the necessity of validating data."

"I understand," she said stiffly, clearly not mollified.

"Doctor, perhaps you'd better fill in the blanks for me," the Admiral said, ignoring her angst at having her background verified.

Tugging the hem of her skirt, she looked at him for a long moment before nodding.

Exodus

19

"Exactly what do you mean by your statement?" The Admiral asked. "*How* is the planet dying?"

"Insect and animal life has decreased by over eighty percent in the past five months. Let me correct that. Not *all* animal life. Only birds and mammals. Amphibian and reptilian communities appear to remain healthy, other than the impact on the populations that depend heavily upon the previously mentioned animals for survival. We have seen a correlating decline in these populations as their food source has become more and more scarce.

"Plant life is suffering as well. We are beginning to see the early stages of the loss of entire ecosystems. This is directly attributable to the disappearance of nearly all the bacteria, molds and fungi in the soil. In essence, the dirt is becoming sterile, as is the ocean."

"I don't understand," Admiral Packard said, shocked. "How does the absence of bacteria harm the plants?"

"Scavengers do the heavy lifting when an animal dies. Bacteria, mold and fungi then go to work, completing the decomposition of whatever is not consumed by a scavenger. That scavenger can be bird, mammal or insect. Typically, all three.

"In the absence of scavengers, as well as the bacteria, mold and fungi, nothing is being broken down to replenish the nutrients in the soil that are required for the vegetation to survive. Even animal waste, what little there still is and which is normally a boon for plants, is not being broken down. It is the cycle of life, gentlemen. And it appears to have been broken."

"Doctor," Captain West interjected. "Please tell the Admiral about your concerns for the oceans."

She nodded and paused a moment to gather her thoughts.

"The same principle applies to the Earth's oceans. There is a cycle of life that depends on many different species playing their part. I have no data on the presence, or lack thereof, of sea life. However, ocean water samples from all around the Pacific Rim are yielding the same results. The presence of bacteria and other microorganisms has dropped to nearly undetectable levels. Based on this evidence, I am comfortable in predicting that if we were to perform a survey, we would find that the presence of higher life forms has plummeted."

"Admiral, this is supported by reports I am receiving from the commercial fishing fleet. If you recall, I briefed you on this last week."

"What reports?" Dr. Hironata asked, sitting up attentively.

Exodus

"The catch has dropped off alarmingly over the past few weeks," Captain West said. "The boats are having to go farther and farther out, fishing in the deepest parts of the ocean to catch even a fraction of what was previously being brought in. Even then, so they tell me, most of what they find in their nets appears diseased, and they are throwing it back."

"That fits with what I was describing," the doctor exclaimed. "Fish and mammals are dying. The deeper the water, the colder, and it's taking longer for the sterilization effect to occur, but it is happening. Very soon, there may be no life remaining in our oceans."

"Wait," Admiral Packard held up a hand to stop the conversation. "How do we know this is happening everywhere? And how do we even know it? There are no global communications that aren't going through a couple of our satellites!"

"The monitoring stations, sir," Dr. Hironata said. "They are completely autonomous. Solar powered and operate on a shortwave frequency, using each other to pass that signal along to my laboratory here in Hawaii. A radio mesh, as it was explained to me."

"But how can we know this is widespread and not a few isolated locations?"

The doctor took a deep breath before answering.

"There are forty-four nations on the Pacific Rim. I have eight hundred and eleven monitoring stations located in thirty-nine of those countries. There is no data for anywhere else on the planet, but it is worth noting that my network provides coverage for nearly forty-five percent of the globe. It is difficult to imagine that the rest of the Earth is not experiencing the same changes."

The Admiral rocked back in his chair, concern creasing his already lined face.

"Should I detail the impacts of this?" Dr. Hironata asked after a long silence.

"Everyone dies," Packard said in a quiet voice. "With no plants or animals, there's no food. No fresh air. Nothing. We simply cease to exist. Am I right?"

The doctor slowly nodded.

"You are correct, Admiral."

"How did this happen?" Captain West asked.

"The virus. It was genetically engineered. From what I've learned, it was originally based on simian rabies. At least that's the predominant theory. But, when it was weaponized, there was a change made to its genetic code. Apparently, there was no concern over the risk of it jumping species and, as it mutated, that is exactly what it has done."

"But, insects? Bacteria?" West asked.

Exodus

"Any living organism is susceptible to a virus, Captain. Even bacteria."

"Other than the fishing reports, are we seeing any sign of it here?" Packard asked.

"Yes, sir. We are," Dr. Hironata said. "Four of the monitoring stations are local. Here in the islands. Each of them is providing similar data. Some locations around the Rim are farther along than others, but every station that is still in operation is detecting the effects I've outlined. I cannot say for sure why there is a discrepancy, but I've spoken with several virologists who assure me this is a normal pattern. There are many variables that go into why one region may be affected first or faster, but the fact is that all regions are experiencing the same thing, to different degrees."

"How long?" The Admiral asked.

"Until all life is eradicated?"

Packard nodded.

"Rough modeling, with the assumption that this is *not* isolated to the Pacific Rim, indicates that there will be no remaining life on Earth within eighteen months."

"So, we have a year and a half," West said, almost sounding optimistic.

"No," she said, shaking her head. "In a year and a half, the Earth will be nothing but a barren wasteland with dead oceans. Long before that, humans will cease to exist, barring those few who may have access to significant food stocks. For the rest of us, the model indicates we will begin dying of starvation within seven to eight months, even accounting for existing food stores. Only very hardy plants will continue to struggle for the remainder of that time, finally succumbing to the virus or a complete lack of nutrients."

"Have you shared this information with anyone else?" The Admiral asked.

"No!" The doctor exclaimed, a look of concern on her face. "Can you imagine the reaction if this were to become public?"

"Yes, Doctor. I can," Packard said. "So, why are you telling me this?"

"I don't understand your question."

"Yes, you do. You're not here to deliver a warning. At least, that's not your sole purpose. What is your agenda, Doctor? Do you have a plan?"

She looked away, an embarrassed smile flickering across her face despite the gravity of the conversation.

"Yes, sir. I have an idea if it's not already too late."

20

Igor made it back faster than I expected, running up and puffing like a freight train. He must have sprinted both directions. A heavy canvas bag was slung over his shoulder, and he thrust it at me as he skidded to a stop. While Gonzales and I had been waiting, the noises from within the pile of rubble had continued as the militia kept digging. It was hard to tell for sure, but it didn't sound like it would be long before they made it through.

"You know that Willie Pete is gonna set all this shit on fire, right?" Gonzales asked as, bag in hand, I hurried towards the debris blocking the corridor.

"That's what I'm counting on," I said, pulling out the first WP grenade.

It only took a couple of seconds to find the right spot. Working the thick bodied munition in between two pieces of shattered concrete, I made sure the spoon was tightly wedged and wouldn't release unless the rubble shifted. When they saw what I was doing, the Master Chief and Igor each grabbed a grenade and began helping.

"Shouldn't have underestimated you, sir," Gonzales said, slipping a grenade deep inside a warped ceiling panel. "These fuckers are gonna get a hell of a surprise when they break through."

"That's OK, Master Chief," I said, placing the final device. "There'd be something wrong if a SEAL didn't think I was doing something stupid."

He grinned as we stepped back to survey our handiwork.

"But it doesn't change my point," he said. "The fire might stop them, but it's going to spread. Unless…"

He turned and aimed his light down the corridor behind us at a heavy steel door that, when closed, would isolate this area of the facility. I'd noted it as we ran past earlier.

"It still might spread," I said. "Got no way of knowing, but it's the best idea I've got at the moment."

Moving back to the debris, I carefully began pulling pins out of the White Phosphorous grenades. It only took a couple of minutes, and when I was done, the only thing keeping them from detonating was the surrounding rubble that was pinning the spoon. As soon as the militia caused a shift in the pile, the spoons would release and ignite the fuse.

White Phosphorous is nasty. Combusting at five thousand degrees when ignited, it sticks to pretty much anything it touches and will continue to burn until it is completely consumed, or deprived of oxygen. About the only way to stop it is to submerge it in water. And, if it touches clothing or skin, it will quickly melt all the way through to bone. If any of the militia came into contact with it, they'd immediately lose all desire to keep digging.

But, in an enclosed space like the corridor, being burned wasn't the only consideration. WP produces a dense, white smoke that is toxic. It has been used for decades by the military to create smoke screens. Just one of those grenades would generate enough choking smoke in the tight confines to send the militia running for fresh air.

"It isn't going to stop them forever," I said, tossing a handful of grenade pins aside. "But it'll sure as hell slow them down and buy us some time."

We both looked at Igor when he chuckled. He met our eyes, grinned and shrugged his shoulders. I had to agree with him. The intruders were going to get one hell of a surprise. But, we still had people missing.

"Let's go," I said, leading the way deeper into the facility. "We've got to find Johnson."

The two men followed, Igor closing and securing the steel hatch after we passed through. Gonzales tried the radio a couple more times, but we didn't get any response from our missing people. He checked with Vance, who verified that his group had made it to the hangar without any issues.

"Where do we start?" I asked, hoping the Master Chief had an idea.

Dirk Patton

"He was two levels down, yesterday," Gonzales said. "That's the last location I know of for sure. Unless you've got a better idea, we should start there."

"Lead the way," I said.

Without another word, the SEAL took off at a jog. I fell in behind him, hoping I wouldn't trip over something that I couldn't judge the distance to or height of. Igor brought up the rear. After a moment, I realized he was keeping the light on his rifle focused on the floor a few feet in front of me.

I appreciated his unsolicited concern, but inside I silently seethed. I've always been the one to take care of others. I didn't like being the one who needed assistance. It just went against the grain for me.

We ran down a long hall, passing seemingly endless doors, then burst into a stairwell and descended. Gonzales quickly pulled away as I slowed to make sure I didn't miss a step. These were industrial type stairs, made of poured concrete with iron caps on the front edge of each tread. A tumble here would be bad news.

He realized I'd fallen behind when he rounded the first landing, pausing to allow me to catch up. My already bad mood worsened as I caused us to waste valuable time. Pushing harder, I started to catch up, and promptly missed a step. If I hadn't been moving with a hand on the steel railing, I would have gone ass over teakettle. The Master Chief did his best to ignore my struggles, and thankfully didn't comment or ask if I was OK.

We made it to the sublevel without any more near-mishaps, bursting into a broad corridor. Our lights swept across the stygian darkness, revealing several high-security doors standing open. Gonzales tried the radio, still receiving no response.

"That way," he pointed, turning and heading to the left.

We moved farther into the facility, every door we passed standing ajar. The electronics that controlled the locking mechanisms were hanging at the ends of wires that disappeared into the walls. Johnson had apparently been very busy.

"Hold up," I said softly.

We had reached a four-way junction and the cross corridor extended in either direction beyond the limit of the lights we carried.

"Just how fucking big is this place?" I asked.

"Can't even begin to guess," Gonzales said. "I found a schematic in the Security office that showed all the tunnels and rooms, but it didn't have any scale markings on it. But, there are well over fifteen hundred rooms, just in the sublevels."

I turned a slow circle, shining my light into the darkness that stretched in every direction. Johnson could well be on this level, in a room he'd opened, examining something. The place was so big, unless we walked right past him we'd never even know he was there.

Taking a deep breath, I shouted his name at the top of my lungs. Getting the idea, Igor and Gonzales quickly joined in. We kept this up for a few seconds, then paused to listen. The silence was deafening.

"More loud," Igor said, stepping forward and raising his rifle.

I looked at him a moment, then nodded my head at the ceiling. Gonzales and I moved away and brought our hands up to cover our ears. When Igor saw we were ready, he fired a long burst of full auto.

Even with my hands over my ears, the noise was brutally loud in the enclosed space. Other than the acoustic ceiling tiles, which shredded under the assault and rained foam down to the floor, every surface was flat and hard. The blast of sound bounced back at us, adding to the hammer-drill that was already pounding inside my skull. But, it was a great idea. If there was anyone on this level, I didn't see how they could fail to hear the gunfire.

We gave it a moment for the echoes to subside, then all three of us began shouting again. I wasn't hopeful that Johnson was close, but there was no reason to not try. Voices growing rough, we stopped and listened. Tomblike silence descended upon us once again.

"Any more ideas, Master Chief?"

My voice was startlingly loud after nearly a minute of a complete absence of sound.

"I think we go deep. The lowest level," he said after a brief pause to think. "Igor's got the right idea. Unless we spooked him with the rifle fire and he's hunkered down."

"What's down there?" I asked.

I hoped he wasn't right about Johnson having heard the gunfire and, not knowing who was shooting, or why, had decided to keep his presence unknown.

"Don't know. Never made it down that far. But Johnson's been on a mission. The few times I saw him come in for some chow, he kept saying he was convinced there would be something here that could turn the tide in fighting the infected. From what I know, he was working his way down, and I haven't seen a door on this level that isn't open."

I considered that for a moment before nodding my head.

"Good a place as any, I suppose," I said, not sure I really agreed. "But when the militia finally breaks through, if we're down there, we're stuck. Right? No other way out?"

"Air..."

We turned to look at Igor, frustration with the English language obvious on his face. When he couldn't come up with the word he wanted, he cursed in Russian and pointed at the ceiling. Through the hole he'd blasted in the tiles, his light reflected off the metallic surface of heavy gauge ductwork.

"Air ducts!" I said when I finally got his meaning.

"Da! Climb up!" He said, smiling.

"Better than nothing if we get trapped," Gonzales said, shrugging.

I nodded again and gestured for him to lead the way.

Exodus

21

I managed all the stairs to the lowest sublevel without a problem. Not as fast as I would have made it before my injury, but my brain seemed to be adjusting to the new normal. I hoped it would continue to get better, then forced myself to quit thinking about it. It had been close to twenty minutes since we'd set up the WP grenades, and I was starting to worry that the militia was going to break through. There was no doubt they'd be slowed, but if they were determined enough…

Pushing through the door from the stairwell, we spread apart to scan around us. Almost immediately, I saw a heavy door standing a few feet open, Johnson's signature wiring job dangling from the wall.

"He's been here."

I kept my light focused on the wires for a moment so Igor and Gonzales could see them. Swinging it up, I could tell that the rest of the doors in that direction had also been opened.

"They're all locked this way," Gonzales mumbled.

I turned and saw half a dozen doors tightly closed, their keypads intact.

"Try the radio," I said.

He did, with no better results than all the other times.

"Lead on, Master Chief," I said, pointing down the corridor with the open doors.

Normally, I'd have been happy to take point. In fact, I would have preferred it. But putting a man on point that has a visual deficit is putting the entire team at risk.

Progressing down the corridor, the doors quickly became farther and farther apart. It took me longer to notice this than it should have, but in my defense, I still had one hell of a blinding headache. Calling a halt, I stepped to one of them that was standing a few inches ajar and pulled it open.

The room behind was cavernous. There was just no other way to describe it. Square, or close enough to not matter, it was easily sixty yards on a side, and the ceiling soared far above.

"How the hell did they do that?" Gonzales asked, craning his head back.

"Must have taken space out of the two levels above us," I said.

"Yeah, but why?" He asked, waving his hand at the empty space then turning to look at the man-sized door we'd come through. "What are you going to do with an area this big when nothing larger than a person will fit through the door?"

Exodus

He had a very good point. Beside me, Igor was aiming his light at the far wall, peering intently. Without saying anything, he strode across the smooth floor, boots ringing sharply on the hard surface. After a moment of watching him, Gonzales and I followed.

We caught up at the far end of the room. He was closely examining a panel with a keypad and several large buttons. I looked at it for a moment, then began slowly moving laterally, inspecting the surface of the wall. A few yards from the edge, I found a narrow gap, no larger than the thickness of a sheet of paper.

Following it with my light, I saw that it went all the way to the ceiling. Watching me for a moment, Gonzales trotted the length of that side of the room and quickly found a matching gap. Nearly the entire wall was a door. I couldn't tell which direction it would move, but it was definitely there to allow very large objects easy access into the room.

"Here," Gonzales said.

He was standing near the midpoint of the wall, shining his light on the floor. I hurried over to see marks most likely left by rubber tires. It only took a few more seconds of looking to find another set, and they were massive. Whatever had been driven out of the room was heavy as hell and riding on some pretty big wheels.

"Where you think that door goes?" Gonzales asked.

I stared at it for a long moment, then shook my head.

"Good question, but we've got more important things to worry about at the moment."

He nodded and headed for the exit. We were halfway across the room when brilliant lights built into the ceiling suddenly sprang to life. Pausing, we looked at each other for a second before hurrying forward. In the corridor, we turned left to continue our search.

I sighed in frustration when I got a look at just how long the hallway was. Before, with only the illumination of flashlights, it had been impossible to gain a perspective of the sheer size. But now, it was easy to see that it stretched into the distance, dwindling to a point before it was possible to see the end.

Continuing our path, we walked for several minutes past partially open doors. I was impressed with how many Johnson had breached, and at the same time was beginning to feel a gnawing bit of concern. Gonzales had told me the man was working around the clock, and I was beginning to worry that devotion to duty may have become an unhealthy obsession. Well, the first step was to find him and the two women. I'd worry about the rest once I knew they were safe.

The Master Chief brought us to a stop with a raised fist. We quickly moved against the walls, rifles coming up as he signed he'd seen movement ahead. We stayed frozen for several seconds, scanning the long corridor. Glancing quickly over my shoulder, I was pleased to see that Igor was facing the opposite direction, covering our rear.

"What'd you see?" I mumbled after nearly thirty seconds had passed.

"Movement at the limit of my vision," he said. "Way down there. Couldn't tell what or who it might have been."

"OK," I said. "Let's go see. Nice and quiet."

"Copy that," Gonzales breathed, staying tight against the wall as he moved forward.

I hoped the Master Chief had just gotten a glimpse of our missing people, but I wasn't going to bet our lives on it. Sure, we'd been holed up inside the facility for several days without running across anything other than the occasional infected Rachel had warned me about, but that didn't mean there weren't other occupants. The place was just too damn big. A mariachi band could have been performing non-stop on a different level, and I doubted any of us would have known.

We pushed forward, our pace suffering as we halted at each open door and carefully checked the room behind it. Actually, that's how we should have been proceeding the entire time, but I'd gotten sloppy. I'd like to blame it on the headache, or the damage to my eye, or any other number of things, but in the end, it was my own impatience.

Five minutes later, we'd covered slightly over half the distance to the point where the Master Chief had seen movement. We'd just finished checking a room that was nearly as large as the first one we'd entered. Igor had stayed in the hall while Gonzales and I cleared it, shaking his head to let us know all was still quiet when we emerged.

As we took the first few steps to resume our search, a blaring siren sounded, seemingly directly over our heads. Each of us jumped, startled by the sudden noise in what had been an almost perfectly quiet environment.

"What fuck?" Igor hissed, looking around.

Before I could say anything, or even shrug my shoulders, a pre-recorded voice began announcing that a fire had been detected on Level A. The militia had made it through, and my little surprises were burning away.

22

The strident alarm spurred us to move faster. We still checked the rooms we were passing, but with a significantly lesser degree of thoroughness. As we reached an open door, I would maintain watch in the hall while Gonzales and Igor entered and took a very brief look around. We were running the risk of missing a hidden enemy that would then be in our rear, but I had a very real sense that we were running out of time.

"Contact," I called as the Master Chief and Igor were about to step back into the hall.

I dropped to a knee and maintained aim with my rifle in the direction we'd been moving.

"What do you see?" Gonzales called, staying concealed behind the heavy steel door.

"Two with rifles," I growled.

"Far?" Igor asked.

"Two hundred yards."

Two figures were clearly visible in the corridor. They appeared to be facing a door as if waiting for something. I couldn't make out many details, only recognizing that they were armed because of the shape of their outlines.

"Try the radio, Master Chief," I called softly.

I heard him speaking as he transmitted. Almost immediately, a nervous-sounding Vance responded, asking about the alarm. The SEAL told him to shut up, and I couldn't help but grin to think how a Commander would take that from a Master Chief. With the radio quiet again, Gonzales broadcasted another message to Johnson.

Moving next to me, he shook his head and handed over the radio. Digging through his pack, he found a small spotting scope and held it up. I nodded and moved aside so he could lean into the hall for a better look.

"It's them," he said, turning to grin at me.

The relief was obvious in his voice. I had to give the man credit. He hadn't allowed his personal feelings to get in the way of acting professionally.

"Let's go," I said. "But stay sharp."

As we began moving again, one of the figures glanced in our direction. There was a brief pause, then something was said and they spread apart, raising their rifles.

"Friendlies!" I shouted. "Major Chase coming in!"

"They can't hear over the goddamn alarm," Gonzales said when they didn't relax.

Exodus

"OK, lower your weapons. Let's not have a friendly fire incident."

We allowed our rifles to hang on their slings as we hurried closer. Soon, one of the figures, which I could now tell was a woman, lowered her weapon and stepped away from the wall. It was Chelsea. She said something to the other, who slowly moved into clear view. Johnson. After a moment, he raised a hand in greeting, then swiveled to face an open doorway. I picked up the pace, and we quickly covered the remaining distance.

"Militia is in the facility," I called.

Chelsea's smile turned to a frown of concern, but Johnson didn't look away from whatever was holding his attention. I pushed past the girl and stopped next to him, freezing when I could see through the open door. A moment later, Gonzales stepped behind me and I heard his breath catch.

"What the fuck?" He breathed, his rifle swinging up.

Johnson gently placed a hand on top and pushed it towards the floor.

"Easy," he said in a quiet voice. "She's got this."

The room we stared into was the largest I'd encountered so far. Far bigger than the one where we'd found the exterior door built into the wall. Encompassing the majority of the room was what appeared to be a containment bubble built of six-inch-thick Plexiglas. Inside was an apparatus out of a movie.

It was blocky, yet cylindrical at the same time, with arm-thick cables that passed through ports in the surrounding walls and disappeared into the floor. A large computer station was located at the base of the machine, and Nicole was seated in front of a terminal, typing furiously. It was none of this that had given us pause. We'd gotten used to seeing the unusual. But, we hadn't gotten used to seeing three infected females standing calmly and watching someone work.

"What the fuck is going on, Sergeant?" I asked, unable to tear my attention away from the scene.

"Those infected were locked inside. Anyone's guess how that happened. Anyway, they treat Nicole like she's one of them. Let her come inside with them and haven't laid a finger on her."

"What the fuck is she doing in there?" Gonzales said.

I could tell he was having a hard time restraining himself from charging in and yanking Nicole to safety.

"That's the power source for the facility. We found it a few hours ago. When the lights went out, Nicole said she might be able to fix it, so we came back and she went inside. Got the lights back on, too."

"Why weren't you answering the radio," I asked.

Exodus

"Battery died. Sorry, sir. Forgot to get a fresh one the last time I was up top."

"We need to get her out of there!"

Gonzales had had enough and started to push forward between Johnson and me.

"Don't go in there!" Johnson said sharply, grabbing the SEAL's arm. "They see one of us in the room, they go batshit. I don't get it, but if we stay out here, they're calm."

"Let's give it a minute, Master Chief," I said in what I hoped was a calming voice.

"Sir! They could attack her at any moment!"

"They could, but they haven't," Johnson said. "She told me about when you guys were bringing her out of Seattle when you first found her. On the way to the boat? Said the females ignored her."

"They did," the Master Chief acknowledged after a long silence. "But I don't fucking like it. She shouldn't be taking the chance."

"Tried to tell her that," Johnson said. "She wasn't listening to me."

As he finished speaking, Nicole removed her hands from the keyboard and looked around. Slowly, she stood, her attention focused on the infected. They watched her the way a cat watches a mouse hole, but didn't exhibit any aggression. A step at a time, she made her way to a door that was more of a hatch set into the clear glass shield. Manipulating the lock, she slipped through and quickly secured it, locking the females inside.

Gonzales couldn't be held back any longer. Shoving past, he raced into the room and swept Nicole into his arms. Inside the containment area, the females went crazy the instant he appeared. They pounded on the walls, pressing their faces against them with lips skinned back from their teeth. I was pretty sure they were screaming, but the thickness of the Plexiglas completely muted all sound. Johnson, Chelsea and I stood there, watching them attack the barrier.

"We need to move," I shouted into the room.

Gonzales broke away from Nicole and, grabbing her hand, led her into the corridor in a rush. I had about a thousand questions, but we were out of time. The enemy was inside the walls.

23

We moved down the corridor at a fast pace, heading for the closest set of stairs that would take us up to A level where the rest of our group waited. I was concerned, as this was the same level where the militia had breached the facility. The fire alarm was a pretty conclusive indicator that they had managed to dig their way through the rubble.

It was always possible that one of the WP grenades I'd set up had popped loose on its own, but I doubted it. They'd been wedged in tight, and I was confident the only way they'd been released was by the debris having been shifted. Now, my hope was that the ensuing fire would buy us the time we needed. And that it didn't spread too far, too fast, and trap us.

Igor was on point, and I followed his broad back as we charged down the hall. Johnson and Chelsea were right behind me with Gonzales and Nicole bringing up the rear. Everyone had lots of questions, but there would be plenty of time for that later. If there was a later.

We were in a bad spot. Multiple levels below ground with only a central bank of elevators and two separate sets of stairs providing a path to the surface. My plan was to rendezvous with the other members of the group in the hangar, then evacuate the facility. Once outside, we'd take the fight to the militia.

Dirk Patton

I wasn't terribly concerned about taking on their numerically superior forces in the hills and rocks of the desert. Not with a Russian Spetsnaz, an Army Ranger and a Navy SEAL on my side. I'd gotten a look at the ragtag band of wannabes that comprised the ranks of the militia. They shouldn't pose a serious threat.

But, if we became trapped in the enclosed spaces inside the facility, their numbers would drastically swing the odds in their favor. Sure, we were better trained and vastly more experienced, but fighting on the enemy's terms goes a long way to offset those advantages.

Igor slowed suddenly, boots slipping on the polished floor and I nearly ran into his back. We'd reached the access door into the stairwell and he was pausing before opening it. Quickly, everyone stacked up behind us and I could hear Johnson and Gonzales mumbling, telling the girls to remain silent and close to them.

With his ear pressed to the steel door, Igor tried to detect any sounds from the stairwell but gave up with a shake of his head.

"Much noise," he said, pointing at the ceiling mounted fire alarm siren that was still blaring. "We go?"

Before I could respond, the alarm shut off and silence once again descended over the facility.

Exodus

"Go," I said, nodding.

Not hesitating, he cracked the door open and peered inside. After several seconds, he pushed it wide and stepped through. I was on his heels, breaking to the side, my rifle aimed up at the first landing above our heads. We held there for a few seconds, then, failing to see or hear a threat, I signed for Igor to start moving.

He had only climbed half a dozen steps when a loud clang from above froze us in place. Rifle aimed and at the ready, I held my breath. Seconds later there was another bang, this time easily identified as a steel door being slammed open against a concrete wall.

Voices floated down to us, too faint to understand what was being said. But, it didn't matter. The militia was in the stairwell. I signed to the people behind me, then tapped Igor on the back. We were retreating. For the moment.

"How the fuck do they know we're down here?" Johnson asked when we were all back in the corridor and the door was closed.

"They don't," I said. "No way they can. They're just spreading out, looking for us."

"Power's back on," Gonzales observed. "If they make it to the security office, they'll find our people in the hangar."

"Call Vance, Master Chief," I said. "Give them a heads up. They may need to bug out without us."

Dirk Patton

He nodded and stepped away to use the radio.

"Other ways up?" I asked Johnson.

"One more set of stairs, and the elevators. That's it, as least as far as I've found, and I've been pretty much everywhere."

"Big door," Igor said, stepping forward and pointing down the hall.

"What..." I started to ask, then the lightbulb flashed on. "Johnson. We cleared a room with a huge door set into the back wall. What's on the other side?"

"Don't know what you're talking about, sir. Show me and I'll open it!"

"Let's go!"

This time I took the lead, retracing our steps and ducking through the entrance into the cavernous room. Rushing to the far wall, I showed him the outline of what I was sure was a door. Nodding his head, he slung his rifle behind his back and grabbed several pieces of equipment out of his pack.

"Never came inside," he said as he began working on an electronic lock. "Opened the outside door and saw the room was empty, then moved on."

While he worked, I looked around. Igor and Gonzales had taken up station at the entrance, keeping watch on the corridor. Nicole had gone with the Master

Chief, but Chelsea had stayed with Johnson, watching closely as he connected his gear to the lock's circuit board. He peered at a small screen for a moment, then turned his head to look at me.

"OK, sir. I can open it. You sure you want me to do that? We've got no way of knowing what's on the other side."

"We're several hundred feet below ground, Sergeant," I said. "Whatever's in there won't be the militia. Open it."

He nodded, then pressed a series of keys on the machine in his hand. For a moment, nothing happened. I was starting to think Johnson's efforts weren't going to pay off when a muted rumble I could feel in my feet started up. I'd expected the door to slide up or to the side, but instead it began descending into the floor.

As the opening in the wall grew, I marveled at the sheer size of the solid slab that was in motion. Easily a hundred feet wide by thirty tall. As the gap at the top widened, a wave of warm, humid air spilled into the room and washed over us. It carried the stench of decay and human waste with it. Uh Oh!

"Johnson, can you stop the door before it's fully open?"

He pressed another key and the motion slowed for a couple of feet before coming to a complete stop.

"What's wrong?" Chelsea asked.

"Smell that?" I pointed at the opening. "That's infected."

She and Johnson both looked up, fear on their faces.

"Then why no screams?"

I turned to see that Gonzales and Nicole had joined us. Igor was still maintaining watch at the entrance.

"Has to be males," I said. "OK. Johnson, bring it on down, but stop it at twelve feet. Can you do that?"

"Yes, sir," he said.

The door began descending again.

"What are you thinking?" Gonzales asked.

Both of us had already stepped back and trained our rifles on the steadily widening gap. Just in case.

"We leave it up enough to keep any infected from flooding out, but just low enough to boost someone up for a look at what's on the other side."

"No disrespect, sir, but do we really have time to be fucking around with this?" He asked quietly.

"You got a better idea, I'm all ears, Master Chief."

24

Newly promoted Chief Petty Officer Jessica Simmons smiled at the Marine who had just finished clearing her through the security checkpoint. With a spring in her step, she walked into a waiting elevator that would take her to the subterranean installation where she worked. A scan of her ID card activated the system, automatically selecting the appropriate level and closing the doors.

As the car descended, she smiled again. She felt wonderful. Not only had she redeemed herself with the Admiral, earning a big promotion, but she'd also gotten sleep. Wonderful, uninterrupted sleep. Having remained on duty for nearly seventy-two hours straight during the crisis with the Russian invasion fleet, she'd finally been able to go to her quarters and fall into bed.

She'd slept thirteen hours straight, waking long enough to pay a visit to the head and remove her uniform, then had gone directly back to her bunk for another ten hours. Now, freshly showered and wearing clean clothes, she felt better than she could remember feeling in some time.

The elevator dinged, announcing its arrival on her level. *Her* level! Not only had she redeemed herself, but she'd also been placed in charge of a very small group of elite people. The Admiral called the newly formed group a proper military name, Navy Task Force 157, but she just called it *The Hive*.

Lieutenant Hunt looked up from his desk as she exited the elevator, giving her a nod and a smile. While she was in charge of The Hive from a technical perspective, the Navy still wanted an officer to be in overall command. So, riding her coattails, her CO had followed her over from the cyber warfare (CW) group.

Pausing to survey the darkened room, she looked at each of the five men and women who were completely absorbed with whatever was on their computer screens. Two of them were in uniform, having come from CW with her, but three, two women and one man, were in street clothing. They were brilliant hackers/coders from the civilian world who lived in Hawaii and had been recruited to help Jessica operate and maintain the limited satellite communications, surveillance and weapons systems that were still available.

Putting her purse away, Jessica walked around the room, quietly greeting each person. At the end of her circuit was Lieutenant Hunt's station and she stopped to speak with him.

"Did you get some rest, Chief?" He asked.

"Yes, sir, I did. Feel like a new woman! What's been going on around here?"

Exodus

"Unusually quiet," Hunt said. "The Russians are keeping their heads down, for the moment at least. Most of them have returned home, but there's still a large presence on the west coast of CONUS. We've got some intercepts and are seeing some activity that looks like they're getting ready to start evacuating large chunks of their surviving population, but nothing definitive about a destination."

"California?" Jessica asked, frowning.

"Maybe," Hunt acknowledged. "NIS thinks that's a good possibility and could explain why they haven't withdrawn from US soil."

"That's what I was thinking. But why not Australia? They move to the west coast, they've got a lot of infected to deal with."

"True, but they've also got empty cities to move into. There's no place for them to go in Australia unless they displace the population. Besides, they've still got the satellite beacon to draw the infected away. Clear the area out before they move in, then their ground forces can mop up whatever's left behind. Anyway, that's just my theory."

"What does the Admiral think?"

"You're asking me, Chief? I'm just a lowly Lieutenant. You're the woman that saved what's left of America. Maybe you should ask him the next time you see him."

Jessica grimaced, irritated at the grin on her CO's face. He was right about her, but she didn't want to be singled out and be special. She had just been doing her job.

"Sorry," Hunt said, not appearing to be sorry in the least. "Couldn't resist."

She smiled, knowing he had only been teasing her a little bit. They'd worked together long enough to develop a strong degree of mutual respect.

"What about Major Chase?"

Hunt's face betrayed his answer before he gave it.

"He's in a bit of a bind. Again. Ran up against a local militia. Several hundred of them, in fact. They managed to breach the facility he's in a little less than an hour ago. That's as much as we know. We've got no comms with him, or any of his group, and no way to know what's going on inside."

"Why didn't someone call me?" Jessica asked, trying to control her voice. "We can fix the comm channel!"

"It's not that," Hunt called, forestalling her dash to a console. "We're green across the board. There's just no one on that end answering our calls."

"Is there help on the way?"

Exodus

Hunt shook his head.

"Our resources are too depleted. We don't have the planes or firepower to fight our way through the Russians. The Admiral isn't happy, but he's not going to send men to die needlessly."

Before Jessica could respond, the phone on Hunt's desk rang. He held up a finger to stop her from speaking and lifted the handset. After a brief and cryptic conversation, he replaced it and looked up.

"Well, something must be in the works. That was Captain West. You're wanted in the Admiral's conference room."

"When?" Jessica asked, surprised.

"Now. Better get going."

"Yes, sir," she said in a distracted voice.

Retracing her steps, Jessica passed through security and into fresh air. Striding purposefully, she headed for the building where Admiral Packard was waiting. Concern for Major Chase warred with curiosity over what the Admiral wanted. Hopefully, she was going to find out that he was ready to send some troops to rescue him and needed her assistance in dealing with the Russians.

Security was tight when she arrived at the rather unimposing structure that housed the Admiral and his staff. She was stopped and checked by two separate roving patrols of Marines as she approached, then three different checkpoints within the building itself.

Clearing the final hurdle, she was met by an imposing Marine Captain named Black. He personally wanded her with a portable metal detector before waving for her to raise her arms. Quickly and professionally, he ran his hands over her body, leaving no curve or crevice unchecked. Satisfied, he instructed her to remove the pins that held her long hair in place. When it tumbled across her shoulders, he thrust his fingers into it, ensuring nothing was concealed.

"My apologies, Chief," he said when he was done. "There's already been one attempt on the Admiral's life. There's not going to be another."

Jessica stood there, blushing in embarrassment from having the Marine's hands touch places on her body that are normally reserved for lovers. When she met his eyes, she could tell that he was as uncomfortable as she was, but had done what needed to be done.

"It's OK, sir," she said, trying to restore her normally immaculate hair.

"No, it's not," Captain Black said, looking away. "I'd normally have a female Marine here, but the Admiral gave me no warning to expect you."

Exodus

"Captain, I've already forgotten it," Jessica said, struggling with her bobby pins.

Black nodded, then escorted her down a long hallway where he paused in front of a closed door. Knocking once, he opened it and stepped inside, motioning for her to follow.

"Chief Petty Officer, thank you for joining us," Admiral Packard said when Jessica entered the conference room. "Please take a seat."

She quickly chose a chair at the far end of the table, glancing around the room. All the Admiral's top aides were in attendance, as well as several other senior officers she didn't recognize. There was also a civilian woman seated to Packard's left. To his right were two civilian men she didn't know, one of them obviously of Native American heritage with a long, black ponytail.

Packard nodded at Captain Black who stepped smartly out of the room and closed the door behind him.

"Chief, what you're about to hear has been classified as compartmented, top secret. It may not be discussed with anyone who is not present in this room. Is that clear?"

"Yes, sir!" Jessica answered, a feeling of dread washing over her.

"Very well. Dr. Hironata, please update everyone."

25

Dr. Hironata spoke for nearly fifteen minutes, detailing the background of her project and ultimately the findings she had already presented to the Admiral. There was stunned silence within the room when she delivered the news that the world was about to perish. The expressions on the faces of the senior officers ranged from incredulity to final resignation to a fate that had been written when the first bomb was detonated in New York. Packard gave them a few moments to absorb the information before speaking.

"We have reviewed Dr. Hironata's data and confirmed what she is telling us. Survey teams are currently spreading out within the Hawaiian Islands to validate the findings, but we have already seen a steep decline in the catch from the commercial fishing fleets, which supports the conclusion. Additionally, I'll offer my own anecdotal piece of information. When is the last time any of you heard a bird singing as you were walking across the base?"

Silence greeted him, several of the men glancing at each other and nodding. The Admiral slowly looked around the room before continuing.

"As bleak as the future looks, there may be a way to survive. Doctor, please elaborate."

"Gentlemen, and lady," she began, acknowledging Jessica's presence. "Since bringing my findings to Admiral Packard's attention, I have consulted with the virologists who have been studying the virus and working to develop a viable cure."

She nodded across the table at Dr. Kanger and Joe Revard.

"They have confirmed my suspicion that the virus can only survive in a temperate climate if it is not inside a host organism. This is validated by the complete absence of infection in the group of Canadians who were above the arctic circle. That is, until they were exposed within the continental US. Conversely, they have also documented that the virus cannot survive in hot, arid environments."

"Excuse me," a Marine General whom Jessica didn't recognize spoke up. "If what you're saying is correct, how do you account for the infection having destroyed the population in the Middle East? That's about as hot and arid as it gets on Earth."

"General," Dr. Kanger spoke up. "Dr. Hironata stated that the virus cannot survive outside of a host organism in those environments. Once it achieves infection in a living creature, it is in large part protected by the very biological system it is attacking. But, in extreme cold, or heat, if the host dies, the virus dies with it."

The General shook his head.

"That may be, but what good does that do us?"

Exodus

Kanger and Hironata exchanged looks before she tilted her head for him to continue.

"If the virus cannot survive in the environment, and there are no infected hosts, in essence, you have a clean area. A safe zone, if you will. Lacking the ability to remain dormant while waiting for an organism to invade, it dies very quickly."

"What are you saying?" An Admiral asked. "All we need to do is freeze it or cook it?"

"That's not practical," Dr. Hironata replied. "Especially when Mother Nature takes care of that for us. All we need to do is be where the virus can't live outside of a host."

There were confused expressions around the table, and Admiral Packard decided it was time to interject.

"Bottom line is, we have less than eighteen months before we're dead. Less than twelve before we begin seeing large portions of the population start dying off. Hawaii is a very temperate climate, especially as far as the virus is concerned. All animal and plant life will succumb until the islands are barren rock. We have no choice other than to leave. A complete exodus before it's too late."

A buzz of voices traveled around the room. The Admiral let it go on for a few seconds before raising his hand to silence the shocked officers.

"Doctor," he said to Hironata. "Please continue."

"Thank you, Admiral," she said, nodding. "Gentlemen, we have two options available to us. Both require the relocation of the entire population of the Hawaiian Islands."

"That's nearly a million people!"

Several voices blurted at the same time. Packard glared at the men who'd interrupted, and they immediately fell silent.

"I'm very well aware," Dr. Hironata said. "However, if we do not have an exodus, as the Admiral put it, they will die. We must choose between an arid desert or the frozen arctic. That is all that can provide us with a safe zone."

"Do you have a recommendation?" Captain West asked, facilitating the conversation.

"I do. The arctic is not a viable scenario. Food cannot be grown, and there are few, if any, natural resources available. That leaves the desert."

"The Middle East?" The Marine General asked.

"No," Packard interjected. "Logistically, this is going to be a nightmare. To relocate a million civilians to the far side of the planet would create an insurmountable task within the timeframe we have. Dr. Kanger has some suggestions."

Exodus

Kanger cleared his throat and leaned forward.

"Admiral Packard asked Dr. Hironata and my team to evaluate possible locations for our exodus. We also worked with Captain West who provided input on logistical issues. In other words, the exponential impact on how quickly we can complete the effort based on the distance we must travel to reach our new home.

"The Middle East has been ruled out. It's too far away, there are numerous radioactive hot zones from the Arab/Israeli nuclear bombs, and a rough computer model that accounts for the availability of ships and aircraft indicates that nearly a third of our population would perish here in Hawaii before we could move them. Australia is better, closer and fallout free, and the western portion of the continent provides ideal environmental conditions, but there is no infrastructure. What do we do? Drop a million people into the desert? Give them nothing more than a tent and a shovel? We'd lose thousands in the first couple of weeks alone. Maybe tens of thousands.

"The only viable solution that the team has come up with is the desert in the American southwest. The climate is favorable for our needs, and existing infrastructure appears to be mostly intact. Supplies and materials are already in place. This negates the need to utilize valuable cargo space for basic necessities such as food, water, medical supplies, etc. The distance is manageable, and modeling indicates we have a narrow window for success. If we begin moving people within the next month."

"Do you mean California?" An Air Force Captain asked.

"No. The coast of California is too temperate for our needs. The inland deserts would be good, but there are no cities large enough to take all our people. We looked farther east and considered southern Nevada and central Arizona. With the collapse of Hoover Dam, water would be a very real concern in Las Vegas, so we selected Phoenix, Arizona. It is the hottest and driest major city in North America. The climate is ideal, and there is more than enough existing infrastructure to comfortably support the entire population. Water is plentiful in the form of a chain of reservoirs to the northeast of the city that are replenished annually by snowfall in the northern mountains."

Glances were exchanged around the room, then slowly heads began to nod.

"Admiral," the Marine General spoke up. "We're forgetting one problem. The Russians are still occupying much of the west coast of CONUS."

"And what happens when they learn about this… this… *new* apocalypse?" A Navy Captain interjected. "Even if we are successful, they're going to be knocking on our door to escape the devastation in California. And, what do we do about the infected? They still have control over the herds. All they'd have to do is send a few million of them in to kill us all, then send them away so they can move in without firing a shot."

Admiral Packard nodded, looking around the room to see if anyone else had a question.

"Gentlemen, allow me to introduce Chief Petty Officer Simmons," he said, gesturing at Jessica.

Every pair of eyes turned to look at her.

"Ms. Simmons is the one responsible for restoring our comms and deploying Thor. She, for the most part singlehandedly, defeated the Russian invasion fleet."

Despite herself, Jessica felt a wave of heat as a blush began at her chest and washed up across her face.

"That's why she is here," Packard said, smiling at her. "Chief, you have one job. I want you to break into the Russian's control systems and seize the satellites that are broadcasting the harmonic that attracts the infected. Captain Thomas is correct. If the Russians continue to have control over the infected, they'll wipe us out before our change of address takes effect. Can you do this?"

"I will do my best, sir," Jessica said, her voice steady under the gaze of the roomful of senior officers.

"So far your best has been better than the Russians'," Packard said. "Report directly to Captain

West. Anything you need, he will ensure you receive without delay. We're counting on you, Chief. Until we have control of those satellites, we can't begin moving people. I'm not going to uproot a million civilians to just have them die in a strange place."

"Yes, sir. I'll make it happen," Jessica said, not at all as confident as she sounded.

26

The massive door trundled to a stop. Well above my head was the top edge and Gonzales and I stayed in place with our rifles ready, just in case. Johnson's eyes were glued to us, his finger hovering over a button that would send it back up and seal the opening if we reacted to any threat. But, after a couple of minutes, nothing came screaming at us.

Lowering my rifle, I called Chelsea over and told her what we were going to do. To the young girl's credit, she didn't even bat an eye, just followed me to the base of the monstrous slab. Kneeling, I grabbed her calves once she was standing on my shoulders, balancing her as I stood. Looking up, I could see that her extended hands were still a foot below the lip.

"I'm going to jump," she said. "Ready?"

"Go," I said, bracing myself.

An instant later she pushed off, and it was all I could do to not stagger backward from the force. Arms extended to catch her if she fell, I watched her grab the edge and pull herself up to slither onto the top of the door. All was quiet for a few seconds, then her head appeared.

"We're good," she called. "Looks like a testing lab. Lots of infected, but they're locked up."

"You're sure?" I asked.

"I'm young, not stupid," she said, rolling her eyes at me.

I grinned, resisting the urge to flip her off.

"Males or females?" Gonzales asked, finally lowering his rifle.

"Females are all I see," Chelsea answered. "They're in some kind of clear glass box. Like the reactor. And there's also a bunch in separate cells along the wall."

They were in an isolation chamber. But then, why had I smelled them when the door opened?

"Chelsea. Take another look. If they're sealed in, why does it stink?"

She opened her mouth, probably to say something sarcastic, then closed it and disappeared from sight. A full minute later she reappeared.

"So, maybe I'm not so smart," she said. "There're males bumping around that are loose. They're all in uniform or scrubs, so must be researchers."

"How many?"

"Eleven."

Exodus

"OK. Hold tight." I looked at Johnson. "Bring it on down."

The door rumbled to life, slowly descending and bringing Chelsea with it. She jumped clear when it was still a few feet above the floor, just as we began seeing the males. Gonzales and I quickly put them down.

Walking forward, I crossed the threshold into another massive room that was obviously an isolation ward. Close to fifty females were secured inside a circular chamber made of thick glass. They threw themselves at the barrier, but the material was so thick I couldn't hear their assault.

The perimeter of the room was crowded with smaller versions of the main holding area, all of them occupied by more females. At least another thirty. Racks of medical and lab equipment filled much of the rest of the space, and at the far end I could see what I was pretty sure was an MRI machine well separated from everything else. Gonzales, Johnson and I walked the entire area, Chelsea and Nicole tagging along, but didn't find any indications of another door.

As we moved, the females followed the interior curve of glass, furiously pounding in frustration when they couldn't reach us. After a second thorough inspection, we regrouped near where Igor was still watching the hall.

"What now?" Johnson asked.

I shook my head, trying to ignore a pounding headache and come up with a way to reach the surface without getting into a gunfight in a stairwell. Slowly looking around, I met Nicole's eyes and paused when a thought popped into my head.

"Nicole, when you were in the containment room with those other females, they didn't try to attack you. Right?"

"Riiiiiight," she said slowly, unsure where I was going.

"Are you able to communicate with them? I mean, do you think you could get them to do what you wanted?"

She stared at me for a long beat before turning and looking at the isolation chamber full of infected.

"I've got no idea," she said.

"Sir?" Gonzales said, concern in his voice.

"Easy, Master Chief," I said. "We've already seen that they won't harm her. What if she can get them to do what she wants? We send them up the stairs to fight the militia for us."

"I don't…" he started to say, going quiet when Nicole looked at him with a raised hand.

"Not your decision," she said firmly before facing me. "I'm willing to give it a try, but don't have a clue if it will work. But, all of you are going to have to be somewhere else."

"Nicole…" Gonzales said.

She stepped close and placed her hand on his arm.

"I'll be fine," she said.

"Master Chief, call Vance and warn him. Tell him to make sure any entrances are secure."

"Yes, sir," he said after a long hesitation.

Stepping away, he raised the radio and did as I'd asked.

"Fuck crazy," Igor mumbled, shaking his head.

"Ing!" Chelsea said, slapping him lightly on the arm. "Fucking! Damn, we've gotta work on your English."

Igor grinned at her and replied in Russian. It was only a few words, but the tone left little doubt of what he'd said.

"Asshole," Chelsea grinned back, slapping him again.

"Let's get in one of the other rooms," I said. "Let them calm down before Nicole opens the door."

We filed out into the hall, Gonzales bringing up the rear after kissing Nicole and squeezing her hand. Moving down the corridor, we entered another empty room and Johnson pulled the door closed behind us.

"Sorry about earlier, sir," Gonzales said.

"No need to be sorry, Master Chief. You're looking out for her. I'd think less of you if you weren't. But, she'll be fine. You saw how those other females treated her."

"It only takes one," he grumbled, moving away to stare at the inside of the door.

I felt for him, completely understanding how he was feeling, but if we could get out of here without a firefight, the odds for all of us making it were much better.

"So, what was that thing Nicole was working on when we found you?" I asked Johnson.

"Some kind of reactor-thingy," he said, shrugging his shoulders.

"She said it was a cold fusion reactor, and she was royally pissed," Chelsea chimed in.

"Pissed? About what?" I asked.

"She said it was her design. She'd been working on it at some lab, then when they had a breakthrough, the project was shut down. The government must have stolen it."

"What's the big deal?" I asked.

"Cold fusion? Seriously? Don't you Army guys ever read?"

She smiled to soften the criticism.

"You're thinking Navy," I said, tilting my head at Gonzales. "The Army's full of scholars."

The Master Chief snorted a laugh, but kept his mouth shut. At least I'd distracted him for a moment.

"Cold fusion will provide nearly unlimited power, and there's no radiation. No nuclear waste. No meltdowns. Just clean power. We've been trying to crack it for decades. Nicole's got to be a genius!"

I looked around when Gonzales's radio crackled to life. He lifted it and listened for a moment, then tossed it to me before dashing for the door. It hit me in the chest, and I fumbled it several times before securing it.

Yanking the door open before I could shout a warning, he jerked back and slammed it when a chorus of screams erupted from the corridor. Turning, he looked at me as he braced his back against the steel surface.

"You hear me? We got your man," a voice I didn't recognize came out of the radio in my hand. "Better bring me those girls you took before we start hurtin' him."

27

There was a brief moment of muted pounding on the door, then the females in the corridor fell silent. Was Nicole able to control them? Right now, that didn't matter.

"What the hell?" Johnson asked. "Our man?"

"Gotta be Vance," I said.

"They want the girls?" Chelsea asked.

We all looked at the door when Nicole's voice sounded faintly from the other side.

"What's wrong?" She called.

"Don't send them up!" Gonzales shouted at the door. "Problems upstairs."

"What do I do?"

"Can you get them back into containment?" I shouted, rushing to stand next to the Master Chief.

"I'll try. Hold on."

"Listen up," the voice on the radio said. "You'd better answer me or we're gonna start fucking this pretty boy up but good. Understand?"

Gonzales looked at me and shook his head.

"You think they really got him?" He asked.

"Maybe. Or they could just be on our frequency, trying to draw us out. But, if that was the case, I'd think he'd be broadcasting, too."

The SEAL nodded but didn't say anything else.

"OK, asshole." We all looked at the radio in my hand. "Guess you don't believe I'm serious. Try this on for size."

There was a brief pause, then a blood-curdling scream of pain blasted out of the tinny speaker. It went on for nearly thirty seconds, finally trailing off into whimpers and labored breathing.

"Hear that, cocksucker? That's the sound a man makes when you slice open his ball sack and pour salt inside. Ready to answer me, or do I get more inventive?"

"Oh, my God! Do something!" Chelsea exclaimed, horror etched on her face.

I waved a hand to silence her and lifted the radio to my mouth.

"What do you want?" I asked.

"Well, hello there! Shame it took you so long to answer. Your buddy here's gonna be plenty pissed you ignored me. It didn't have to go this way."

There was a brief chuckle before he released the transmit button.

"Tell him to stop!" Chelsea said. "Tell him what's going to happen to him if he doesn't!"

"Chelsea, I need you to be quiet," I said in a calming voice. "Blustering on the radio isn't going to do any good. Now, let me think."

She looked like she was ready to argue the point, but Johnson stepped close and leaned in to whisper in her ear. I turned my back on them, not needing the distraction.

"It's time for us to meet," the voice said a moment later.

"Why?" I asked.

"Why? Don't be a smart ass. Your buddy here's got plenty more parts that can be slit open or maybe even cut off. Don't test me. Just come on into the hangar where he was hidin' and we'll have a little chat. And don't forget those girls you stole from me!"

I stood still in thought for several moments, then pressed the talk button.

"Let me speak to the General."

There was a long silence before the voice replied.

"She ain't got nothin' to do with this. We don't take orders from her, so no point in wastin' time talking to the bitch. I'm getting impatient. Where you want me to start cuttin' next?"

I shook my head in frustration.

"I'm on my way, but it's going to take a bit. This is a big place."

Gonzales stared at me with surprise on his face as I finished speaking.

"Five minutes," the voice answered. "Any longer and I start removing protruding body parts."

I checked my watch as I stuffed the radio into a pocket.

"What the hell are you doing?" Gonzales asked. "You can't turn yourself over to them. You know that!"

"Not what I have in mind, Master Chief," I said, turning to see Chelsea sulking and Johnson watching me closely. "Johnson, how do I get to the outside?"

"You don't," he said, shaking his head. "At least, not from down here."

"There has to be a way," I said. "They didn't bring all those females in through the halls. There's got to be another way."

"Not that I've found."

Exodus

There was a sudden banging on the door and Nicole's voice called out. Gonzales spun and yanked it open, reaching out and pulling her into the room.

"You get them to go back?" I asked in surprise.

"I did. Not sure how or why, but they do what I tell them. Sort of. Kind of like getting a pack of dogs to listen. Why'd you stop me?"

"Militia's got a hostage," Gonzales said.

"Where do you think the girls are?" Johnson interrupted.

"I'm thinking I may have underestimated Vance," I said. "It sounds like he either hid them or got them out of the facility and stayed behind to distract the enemy."

Everyone began to speak at the same time, but I stopped them with a sharp gesture. Discussing the situation was fine, but we didn't have time. I turned to Johnson when a thought occurred to me.

"What about air shafts or maintenance tunnels? Any way to get to the surface that they won't be watching?"

He started to shake his head, pausing with a contemplative look on his face.

"There's a maintenance hatch in the room with the reactor. Set in the back wall. Maybe it goes up."

"Let's go," I said, brushing past Gonzales and through the door.

I led the way to the reactor chamber, ignoring the frenzied females trapped inside the containment area as we entered. Johnson hurried past me, gave the infected a wide berth even though they couldn't get to him, and stopped at a large, steel hatch set into the rear wall. Within a few seconds, he bypassed the lock and tugged the heavy door open.

Cool, musty air flowed out of the pitch black opening. Grabbing a flashlight off the rail of his rifle, Johnson leaned into the void and looked around, finally twisting to look straight up. After a couple of seconds, he withdrew and handed the light to me.

"It goes farther than I can see," he said.

Sticking my upper body through the opening, I did as he'd done and looked up. Iron rungs were set into the concrete wall, ascending farther than the beam of light could penetrate. At least a hundred feet above my current position, I could make out what looked like another hatch that opened into the shaft.

Pulling back, I examined the inside of the door Johnson had opened. There was a simple release mechanism that didn't require anything other than the pull of a lever. That made sense. If someone was inside, they were likely clinging to the ladder and didn't need to be trying to enter a security code to open a door.

Exodus

"Two minutes," the voice sounded over the radio.

"I need more time," I answered. "Ran into some infected and they slowed me down."

He took his time responding to my message.

"Five more minutes," he finally said. "Not one second more or I'm carving up your buddy. Don't test me. You won't like what happens."

Turning the radio to silent, I shoved it into a pocket. There wasn't any point in continuing to listen to the militia's threats or trying to talk to them.

"Igor and Johnson with me," I said, working my rifle around so it was hanging down my back. "Master Chief, stay here with the ladies. Just in case. Nicole, can you shut the power off again?"

"Yes. No problem. The fuckers used my design…"

I held a hand up to stop her, and she nodded an apology.

"Exactly four and half minutes from now, I want you to cut power to the entire facility. Got it?"

"Got it," she said, nodding.

28

I entered the maintenance shaft first, swinging my feet onto the closest rung. Reaching up, I nearly missed the next higher one and reminded myself that I had to focus my attention on what I was doing. Rachel had been correct. My depth perception was for shit, and if I wasn't careful, it was going to be a fast trip to the hard concrete below.

The climb was slow and arduous, reminding me of ascending the elevator shaft in Los Alamos with Martinez, Scott and Irina. A sense of loss spread through me as I thought about my friends, but I didn't have the luxury of continuing to mourn the fallen. Right now, I wanted to wrap up the happy horseshit with the militia and find a way to Australia. Once my hands were wrapped around Barinov's throat, I'd let myself think about all the people I loved who were gone because of him. I'd recite their names as I choked the life out of him. If I let him pass that easily.

Nearly missing another rung, I cursed at myself and shoved all those thoughts aside. Pushing, I climbed faster, finally reaching a hatch labeled simply as B. I didn't know the facility well, but was certain this would open into the level immediately below where Vance was being held in the hangar.

Glancing down, I made sure Johnson and Igor were ready, then released the locking lever and

Exodus

cracked the door open a couple of inches. I could see a narrow slice of another large room. It was well lit, and various machines I couldn't identify were sitting in the middle of the shiny floor. There was no sound, and with no time to waste before the power was cut, I shoved the hatch fully open and scrambled through.

As I crossed the threshold, I pulled my rifle around and moved to the side to make room. Scanning, I noted a faint sound as first Johnson, then Igor, joined me. I saw them raise their weapons from the corner of my good eye. We gave it a few seconds, circling the stored equipment in opposite directions. We were alone.

Johnson dashed back to the maintenance hatch and gently closed it, the lock automatically engaging. We moved to the exit and tried to listen for sounds of the enemy on the far side, but the steel was too thick.

"Which direction to the hangar?" I mumbled, hand on the lock release.

Johnson thought for a second before pointing to what would be our left when we stepped into the corridor. Nodding, I tugged on the thick handle, gratified when it moved with no sound other than a faint snick as the locking bolts retracted. With a deep breath, I pushed, and it swung out an inch.

The clock was ticking, and I didn't have the luxury of standing there and thoroughly listening. When I didn't see or hear anything, I pushed it open and stepped quickly into the hall, rifle up, seeking a target. But, once again, there weren't any members of the militia waiting to ambush us.

Igor came next, then Johnson followed, closing the door behind us. We set off in the direction he'd indicated. Moving fast now, I took the lead and bypassed doors that were standing ajar. Not exactly the right way to move through hostile territory, but the circumstances demanded speed. All of us were carrying suppressed rifles, so we wouldn't make as much noise if we had to fire. Besides, by now, I was more than a little pissed off and spoiling for a fight.

I slowed as we approached the intersection of the corridors. There were four elevators that serviced the central hub, housed in a cylindrical shaft. Now at a walk, I moved with the rifle up and my eye to the scope. This was a bitch as I'd normally have my left eye open and watching as well, but with it out of commission, I was limited to the narrow field of view afforded by the optic.

A subtle sound from ahead caused me to slow and quickly scan back and forth. I didn't see anything, then heard the sound again. A foot scraping on the floor. Pressing forward, I saw movement as a man stepped into view from the far side of the elevator tube. He was wearing jeans and a camouflage T-shirt, a rifle held loosely in one hand. A bored guard.

I fired once, my round punching through his skull. The noise of his body and weapon falling to the hard floor was louder than my shot. Igor and I rushed forward, Johnson peeling away to circle the elevators and meet on the far side. The one guard had been alone.

"Which way?" I asked.

"You know we're a level down, right?"

"Yes. Which way?" I hissed.

"Follow me," he said and took off at a fast trot.

Igor and I fell in behind him. As we ran, I hoped I remembered correctly. When we'd first begun searching the facility, one of the teams had found a hypersonic stealth aircraft in the hangar where Vance was being held. When they'd taken me to see it, I'd noted several maintenance hatches in the walls. I was betting everything on the hope that they opened into shafts like the one we'd just used and we could access them from this level. Climb up and surprise the assholes that had broken in.

Of course, I was counting on a lot, not to mention the fact that I had no idea how many we were going up against. And, I was hoping that we'd be the only ones with night vision scopes on our weapons. Maybe I should hope for Santa Claus to show up and give us all a ride to safety while I was at it.

"Hangar's up there." Johnson pulled to a stop and pointed at the ceiling.

Without slowing, I raced through an open door and quickly looked around, not seeing any access hatches.

"What looking for?" Igor asked.

"Maintenance shaft entrance," I said as I ran to the next room. "Saw some in the hangar. Betting there's some down here."

Johnson grinned when he understood what I had in mind and ran into the room next to the one I was headed for. Igor was already conducting his own search. None of us found a hatch and moved farther down the hall.

"Here!"

Johnson's voice floated out of the space next to where I was searching. Turning, I dashed through the door, nearly colliding with Igor. Johnson was already at work defeating the electronic lock. It only took him a few seconds, the bolts releasing with a muted thud. He pulled it open and stuck his head inside, twisting to see higher up the shaft.

"Got it," he said. "Door's about twenty-five feet up!"

He moved aside, and I stepped through onto an iron rung. Three steps later, the power went out, and we were again plunged into darkness. There was a muttered curse in Russian from beneath my feet, but that was the limit of their reaction. A moment later I heard a click and Johnson's light came on, allowing me to see well enough to resume climbing.

I quickly scaled the remaining distance, locking an arm through a rung when my feet were level with the bottom of the hatch. There was a vibration from within my pocket that I ignored. The radio. Probably the asshole who'd I'd talked to, calling to issue some additional ultimatums. I just hoped the lights going off didn't goad him into doing anything further to Vance.

"I'm going left, Igor right, Johnson middle. Ready?" I mumbled just loud enough for them to hear.

I received a da and a yes. Reaching out, I grasped the locking lever and took a deep breath. This was going to be the riskiest moment. I was clinging to an iron rung, had to unlock and open a door a foot to my side, then swing through. And I had to do all this silently, and with my rifle still slung down my back. I wouldn't be able to bring it around until I was in the hangar, and if the militia saw me while I was entering, I'd be a sitting duck.

"Light," I hissed, looking down.

An instant later we were in darkness, and I gently tugged on the lever. It took some force but moved smoothly and silently. The only sound was the faint click as locking bolts released. Shifting my weight until one foot was swinging free and ready to step through, I carefully pushed the hatch open.

Dirk Patton

Immediately, I began hearing the undisciplined shouts of several men. They were cursing, checking on each other and repeatedly asking what had happened. Swinging out, I stepped through, noting several flashlight beams playing around far across the massive hangar. Sliding sideways, I brought the rifle up and looked through the night vision scope as Igor, then Johnson clambered into the space.

We had come out on the wall farthest from the entrance off the corridor. The giant, active camouflage plane squatted between our position and the militia, a set of roof-high steel doors to our right. A quick scan reassured me that we were well removed from the enemy, then I settled in to look them over.

There were fourteen men wandering around, all armed with various makes and calibers of rifles. Really? You raid the armory at an Air Force Base and don't bother to make sure that all your troops are using the same style and caliber of weapon? Well, that just reinforced my assessment that these guys didn't really know what the hell they were doing. Unfortunately, that didn't necessarily make them any less dangerous.

Most of the men were running around like frightened children, but there were three of them that had stayed in place near a table. Another form lay on its surface, and it wasn't a long shot to guess it was Vance. As I watched, one of them lifted his hand. A moment later, the radio in my pocket vibrated. Hello, asshole. Unfortunately, he was still a little too far away for me to take a shot.

Exodus

Surveying the open space between them and us, I paused with my eye trained on the plane's oversized landing gear. The tires looked like they were at least five feet tall, and the heavy wheels and struts would provide ideal cover from which to launch an attack. Lowering my rifle, I scooted to the side and pulled Igor and Johnson close.

In clipped sentences, I told them what we were doing, and they each mumbled an understanding. The radio vibrated again, and I ignored it as we hurried forward. The militia was starting to settle down, but lights were still being nervously played across the floor and walls as we took up positions beneath the belly of the jet.

Aiming my rifle, I focused in on who I assumed was their leader. He was slightly taller than the rest and began shouting for his men to be quiet. It took several commands before they complied and even though I couldn't read his facial expression through the night vision, I had little doubt he was pissed off by the way he looked around. Finally calming, he raised the radio and barked into it. I couldn't understand the words but could hear his voice across the echoing room.

"I'm taking the leader," I hissed. "Igor, left. Johnson, right."

We were targeting the three men standing around the table that held the figure I believed was Vance. I had received their acknowledgment and was opening my mouth to give the order to fire when the main entrance door suddenly opened with a loud clang.

Instantly, lights swiveled to the opening, spotting a large man as he walked into the hangar. Right behind him was a woman, three more men bringing up the rear. All four of the men moved and handled their weapons like professionals, and I was willing to bet the woman was the General.

"What the hell are you doing?" She called in a loud voice.

29

The Governor of Hawaii sighed deeply and rolled his eyes as Captain Black made him remove his suit coat for a more thorough inspection. Handing the garment off to another Marine to be cleared, the head of Admiral Packard's personal protection detail slipped on a pair of latex gloves and expertly ran his hands over the politician's rotund form. Leaving no area unchecked, he snapped the gloves off when he was complete and nodded for the Sergeant to return the jacket.

"This is absolutely inappropriate!" The Governor said, yanking his suit back into place. "The Admiral will hear about it, I can promise you that!"

"Thank you for your cooperation, sir."

Captain Black was unfazed by the complaint. Turning around, he knocked sharply on the Admiral's office door, opening it when permission to enter was granted. He announced the Governor and held the door for the pompous man, closing it quietly after he stormed through.

"Admiral Packard, I really must protest being treated in this manner. Being groped by that thug is quite unnecessary!"

The Governor was obviously upset, his voice strained as he stood in front of Packard's desk. Staring at him, the Admiral slowly rose to his feet.

"Governor, I do not tell my security detail how to do their job. They know far better than I. And, I would suggest you refrain from calling any of my Marines a thug in the future, especially if they can hear you."

The man gaped at the rebuke, his face turning a deep shade of crimson.

"Have a seat," Packard said, resuming his and ignoring the man's anger. "I'm quite busy so let's dispense with the pleasantries and get to the reason for your visit."

The Governor glared at him, then, acting like a true politician, swallowed his angst and smiled as he sat down. Leaning forward, he placed a thick file folder on the large desk.

"What's this?" Packard asked without picking it up.

"This, Admiral, is a legal brief prepared by my Attorney General."

"For what purpose?"

"For the legal and Constitutional purpose of you placing yourself and the remaining United States military under my command. You see, Admiral, for several months now you have acted unilaterally. You have made all the foreign policy decisions for the country. You have declared and fought a war. Sent men and women into battle. Spoken directly with foreign leaders. Violated sovereign Australian territory. The list is quite extensive.

"But, this is the United States of America, Admiral. The military does not dictate foreign policy or when we will or will not go to war, or with whom. That is the job of the *civilian* Commander in Chief. A duly elected Commander in Chief. At the moment, you are in violation of the Constitution as well as numerous federal laws.

"Now, I understand that times have been, well, unusual, and you've done the best you could under the circumstances. But, the Constitution must be honored and the rule of law restored. Since the threat of a Russian invasion has been resolved, it is time to move forward.

"As such, I have instructed the Hawaiian Secretary of State to prepare for an emergency election. We will select a new President, who will appoint a cabinet and assume rightful control of the military. Until then, since I am the most senior surviving elected official in the United States, I will be taking command of all aspects and components of the federal government until such time as a new President is sworn in."

The Governor leaned back in his chair, unable to suppress a smug expression. All the earlier anger was completely gone.

"And I suppose you will be running for the presidency," Packard said, his voice neutral.

"I haven't made that decision. Yet."

The Admiral was met with another smug smile.

"I see," he said. "And, when will this emergency election take place?"

"As quickly as possible," the Governor said, encouraged by the lack of resistance. "It's quite important that we restore the leadership of our men and women in uniform to the people, where it belongs."

The Admiral nodded slowly as the man finished speaking.

"I cannot agree with you more," he said, earning a surprised expression from his visitor. "And, as soon as there is a lawfully elected President, I will acknowledge his authority and constitutional position as the Commander in Chief of the military."

"I must say, Admiral. I am rather surprised and pleased with your reaction. Honestly, I'd expected resistance."

"Mr. Governor, my oath to the constitution did not end when we lost the President and his cabinet. I will support whoever is elected and would be more than happy to lend any assistance you may need in ensuring the election is fair and legal."

"Very good, Admiral! And, I appreciate your offer, but no assistance from the military is required. Now, in the interim, I will be placing my Lieutenant Governor here in your offices. He will be the liaison between my office and yours. A poor man's Secretary of Defense, if you will."

The Governor was smiling ear to ear, unable to restrain his excitement at how well the meeting appeared to be going. That smile vanished quickly as Admiral Packard began shaking his head.

"That's not going to happen, Mr. Governor," Packard said firmly. "I will not acknowledge your authority in any matters other than the governance of the civilian population of Hawaii. You are not the Commander in Chief. At least, not yet."

"Admiral," the Governor began in a low, dangerous voice. "Before you make any decisions, I would highly suggest you review the legal brief I had prepared. You do not want to be on the wrong side of history when a new President takes office."

Packard held his gaze for several seconds, finally looking down at the file. When he broke eye contact, the Governor nodded and smiled. Reaching out, the Admiral picked it up, examined the cover briefly, then leaned sideways and dropped it into a waste can.

"I believe I've made myself clear, Mr. Governor," he said as the politician leapt to his feet with indignation on his face.

"You will regret this, Admiral! You are paving your own road to charges of sedition and treason!"

"I'm willing to take that chance," Packard said, his eyes boring into the Governor's. "Now, if there's nothing else, I must get back to work. I trust you will keep me informed on the status of the election."

As the Governor stared at him with his mouth hanging open, the Admiral pressed a button on his desk. Within a second, his office door opened and Captain Black stepped through.

"Sir?"

"Please escort the Governor to the main gate, Captain," Packard said, turning his attention to a stack of reports on his desk.

"Yes, sir. Sir, if you please." Black moved to the side of the open door, eyes boring into the politician.

The Governor glared at Packard for several seconds, then snorted a loud humph of indignation.

"This is far from over, Admiral," he spat, venom in his voice.

Exodus

Packard ignored the man, only looking up as he stormed out of his office with Black close behind. Before the door closed, Captain West stepped in, looking over his shoulder at the enraged Governor.

"What did he want, sir?"

"Wants to be the leader of the free world, or at least what's left of it."

"That idiot? Wasn't he facing a federal racketeering investigation before the attacks?"

"He was," the Admiral said. "He says he's ordered an emergency election to pick a new president."

West's eyebrows shot up in surprise.

"With everything that's going on? That's nuts. We don't have time for this, sir! What did he have to say about the exodus?"

"I didn't tell him," Packard said. "I don't trust that he won't go on TV and try to use that as a platform to get himself the presidency. It's going to be bad enough when word gets out, but at least we'll have plans in place and be ready to start moving people. That will go a long way towards calming fears. But, if the information gets out too soon, I'm worried the civilian population will descend into chaos."

"I'd like to think the people have been through enough that they would understand the need for a rational approach, but I'm afraid I have to agree with you, sir. But, what about the Australians? And, there are a few other lightly populated islands in the South Pacific that were given the vaccine for their people. They don't know what's coming."

Packard dropped the report he'd picked up and leaned back in his chair.

"That's one of the many things that keeps me up at night," he said. "Informing the Aussies. Their PM is no better than that slimy politician that just left. If we tell him, you can bet the Russians will hear about it as soon as I get off the phone. If that happens, they're going to be looking for a new place to live and will arrive at the same conclusions we did. They're going to want the same chunks of land, and we don't have time for a war."

"Sir, with all due respect, we can't *not* tell them. There's not much time, and there are millions of people that will die. Maybe, if they start now, they can get emergency shelters set up in their western deserts that will take most of their population. Maybe we can convince the Russians to abandon North America and move into the Middle East. There are several large cities that are sitting empty. Riyadh or Baghdad are more than large enough."

The Admiral waved Captain West into a chair.

"The last I heard, there are still high levels of radiation in the region. Remember, Israel was attacked shortly after we were, and they unleashed hell on the more radical countries. The Russians aren't going to accept that. Not after they think they've conquered the world.

"Put yourself into Barinov's shoes, Captain. He thinks he's in complete control. But, as soon as he gets word that the world is dying, he's going to be looking for an out. At that point, the Australian citizens are just going to be in his way. A fresh release of the nerve agent will solve that problem for him."

"What good will that do?" West asked, obviously having failed to consider the scenario the Admiral was describing.

"It makes room for more Russians to be brought into Australia. Consider this. He kills a few million citizens. Suddenly, there are homes aplenty for the people he allows to come in. And, not only that, he's put the fear of God into the surviving population. What do you think parents will do to protect their children, Captain? Don't you think they'd be willing to become Barinov's slaves? Move out into the deserts to cultivate food for their masters who will continue to live in comfort in the cities?"

West sat quietly for a long moment, considering what Packard had said.

"So, we don't tell the Aussies, and when Barinov figures out what's happening, we'll have a fight on our hands to defend our new home. But, if we do tell them, there's a very real chance that millions of their citizens will be murdered. Those are our only choices, sir?"

Packard nodded and picked up a file folder, gently waving it in the air.

"That's what intel has gamed out, and I agree with their conclusions. Millions of dead Australians, or a protracted battle in Arizona and we lose tens, if not hundreds, of thousands."

"That hardly stacks up against millions in Australia, sir."

"You think I haven't anguished over this?" Packard snapped, slapping the folder back onto the surface of his desk. "We're almost gone, Captain. The best estimates are that there're slightly less than one million Americans still alive. Regardless of that fact, I'm not willing to be even indirectly responsible for a mass genocide in Australia, so I'm going to keep my mouth shut. We'll lose people. A lot of people. But, we're not going to let others die so we can be safe. I couldn't live with that. Could you?"

"No, sir," West said. "I couldn't. But, the Aussies and the Russians are going to notice something is up when we start moving people to CONUS. What do we say when they ask? And there's still the problem of the enemy occupying California. How are we going to get past them?"

Exodus

"Good questions, Captain. And, I'm sure you'll have good answers for me when you present your plans tomorrow morning."

30

Jessica leaned closer to the monitor, peering at a string of computer code as it scrolled across the screen. She watched intently for nearly a minute, then blew out a sigh of frustration. Stretching her sore back, she twisted until it popped in several places, giving her a small degree of relief.

Looking up, she surveyed the darkened room. All her staff were intently hammering away on keyboards, working to help her bypass the multiple layers of encryption that protected the Russian system she was attempting to breach. She could tell with a glance that none of them were having any better success.

"Stuck?"

Jessica looked around to see Lieutenant Hunt staring at her from his workstation.

"Yeah," she said, swiveling the chair so she didn't have to turn her head. "Say what you will, but the damn Russians know what they're doing when it comes to cybersecurity."

"What's stopping you? You've cracked their systems before."

"Yeah," Jessica nodded. "But I've never seen anything like this. None of us have."

Exodus

She flapped a hand at the other people who were still working.

"So, what's the problem?"

"Multiple, rotating layers, and they're self-healing. I crack the first one and get through, then have to back out to get to the next. As soon as I do, the first one repairs itself, and I'm back to square one. Similar to how the NSA did it. Too similar. Someone copied someone's idea, but the Russians did a better job."

"Are you going to be able to get in?" Hunt asked.

"I'll eventually get it," Jessica said. "Just need a reset and to let my mind work on the problem."

Hunt nodded as she stood up and stretched.

"I'll be back," she said, grabbing her purse and heading for the door.

Jessica checked out through security and made a stop on her usual bench for a quick cigarette. She only smoked half of it, memories of her boyfriend intruding on what she had hoped would be an opportunity to relax. Giving up, she started to head back to work, but at the last moment detoured to the CIC. She wanted to check on Major Chase.

Stepping into the cavernous room, she greeted the duty officer and asked for permission to use a terminal. The Navy Commander knew her well and agreed without hesitation. Taking a seat at a vacant workstation, Jessica nodded to the Master Chief Petty Officer at the adjacent position and quickly logged in.

"What's going on Chief?" The older man asked as she waited for the system to finish loading.

"Needed a break and thought I'd check on that Army Major in Nevada."

"Lookin' at it now, if you want a peek," he said.

Jessica smiled and rolled her chair next to his. She wasn't happy to see what was displayed on a large monitor.

"Didn't realize there were that many in the militia," she said, staring at the screen.

"Four hundred and eight surrounding the facility," the Master Chief said. "And they're inside, too."

"How?"

"Big bomb they must've brought up from Nellis. The initial flash was so bright it tripped our nuke monitors, but it was just a damn big conventional explosion."

"Any contact with our people?"

"No. No one's come out, neither. Twenty militia went in when they breached, and just a couple minutes ago an SUV pulled up and five more went inside. Woman and four operators."

Exodus

"Whadya mean? Operators, not militia?"

"Just my gut," he said. "Way they carried their weapons and how they moved. Not like these hicks. I mean, check this out."

He clicked a mouse a few times and the view zoomed to a group of men standing near a pickup.

"See that?" He pointed at the screen. "They're dressed like a teenage gamer's idea of a soldier, and they piled all their rifles into the bed of the truck. Idiots don't think they'll need 'em and must not like holding them. Probably too heavy for their delicate little arms."

Despite her worry for Major Chase, Jessica snorted a laugh.

"Heard anything about a rescue mission?" She asked.

"Nope. Look here."

The man manipulated the controls and zoomed out before panning west. A few more commands and the view changed to display a thermal image of Southern California. Multiple, fast moving heat sources were patrolling the coast, and several heat blooms were clear to see in San Diego and Los Angeles.

"What are those?" Jessica asked. "Russians setting up shop?"

"Exactly. And we ain't getting any planes through. They've got the whole region locked down tight."

Jessica stared at the monitor, wondering how Admiral Packard planned to get around that problem when it was time to begin the exodus. The very harbors that they would need to use on the California coast were currently occupied by the enemy. But that problem wasn't public knowledge yet, and she couldn't say anything to the Master Chief.

Exodus

31

"Hold fire," I mumbled.

Four new shooters had just arrived, tilting the odds even more in the militia's favor. We needed to give things a minute to see what was going on before we started a firefight with a vastly superior force. I just wished we were close enough to hear what was apparently an angry conversation. Straining to listen in as I watched through my night vision scope, I looked up in surprise when there was a muted thud over my head.

"Hear that?" Johnson mumbled.

Shit. There was someone inside the goddamn aircraft! What else had I missed? Now, not only was there a hostile force on the other side of the hangar, we had a problem directly over our heads.

Tilting the rifle up, I scanned the belly of the plane and spotted a seam that looked a hell of a lot like a bomb bay door. Set into the smooth skin was a latch that wasn't completely locked. So, someone had climbed inside and managed to pull the door shut, but not secure it. If we'd started firing on the militia members that were in the open, they could have quietly opened the bay and attacked from the rear. We'd have been chewed up before we even knew there was a problem.

Dirk Patton

It was too dark to see Johnson or Igor, and I had to settle for mumbling instructions to them. We needed to clear the plane but had to do it quietly, so the other assholes didn't hear and come charging in on the attack. That meant no firearms. Even suppressed, they would make enough noise to give away our presence.

Leaving Johnson huddled behind the heavy landing gear to keep an eye on the militia, Igor and I silently made our way towards the far side of the large jet. There was an exterior hatch we could open and climb through, hopefully without alerting the occupants that we were coming to kill them.

It was a very high risk proposition, but other than retreating and leaving Vance to further torture and death, I wasn't coming up with a better option. At least it was pitch black in the hangar and my damaged left eye wasn't going to be a disadvantage.

Ducking beneath the wing, we moved forward along the fuselage until reaching the door. Igor backed a couple of steps away, raising his rifle and drawing a bead on the hatch. My rifle was slung, Ka-Bar knife in my hand. I didn't want him to fire and give us away, but if I opened the plane and there was a bad guy waiting and ready to drill a round through my skull, he'd take the shot.

Reaching up, I fumbled my hand across the smooth skin until I found the right spot. A spring-loaded section was flush with the exterior surface and when pushed, it manipulated the interior lock. Unless

Exodus

whoever was inside had thought to secure the door so it couldn't be opened from the outside. I was counting on that not being the case.

Pressing slowly and smoothly, a section slightly larger than my hand sank into the side of the plane. As it moved, I could feel a moment of extra resistance as the locking bolts retracted, then it hit bottom and the door suddenly bulged out from the surface. I released the breath I'd been holding. There had been almost no sound, which was probably only because the aircraft was new.

Slowly allowing the lock release panel to return to its normal position, I trailed my hand across the surface until finding the lip of the door which now extended a couple of inches from the plane. Gripping it with my fingers, I pulled. Slowly, it began to pivot out.

It was just as dark within the aircraft as it was outside, and this was going to be a problem. I'd been repeatedly kicking myself that we hadn't taken night vision goggles from the armory when we had the chance, but there was no point in dwelling on missed opportunities. All I could do was get the door open far enough to slither inside, then go to work with the knife. At least it didn't matter that I could only see out of one eye.

The door continued to swing open, and I suddenly jerked my hand away and jumped back when something touched it. Whatever it was had been cold and damp, almost clammy. Infected went through my head as I grabbed my rifle, looking around in surprise when I heard a low chuckle from Igor.

Ignoring him, I whipped the weapon up and looked through the scope, smiling in surprise. The door was a little more than a foot open, and Dog was sticking his head through to greet me. I'd felt his nose on my hand. Stepping closer, I rubbed his neck and pressed my face to his for a moment before tugging the door farther open.

"It's me. John," I hissed into the impenetrable darkness inside the aircraft.

There was the faint sound of bodies moving around, then a hand fumbled across my arm before following it down to my hand.

"Thank God," Rachel breathed a few inches from my face. "What happened to Vance? We heard screaming."

"They've still got him," I mumbled. "On the far side of the hangar. You got everyone else?"

"Yes. He hid us in here when they started breaking through the door. Wouldn't hide with us. Said they needed to find someone so they wouldn't keep looking."

I shook my head, more than a little surprised. Vance had been an ass when we'd first met. Had hit on Rachel and made it clear he intended to take a run at Tiffany. Seemed all he was worried about was getting his dick wet. But when it mattered, he'd stepped up. Big time. Maybe I owed him an apology.

"Stay put and stay quiet," I said. "We're going to see what we can do."

Rachel trailed her hand up my arm and cupped it around the back of my head, pulling me forward. In the dark, her lips found my chin. She corrected quickly, kissing me deeply before letting go. Stepping back, I ruffled Dog's ears and pushed his head inside the plane before gently shoving the door closed. Igor following, I returned to where Johnson was closely watching the militia through his night vision scope.

"The girls are in the jet," I mumbled close to his ear.

He nodded but kept his attention on the enemy.

"Anything happening?" I asked.

"Whoever the woman is, she's getting a lot of shit from the guy with the radio in his hand, but she's not backing down. Those four that came in with her are acting as bodyguards, and I think the guy is scared of them."

I raised my rifle and peered through the scope in time to see one of the men who'd arrived with the General looking directly back at me. We were too far apart for me to make out features, or even be certain that he'd seen us. But the very fact that he was scanning with his weapon told me he either had a thermal or night vision scope.

Remaining frozen, I hoped he would fail to spot me. I was mostly concealed behind the landing gear, only my head, arm and rifle exposed. It was possible, no matter how slim the chance.

After several seconds, he swung the rifle away, completed his sweep and lowered it. Casually, he took a few steps forward and leaned in to speak with a very large man who seemed to be in charge. Fuck! We'd been seen, and the guy was playing it as cool as he could.

"Get ready," I hissed, moving my finger onto the trigger.

Shit was about to start going sideways, and at the moment there were only two of the enemy that knew we were in the hangar with them. My first shot would take out their leader. Applying pressure, I paused when a shout rang out.

"It's none of your business, bitch!"

I clearly heard the words, seeing the heads of all four of the General's guards snap in the direction of the argument. Lights were directed onto them as the other militia soldiers moved in, forming a loose circle around the group. The leader grabbed the General's arm and pulled her inside a small bubble he and his men formed, each facing out with their rifles up and ready.

Exodus

One of the flashlights was aimed directly at the leader, brilliantly illuminating his face. It washed out in my night vision, appearing as a bright blur. Deactivating the scope, I dialed up the magnification on the daylight optics and took another look. For several seconds, I was frozen in disbelief. I knew the man. Had fought and bled with him.

Without turning my head away, I hissed instructions to Johnson and Igor. They acknowledged, and reactivating the night vision, I tracked the muzzle back onto the man who had been torturing Vance. He stood with a pistol at arm's length, pointed at the General. OK, enough fucking around with these guys.

"Now," I said, pulling the trigger an instant later.

On either side of me, Johnson and Igor both fired. My guy dropped to the floor, minus a chunk of his skull, and two more of his assholes tumbled down as well. Each of us shifted aim, taking out three more men before they realized they were under attack. The four men surrounding the General opened up as we continued picking off targets. Within less than ten seconds, they were the only ones still standing.

I scanned each of the bodies quickly, satisfied to see that none of them were moving. Checking on the group protecting the General, I wasn't surprised to see that they had taken cover behind some equipment and had their weapons trained on us.

"Should have guessed you'd survive, Nitro," I shouted into the darkness.

There was no reply for several seconds, and I could well imagine the confused expression on my former teammate's face.

"Who the fuck're you, esse?" He shouted back.

"John Chase," I answered, stepping around the landing gear into full view.

"No fuckin' way! Boss? That really you?"

"They're lowering their weapons," Johnson reported in a quiet voice.

Mine was lowered, too, and I couldn't see anything other than the small areas that were lit by the flashlights the militia had dropped when they'd died. A few seconds later one of them was picked up and slowly began coming towards me. Leaving my rifle hanging, I walked forward.

"Goddamn, Nitro," I said with a grin when we met halfway across the open space. The light reflected off the smooth concrete, giving each of us a good view of the other's face. "How the fuck did you get uglier? I didn't think it was possible!"

"Barrio handsome, Wedo," he said, laughing as he stepped close and wrapped me into a bone crushing hug.

32

I stepped back from Nitro and waved my small team forward.

"Johnson," I shouted. "Get Rachel to check on Vance!"

He nodded as Igor stepped into view. As he popped the bay doors open, Nitro turned and signaled for his people to approach. They came forward with caution, and no small degree of trepidation, weapons pointed at the floor but firmly gripped in their hands.

"Wanna tell me just what the fuck is going on?" I asked.

"Bunch of fucking half-wit wannabes," Nitro growled. "It's a long story, but we got bigger problems at the moment."

"More of them inside?" I asked, looking over his shoulder as the other three operators walked up, the General leading the way.

The woman was even more beautiful than I'd realized from viewing her through a rifle scope a few days earlier. She was roughly my age and was still a stunner. She stepped forward, stopping next to Nitro's bulging shoulder and looked me up and down.

"Yeah," he said, watching Rachel, Irina and Tiffany hurry past to check Vance.

Dirk Patton

Without even looking at her, I could tell Rachel had noticed the General standing in front of me. It's kind of like you can feel the vibes when a woman is jealous. Maybe, someday, I'll figure out how the hell that works.

"Seems like you know them," I said, staring at Nitro and the General with hooded eyes.

"And you are who, exactly?" The woman asked in a low, husky voice.

"John Chase," Nitro replied, introducing me. "He was my team leader in Delta, ma'am."

"You didn't answer me, Nitro. What are you doing with the militia?"

Nails clicked on the smooth floor and a second later Dog sat down next to my leg. He stared at Nitro and the other men who had formed a half-circle behind him and the General. His lips peeled back to expose his teeth and a low growl rumbled in his chest.

"Easy," I said to him, placing a hand on his head.

Igor and Johnson took up positions on either side of us, staying back and eyeing Nitro and his small group.

"Look," I said to Nitro and the General. "Are we gonna have a problem, or not? You're either with them, or you aren't. Where do we go from here?"

Exodus

"We were with them," the General said. "Or, they were with us. Things have changed. You stumbled into me trying to set things right. Do you have a way out of here?"

I stared at her long enough to make her uncomfortable. She shifted her weight and began to look away before catching herself and crossing her arms across her chest in defiance.

"Maybe," I said. "That man strapped to the table over there is our pilot. The woman working on him is a doctor. Hopefully, he'll be able to fly. But, first things first. How many militia are inside and what are we up against?"

"Wait," the woman said, eyes flashing. "These are my men. You're not going to start…"

I took my hand off Dog's head and held it up like a stop sign.

"Lady, if you want to walk out that door, be my guest," I growled, patience wearing thin. "The only reason we're even talking is because of Nitro. Him I know and trust. You? And these guys? I've got no idea who you are or what your agenda is, and I don't care. But, I'm going to get my people out of here. If you want to come with us, I'm happy to have you along, but we're going to do things my way. Take it or leave it!"

She glared back at me, the three men behind her subtly shuffling their feet, spreading out in case things went sideways. Dog growled again, and I saw movement to my right as Igor took a step to the side.

"Ma'am," Nitro said, turning to her. "You trust me, and I trust him."

After a few seconds, her eyes shifted from me to Nitro. Finally, she nodded and turned back to face me again. The men behind her visibly relaxed a notch when Nitro looked at each of them and nodded.

"So, where will we go?" She asked.

"One step at a time, General," I said, noting the surprise on her face when I called her by her rank. Without turning my attention from her, I said, "Johnson, get your ass down the shaft and bring the Master Chief and the rest of our people up here."

"You want the lights back on?" He asked.

I thought about that for a second, then nodded. It would be easier to hunt the militia if we could see without having to depend on our rifle scopes.

"Yeah, have Nicole restore power."

"Yes, sir."

He was to my left, and I couldn't see him move away but could hear his boots on the floor as he ran for the hatch in the far wall.

"Sir?" Nitro asked, squinting at me.

Exodus

"I'm a Major, now," I said, shrugging. "Long story. So, how many are we facing and where are they?"

Nitro stepped forward and pulled a sharpie out of a pocket. Kneeling, he began sketching a crude outline on the floor, talking as he drew.

"Here's the exterior entrance they breached. The corridor is in bad shape, nearly impassible between the bomb damage and fire, but you can get through. That's where they came in. They've got ten men outside, guarding the hole, and another five on the interior side of the damage. Pretty sure they put a guard on each level at the central elevator shaft. At least, that's what one of the ones pulling duty at the breach said. And, they've got others spreading out to see what's worth taking."

"They have anything other than small arms?" I asked, kneeling next to him.

Dog had wormed his way under my left arm, on the opposite side of my body from Nitro. He'd stopped growling, but every time I looked at him, his teeth were exposed in a silent snarl.

"Not inside," Nitro said. "They got their hands on some medium and heavy weapons at Nellis. We were there, trying to direct them away, but they found them anyway."

"OK," I said, looking at the sketch and nodding as I thought. "Take two of your shooters and clear out the guards on the inside of the breach. Leave one of them here to guard the civies. I'll take two of mine and take out the searchers and have the fourth stay here with yours."

We all reflexively looked at the ceiling when the lights suddenly popped to life, buzzing loudly as they warmed up. When I lowered my eye, Rachel was approaching at a fast walk. She came to a stop next to Dog, and I didn't miss the look that passed between her and the General. I had no idea what it meant, but they probably did.

"How's Vance?" I asked.

"Hurting," she said, scratching Dog's ears. "They cut open his scrotum and poured salt directly into the wound."

All the men around us grimaced, several of them muttering quiet curses.

"He OK?"

"I just sewed him up, and he's asleep at the moment. The salt, as bad as it had to hurt, will probably wind up saving him from a nasty infection. But, he's got a lot of swelling already and lost quite a bit of blood. I need to get him to medical and on IV antibiotics."

"That's going to have to wait," I said. "We've got intruders wandering the halls. Think he'll be able to fly when the time comes?"

"Maybe," Rachel said, lifting her hands in a shrug. "If he's able to sit in a cockpit. How soon can you get me to medical? He's going to need some pain meds, too."

"Soon as I can," I said, standing.

"Sooner is better," Rachel said, putting her hand on my arm.

"Got it," I said, turning as Johnson, with Gonzales, Nicole and Chelsea trotted up.

Nitro and his men noticed the thick swaddle of bandages on the Master Chief's face but didn't comment or ask any questions.

"OK, people. We've got work to do," I said. "Nitro, get moving. Johnson and Igor, you're with me. Master Chief, stay put and keep everyone quiet. We've got militia searching the facility, and you don't want to draw their attention. Questions?"

"I did find something yesterday that might help," Johnson said. "I think it could seal off areas if we needed to."

"What'd you find?" I asked.

"Took a while to figure out what it was," Johnson said, stepping forward. "Guess they were developing some sort of system to seal up a breach, or maybe disable a vehicle. I pressed a button and damn near glued Nicole to the wall. Damn thing shoots out a jet of high-pressure foam. Sticks to cement like a fuckin' barnacle, then expands and hardens. Don't know how the hell you'd get someone out of it if they got trapped."

"How big of an area will it seal?" Nitro asked.

Johnson looked at me, and I nodded for him to answer.

"Covered about fifty square feet in less than a second, then the foam expanded and doubled in size."

"We take out the guards inside the breach, that could seal it up," Nitro said, reaching out and tapping a spot on the sketch he'd drawn on the floor. "At least until they bring in some more explosives."

I nodded, liking the idea.

"You could have mentioned that before I set up the Willie Pete," I groused at Johnson.

"Sorry, sir. Didn't think about it at the time."

He shrugged and gave me a half-assed grin.

"Where is it?"

"Couple levels down," he said after thinking for a few seconds.

"Do you need help moving it?" I asked.

"No, it's on some sort of wheeled platform. I can move it by myself. But I'm going to have to use the elevator to bring it up. It's not *man-portable*."

"Alright," I said. "New plan, everyone. I want two men in the corridor to keep watch and make sure no more militia make it beyond the guards and into the facility. Two men stay here. The rest of us are going with Johnson to get the… thingy."

There were a couple of muted laughs when I said that last word.

"Then what?" The General asked.

"Then we seal up the breach and go hunting," I said, earning nods from all the warriors.

33

We quickly got our shit together and prepared to head out. Nitro barked some commands, and two of his men, called Bunny and Monk, took off at a trot. They'd set up around a bend from the breach and keep an eye on our uninvited guests. I told them to make sure that no more of the militia made it into the facility.

We already didn't know how many we'd be facing, and sure didn't need that number to grow. Everyone huddled and pooled resources, and when they headed out, they were equipped with nearly a dozen fragmentation grenades and a couple of WP grenades that Igor had held back.

A tall, thin man that Nitro referred to as Goose was selected to stay behind with Gonzales to protect the girls. He was a former SEAL, and it took him and the Master Chief all of half a second to bond and begin sharing sea stories. The rest of us, me, Nitro, Johnson and Igor would go collect the foam machine. But, before we could head out, Tiffany came running up.

"Here," she said, thrusting what at first I thought was a bra into my hand.

"What the hell's this?" I asked, holding it up to unfurl.

When it did, I was confused for a moment. It was a bra or had been at one time. A small, black, frilly thing. But she had cut the fringe off as well as one of the cups, done some reshaping of the remaining one and stitched the whole thing back together. She'd made me an eye patch.

"Don't even look at it like that," she said, hands on her hips. "I had to talk one of the girls out of her bra, then it took some time to make it work."

I looked at it for a few moments, then up at Tiffany.

"What?" She said, challenging.

"Thank you," I said, smiling. "I'm actually touched that you went to all this trouble for me, but I really don't think I need it."

"It will give you some protection," Rachel said. "You need to guard that eye until we can get you to what's left of civilization and a good surgeon. Right now, you won't even see something coming that could cause more damage. Wear it!"

After a beat, I worked it over my head, settling the modified cup over my damaged eye. It wasn't perfect, and I probably looked ridiculous, but if it would prevent any more damage, I was willing to give it a go. Adjusting the fit, I noticed Igor turn away, but not before I saw the grin on his face. Nitro was doing his best to ignore me.

"Thank you," I said again to Tiffany.

She beamed before heading back to join the other girls who were clustered around the still unconscious Vance. Rachel squeezed my hand and followed her. I turned to lead the way to the door, coming face to face with the General.

"Bring my men back," she said softly.

I saw something in her eyes that changed my impression of her. Genuine concern for the well-being of the warriors under her command. That, more than anything else she could have done or said, softened my attitude towards her.

"I'll do my best," I said.

She nodded and stepped out of the way as the four of us took off at a trot. Dog fell in beside me, seemingly happy to be heading out to wreak mayhem on our attackers. I'd considered leaving him with Rachel for an extra layer of protection, but knew he'd be an asset. And, if we did our jobs, he wouldn't be needed in the hangar.

"Hey, boss. How's it feel to have a bra on your head?" Nitro asked as we ran across the hangar.

"Shame she didn't use a pair of panties," Johnson quipped.

Igor snorted a laugh and I sighed in resignation. It was going to be a long day. And the worst part was I had no doubt Nitro was going to rub off on both of them.

Exodus

I slowed at the door, leaning out to scan the corridor before stepping through with my rifle up and ready. The rest of my team followed close behind, the hatch closing softly behind as Gonzales secured it. The heavy locking bolt refused to go home. It was bent from the militia having forced their way in earlier.

It took some time to reach the central hub where the elevator shaft was located. The smell of fire was strong in the air from where they had tripped the WP grenades I'd set up. It was carried to us on a gentle current blowing in from the corridor where Nitro's men had set up.

"That WP wasn't a half bad idea," he mumbled to me as we paused. "Killed a couple of 'em, too. But, it really pissed off the rest."

"How many are outside?" I asked.

"'Bout four hundred," Nitro said, shrugging like it didn't matter.

Shaking my head, I moved to the stairwell entrance and peeked through the tall, narrow window set in the door just above the handle. We'd have to use the elevator to bring the equipment back up, but I didn't want to ride it down and alert any of the militia that we were on the move. Seeing nothing, I cracked the door open and gave Dog a moment to sample the air. His nose twitched briefly, then he looked up at me, waiting to see what I wanted to do.

Trusting his senses, I pushed through and began descending, happy to have him. If I'd left him behind, there was no way I'd be taking point with only one eye. Nitro, Johnson and Igor stayed close behind as we silently padded down the concrete stairs. I paused at each landing, carefully looking out through the window. On level C, I pulled back quickly when I saw movement. Two men carrying rifles were approaching a door Johnson had left open during his search.

"Scroungers," I mumbled to my small team. "Two, going into the first room on the left."

"Kill them," Igor said, earning nods from the other two men.

I made my decision in less than a second, signing our stack order to the men before turning to approach the door. Nitro's big hand on my arm stopped me.

"Boss, you know I trust you, but you the right one to go through the door first?"

He reached up and tapped his left eye, then pointed at mine.

"Sorry, boss," he said softly.

I was immediately angry. Nearly told him to go fuck himself since I had Dog by my side. But, he was right, and I had no business being mad at him. Swallowing my pride, I stepped aside.

Exodus

"OK. Nitro takes lead, Igor then Johnson. Dog and I have got rear security."

Everyone nodded and we took a couple of seconds to re-shuffle our positions, then Nitro pushed out of the stairwell. Igor and Johnson were tight on his back. They quickly moved to the door, pausing just before the jamb. While they were focused on their entry, Dog and I put our backs against the wall, scanning up and down the corridors for any threats.

When Nitro was ready, they moved quickly, flowing through the opening without a detectable sound. I slid along the wall to where they had been stacked, keeping my rifle up and moving as I scanned for threats. This wasn't something I was used to doing, and it pissed me off. But it was nobody's fault. It was just one of those things that can happen in combat.

I heard several suppressed shots from the room, then Nitro's voice softly calling the all clear. A moment later he spoke from around the door, letting me know they were coming out. Still scanning, I headed for the stairs, Dog tucked tight against my leg. We were back in the stairwell in seconds, Nitro maintaining point as we descended another level.

"This is it," Johnson said quietly when we reached the landing for D.

"Which way?" Nitro asked.

"I'll take point," Johnson said, slipping past him and placing his hand on the door.

Nitro shot me a glance. I nodded, confirming Johnson knew his shit. Shifting around, we followed him through the door. He circled the elevator shaft and quickly scanned each of the corridors before heading down the longest one. Dog and I were still on rear security, moving with the group but making sure we didn't get surprised from behind.

Several dozen open doors later, Johnson led us into a room. A large machine rested on a wheeled platform, but what caught my attention was the large blob that covered almost an entire wall. Telling Dog to stay at the door, I walked over and tentatively tapped on the substance with the hilt of my knife. It felt like concrete.

"This is it?" I asked, even though I didn't need to.

"Yep," Johnson said, bending to release the locks on the platform's wheels. "That was a one-second blast."

I looked up at the machine, shaking my head in amazement. Calling it a machine was perhaps being too optimistic. A six-foot tall tower that encased several pipes was bolted to the center of the platform, a pair of fifty-five-gallon drums strapped to either side of it.

Exodus

A large motor was attached at the rear, its shaft connected to a steel encased pump that fed the pipes. At the top of the tower was what looked just like the nozzle on a fire hose, and there was also a wand, similar to what you'd see in a car wash, at the end of a long, braided steel hose. Finally, a large bank of batteries to power the unit was bolted down to the side.

"You can switch between the tower mount or the handheld, right here," Johnson said, pointing at a large lever on the front of the pump.

"Plenty of foam in the barrels?" I asked.

"Two different substances," Johnson said, tapping the one closest to him. "They're mixed together when you fire, as best I can tell. Probably like a two-part epoxy. And yes, both are mostly full."

"OK, let's get..."

I spun around when Dog emitted a low growl. He was inside the room with us but had his nose extended into the corridor. Rushing to his side, I put my hand on his back and carefully poked my head out for a look.

34

Jessica looked up when a shadow fell across her workstation to see Admiral Packard and Captain West standing behind her. Fingers poised over a keyboard, she returned the Admiral's warm smile. She'd never really figured out why he had taken a liking to her but wasn't about to question her luck. If it wasn't for him, she'd most likely be in prison instead of still doing her job.

"Progress, Chief?" Packard asked.

Jessica couldn't help but smile broadly.

"Yes, sir! I just defeated the last layer of encryption. Well, to be accurate, my team and I did." She waved at the other people in the room who were staring curiously. "Without their help, I'd never have found the way through."

"Excellent work, everyone," the Admiral said in a loud voice. "Chief, when will you have control?"

"I can't say, yet, sir. I quite literally just made it into the control system and haven't even begun poking around. Once I get a look under the hood, I'll be able to give you an estimate. Where do you want me to send the infected?"

Exodus

"That's the big question, isn't it, Chief," Packard said. "Considering our plans, do you have a suggestion?"

"As far away as possible," Jessica said with a shudder.

"Amen to that," Captain West muttered, drawing a grin from Packard.

"Come find me when you know what you're dealing with," the Admiral said.

"Aye, aye sir. Will do."

Packard and West quickly exited the room, immediately being surrounded by the Marine protection detail led by Captain Black. They all squeezed into an elevator and rode to the surface, exiting into a beautiful, tropical morning. A rain storm had just passed across the island, washing the air clean and leaving behind a calm sea and a brilliant blue sky.

"Let's make a detour to the bench, Captain," Packard said to Black as he reached into his pocket for a pack of cigarettes.

"Sir, everyone is assembled for the briefing and waiting for us," West reminded him.

"Captain, you're giving the briefing, and they all work for me. I think they'll wait."

West grinned and shook his head. It was impossible to argue with the old man's point.

"What do we know about our wayward Major?" The Admiral asked as they strolled across the lush grass.

"At last update, he was still unconscious with a head wound, but I don't have any details on the severity of his injury. However, we've lost comms with the facility they're in, and they have some big problems. There is a large contingent of a local militia that has surrounded them and is attempting to breach the exterior. They acquired some large munitions from Nellis and have employed them in their attempts. That is likely the reason for the loss of comms."

"Can we get to them?"

"Not easy, sir," West said, shaking his head. "The Russian build up along the California coast is blocking our access, and they are patrolling a large area, including all the way to the tip of Baja in the south. We would have to attempt to fight through, and our losses would be significant whether or not we were successful. The odds of an extraction are very low."

The Admiral stared at the harbor below, chewing on his lip in thought.

"What about the Reagan and its strike group? How are they coming along?"

Exodus

"As you know, sir, they were heavily damaged when the Russians struck the Bahamas with nuclear weapons. They've put in to Norfolk Navy Yard to effect repairs, but are dealing with residual radiation from the bombing of D.C. as well as a large population of infected. However, Captain Morrow assures me they are making progress, albeit painfully slow.

"At my request, he dispatched a squadron of F-18s to lend assistance to our people in Nevada, but they were met by a vastly superior enemy force in the southeastern US and turned back with no losses. On my orders, sir. We cannot afford to lose those pilots and aircraft."

"Agreed," Packard grumbled. "But, speaking of pilots, have you been able to debrief Commander Vance?"

"Yes, sir. I was able to speak with him before comms went down. He confirmed that the Athena Platform is still functional and in control of American personnel."

"Have you contacted them?" Packard asked, surprised at the news.

"No, sir. They communicated with Vance via a low powered transmission on the guard channel and informed him that they are resuming EM silent status. They are mostly unprotected, and if they utilize any of our data links, it will alert the Russians to their presence. I have instructed the Reagan to deploy to the gulf immediately when the strike group is sea and battle ready."

"What do you make of that file the Major retrieved from SAC? Pie in the sky, or is there really a time machine sitting off the coast of Texas?" The Admiral asked.

"Sir, at first I was of the opinion that the project was a false flag, designed to distract and demoralize the enemy. Kind of like Reagan's Star Wars project in the early 80s. But, the presence of personnel on site isn't consistent with that theory. Now, I just don't know what to think."

Packard nodded and lit a smoke, settling onto the bench.

"So, give me a preview, Captain," he said. "What's your plan to get us to Arizona?"

Both men looked up when a Marine Super Cobra roared overhead. It was another layer of the Admiral's protection, ensuring no one and nothing was going to get close enough to harm him again.

"Well, sir, if you'll bear with me, I'm going to recite what is almost certainly obvious to you, but I need to set the stage."

"Proceed, Captain."

"Sir, the Russians have occupied the California coast from San Diego to north of Marin county near San

Exodus

Francisco. Currently, they are conducting surface, subsurface and flight operations out of all of our naval bases on the coast, as well as having moved two divisions of heavy armor into Camp Pendleton, just north of San Diego.

"They maintain a strong presence in Oregon and Washington state but appear to be slowly drawing down their strength to augment the forces that are already in California. All the Russian civilians who had taken up residence in the Seattle area have evacuated, most likely due to the radiation from the breached reactor aboard Peter the Great. We had hoped they were relocating to Australia to join Barinov, but they have gone south to the LA area. Malibu and Santa Barbara are quite popular.

"As the enemy strengthens its hold on the region, we are beginning to monitor flights coming out of Russia, bringing more civilians. These are not the business or political elites, who are already in Australia with Barinov, but are well connected nonetheless. Our current estimate is there are roughly fifteen thousand Russian citizens in California. And that number is steadily climbing. The damage to their country's infrastructure and environment from our attacks is driving a mass exodus.

"In fact, when we are in the briefing room, I have several intercepts of government officials discussing the situation for you to review. Radiation is still spreading from the nuclear power plants we targeted, and as winter is settling in, people are already suffering from the lack of basic services such as running water and power for heat. Additionally, the Russian authorities are dealing with food riots in every major city. As a result, their consensus, with President Barinov's blessing, is to relocate a large portion of the civilian population to California where our infrastructure is still intact."

"Hold on, Captain," Packard said, lighting another cigarette. He seemed to show no sign of being interested in heading inside. "You said a large portion of the population will get relocated. What does that mean?"

"It means, sir, that Barinov has left it up to his cronies and commanders to decide who is worth saving and who isn't."

"Excuse me?"

"Sir, his exact words were, *'Save the ones worth saving. The rest can freeze or starve. We've got too many people that are nothing more than a burden.'*"

Packard sat staring at his aide, shock and horror on his face.

"How many people is he planning on leaving behind?" He finally asked.

"Unclear, sir. However, based on intercepts it appears that anyone not of pure Russian heritage will be left to fend for themselves. That's the first cut. After that, they seem to be prioritizing scientists, engineers and doctors. The result will be a population not unlike what we've gamed out in the War College."

Packard nodded, slowly smoking his cigarette.

"Save the people that can perpetuate your society. A spot on the lifeboat is based on your value to the larger group," the Admiral said, understanding what West was telling him. "What about the service sector? Mechanics, maids, cooks, laborers; that sort of thing?"

"I had a long conversation with our senior intel people last night, sir. They are of the unanimous opinion that was the purpose behind the attempted land invasion of Hawaii. The Russians intended to capture our civilians and force them to fill these roles. In their eyes, nothing would be more prestigious than having American citizens cooking their food, cleaning their toilets and mowing their lawns."

"What's their plan now that the invasion is defunct? Do they have enough assets to mount another attempt?" Packard asked.

"No, sir. Not a successful one, at any rate. They would have to be willing to accept heavy losses which would degrade them to the point of no return. Again, after discussing this topic with intel, we are of the consensus that the current plan is to starve us out.

"We have roughly a million people here in the islands. We're getting by for the moment, but very soon the cupboard is going to be bare. As you know, we had plans to make supply raids into CONUS as well as restarting much of the agriculture in California's central valley. That would be more than capable of meeting our needs. In fact, estimates were that we would have plenty of excess to use as a trading commodity with Australia. But, the Russians have successfully cut off our access. That, of course, no longer matters now that we are facing a planetary blight because of the virus, but the Russians don't know that. Yet. They're working on the assumption that when we get hungry enough, people will be lining up to come to work for them."

"So, if we move all our people to Phoenix, we'll have most of what's remaining of the Russian military only a few hundred miles away. We already expected to have to fight another war when they figure out what's happening to the planet, but this is going to be worse than I thought."

"Agreed, sir," Captain West said. "But, we have time to prepare, if we can get our people moved. There are still significant quantities of materiel within CONUS that we can use. Many of our civilians will volunteer to be trained and fight. And, I do not believe the Russians will bomb the city. They need the infrastructure intact, or there's not much point in fighting for it. I think we're going to be looking at a major land battle in the deserts between LA and Phoenix."

"Did you put together estimates on what we have available in CONUS, as well as the personnel we're going to need?" Packard asked, lighting his third cigarette.

"Yes, sir. It's in the conference room in my briefing folder. But, I have an alternative suggestion."

"Do tell, Captain."

"Well, sir. We haven't met her, but this has to do with the Russian GRU agent that's with Major Chase. Captain Irina Vostov."

"What can she do?" The Admiral asked in surprise. "Her uncle was the power in Russia, and his role was discovered. I've no doubt that Barinov had him drawn and quartered."

"Not entirely accurate, sir," West said. "That was our initial belief. Firing squad was our assumption, but we did believe he had been executed. In my discussion with intel, they dropped a little nugget on me. Fleet Admiral Shevchenko, Captain Vostov's uncle, is still alive and being held in Detention Camp 7 in Siberia."

"If we get our hands on him, would the Russian commanders follow his orders?" Packard asked.

"Not if Barinov is alive, no sir. But, if we can take Barinov out and release Admiral Shevchenko, the odds are good. Especially if he has an offer in hand when he talks to them."

"What offer would that be, Captain?"

Dirk Patton

"We share with the Russians. Allow them to move into the Phoenix metro area with us. There's enough land and water to accommodate food production for millions of people. Things will be cramped, but new houses can be built."

Packard stared at his aide in silence. His initial reaction was to flatly refuse the suggestion, but he'd been around too long to quickly dismiss any idea, no matter how repulsive it was. West saw his hesitation and continued.

"Sir, I don't like the idea, either. And, it's going to take some convincing to get the people to go along with it. But, we must remember one thing. It was not the Russian people who did this to us. It was a madman, and his sycophants, who were in control of their country. We can dictate who is allowed in, and I believe that Admiral Shevchenko would have a vested interest in excluding anyone who supported Barinov."

"You're trying to tell me we don't have any other options, aren't you, Captain?" Packard asked, staring at his hand as he rolled an unlit cigarette between his fingers.

"Sir, there are options. We can fight. And very likely lose tens, if not hundreds of thousands of people. But, we're dwindling fast, sir. One of the reports in my briefing folder provides details on the demographics of the surviving population of America. Less than thirty percent are of childbearing age. That's less than three hundred thousand people, and unfortunately, the numbers are skewed against us. Of that group, sixty-one percent are male.

"Even without fighting another war, or the effects of the coming blight, we are going to lose a significant portion of our people over the next one to two decades to disease and old age. And, if we were to keep fighting, the majority of those who will die on the battlefield fall within the age group that should be home making babies. We cannot sustain ongoing conflict if the human race, well, the American part of the human race, is to survive, sir."

"Make love, not war? Is that it, Captain?" Packard asked with a sardonic grin.

"Your words, not mine, sir," West said, chuckling.

"Taking out Barinov without starting a shooting war with Australia will be very difficult," Packard said.

"Perhaps, sir. But, perhaps not. After the incident in Sydney where their PM ordered the military to stand down while Barinov executed our SEALs, there are some fractures appearing. He has lost the confidence of almost all his senior commanders, and as word spread, well over ten thousand troops are refusing to leave their barracks.

"Barinov is currently the power in that country, and only because he supposedly has his thumb on the trigger to release the nerve agent in all of their major cities. The PM is weak. He wasn't popular before all of this, and I believe that if we could take Barinov out without the nerve gas being deployed, there is enough anger and disillusionment amongst the Australian senior officers for them to seize power. At the very least, they wouldn't follow the PM's orders. Ideally, they take control until elections can be held."

Packard was quiet for a long time, absorbing everything he'd just been told. Hunched over, elbows on his knees, he continued playing with the cigarette as he considered options. Finally, he sat up straight and lit it, inhaling deeply.

"Just so I understand, Captain. We have two choices. One, we fight our way through the Russians in California so we can land and transport one million people across hundreds of miles of desert to our new home. And once we get there, the fighting won't stop. We'll have to defend our territory, and even if we're successful and win the war, we'll lose so many young people that it won't matter. About all that will be left will be senior citizens, like me, who can sit in our rocking chairs and watch our population die off until there's not anyone left.

"Or, we go into Australia and kill Barinov, then rescue Admiral Shevchenko from the gulag in Siberia in the hope that he'll be able to convince all of the Russian commanders to follow him and come live arm in arm with us. You're going to put two groups of people together who hate each other. Who destroyed each other's country and killed millions in the process. And, somehow, we've got to find a way to get along without killing each other. Is that pretty much it?"

"In a nutshell, sir," West said.

"And, why do you think this will work?"

"Because there's no other choice, sir. Yes, we hate the Russians, and they hate us. Good reason on our part, and I'm sure they think they have a legitimate beef as well. But, if we don't do this, there won't be enough of America left to justify continuing the fight. Sir."

"And, who exactly is going to sell this to the American people? Tell them to put aside their hatred for what's been done to us, to the entire planet, and buddy up with the people they hold responsible."

"You are, sir," West said with a grin.

"Captain, when we're through here I want you to report for drug testing," Packard said with a snort.

"Happily, sir," West said, smiling. "But, I'm serious. You've led us through everything that has happened to our country, and the people know that. Without you, I don't believe we'd still be here. They know that, too, and they'll listen to you. That's why I took the liberty of leaving a form on your desk. It's already filled out, and all it needs is your signature."

"What form? What are you talking about?"

"Seems the Governor wasn't just posturing when he said we were going to have elections as quickly as could be arranged. I went down to the Hawaii Secretary of State's office early this morning and picked up the paperwork to declare candidacy for President."

Packard paused with a cigarette halfway to his mouth, staring in surprise.

"I'm not a politician, Captain," he said, shaking his head.

"No, sir. You're not. And that's exactly why we need you right now."

35

A single, distant figure was in the corridor, slowly moving in our direction. It was too far away to make out details, but I was willing to trust Dog's nose. If he thought it was an infected, who the hell was I to argue with him?

Moving cautiously, I raised my rifle for a look through the scope. Finding my target, I saw a woman dressed in an Air Force enlisted uniform. I couldn't see her eyes, but within a few seconds, she hitched her shoulder while ticking her head to the side. This confirmed I was looking at an infected.

As she paused to test the air at an open door, I pulled the trigger. The rifle emitted a muted report as it spat out a bullet and an instant later the female's head snapped back and she tumbled to the shiny floor. I kept my eye to the scope for several more seconds to see if she had any companions that would emerge into the hall, but it seemed as if she was alone.

"Female infected," I said to the team, lowering my weapon.

"How the fuck did she get in?" Nitro hissed.

"Found a few," Johnson said. "So far, always in the lower levels."

"Probably been here all along," I said. "She was in uniform. We'd better be sure we're watching our asses. Don't need a surprise to come screaming out of one of these rooms. Now, let's get moving and get this thing upstairs."

Dog and I stepped out into the hallway, Igor joining us. We took up guarding positions on either side of the door as Nitro pushed and Johnson pulled and steered the large contraption. It must have been even heavier than it looked because Nitro was puffing and sweating within a few yards. Igor glanced down at the machine. Leaning sideways for a better look, he raised a hand to stop them and picked up a control module connected to the unit by a heavy, black bundle of wires.

He clicked a button, then pressed on a small, rubber encased joystick. With a faint whine of electric motors, the platform began rolling down the corridor under its own power. When he released the control, it quickly came to a stop. Grinning, he handed the module to Johnson and went back to scanning the corridor.

"You guys are making America look bad," I grumbled.

"Piss off, boss," Nitro said with an embarrassed grin on his face.

Johnson made a few false starts but quickly figured out the little nuances in driving the machine.

Exodus

Soon he had it humming down the middle of the corridor, walking behind it with the controller in his hand. Nitro joined Igor on point, moving ahead and paying close attention to each open door. Dog and I trailed behind, keeping a close eye on the long stretch of hall to our rear.

We spread out in the central hub, covering all the corridors as Johnson maneuvered the platform into an elevator. Igor stayed with him as Nitro, Dog and I raced up the stairs to level A. Our job was to make sure there hadn't been any bad guys, or infected, come into the area. Putting all of us into the elevator could result in a nasty surprise when the door opened at our destination.

It was a matter of less than a minute for us to clear the immediate area, then Nitro ran back down to give them the go ahead as Dog and I kept watch. Walking a slow circle around the central bank of elevators, my mind immediately drifted to Katie and my burning need for vengeance. I experienced a momentary flash of guilt when I thought about Rachel, but dismissed it as quickly as it came over me. I had something to do before I could let myself even consider what the future might hold for us.

The elevator dinged softly, pulling me out of my thoughts. Nitro and Igor stepped out, moving in opposite directions as Johnson piloted the machine into the open. He steered it to the entrance of the breached corridor, letting it roll to a stop.

"How are we going to do this?" He asked, looking at me. "This thing isn't exactly fast, and I don't expect the militia is just gonna let me drive it close enough to hose them down."

"I'll do it," Nitro said. "They know me. Don't like me, but they know me. I can get close before they realize there's a problem."

"Do it," I said without hesitation.

Johnson handed the controller to Nitro and stepped to the side. We fell in a few yards behind him as he piloted it into the corridor. It took several minutes to cover the distance to the bend where Bunny and Monk were hunkered down. Both looked at Nitro in surprise when they saw the machine.

"What the fuck's that?" Monk asked.

He was a little guy, no more than five foot three or four and built like a gymnast. The top of his head didn't even reach Nitro's shoulder. I didn't know him but was willing to bet he was hell on wheels in hand to hand combat. Never underestimate the little guys.

He reminded me of a time I'd been in Thailand on leave. Young, dumb and full of... well, you know what I mean. Anyway, here I was, this great big, strapping Green Beret who thought he was the toughest guy to ever walk into a bar. Like the wet behind the ears idiot I was, I wound up challenging this skinny little local guy who couldn't have weighed more than a hundred and twenty pounds soaking wet. He was nothing more than sinew stretched over bone, and I'd taken exception to how he looked at me.

What I didn't know at the time was just how popular the martial arts in general, and stick fighting specifically, were in Thailand. And, in my defense, I had no way of knowing the guy I'd just shoved off a bar stool was a nationally ranked stick fighter. As I found out, they are blindingly fast and know exactly where to place their strikes to cause the most damage.

Well, I think he hit me about thirty times before I managed to land a glancing blow on his shoulder. With my size, if the punch had connected solidly, I'd probably have broken his neck. But, that's the thing about the guys that practice this type of combat art. They train and train and train on being able to avoid blows from big, dumb guys like me. So, he hit me about twenty more times, and I was in real trouble before the other Americans in the bar finally intervened. Other than the one near miss, I'd never laid a finger on the guy.

I was nearly out on my feet when half a dozen guys hustled me out of there before I wound up in the morgue. Fortunately, I learned a few valuable lessons that day. First, don't start shit with someone over something stupid. More importantly, never underestimate an opponent. Oh, and one other thing. If you're facing a ridiculously fast little guy like that stick fighter, just shoot the fucker rather than get your ass kicked. Saves a lot of wear and tear on the body and face.

"Heard you needed an enema," Nitro answered Monk. "Bend over!"

"Can we focus on the bad guys?" I asked.

"Sorry, boss," Nitro said, sounding anything but. "Bunny, you're with me."

"Doing what?" The other man asked.

"You drive this thing. I'm going to walk beside it."

"Yeah. What does it do?" Bunny asked, slowly taking the controller.

"Easier to show you than tell you," Nitro said. "Johnson, what do I do?"

Johnson stepped forward and leaned over the pump. He pressed a couple of buttons that were protected by clear plastic covers. A low-frequency hum started up as he opened valves on the top of each drum.

"Point it and pull the trigger," he said. "Be ready. It comes out damn fast. Kind of like a fire hose."

Nitro nodded and picked up the wand. It looked like the sprayer from a pressure washer, but the pipe was about an inch in diameter with a complicated valve on the end. The inert half of the foam was probably pumped through the pipe, the valve at the end mixing it with the contents of the other barrel as it shot out.

"Let's go," he said to Bunny.

Together, they set off down the corridor at a slow pace that matched the trundling platform. The rest of us stayed back, hidden from the guards by the bend. Quickly, the whine of the drive motor and pump faded away. I wanted to watch, to see what the thing looked like in action, but couldn't expose my head and risk alerting the militia that something wasn't quite right.

A couple of minutes later there were several shouts of alarm from down the corridor. They were cut off by a scream of pain and fear that didn't stop.

"Let's go," I said, standing and leading the way around the bend.

Dog at my side, I charged down the hall. Ahead, I could see the large machine, Bunny unmoving behind it. Nitro was to the side and slightly ahead of the platform. Drawing closer, I got my first look at the results of his attack.

A large blob of foam nearly filled the corridor from floor to ceiling. In several places, I could see feet and hands sticking out of the surface. As I skidded to a stop beside Nitro, one of those hands opened and closed a couple of times before going still.

The screaming continued, coming from a man who was completely encased in the substance up to his neck. His eyes were wild with fear as he bellowed in pain. Nitro simply stood staring, the sprayer hanging limply from his big hand. Raising my rifle, I shot the man between the eyes, silencing his screams and ending his pain. After that, we all stood there, staring at what the device had done.

"Two seconds," Nitro said in a quiet voice.

"What?" I asked.

"Two seconds," he repeated. "That's all it took. The shit hit them and just swallowed them up as it expanded. Never seen nothin' like it. Fuck of a way to go."

There was still an opening through the debris field caused by the bomb and before I could say anything I began hearing sounds of movement. The guards outside were coming to see what had happened.

"Seal that up," I said, pointing.

Nitro nodded and stepped closer, aiming the end of the sprayer into the void. Depressing the trigger, he held it down for a couple of seconds, sending a thick, grayish stream of foam into the opening. Wherever it came into contact with any surface, it immediately stuck and expanded incredibly fast, completely filling all of the empty space, the debris becoming embedded.

Exodus

By the time Nitro shut off the stream, the breach was completely sealed and impassible.

36

"How's he doing?" I asked Rachel.

We had returned to the hangar. Well, Dog and I were there already. The rest of the team was busy adding more foam to the corridor to ensure the breach remained sealed. Once that was complete, they were going to perform a sweep of the A level and make sure we had a clear path to the medical suite.

"Still unconscious," Rachel said.

"I meant, is he going to be able to fly? We've got about four hundred assholes out there, and I don't see how we're going to fight our way clear."

"I can't tell you that," Rachel said.

"I can fly if you've got a helicopter."

We turned in surprise when the General spoke from behind us.

"You can fly a helo?" I blurted.

"My dad was an Army pilot. Taught me to fly before I could drive," she said, crossing her arms in defiance. "It's been a while since I've been in the cockpit, but I can get us out of here. Where would we go?"

Exodus

I looked back at her without saying anything, feeling the tension rolling off Rachel. There was something about the General she didn't like, and I was only assuming it was jealousy of another attractive woman. Maybe there was more to it than that. We needed to have a conversation, but first I needed to know what the hell was going on.

"I'm not sure I'm ready to board an aircraft that you're in charge of," I said bluntly.

Her eyes opened wide at the blatant statement of mistrust.

"You really think Pablo would trust me if I had an agenda?" She asked, surprising me that she knew Nitro's real name.

"He wouldn't be the first man to be seduced by a pretty face and big tits!"

It was my turn to open my eyes, well, eye, wide in surprise when Rachel spoke. Dog was sitting between Rachel and me and, picking up on her mood, flattened his ears and showed his teeth. Anger flashed across the General's face, and I quickly raised my hand to stop both of them before things got out of hand.

"Enough!" I barked, also placing a hand on Dog's head. "General, you and I need to have a chat. We've got nothing else to do until the team returns, so we might as well get some things out in the open."

Her eyes were locked on Rachel's, and I was afraid I was going to wind up having to pry them apart if I didn't get some space between them. Irina, standing to the side, caught my eye and tilted her head. I nodded, and she stepped forward, wrapping her arm around Rachel's shoulders. After several long seconds, and another withering glance, she allowed herself to be lead away.

"That woman is crazy!" The General said when they were out of earshot.

"I'd advise you to watch your mouth," I said. "You don't know her story."

"And she doesn't know mine!"

"Fair enough," I said after a moment. "So, why don't you tell me? And what's with the pearl handled .45s?"

I pointed at the twin pistols she wore on her belt.

"They were my dad's," she said, a brief flicker of sadness passing across her face.

She seemed about to continue talking, but hesitated and shook her head.

"I want to talk to Pablo, first. I'm feeling a little like I've gone from the frying pan into the fire."

"Suit yourself," I said. "Just remember what I said about watching what you say. My people have been through hell and aren't going to take too kindly to any disrespect."

"Oh, give it a break," she said. "You don't see what's going on with her?"

"What the hell are you talking about?"

"My God. You're just as thick as Sean! That woman is in love with you. Can't you see that? What I don't get is why I'm a threat and that little blonde that took her aside isn't."

The name rang a bell, and it took a few seconds for the low wattage light bulb in my head to come on.

"Sean? Who was that?" I asked.

She stared at me, trying to figure out why I was asking.

"My husband," she eventually said, her pain clear.

"Where is he now?"

She shook her head and looked away before answering, "He's gone. Died in the D.C. area on the night of the attacks."

"I'm sorry," I said after a pause. "I think I talked to him. Once."

She blinked, all traces of anger gone from her eyes. Reaching out to touch my arm, she stopped herself and let her hand drop to her side.

"You talked to him? When?"

"The night before the attacks," I said, not seeing any reason to keep the information to myself. "Nitro called me at home, asking if I'd talk to Sean. He had questions about somebody I'd worked with in the past. I agreed, only because it was Nitro, and talked to your husband for about half an hour."

"Delker!" She exclaimed. "He called you about a man named Delker!"

"Yes," I said, a chill passing through me. "What do you know about him?"

"He was involved," she said in a low voice.

"Involved? With what?"

"The attacks. Somehow. It was a conspiracy within the government. Something like that. That's all I know."

I stood mute, remembering the abrasive CIA officer I'd worked with on an operation in Central Africa in what seemed another life. The fucker had been a thorn in my side, and we hadn't parted friends.

"Where is she?"

Exodus

The General startled me out of my thoughts, and I realized she was pointing at the wedding ring on my left hand.

"She's gone, too," I said, successfully compartmenting the pain that came with memories of Katie.

"I'm sorry," she said. "We've all lost too much."

I just nodded, absently rubbing Dog's head. Petting him helped me to focus my mind on something other than Katie, and he pressed against my leg. Maybe he understood that he was providing comfort, or perhaps he just enjoyed the attention. Either way, it didn't really matter.

"Maybe we should start over," the General said, extending her hand. "I'm Anna Thompson."

"John Chase," I said, taking her hand in mine.

Something I didn't understand passed between us at that moment. Maybe it was the mutual pain of having lost someone we loved, or maybe it was nothing.

37

Half an hour later, the team returned to report that A level was clear. They'd encountered three different militia search teams, taking each one out. Johnson had found a way to shut down the elevators and wanted to foam all the doors that allowed access into stairwells. While I didn't disagree with his sentiment, I didn't want to cut off easy access to the lower levels. Instead, I made assignments that would split the team up and put a guard on each door.

"Johnson, we need radios," I said. "Get your ass to the armory and see what you can scrounge."

"Already ahead of you, sir," he said, spilling a cache of digital transceivers with earpieces onto a bench.

"Good. Get one issued to everyone and make sure we're all on the same channel."

He set to work on the radios as Igor unfolded a portable litter on the floor next to Vance. When it was ready, he slipped it in place as Rachel and Irina gently rolled the unconscious man to the side.

"He be OK?" He asked as Rachel tucked the patient's hands beneath his hips for the trip to medical.

Rachel shrugged her shoulders and stepped aside as Goose and Igor moved to either end and lifted the injured man. She wasn't speaking to me, at the moment, and apparently wasn't talking to anyone else, either. I sighed and kept my thoughts to myself.

The General, Anna, followed them out of the room as Rachel and Irina gathered up the girls and got them moving. Bunny, Monk and Gonzales headed out to their assigned posts, Nicole electing to go with the Master Chief. Nitro hung back, waiting for me. Johnson would take the foam machine with him and go to the security office to see how many exterior cameras were still functional. The militia might have lost the first battle, but the war was far from over, and I needed to know what they were up to.

"Keep them in the cafeteria," I said to Rachel before she could walk away. "I don't know when we're going to move, but it may have to be in a hurry. We don't need to be searching for missing people."

"Where are you going?" She asked in a cold voice.

"Comms," I said, frowning at her. "Going to see if I can get through to Hawaii."

She nodded and turned without saying anything else. Dog, lying a few feet away, raised his head and looked back and forth between us.

"Hold on," I said, reaching out and gently touching her arm.

"What?" She asked, turning towards me but looking at the floor.

She was obviously upset. I didn't need the experience of years of marriage to recognize when a woman is unhappy about something. Over her shoulder, I saw Irina give us a glance before ushering the girls through the door. Nitro quickly followed. I waited until they were gone, leaving me and Rachel alone in the hangar.

"Why are you upset at me?"

I know, I know. Keep my mouth shut and let her stew until she was ready. That's fine when the most pressing thing you have to worry about is what's for dinner. It's not fine when you're surrounded by hundreds of people who want to do you harm.

"It's not important," she said, looking at me after several seconds of silence.

"It obviously is," I said, trying a disarming grin that failed miserably.

"Look," Rachel said with a dramatic sigh. "You do whatever the hell it is you want. I've got no claim on you. Just don't do it in front of me!"

She turned and headed for the door, leaving me standing there with my mouth hanging open. After a stunned moment, I rushed to catch her.

"Wait," I said, moving into her path.

Exodus

Coming to a stop, Rachel crossed her arms and glared at me.

"Whatever you're thinking, it's not true," I said softly.

"And what am I thinking?"

Oh, for fuck's sake! I hesitated, taking a deep breath to calm myself and collect my thoughts before I opened my mouth again.

"I think you're thinking I'm going gaga over the General, and that's just not true."

"Sure looked like it," she said petulantly. "And if that's what you want, go ahead. Just don't expect me to be around to watch it!"

"Goddamn it!" Frustration got the better of me. "I don't know what you think you saw, but you're way off base. We were talking about her husband, who died in the attacks on D.C. Then she saw my ring and asked. I told her Katie was dead. That was it. Some mutual pain, but nothing else! Jesus Christ!"

It was almost certainly the raw wound from the loss of Katie that was being torn open again, but I was getting mad. Breathing hard. Heart pounding. Katie and I had gone through a few of these kinds of *discussions* early in our marriage, but it had been a long time since I'd had to deal with another person's irrational jealousies. And this sure as hell wasn't the time or place. I looked down when Dog bumped his nose into my leg then pushed his shoulder against me hard enough to move me a step to the side. He doesn't like discord, either.

Rachel was looking at the floor again, refusing to meet my eyes. Not responding. Pain and anger coursed through me, and I'd had enough.

"Dog, stay with her!" I commanded, spun and strode for the door.

"You're just going to walk away?" Rachel called before I'd gone ten feet.

I stopped and whirled, ready to unleash verbal hell on her. She probably didn't deserve it, and maybe she had good reason to be upset, but this wasn't something I could even remotely deal with at the moment. As soon as I turned, Rachel rushed across the distance separating us, slammed into me and threw her arms around my neck. I wrapped my arms around her waist as she buried her face against my shoulder.

"I'm sorry," she said, voice muffled.

"Me too," I said after a long pause.

We stood there for several minutes, just holding each other. I wanted to stroke her hair. Trail my hand across her face and tell her I loved her. Press my lips to hers as I pulled her body against mine. But, I couldn't. Not yet. Just the thoughts of doing those things made me feel like I was betraying Katie. Unfortunately, I couldn't find the words to tell Rachel what was holding me back from giving her what she wanted. To explain that the only woman who was coming between us was my dead wife.

Dog, sensing the change in mood, walked up and shoved his muzzle between us. He wasn't satisfied with just a nose and kept pushing until his entire body separated us. With a giggle, Rachel released her hold on me, kissed me lightly on the lips and stepped away.

"We have to be together," she smiled sadly, rubbing Dog's back. "For the sake of the child!"

Despite myself, I snorted a laugh. Extending my hand, I took Rachel's and led her out of the hangar. Dog, seemingly relieved, was happy to walk between us.

"You two kiss and make up?" Nitro asked when we entered the corridor.

He'd been waiting outside the hangar, pushing off the wall when we appeared.

"Fuck off, Pablo," I said.

"No, no, boss," he growled, falling into step with us. "Only my mother and the General can call me Pablo. You know better!"

"But I like Pablo so much more than Nitro," Rachel said, giving him a brilliant smile. "Can I call you Pablo? Please?"

Well, she'd certainly gotten over being upset in record time. I wasn't still angry, but I couldn't say I was necessarily in the mood to be playing around, either.

Nitro looked at Rachel for several seconds before sighing and shaking his head.

"OK, fine," he finally said, then jabbed a thick finger in my direction. "But not him! First, he'll be calling me Pablo, then the next thing you know he'll be cracking Puerto Rican jokes. It'll never end once it starts."

"What's the difference between a smart Puerto Rican and a Unicorn?" I asked, just to get under Nitro's skin. "Nothing. They're both imaginary creatures!"

"That's mean," Rachel said, trying not to laugh. "You should be nicer to your friend!"

She released my hand and slapped me on the arm.

"How do you make an Irishman dizzy?" Nitro asked, refusing to take the bait. "Put him in a round room and tell him there's a drink in the corner."

I'd heard that one a few times in my life and was racking my brain for a comeback when Dog suddenly growled. We immediately came to a stop, rifles snapping up. Nitro covered the corridor behind us while I scanned to the front. Rachel moved to the opposite wall, looking both directions with her rifle pointed at the floor, ready to be brought into action in an instant.

"Clear," Nitro mumbled after several long seconds, and I answered with the same assessment.

Taking my eye off the hall to my front, I glanced down at Dog. He was rigid, looking in the direction I'd been scanning, nose lifted slightly. Something he didn't like was in that direction.

"Thought you guys cleared this level," I said quietly to Nitro.

"Cleared the open space," he responded. "Lots of goddamn nooks and crannies. Would take a whole platoon a full day to check every single spot."

Nodding, I reached up and activated the radio and broadcast a message that we might have infected on the level. I received an acknowledgment from everyone.

"I've got point," I said quietly. "Rachel, you're in the middle. You know the drill."

Moving forward, Dog stayed close to my side. He was alert and tense as we slowly progressed. We passed several doors, and I paused at each one to give him an opportunity to test the air, but he kept his attention focused straight ahead. As we passed another room, there was a flash of motion ahead. A figure dashed out of an open door, crossing the corridor and disappearing into another.

"Contact," I said.

Dog suddenly whirled with a loud growl, and there was the sound of bodies colliding from behind us. Spinning, I saw both Rachel and Nitro on the floor, two females attacking him and another on top of her. Dog leapt into the fray, tearing the infected off Rachel as I began to rush forward, but screams from down the hall stopped me in my tracks.

Turning to face front, I cursed when I saw five females sprinting directly at us. Coming fast, they were damn close by the time I brought my rifle on target and began shooting. There were too many and the distance separating us was too short for well-placed head shots, so I chopped their legs out from under them with brief bursts of fire.

Risking a glance behind, I saw that Dog had finished off the female he'd attacked, but Nitro was still struggling with the pair on top of him. He's huge and immensely strong, and I was surprised he was having trouble, even with two of them. Rachel scrambled across the floor and grabbed the closest one's long hair, yanking her head back so Dog could lunge in and tear her free of Nitro.

Turning back, I quickly dispatched the crawling females, the final one going still only feet from where I was standing. Spinning to help Nitro, I paused as he lifted the last infected into the air and with a grunt of effort twisted her head far enough to snap the bitch's neck.

Exodus

Dog had torn out the throats of the other two and the floor was awash in blood. Stepping around a puddle, I reached down and pulled Nitro to his feet when he grasped my hand. Rachel seemed none the worse for wear, and Dog trotted over to check the females I'd shot.

"You OK?" I asked Nitro.

"Landed flat on my back and got the fuckin' wind knocked out of me," he said sheepishly. "Ain't as young as I used to be."

"Join the club, brother," I said, slapping him on the shoulder before turning to Rachel. "Good to go?"

"I'm not ancient like you two," she said, adjusting her rifle's sling which had gotten twisted in the struggle.

I shook my head and checked on Dog. He was standing a few yards down the hall, ignoring the dead infected sprawled around him. His stance was alert, but not tense and he wasn't growling, so I hoped we were done with being attacked for a while.

"OK, we need to get her to medical," I said. "Let's move. Fast and quiet."

38

Nitro and I delivered Rachel to medical without any further drama. The General, Igor and Goose were waiting, Vance already resting on a bed. The pilot was awake, bathed in sweat from the pain of his injury.

"You're either a very brave man, or a stupid one," I said to him.

"Little of both," he said, then nodded at Igor. "He told me what happened. Thanks for coming for me."

"You got lucky," I said, grinning. "I came for Rachel. You just happened to be in the same place."

"OK. Out!" Rachel said, shooing all of us away after hanging an IV bag on a tall pole mounted to the head of the bed. "I've got to check his wound and change the dressing, so unless you want to see what a split open…"

"We're going," I said quickly before she could finish the sentence.

Giving Vance a nod, I went out into the hall, Nitro, Goose and Igor following. I was surprised when the General didn't come with us. Poking my head back inside, I saw her holding Vance's hand and speaking with him as Rachel started an IV. Well, there was apparently more to her than I'd thought.

Exodus

The cafeteria was only a few doors away, and I stepped over and checked to make sure the girls were safely inside. Irina was acting as den mother, looking up and waving when I cracked the door open.

"Alright, Goose and Igor, you two stay here in the hall. We ran into eight females on our way. They had a decent little ambush set up for us, so keep your eyes open."

Goose glanced at Igor before nodding. I saw something in that look that I didn't like.

"Is there a problem?" I asked.

"Didn't realize he was a fuckin' Russian," Goose drawled in a deep Georgia accent.

"Well, he is. And he's proven himself. More than a few times. You got a problem with him because of where he was born, you'd best nut up and forget about it. We've got a job to do."

"I don't work for you," Goose said, giving me a challenging look.

To my side I could see Nitro swell up, ready to jump in. Igor, scowling, had swiveled slightly, so he was facing the man. Dog, sitting outside the door to medical, ignored us. I reached out and placed a restraining hand on Nitro's arm, taking a step closer to Goose and invading his personal space.

"If you're with this group, you work for me," I said in a quiet voice, meeting his glare. "You don't like it, we'll find a door and you can go out there with the militia. Make your choice now. I don't have time for petty bullshit!"

He stared back at me for several seconds, then his eyes slid to Nitro. Not finding any support, he finally looked away and nodded.

"I'm good," he mumbled, sounding distinctly like he was anything but.

I let several more seconds pass before moving back.

"You change your mind, let me know," I growled before turning and walking away.

Behind me, I could hear Nitro speaking in a low voice, but couldn't understand what he was saying to Goose.

"Dog!" I called.

A moment later his nails clicked on the floor as he ran to catch up. A few seconds after that, Nitro trotted to fall in beside me.

"He'll be fine," Nitro said. "Actually a good guy, even if he is wound a little tight."

"Hope so," I said. "For his sake."

Exodus

"Goddamn but you're even starting to sound like an officer," Nitro said with a chuckle.

"Now why'd you have to go and start insulting me," I asked, earning a snort.

"Where we going?" He asked.

"Stopping off at security to see what your buddies outside are up to, then on to the comm room."

"Not my fuckin' buddies," Nitro said, sounding offended. "I wanted to start killing them in their sleep, but the General wouldn't let me."

"So, what's the story, Nitro? You call me the night before all this shit starts, asking about that fuck stick Delker, then months later I find you bunking with a bunch of limp dicks."

"Long story, boss. I'll tell you the whole thing when we got time. But, those assholes outside weren't my idea. The General's dad was some big shot DOD contractor. Somehow, he knew what was coming and decided it was time to put together a bunker. He didn't want the government to find out about it, so he hired these fucks and financed the build."

"Had a chance to talk to one of them that tried to ambush us a few nights ago," I said. "He said they'd been prepping for a long time."

"Well, they were just some fringe militia group. You know the type. Bunch of looney tunes that think the government is gonna herd them into a FEMA camp and start going all Nazi. Feed 'em to the ovens and perform experiments on them. Shit like that.

"Anyways, they wasn't on anybody's radar, so he funneled money to them with instructions on what he wanted built. They got it done, but he had to agree to build additional shelters for them, too. The guys and I showed up with the General a few hours before the attacks started. We were hired to protect her.

"She was supposed to be in charge, was for the first couple weeks, but the militia leader had different ideas, and we were a bit outnumbered. Guy in charge thinks he's some sort of apostle or somethin'. Made it real clear he wasn't takin' orders from a woman, and his people have been doing their own thing ever since."

"Why didn't you leave?" I asked.

"Thought about it, but go where? Far as we could tell, nothin's left."

I nodded as we kept walking.

"What about those girls they took, Nitro?"

I turned my head to look at him as we moved. He lowered his head before answering.

"We didn't know," he said. "Only found out about it after your big Russian friend back there came and got them. He took out a bunch of militia guards doing it, and they went apeshit. That's when we knew.

Exodus

That's when the General decided she'd had enough. We came here today to push the issue."

"Push the issue? You were a bit outnumbered and outgunned."

"Fuck that," Nitro grumbled. "We found out about those girls, somethin' had to give. I ain't sittin' back while shit like that's goin' on, and neither was the General."

"You're pretty attached to her, aren't you?" I asked gently.

"She's a good person," Nitro said. "Got caught by surprise, just like the rest of us. Lost her husband during the attacks. Sean, the guy you talked to when I called. He was a good guy, too."

We walked in silence for a bit as I thought about what he was saying. I believed him, but only because I knew him.

"So, was their leader one of the guys we put down in the hangar?"

"No. Those were just some assholes that were itching to set off that fuckin MOAB they found at Nellis. William, their leader, is off somewhere. Don't know where, or what he's up to, but you can bet it ain't good, whatever it is. If he'd been here, he'd of had a couple hundred men inside with him, and we'd be in a world of shit. He may be a whack job, but he ain't stupid."

I didn't have anything to say to that. Was just glad the asshole hadn't been here. But, the news lent a new sense of urgency to getting the hell out of here. As I was still thinking about what Nitro had told me, we arrived at the security office. I was surprised, and unhappy, to find Tiffany in the corridor, crawling all over the foam machine as she examined it. She was alone and unarmed.

"What the hell do you think you're doing?" I asked, a little too brusquely.

She stopped her inspection and looked at me, eyes reflecting the fact that I'd hurt her feelings.

"Sorry," I said. "Didn't mean for it to sound like that. Didn't anyone tell you there are infected on this level? We ran into eight of them on the way to medical."

The hurt was replaced with fear as she glanced around at the empty corridor that stretched away from us into the distance.

"No one told me," she said.

I bit back several things I wanted to say. I'd transmitted a warning. Everyone who had a radio had acknowledged they'd received it. For some unknown reason, they hadn't bothered to pass on the information, and now Tiffany was out here without any protection.

Exodus

"Come on inside with Johnson," I said, pulling her to her feet.

Without argument, she followed us into the security room and headed for a chair in the far corner. Dog went with her, sitting close and putting his head in her lap for attention. Johnson was bent over the control console, working on something, and didn't bother to look up.

"When I tell you there're infected running around, I expect you to not let someone that's unarmed go hang around out in the open," I said.

He looked up in surprise, then turned towards Tiffany when I nodded in her direction.

"Don't yell at him. He didn't know I was out there," she said.

I took a deep breath and shook my head.

"Sorry," I said to Johnson.

"No worries, sir," he said. "If I'd known, I'd have made her come in here with me."

"So, what's the militia up to?" I asked, ready to change the subject before I offended anyone else.

"Still have us surrounded," he said, pointing at several monitors that showed pickup loads of armed men slowly driving patrols around the base. "I can't tell what's happening in the area where they breached.

That damn bomb blew out a shitload of cameras. We've got a huge blind spot. But, that's not all."

He hit a few keys and the view on one of the monitors changed to show a fenced area that held multiple satellite uplinks. It was a long view from an odd angle, but I could still tell that the equipment had taken heavy damage from the shockwave of the blast. The fence was down in several places, and all the dish antennas knocked to the side. Several of the larger ones had been completely ripped off their mounts and lay on the sand.

"Son of a bitch," I breathed. "Is that all of them?"

"As far as I can tell, yes, sir. And, the gear that's in here is down. There's an uplink for real time sat surveillance of the base, and it's not connecting."

"That something that can be fixed?" Nitro asked.

I looked around when Tiffany bumped into my arm. She'd come forward to see what we were talking about.

"Maybe," she interjected. "But those dishes that have pieces missing or are bent are just scrap. Nothing can be done other than replace them with new ones."

"And, to add to the fun," Johnson said. "That's about two hundred yards from the closest working exit, and there's a bunch of pissed off guys out there who might have something to say about us trying to get to them."

"So, what do we do?" Tiffany asked.

I stood there staring at the damaged equipment, not saying anything. My head still pounded, and frustration threatened to get the best of me. I was tired of this. All I wanted to do was go find Barinov and introduce him to some American steel.

"What else did you find while you were poking around," I asked Johnson. "Anything we can use to clear out all those assholes?"

He swiveled around in his chair to look at me.

"I found so much shit that I don't even know what it might do, it's not even funny. Nicole was stumped by most of it too, and she's pretty smart."

"Place like this, they've gotta be working on some kind of weapons systems," Nitro said.

Johnson looked at him and shrugged his shoulders.

"This is actually an Air Force Base, right?" Tiffany asked.

"Yeah. Why?" I asked.

"Because you guys are thinking like Soldiers," she said, as if that explained her point.

"Well, that's what we are," I said. "What are you getting at?"

"Think about it! You guys want some kind of super gun, or tank or something like that. But, this is the Air Force. What kind of weapons do they use?"

"They use rifles and grenades, too," Johnson said.

"OK, but what do they *mostly* use?" Tiffany asked patiently. "They use weapons from the air. Bombs. Missiles. Stuff like that. Maybe you were looking in the wrong places, or maybe you were finding stuff that didn't make sense because it's supposed to be aboard an *aircraft*, not on a battlefield at ground level."

I looked at the girl in surprise, once again reminded just how smart and logical thinking she was.

"That's good," I said. "But if we don't know what it is, we won't know what kind of aircraft to put it in or what it does."

She was shaking her head before I finished speaking.

"No, you're not thinking. Things that are sitting in a room probably aren't ready to even be tested. Have you checked the planes? Other than the one with the adaptive camouflage? If there's a working prototype, it'll most likely already be installed for field tests."

We all looked at Johnson. He shook his head.

Exodus

"No, I didn't," he admitted. "Just the one plane because it was so odd, but there's a lot of others in a bunch of different hangars that I didn't even give a second look."

"Then that's where we should start," Tiffany said, beaming that she had thought of something the rest of us had missed.

"Forgetting one thing," Nitro said. "Even if we find an armed plane, how the hell do we get it out of the hangar and onto a runway? The militia's gonna open up on us the instant they see us."

"Helicopters don't need runways," Tiffany said smugly.

That earned her a scowl from Nitro. She stuck her tongue out at him and held it there until he smiled at her.

"Johnson, are there cameras in the hangars?" I asked.

"I think so," he said, spinning around and attacking the keyboard.

We lost sight of the exterior, and soon several monitors displayed images from a variety of hangars that I hadn't been in. I saw a couple of C-130s, several different fighter jets and an A-10 warthog that had some extra bulges that weren't normal. The screens continued to cycle through, and we finally had a view of a large space occupied by several helos.

I recognized the Apaches, Black Hawks and Super Cobras, but there were a couple of machines that I'd never seen before. They looked like something Hollywood would have thrown together for a big budget sci-fi movie. Kind of a cross between an Osprey and a fighter jet.

"What the hell are those?" I asked, leaning in for a better look.

"Nothin' I ever seen," Nitro said.

"Johnson, keep an eye on things. Nitro, get your ass down there and take a closer look. See if you can tell if those things will actually fly, and whether or not they're armed. Take Tiffany with you. She's smarter than all of us put together. I'm going to go back to medical and see if our pilot can do his job with a sore ball sack."

39

"Are you bringing me good news, Chief?"

Admiral Packard looked up from a stack of reports when Jessica walked into his office. He paused when he saw her appearance.

"Chief, this is the second time you've arrived in my office looking disheveled. Is there something going on I should know about?"

Jessica paused, unsure how to answer the Admiral's question. Captain Black, standing in the open door, spoke up.

"My fault, sir," he said.

"Excuse me?" Packard barked. "Exactly what do you mean, Captain?"

His eyes had hardened to flint and bored into the young Marine.

"Security inspection before she's allowed into your office, sir," Black said, unfazed. "Unfortunately, the Chief has a lot of hair, and I may have been a tad overzealous when I checked it."

The Admiral visibly relaxed but still glared at the head of his security.

"Going forward, Captain, consider Chief Simmons as already cleared. No need to rumple her up before she comes in."

"Yes, sir!" Captain Black said, stepping out and silently closing the door.

"You realize he'll ignore my order," Packard said, smiling. "Now, what do you have for me, Chief?"

"Sir, I've achieved full control of the Russian system that transmits the harmonic. There are actually three satellites in geosynchronous orbit over North America that are equipped to do so. Targeting is as simple as entering the desired coordinates and enabling the broadcast."

"Outstanding work, Chief!" The Admiral said. "Have you considered my question of where to direct the infected?"

"Yes, sir. I have. I believe our best course of action is to draw them as far north as possible. Winter is setting in across the continent, and we've seen that the infected cannot survive harsh conditions. At least conditions as harsh as a Canadian winter."

Packard rocked back in his chair, silent as he considered her proposal.

"Are the Russians aware that you have penetrated their system?" He asked, surprising her with the question.

"Not so far, sir," she said, shaking her head. "Or if they have detected the intrusion, they have made no efforts to stop me."

"Why do you think that is?"

"My opinion is they are unaware, sir," Jessica answered, wondering where he was going with this line of questioning.

"If they did become aware, would they be able to successfully lock you out again?"

"No, sir. I've already installed a hidden back door. For them to lock me out would require a complete wipe and reinstallation of the core code running the system. That's possible, but I'd see what they were attempting to do and be able to stop them."

Packard stared at her for a long beat before smiling broadly.

"You truly are talented, Chief."

"Thank you, sir. How would you like me to proceed?"

"For the moment, do nothing. Select the target locations to the north you want to use, but do not retask the satellites at this time. Dismissed."

"Thank you, sir," Jessica said, making a smart about face and marching out of the Admiral's office.

She nearly collided with Captain West, apologizing and stepping aside for the officer to come through the door.

"Captain?" Packard asked when his aide closed the door and approached his desk.

"Sir, the Governor is at reception, demanding to speak with you."

"Did he say what he wanted?"

"No, but I'm willing to bet he's upset over you having filed for candidacy in the upcoming election."

"Probably," Packard chuckled. "Wish I could have seen his face when he got the news. What's the progress on our plans for Barinov and Shevchenko?"

"We're into planning a raid into Sydney to target Barinov. We're also putting together options for a lightning strike into Siberia to retrieve Admiral Shevchenko, but we still haven't come up with a viable plan to pull Captain Vostov out of Nevada."

"Captain Vostov? I was unaware we needed her, Captain," Packard growled, irritated at the surprise.

"My apologies, sir. I've been working directly with NIS and the SEAL teams and have failed to update you. The consensus among our Russia experts is that Captain Vostov's presence will be necessary to fully persuade her uncle to agree to our proposal, as well as help him convince the other Russian commanders."

Exodus

"How important is she?" The Admiral asked.

"Potentially, vital, sir. She is known to most of the senior military officers in Russia and legitimizes our intentions, which should allay their concerns to a large degree. This proposal will only work if there is trust, or at least the desire to trust. She has lived and fought with us for months. She will be a strong advocate for ceasing all hostilities and moving forward together."

Packard nodded at Captain West's explanation.

"And, that's why I'm glad I'm in the election, Captain," he said. "It was actually a stroke of genius. Because of my candidacy, the Governor will be distracted, trying to figure out how to defeat me, and not creating other problems for us."

"Yes, sir," West said, a sly grin spreading across his face.

"Now, please have him brought up."

It was most of ten minutes later before Captain Black knocked, opened the Admiral's door and announced the Governor. The man stormed in, Captain West slipping in behind and taking up position against the wall. The Governor looked nearly as disheveled as Jessica had. Packard had to suppress a grin, suspecting his Devil Dog gatekeeper had been especially thorough in checking the politician before allowing access.

"What can I do for you, Governor?" The Admiral asked in a congenial tone.

"Exactly what do you think you're doing, Admiral?"

He slapped a sheaf of papers onto Packard's desk and stood glaring. They were copies of the declaration of candidacy that the Admiral had signed.

"I believe those documents are fairly self-explanatory. Is there something you don't understand?"

The Governor's face turned an interesting shade of red, and he had to gulp several deep breaths before speaking.

"This is unprecedented, and it is illegal!" The man nearly shouted. "You know as well as I that active duty military personnel are prohibited from running for public office!"

"That's not correct, Governor," West said with a condescending smile. "There is no such prohibition. The restriction is against campaigning. The Admiral can run for any office he so chooses, as long as he doesn't participate in the campaign."

"And I have no intention of doing so," Packard said.

"You're not going to campaign? Then why the hell are you doing this? You can't win without campaigning! The voters have to know you're running and what your position is on the issues. There will be debates! You're just muddying the waters and making a mockery of the election, and I won't stand for it!"

"Governor," the Admiral said, getting to his feet. "I frankly couldn't be less interested in what you will or won't stand for. My paperwork has been legally registered with the Secretary of State, and my filing fee has been paid. Other than campaigning against me, there is nothing you can do."

"We'll see about that!" The man spat, nearly apoplectic in his anger. "This is *my* world, and you have no idea the can of worms you've opened by pulling this stunt! Trust me. It will be remembered when I'm sworn into office!"

Turning, he stomped out of the room. He attempted to slam the door, but Captain Black's thick arm snaked out and grabbed it, guiding it gently closed.

"He's worried," Captain West said.

"He shouldn't be," Packard said. "You don't really think I have a chance in hell of winning, do you?"

"Sir, there's no one in the islands that doesn't know who you are. Not after the past several months. Besides, there're about thirty thousand Soldiers, Sailors, Airmen and Marines that will be talking you up every time they're in town. The troops love you, sir. That's your campaign, right there."

The Admiral shook his head and resumed his seat.

"Never wanted to be a politician," he said. "You know, it's been forty-one years since I put on the uniform. I was ready for retirement. Move to Montana. Fish and hunt. Sleep late, eat and drink too much and act like a civilian in general."

"If you'll forgive me, you'd be bored to tears inside a month. And as far as forty-one years of service, well... that just means your well-seasoned, sir," West said with a perfectly straight face.

"Don't you have somewhere to be, Captain?" Packard asked, shaking his head in resignation.

"Yes, sir. I need to go check on what I hear is the misappropriation of Navy resources. Seems our printing office is churning out a bunch of political signs for the upcoming election. But, I doubt I'll be able to identify the perpetrators. I'd also better check on the rumors that our people are putting up those signs all around the island. Don't worry, sir. I'll stay on top of this illegal activity throughout the election!"

40

"Goddamn it! Take it easy, will you?"

Vance yelled as the wheelchair gently bumped into a piece of equipment sitting near an Apache helicopter. I didn't blame him one bit. In fact, I truly felt sorry for the poor bastard.

"Going to be Christmas, soon," I said, pushing him across the smooth floor to where Nitro and Tiffany stood.

"What the hell's that got to do with anything?"

"Just wondering if you'd like to go see the Nutcracker."

He was quiet for a beat before tilting his head back to look at me.

"You're not a nice man. Anyone ever tell you that?"

"I prefer the term 'asshole,' " I said, chuckling.

Vance laughed, then groaned as the movement tweaked his injury. Dog raced ahead to greet Tiffany who went to a knee to wrap her arms around his thick neck.

"Sure you're OK to fly?" I asked, all levity gone.

"I'm good to go," he gasped.

I softly clapped him on the shoulder and didn't say anything else.

Earlier, when I'd walked into medical, Rachel had been inserting a catheter into his penis so he didn't have to walk to the latrine. The General was standing on the far side of the bed, her back turned to give him some privacy, or so she didn't have to see his wound. I'd gotten a quick look, turning away and involuntarily shuddering. His scrotum was bright red and had swollen so much it looked like two softballs were hanging between his legs.

"It's worse than it looks," he quipped when he saw me turn my head.

"Nothing's worse than that looks," I said, facing the wall.

"You're not helping," Rachel said as she taped the catheter tube to Vance's leg.

"Can you fly?" I asked him, ignoring her rebuke.

"Depends," he said. "No way I'm squeezing into a G-suit and getting into an F-18, but give me a bag of ice and I could probably handle a C-130. Why?"

"OK, he's good," Rachel said.

I turned around, glad to see Vance's privates were covered by a sheet. There was no way I wanted another look at what had been done to him. In fact, just thinking about it made my boys ache.

"I'm more than good, sweetie," he said, winking at Rachel. "Ever seen a pair of balls this big before?"

Despite my history with the man, I couldn't get mad at him. In fact, I snorted a chuckle, earning a faux dirty look from Rachel. She patted Vance on the shoulder and moved aside, shaking her head and trying not to smile.

"So. Flying?" I prompted. "What about a helicopter?"

"Maybe," he said. "Again, why? What's the rush?"

"The fuckers that did that to you are still outside," I said, waggling my finger in the general direction of his crotch. "They're still trying to get inside, and I'd rather not be here when they do."

"Why didn't you say so?"

He started to sit up, his face immediately registering pain. Gently, he laid his head back, breathing deeply through his nose.

"What about it, Doc?" He asked several seconds later. "Got something you can shoot my sack up with that'll numb the pain? Something that won't fuck with my head so I can fly?"

"I can give you a local, but I'm worried about you tearing open those stitches and causing more damage," Rachel said.

"More damage than what will be done if we don't get out of here?" He asked, one eyebrow arched.

Rachel had her arms crossed over her chest, staring at him. She turned to look at me, but I didn't say anything. She knew the situation and didn't need any prompting on my part.

"When do we need to do this?" She finally asked.

"Now would be a good time," I said.

After another pause, she nodded and moved to a cabinet that held multiple vials of various drugs.

"So, where are we going?" Vance asked as Rachel began preparing some syringes.

"Hawaii," I said.

"How? Russians got the whole coast locked up. At least they did the last time we talked to Pearl, and that was just yesterday."

"Go south and loop around Baja?" I asked.

"Again, how? I haven't seen anything that will hold enough fuel to go that far out of our way, and there sure as hell aren't any gas stations between here and there."

"Why Hawaii?" The General asked.

Exodus

"Last outpost of America," I said. "Things are still relatively normal, there. Or, at least that's what I'm told. And, it's a stop off for me to get to Australia."

"Is Australia OK, too?" She asked.

I nodded.

"What's there? Why not stay in Hawaii?" Vance asked.

"Personal business," I said, not wanting to go into details.

They both looked at me for a moment, and I could tell they wanted to ask questions. Rachel forestalled that by stepping to the side of the bed with two syringes in her hand. She glanced at each of us as she reached for the sheet covering Vance's body. I quickly turned my back.

"OK," I said, facing the wall. "What about at Nellis? It's what... maybe a hundred air miles from here?"

"Maybe," Vance said, grunting in pain as Rachel began injecting him. "Depends on what's sitting there. We could also try the Vegas airport. Probably a few big commercial jets still on the tarmac. One of those should make the trip, as long as we can top it off before we leave."

"We'll start with Nellis," I said. "General, you said you can fly a helo?"

"It's been a lot of years, but yes, I can."

Vance grunted again, then there was the rustle of fabric as Rachel pulled the sheet back up. I risked a glance over my shoulder, turning around when I saw she'd finished administering the local anesthetic. The pilot looked at me, his face waxen and covered in a sheen of sweat.

"You sure you can fly?" I asked him, worried.

"I can do it," he said, nodding. "But, if I'm flying, why are you asking her if she can?"

"Because we've got a few hundred armed men outside," I said. "I know they've been into the armory at Nellis, and I'm a little worried they have more Stingers. Remember at the lake?"

"They do," the General said.

"How many?" Vance asked. "They popped one off at me when we picked up the girls in the lake."

"I saw six," she said. "So, what's your plan?"

She looked at me, Vance and Rachel doing the same.

"Found a couple of hangars full of helicopters," I said. "Apaches, Cobras and what I'm pretty sure are next-gen prototypes. I'm thinking Commander Vance here uses an attack helo to clear out the enemy at the gate. Once things are safe, well, a little safer, you fly the rest of us out in the Chinook we brought with us. Can you handle something that big?"

"Do I have a choice?" She asked. "There's nothing else that will hold all of us."

"What about it, Vance?" I asked. "Think you're up to kicking some ass?"

"You do remember that the Chinook is outside, right? That you're going to have to go out there with *them* to get to it?"

I didn't remember that. I'd been unconscious when he'd brought us to Groom Lake.

"Fuel status?" Anna asked.

"Should make it to Nellis, no problem," Vance answered. "But that'll be it. Flew from Luke in Arizona with a little detour and some time on station at Lake Meade. Burned a lot of gas with the low altitude maneuvering."

"Where is it?" I asked, drawing a blank look from him.

"Outside on a helipad," he said. "Other than that, I can't tell you."

"We landed near the entrance the Rangers breached when we first got here," Rachel said.

Reaching up to my ear, I activated the radio and called Johnson. It didn't take him long to respond that he had spotted the Chinook on a security camera and it didn't appear that the militia had messed with it.

"Well, then that's what we're going to have to do," I said, turning to the General. "Anna, did the militia get any night vision from Nellis?"

"Not that I know of," she said. "I was focused on the munitions they were taking. Trying to make sure the idiots didn't blow themselves, and me, up. But, they do have some low-grade civilian units. I'm not sure how effective they are."

I stood there for close to a minute, thinking about the tactical situation before making a decision.

"OK, we're going at dusk," I finally said, glancing at my watch and noting we had less than an hour to be ready. "Anything they've got will be limited compared to military grade, so it won't do them much good, if any, as the light is fading. Questions?"

There were several, but none of them had to do with the immediate task at hand. Putting them aside, I called Igor into the room, and together we assisted Vance into a wheelchair. Even with the injections, he was hurting like hell by the time we got him situated.

I gave instructions to Igor, Goose, Rachel and Anna. They would be responsible for having all the girls waiting near the exit, ready to go. Bunny, Monk and Gonzales would stay at their posts, guarding the stairwell entrances, until the last moment. Johnson

Exodus

would remain in security, keeping an eye on the activity outside the building while Nitro and Tiffany waited in the hangar for me and Dog to arrive with Vance.

41

"Holy shit!" Vance breathed when we circled around a Super Cobra and he got a look at the aircraft Nitro and Tiffany were standing next to. "That's a fucking FVL!"

I came to a stop, looking at the machine. The fuselage was roughly the size and shape of a Black Hawk but had been severely streamlined. Looking up, I could see that it held two main rotors, stacked on top of each other. The other main difference was that the tail rotor had been replaced by a rear-facing propeller.

"What's an FVL?" I asked.

"Next generation helicopter. Future Vertical Lift. I've heard rumors but didn't realize they had a working prototype. See that?" He asked, pointing at the main rotors. "Coaxial. Counter rotating! Know what that means?"

"No clue," I said.

"Less speed loading and almost no rotor wash! Ever landed in the desert and been blinded by all the sand being blown around? Well, of course you have. And look at that! A pusher prop in place of the tail rotor! This baby has gotta be fast and agile as hell! Probably damn quiet, too!"

Exodus

"OK," I said, slightly amused at his enthusiasm, which seemed to have made him forget about his injury. "That's fine, but which one will get the job done?"

Nitro and Tiffany had walked over as Vance was gushing about the helicopter.

"All are fueled," Tiffany said.

"What about ordnance?" Vance asked.

"The Cobra," Nitro said, turning and pointing. "Two Apaches, and whatever the hell that thing is."

"That's an FVL," I said in an important voice.

"Give it up, boss. You wouldn't know that if he hadn't already told you."

Vance stared longingly at the FVL before sighing and twisting around to survey the other options.

"Better go with what I've flown before," he said, nodding at the Super Cobra. "Wheel me over so I can see how it's armed."

I did as he asked and a few minutes later he declared he was satisfied.

"So, what's the plan, boss?" Nitro asked after we helped Vance out of the chair and into the cockpit.

"How's he going to fly?" Tiffany interrupted. "Can't fly a helicopter without your legs."

"Legs work fine, sweetie," Vance said, smiling down at her. "I just like making him help me."

I shook my head and pulled the wheelchair well away from the aircraft as I quickly filled Nitro in on our plans.

"Hey! Knuckle draggers!" Vance shouted. "You gonna hook up and give me a tow, or what?"

"Gonna make your face look and feel like your balls if you don't shut up!" Nitro yelled back.

I glanced up at the pilot's grinning face as Nitro jogged to an electric powered tug that was parked near the closest wall. Far across the hangar was a broad tunnel that led to a helipad with a retractable roof. Seemed a little too sci-fi movieish to me, but I suppose it was one of the ways Area 51 kept secret test aircraft under wraps.

"Sir, we've got a problem."

Johnson's voice in my earpiece.

"What's wrong?" I asked, pressing the bud deeper.

"Militia's gathering around our ride. Must be fifty of 'em huddled around the Chinook, and more comin'."

"Say that again," I ordered.

Exodus

I'd heard him, it just didn't register. Not at first. I listened carefully as he repeated himself.

"Stand by," I said after he'd finished giving me the bad news a second time.

What the fuck? Why would they do that? Unless…

"What's wrong?" Tiffany asked, but I ignored her.

"Nitro!" I bellowed.

He had already boarded the tug and pulled to a stop next to me.

"Militia's gathering around the Chinook," I said.

"What? Why the fuck they doing that?" He asked, surprise clear on his face.

"Only one reason I can think of. If they're close to the aircraft we need to escape, that means we can't put Vance in the air to shoot them and risk damaging our ride out of here."

"Yeah, OK, but how the hell would they…" his voice trailed off as realization dawned on his face. "We got a fuckin traitor!"

I nodded slowly, seething inside as I stared at him.

"Who?" Tiffany blurted, but both of us ignored her.

"I know what you're thinkin', boss," Nitro said, staring back at me. "No way. He wouldn't do that."

"What am I thinking, Nitro?"

"You're thinkin' Goose because he was a prick about your big Russian friend. I'm tellin' you, he's a stand-up guy."

"How long you known him, Nitro?" I asked.

"Couple years."

He shrugged.

"If not him, then who? He obviously isn't happy with Igor or me, or any of this. Who the fuck else would have a reason to alert the militia to our plans?"

"Not my guys!" Nitro said, stepping off the tug and coming to stand directly in front of me. "How well you know your people?"

"Careful," I growled.

"Fuck careful," Nitro said through his teeth. "You know me better'n this. Don't go fuckin' making accusations until you've checked your own goddamn house!"

"Stop!" Tiffany stepped between us and put a hand on each of our chests, pushing. Neither of us budged. "Jesus, you two are like a couple of wild dogs protecting your turf. Quit flexing and think about it for a minute!"

She pushed again, this time both of us allowing her to move us back a step.

"Say what you're thinking," I said to her without taking my eye off Nitro.

I was pissed, but not at him. He was just the recipient of my anger.

"How many people knew about the plan to use the Chinook?" She asked, glaring up at me with her arms crossed over her chest.

"Everyone," I grumbled, then realized that wasn't accurate. "Well, not everyone. Rachel and the General were there when I came up with it. And I told Igor and Goose and Irina so they could get the girls moved to the exit and ready to go."

"Who else?" Tiffany asked.

"Johnson."

"What about Gonzales and Nicole, or Bunny or Monk?"

I shook my head. All I'd told them was to be ready to haul ass to the exit when I called.

"And you just told us two minutes ago," she continued. "That means we couldn't have done it. Not with you standing here with us."

"Fine," I said. "Now we know who couldn't have betrayed us. How do we find out who did?"

"Wow, didn't you ever read, or watch TV? Like a mystery novel or a detective show? Motive, means and opportunity! That's what it always is. So, motive. Who would want to sell us out? Help the militia?"

I stared at her for a long moment, finally shrugging my shoulders. She turned and looked at Nitro who shook his head.

"Well, what about means, then? How did someone do it? We're locked down, right? So, they had to have used a radio. Who has a radio that can talk to the militia?"

I looked at Nitro and raised the brow over my good eye.

"You guys lived with them for months. Sharing radio freqs?"

After a long pause, he lowered his gaze and nodded.

"And maybe someone got a little friendlier than you realized? Sympathetic, even?"

Exodus

"No way, boss," Nitro said. "I'd have seen something. I've been through a world of shit with these guys, before and after the attacks. I'd know if one of them was betraying me."

"Hey! Grunts!" We all turned to look up at Vance when he shouted. "Has to be a radio, right? Well, the Navy monitors and logs every single radio transmission on and around its bases. This is Air Force, but I'll bet they do the same. Especially at this place."

I stared at him with my mouth open. He was right. If that part of the security system was still operating, we'd be able to hear the transmission that warned the enemy of our plans!

Nitro and I quickly got him out of the cockpit, returning him to the wheelchair when Tiffany brought it over. I pushed as we hurried out of the hangar, on our way to the security office.

42

"You want what?" Johnson asked when we all crowded around him.

"Logs of every radio transmission in the past hour," I said. "Know where to find that?"

"No," he said. "Didn't even know there was such a thing."

He pulled a keyboard closer and began banging away. Nitro and I pushed in, one of us on either side of his chair. I was sure it wasn't Johnson but wasn't about to not be watching closely as he searched for the evidence we wanted.

It took some time, and lots of clicking through menus, but he finally opened a folder that contained numerous audio files. Each had a long, numerical name followed by a time stamp. I was surprised at how many there were for only the past sixty minutes.

"Play them, one at a time," I said.

Johnson clicked on the first, and I heard my own voice coming from hidden speakers as I issued the warning that infected were on the A level. He kept going, playing one file after another. Most of the way through the list, I was starting to think this was going to be a bust when a young girl's voice sounded in the room. She was whispering, talking to a male that I didn't recognize, telling him our plan. I blinked in surprise when they ended the conversation by saying "I love you" to each other.

"What the hell?" Johnson asked, looking up at me.

"Our traitor," I said, turning to Tiffany. "Recognize the voice?"

She nodded, tears springing from her eyes.

"That's Angela. She's the little sister of one of the girls on the team. Hasn't been the same since we got her back. Now I know why."

"Where the fuck did she get a radio?" Johnson asked.

"Who the hell knows," I said. "Maybe she brought it with her when Igor rescued her. Maybe she picked it up off one of the bodies in the hangar. Doesn't matter at this point."

"What are you going to do?" Nitro asked me.

"Tiffany," I said. "I need your help. We're going to go up to where the girls are, and I want you to point out Angela for me."

"Why? You can't hurt her!" She took a step away from me.

"No," I said softly. "You're right. I can't. But we need to take that radio away from her before she hurts us any more than she already has. OK?"

"You promise you won't hurt her?" She sniffled.

"You have my word," I said. "Now, we need to go."

After a few moments, she nodded and wiped her nose on her sleeve.

"Johnson, stay put and let me know if anything changes outside. Nitro, get Vance back down to the hangar and ready to go."

"Ready to go?" Vance asked in surprise. "What the hell am I going to do? Fly around and impress them into letting you get to the Chinook?"

"Just be ready," I said, pulling Nitro to the side. "Sorry 'bout that. I should have trusted you."

"Damn right you should have," he grumbled. "I know you've got a lot of shit to deal with, but don't forget who your friends are."

Properly chastised, I nodded and called Dog as Tiffany and I headed out the door. I was setting a fast pace and she had to alternate between walking and skipping to keep up.

"What are you going to do to Angela?" She asked.

Exodus

"Already told you," I said, sighing. "I'm not going to *do* anything to her. Just going to make sure she can't keep feeding information to the enemy."

We were quiet for the rest of the walk to where the girls were huddled near the exit. Igor and Goose stood watch at opposite ends of the group, Rachel, Irina and Anna sitting on the floor with them.

"The blonde sitting next to Chelsea," Tiffany said as we approached.

Igor looked at me questioningly but didn't say anything as I breezed past. Stopping directly in front of the girl, I held my hand out.

"Give it to me," I said.

The rest of the girls stared, and the three women who had been sitting with them got to their feet. Angela met my eye, remaining perfectly still.

"What's going on?" Chelsea asked, standing and looking back and forth between us. I ignored her.

"Angela," I said. "Give me the radio. Now!"

"What radio?" Chelsea asked, looking down at the other girl. "Ang, what's he talking about?"

The girl still refused to say anything.

"I'm talking about a radio she used to tell the militia what are plans are to get out of here. Now, they've got the helicopter surrounded and we can't escape."

I didn't have to check to know that every pair of eyes was locked on Angela.

"Is that true?" Chelsea asked her friend.

"It's true," Tiffany said when the girl remained silent. "I heard a recording of her talking to them."

"Why?" Chelsea asked her. "Why would you do that?"

Angela lowered her eyes to the floor and spoke in a choked voice.

"I don't want to leave. I'm pregnant."

I can't say I was terribly surprised after having heard her conversation. A buzz started up amongst the other girls as they reacted to the news. I took a big breath and let it out slowly as I looked at Rachel. She shook her head, but I had no idea if she was trying to tell me something.

"Angela," I said, kneeling in front of her. "You don't have to do anything you don't want to do."

She looked up at me through tear-filled eyes, surprise written across her face.

"What?"

Exodus

"If you wanted to stay, all you had to do was say so. I'm not going to make you, or anyone, go with us if they don't want to. But, are you sure you really want to?"

"I love him!" She said, sniffing. "I'm going to have his baby. I have to stay!"

"OK," I said. "Just give me the radio. You don't have to leave."

She stared back at me for several seconds before digging a small handset out of her sweatshirt. I took it and turned the power off before standing and slipping it into a cargo pocket in my pants. Stepping away, I came face to face with Tiffany, who looked decidedly distressed. Rachel grabbed my arm and led me down the hall near where Igor was busily scratching Dog's belly. Tiffany followed.

"You cannot leave her behind!" Rachel whispered.

Tiffany, standing next to her, nodded emphatically. Before I could respond, Anna and Irina joined them, the four women facing me down.

"She's an adult. She can do what she wants," I said.

"No, she's not!" Tiffany hissed. "She just turned sixteen, for Christ's sake! She doesn't have any idea what she's doing!"

Dirk Patton

I looked over my shoulder at Angela. She was curled into Chelsea's arms, sobbing, as the older girl gently rubbed her arm.

"We take her with us," Rachel said, Anna and Irina nodding their support.

"You're going to force her?" I asked.

"If we must, then that is what we will do," Irina said firmly.

"What about bringing the boy along?" Anna asked, earning shocked looks from the others. She looked at their expressions before offering an explanation. "It would make it easier."

"Are you kidding me?" I asked, trying to keep my voice down so Angela couldn't overhear our conversation. "This whole thing is about them wanting the girls back. That, and revenge for the ones Igor killed while rescuing them. You really think they're going to just let us go, and take one of their kids with us?"

"Look. I don't care about the boyfriend," Tiffany said. "But, we're not leaving Angela behind!"

I wanted to throw my hands up in the air in frustration. Gave it serious consideration for a few seconds. In fact, I was seriously considering sending Vance out in the Super Cobra to wipe out the militia and not worry about the Chinook. Once the enemy was finished off, we could drive to Nellis and find another aircraft.

"We can't leave her!"

I sighed in exasperation and turned to see Chelsea standing on my blind side.

"Yeah, that's what I've been told," I said sarcastically. "Don't need to hear it from you, too."

"Stop being an ass," she said. "I got her talking after you walked away. The father is one of the guys that was guarding them."

"That's not a surprise," I said, earning a dirty look from all the women surrounding me.

"Well, when she said who it was, Chris, one of the other girls who was held captive, remembered him. This isn't what you're thinking. This guy's an adult. Your age, or older. He raped every one of them. Angela's the one that got pregnant."

"No way we leave her with him!" Rachel said, stepping close and thrusting her face at me.

"Agreed," I said, gut churning in anger. "OK. Tiffany and Chelsea, she's your responsibility. If she fights when the time comes, Rachel and Irina will help."

"Me too," Anna said.

I nodded.

"How we go?" Igor asked.

"Haven't figured that one out," I said. "Not unless we sacrifice the Chinook to take them out."

"They're all in a tight group around the helicopter?" Chelsea asked.

"Yeah."

"The infected downstairs," she said. "Remember? Nicole can control them. There's a bunch of them. Let's send them out to do the fighting for us!"

I looked at her for a moment, a big grin slowly spreading across my face.

Exodus

43

Dog and I stood in security, looking over Johnson's shoulder. Our best guess was that over two hundred militia soldiers were clustered around the Chinook. The remainder of their forces were still circling the perimeter in a variety of vehicles. They would be Vance's primary targets once he was airborne. The others were about to get a nasty surprise.

Igor and Goose had taken everyone else into the cafeteria, securing the doors once Bunny and Monk joined them. Gonzales had escorted Nicole back to the sub level, propping open stairwell doors along the way, creating an unimpeded path for the infected to reach the surface. Once he was safely behind locked doors in an adjacent room, Nicole freed the females.

I watched in amazement on a monitor as they flooded out of the containment cells and surrounded her. At first, my heart rate shot up as I thought they were going to attack, but my fears were unfounded. Forming a large circle around Nicole, they quickly calmed and stood watching her. While they were still, I made a rough count, coming up with nearly a hundred. I was glad I wasn't out there with the militia.

At first, I thought Nicole was just staring back at them, but soon I realized her mouth was moving. Not like she was talking, but almost as if she were singing to them. The surveillance camera didn't have audio so I couldn't hear whatever sounds she was making, but the females did. After several seconds, they turned as one and raced down the corridor to the open stairwell.

Johnson tracked them as best he could, but they flew up the steps faster than he could change views. In far less time than I could have, they reached A level and bunched up at the exit.

"Clear to launch," I said into my radio, releasing Vance to take off.

On another monitor, we watched as the roof of the indoor helipad began to retract. It was thick, heavy steel and trundled slowly open.

"Kill exterior lights," I said.

Johnson already had the controls up and ready, the entire outside of the facility plunging into darkness. A couple of seconds later the cameras automatically switched to night vision and our view was restored. Vance would be flying without any lights showing, taking full advantage of the Cobra's advanced systems to maneuver and engage the enemy at night.

That didn't help him with any Stinger missiles the militia had, but it's not that easy to lock onto a target you can't see. Especially if that target is low to the ground and dancing all over the place. Not that the weapon needs visible light to operate, but the human hand on the trigger has to be able to line up on target for the IR seeker head to achieve lock. Without that lock, the missile won't fire. I was counting on the militia to fall victim to a lack of training and experience.

"Let them out," I said when the shield covering the helipad was fully open.

Johnson pressed several keys. First, a thick blast shield retracted from the exit where the females waited, then the door lock released which allowed them to push through. On the other monitor, the Super Cobra appeared as it ascended out of the hangar.

The large group of females charged through the door, immediately zeroing in on the militia standing near the Chinook. We could see them clearly in shades of black and green on the monitor as they raced across the smooth tarmac. They were only three hundred yards from their prey when they exited the facility, and were in a full sprint.

Around the helicopter, the militia wasn't aware that death was racing towards them. They'd been smoking and drinking beer for the past hour, waiting for something to happen. And, when they heard the Super Cobra take off, they thought that was their only threat.

They all stood and faced the direction of the aircraft's noise. Rifles were raised and aimed. In the rear of a pickup, a man stood and shouldered a boxy device with a long tube extended from the rear.

"Vance, you've got a Stinger near the Chinook!" I shouted into the radio.

"Copy," he answered immediately, his voice tight with concentration.

By now the females had closed half the distance to the closest militia troops. We were still working without audio, but I was certain they were attacking without screaming. Everyone was still focused in the direction of the attack helo, apparently unaware of what was bearing down on them.

There was a brilliant flash of light from off camera that lit up the area around the Chinook. It was quickly followed by a second. Vance taking out roving pickups.

The explosions and light must have been too much for the females to contain the urge to scream. In almost comedic coordination, every head amongst the militia turned in the direction of the attackers. For an instant, they remained frozen in shock, mouths hanging open, then there was a mad scramble to bring weapons around.

But, they were too late. The speed of the females prevented them from getting more than a short volley of gunfire off before the leading edge slammed into them. From that point, carnage ensued. The infected tore into the surprised people with savage efficiency. Throats were ripped open by slashing nails. Bodies were ridden to the ground and rent open.

Exodus

Some of the females were killed by panic fire, but the militia was unable to mount a coordinated defense. Two trucks tore away, one of them spilling terrified men out of the bed as it accelerated. The infected were on the hapless people in a blink, seemingly exultant in tearing them to ribbons. As the massacre continued, it was regularly lit by flashes as more vehicles were targeted and destroyed by the Super Cobra.

"Fuck me!"

I turned to see Nitro looking over my shoulder at the monitor. He'd hurried up from the hangar after closing the roof behind Vance.

"I've never seen this many at once," he said, his face slightly pale.

"Boy, have I got some stories to tell you," I said, turning my attention back to the screen.

Within minutes, the females had killed every single militia member that had been near the Chinook. Their prey down, they fell on the bodies and began feasting. Behind me, I could hear Nitro reciting what had to be a prayer in Spanish. Didn't blame him. Even though I'd seen this more times than I could count, it was still a horrifying display.

"All targets destroyed!" Vance's voice over the radio. "Got a few running out into the desert. Want me to go after them?"

"Negative, stay on CAP," I said after thinking about it. "Are we clear other than the infected?"

"Looks like. Stand by, and I'll make another orbit."

Five minutes later, he came back on the radio to confirm we were clear. Now came the part that really worried me. Nicole going out to send the infected away. Sure, she'd been able to control them inside the facility, but now their blood was up.

They'd just killed two hundred people and were busily feeding. Would they listen to her, or would they attack? And, going out there to protect her wasn't an option. That would just enrage the females and make things worse. I tapped my radio to transmit.

"Gonzales, you upstairs yet?"

"Yes, sir. With Nicole, near the exit."

"It's time, Master Chief."

There was no immediate response, and I resisted the urge to repeat my order. I imagined that he and Nicole were arguing. He didn't want her to go outside, and I didn't blame him. But, we needed the infected gone so we could board the Chinook, and short of an extended fight to kill all of them, I didn't know of any other way to accomplish that.

"Copy, sir. She's going out now," he finally said after several minutes.

Exodus

Nicole appeared on the exterior camera, cautiously exiting the facility.

"Lights," I said to Johnson.

A few seconds later the cameras had to adjust back, once again giving us a sharp, high-definition color view. Nicole paused when they came on, then purposefully strode directly towards the bloody carnage near the helicopter. She covered the distance much slower than the infected had, coming to a stop a dozen yards from the closest corpse that was being consumed.

Her back was to the camera, but from the way her head moved it was obvious she was communicating with the females. At first, I didn't think they were going to respond, but slowly they began to look up, blood dripping from their faces. Nicole seemed to falter, then gathered herself.

One by one, the infected rose to their feet, abandoning their fresh kills. Slowly, they drew together around Nicole. How she didn't break and run at that moment, I'll never know. Instead, she stood her ground and faced their blood slicked faces and arms. She kept at it, finally lifting her left hand to point at a spot on the horizon and holding the pose.

At first, there was just a trickle, but soon the entire group was running away in the direction she had indicated. Nicole watched them race across the tarmac towards the desert, slowly lowering her arm as they left the pavement and charged across the sand. There was a flash of movement near the exit, then Gonzales appeared, running to where Nicole still stood.

44

A chilly night breeze was blowing steadily across the tarmac as we loaded everyone aboard the Chinook. Dog, Rachel and I stood to the side as Igor and Goose wheeled an unconscious Angela into the aircraft. She'd become frantic, and after the two men physically restrained her, Rachel had given her a sedative.

"The baby will be OK?" I asked.

"Should be," Rachel said, not sounding completely confident. "Either way, it's better off than having the mother fighting with everyone and trying to escape. She took a chunk out of Igor because he was trying to be gentle with her."

I nodded, looking over at where Nitro and Gonzales stood guard over five men who were on their knees. They had managed to shelter inside the Chinook when the females attacked and hadn't tried to fight when we found them.

"What are you going to do with them?" Rachel asked.

I paused at the roar of a helicopter passing directly overhead, but couldn't see it in the dark. Vance was making repeated, slow orbits around us, keeping watch with the Super Cobra's night targeting system.

"Still thinking about it," I mumbled when the sound receded, then turned when there was a shout from behind.

Anna was hurrying forward, Chelsea at her side, and from the look on her face she was ready to tear someone a new asshole. I stepped around Rachel and intercepted her with both hands raised.

"You know them?" I asked, meaning the prisoners we'd taken.

Anna started to open her mouth, then paused as the girls approached. Several of them hurled curses towards the men on their knees, one of them rushing forward and getting close enough to spit in one's face before I could grab her. Chelsea and Tiffany moved in on either side and guided her into the waiting helicopter. A minute later, the last of the girls disappeared inside with Irina bringing up the rear.

"That him?" Rachel asked.

"That's the animal," Anna hissed.

The exit door from the facility banged open, Bunny, Monk and Johnson running to join us. They gathered around Nicole, asking her in a whisper what was going on.

"What do you want to do with him?" I asked Anna, resisting the urge to draw my knife and perform a castration.

Exodus

"Them," she said with barely controlled anger. "They were all involved in taking the girls."

I turned and looked at the group of frightened men. They were all in their forties and before the attacks wouldn't have drawn a second look from anyone. But, dire events bring out the best in some people, and the worst in others. I've always thought it's simpler than that. Difficult times reveal a person's true colors, no matter how well they were hidden from polite society.

Turning towards them, I clicked off the safety on my rifle. There was no longer a decision to make. These assholes had made it for me. Before I could take a step, Anna placed her hand on my arm.

"If I'd been stronger, this wouldn't have happened," she said. "I'll clean this up."

I looked at her, seeing the determination in her eyes. Rachel stood slightly behind her, catching my eye and nodding. Anna drew one of her pistols and turned to face the frightened men. When they saw her with a weapon in hand, they began begging for mercy. They shouted apologies as the reality of their situation dawned on them. One of them scrambled to his feet and began running.

"Nitro!" Anna spoke, her voice low and hard.

Nitro snapped his rifle up, took half a second to adjust aim and pulled the trigger. The bullet punched into the middle of the man's back, sending him sprawling face first onto the tarmac where he didn't move again.

Anna walked directly to the first man in line. The one the girl had spat on. He shrank away, tears on his face as he begged her not to kill him. She stared down for nearly half a minute, then stepped sideways and shot the prisoner next to him.

Before the body hit the ground, she turned slightly and killed the next man. The last man, other than the confirmed rapist, fell back and began crawling away, snot bubbling from his nose and voice cracking as he begged for mercy. Anna gave him none, striding forward and firing a single bullet into his head.

Rachel had moved next to me and when Anna killed the fourth man, she took my hand in hers and squeezed tightly. I glanced at her, seeing the anger and determination on her face. If Anna hadn't done this, I didn't doubt Rachel would have.

"Watch him!"

Anna barked the order to Nitro as she brushed past him and walked up to Nicole. The conversation was brief, Nicole hurrying away around the far side of the helicopter as Anna returned to stand over the terrified man.

"Run!" She said through clenched teeth.

"Wh-wh-what?" He stammered.

Exodus

"I said RUN, goddamn it!" She hissed, raising the pistol. "Run, or so help me God, I'll shoot your fucking balls off, one at a time!"

He didn't immediately move, hesitating out of fear and confusion.

"NOW!" Anna screamed, firing a round into the asphalt right next to him.

The man jerked as if hit by a jolt of electricity, crawling away from her before leaping to his feet and running towards the desert. He looked over his shoulder, waiting for the bullet he knew was coming, but Anna hadn't raised her weapon. He faced forward, put his head down and ran, fear lending speed to his feet.

"What the hell's she doing?" Rachel whispered.

I shook my head, not understanding either, then movement at the edge of the bright lights caught my attention and I raised my rifle. Nitro and Gonzales had seen it too, both starting to raise theirs, then hesitating when Anna held up her hand.

"Don't," she said, eyes fixed on the fleeing man.

He didn't see the three females that were charging in from a steep angle. They were in a full sprint, covering ground at a terrifying pace. There were no screams, but he must have heard their feet a moment before they caught him. He looked to his left and slightly behind, and even if they weren't much faster, that distraction would have been his undoing.

While his head was turned, he missed a step and tumbled forward with a shout. Scrambling, he tried to get up and keep running, but the lead female slammed into his body with a flying tackle before he could regain his feet. They rolled several yards from the momentum of her attack, then the other two arrived. There was brief scream as he tried to fight, but it was cut off when one of the infected tore his throat open with her teeth.

Without a word, Anna holstered her pistol and turned away. Stepping gingerly over the ravaged bodies of the militia that surrounded the Chinook, she performed a quick walk around before climbing into the cockpit.

"Fuck me," I breathed, glancing around to see stunned expressions on every face.

Nicole reappeared from the far side of the helicopter, disappearing up the ramp without saying a word. For several seconds, we all just stood there, watching as the females feasted on the man Anna had sent to them. Finally, I shook myself and barked for everyone to get on board. I led the way, still holding Rachel's hand in mine. Johnson was the last one to walk up the ramp and paused to count heads.

"That's everyone, sir," he said quietly.

Exodus

A loud whine sounded as Anna activated the starters. The engines caught quickly, and the twin rotors began to spin slowly.

"Ready?"

Anna yelled to be heard over the racket. I hesitated a moment, looking over my shoulder at the desert.

"Something wrong?" Rachel asked.

"No," I shouted. "I'll be back in a minute. Tell Anna to wait."

Rachel looked at me for a beat, then nodded and released my hand. She headed for the cockpit as I went down the ramp.

It was a long walk across the tarmac to the edge of the desert, especially since I gave the three females a very wide berth. Also, I was walking slowly. I should have been in a hurry. We needed to get out of here, but I wasn't in the mood to be rushed. Dog had come with me, without an invitation, and walked on my left side, growling and looking in the direction of the macabre dinner party. It was good to have his keen senses on the side of my body where I was blind.

Several minutes later I knelt next to Katie's grave. As I'd approached the spot, I was reminded that I'd never installed any sort of marker. Well, it was too late now. Besides, I had no idea what I'd use.

Dog at my side, keeping watch, I closed my eye and thought about my wife. Remembered the time we'd had together. Pictured her face as I said my last goodbye. Looking up, I wiped away tears and began to stand, pausing when I spied a small pile of rocks that I'd tossed aside when I'd dug into the Nevada dirt.

Removing the gold band from my left hand, I placed it on top of the grave and pressed it into the soil, directly above where I thought Katie's heart would be. One at a time, I piled the rocks on top of my wedding ring until I'd created a foot-high pyramid. When it was complete, I stood and took another minute, then turned and headed for the idling Chinook with a lump in my throat and a spear of ice in my chest.

Dog, sensing my pain, rubbed the side of his head against my leg and nuzzled my hand with his nose. I can't say I didn't think about telling Anna to take off without me. Part of me, the part that couldn't deal with my pain and loss, wanted to stay. To visit Katie's grave every day and talk to her. Or maybe even to dig a second one next to her and…

Fuck that! I gritted my teeth so hard my jaw ached. Maybe someday, but first I had an appointment with Mr. Barinov. A Reaper was coming for him. Perhaps not tomorrow, but soon. He desperately needed to be properly sent off to that special place in hell.

We were halfway back to the Chinook, picking up the pace, when Rachel appeared at the bottom of the ramp. She seemed to hesitate, then walked forward to meet us. As I stepped up to her, I realized that tears were still streaming down my face. She moved in front and put her arms around me, burying her face against my neck. I held her for a few moments, then got us moving towards the helicopter. It took a while for surprise to nearly stop me in my tracks. For the first time, ever, I had touched her without feeling like I was betraying Katie.

Aboard the helicopter, I sank into a sling seat next to Nitro, Rachel on the other side. Dog promptly curled up with his chin on my boot and went to sleep.

"What was that?" Nitro asked as the aircraft slowly lifted into the air.

"Long story," I said, closing my eye and tilting my head back against the vibrating fuselage.

"Got anything better to do for the next hour?"

"My wife," I said without opening my eye.

"What about her?"

"She's buried out there," I said, appreciative that neither Irina nor Igor had told him.

Nitro was quiet, recognizing that I was hurting. Finally, several minutes into the flight, I started talking. Told him about everything that had happened to me since the night before the attacks when we'd talked on the phone. Told him about Katie, and Martinez and

Scott and Colonel Crawford, and all the other people I'd lost in the past several months.

When I was finished, I opened my eye and sat up, surprised to see everyone gathered around. Several of the girls were crying softly. Nitro, Goose, Bunny and Monk were very still, staring at the deck. I noticed that Igor and Irina were sitting very close together, heads inches apart as they spoke. And, I felt better. Not that I didn't acutely feel the loss of my wife, but talking about it had begun the process of healing the wound. A process I hadn't allowed myself to start.

To Nitro's credit, he kept his mouth shut. I didn't want anyone's sympathy, or pity, and he instinctively knew that. Rachel had rested her head on my shoulder as I spoke and left it there, also saying nothing.

"Nellis ahead!"

Anna's shout from the cockpit jolted all of us back to the moment. Freeing myself from Rachel and Dog, I picked my way forward and slipped into the copilot's seat. I could see nothing other than darkness through the large windscreen. It took a moment of looking around to find the flight helmet and slip it on, which activated the night vision display. Now I could clearly see the massive air base less than a mile ahead. Activating my radio, I contacted Vance. He was flying above and behind us, ready to spring to the defense of the Chinook if needed.

Exodus

"Take a look and see if there's any aircraft that'll meet our needs," I said to him.

He acknowledged, the Super Cobra roaring past a few seconds later.

"Let's stay out here, beyond the perimeter fence, for now," I said to Anna.

She nodded and killed our forward speed, bringing the hulking aircraft into a hover.

"You handle this thing pretty good," I said in admiration.

"My dad wouldn't have it any other way," she said. "Wanted me to fly for the Army. Said I had it, whatever *it* is."

"So, why didn't you?" I asked. "And, by the way, are you really a General?"

"Guess I wanted to make my own path," she said, shrugging slightly. "And, yes I am. Kind of."

"What does that mean?"

"I served as a Lieutenant Colonel. The star was a parting gift from General Olber and SECDEF when I was forced to retire."

"Chuck Olber?" I asked in surprise.

"You know him?"

"Knew him," I said. "He was a Special Forces officer, a Light Colonel when I knew him. Well, knew of him. I was a buck Sergeant at the time, so we didn't exactly travel in the same circles. But, what I remember of him, he was a good man."

"He was," Anna said. "Anyway, that's how I got my star, but it was all my dad's doing."

I started to ask another question, but Vance's voice over the radio cut me off.

"Got a couple of B-52s sitting on the tarmac. That's all I see that could make the trip."

"They can do it without refueling?" I asked.

"No problem," he said. "They've got something like a ten-thousand-mile ferry range."

"What's that mean?"

"One-way flight. Only thing is, for as big as they are, they aren't made for passengers. Gonna be cramped and uncomfortable as hell. And, only the cockpit is heated. We should probably go check the civilian airport."

"Agreed," I answered without hesitation. "Lead on."

"Copy," he said, the circuit falling silent.

Exodus

    Anna had been listening, and a few moments later we were tucked in behind the Super Cobra, heading south over the city of Las Vegas.

45

"See? I knew once you got a feel of my balls, you wouldn't be able to resist coming back for more!"

Vance was stretched out in the back of the Chinook, grinning up at Rachel as she gently worked the pair of warm-up pants over his hips. He was hurting like hell and had asked for another injection of the anesthetic. How he was still able to joke was beyond me.

"Keep being a smart ass and I'll let him give you the shot," she said, tilting her head in my direction.

Vance looked at me, and I grinned back. He made a production of shuddering.

"Sweetie, as long as you rub the sore spot when he's done…"

"You're incorrigible," Rachel laughed.

We'd finally figured out that despite the man's crude approach to women, he was actually a decent guy. He was just trying to live up to the image of the shit-hot fighter pilot. Maybe he crossed the line more often than not, and there was no doubt he was a letch of the first order, but he'd earned my respect when he'd put himself on the chopping block to protect the girls. Like my grandpappy used to say, "Watch their feet. Don't much matter what they say."

Exodus

It had taken me a lot of years to fully understand what he meant, and even longer to adopt it. Not that words don't give you some insight into a man's character, but I'll take an obnoxious jerk any day when he places the safety of others above his own. Especially when there's nothing to be gained by doing so. So, Vance had earned a pass from me, and apparently, Rachel as well.

We were on a runway at the Vegas airport, both helicopters not far from a Virgin Atlantic 747. The giant plane had apparently been abandoned in a panic, all the inflatable slides deployed and hanging to the tarmac far below. I'd sent Goose, Igor, Johnson and Monk aboard to clear the aircraft and make sure there wasn't any damage. They were still on the plane but had radioed a report that other than a mess in the passenger cabin, everything seemed in order. I wanted to get Vance aboard to give it a professional's inspection, but he'd needed some medical attention first.

Anna and Nicole were waiting just outside the Chinook while Nitro, Gonzales, Bunny and Irina had the girls gathered near the 747's front landing gear, keeping a close eye on them as well as watching for infected. Angela had regained consciousness as we were landing and was proving to be quite the handful. She'd lost it, for lack of a better description, screaming and spitting at anyone that came near and trying to attack them. Rachel, hesitant to sedate her again and risk damage to the fetus, finally suggested we restrain her before she harmed herself or someone else. So, I'd gotten creative with a couple of the web sling seats from the big helicopter.

"We're going to need to fuel it," Vance said, grunting as Rachel pushed a needle into his scrotum.

"How do you know?"

I turned to face him then quickly looked away. The sight of a man getting an injection into his grossly swollen scrotum was something I could do without.

"Plane's facing the terminal, not out," he said through gritted teeth. "That most likely means it just landed and they popped the emergency exits the instant the pilot could get it stopped."

I nodded, accepting his logic, then cursed silently to myself. I'd done this whole fueling thing before, and it had been a pain in the ass.

"What else will we need?" I asked.

"As long as there's no physical damage and the cockpit is intact, that'll do it," Vance said. "Won't know until I can get aboard and check."

"Alright," I said. "Let's go, Dog."

I walked down the ramp, Dog at my side. Anna looked at me and nodded at Nicole who was standing a few feet away. Her head was tilted back, eyes closed. She appeared to be listening to something. Before I could say anything, Dog emitted a loud growl. I looked at him then snapped my rifle up to point in the direction he was facing.

"Stay sharp," I transmitted on the radio. "We have infected in the area, most likely to the south."

I scanned the direction but didn't see anything other than hangars and the ground equipment normally found at civilian airports. Dog continued to growl as I searched for the threat.

"Nothing," Nitro said over the radio a minute later. "What'd you see?"

"Not me," I answered. "Dog. He's got their scent. Break. Johnson, you guys get your asses back down here."

"Already down," he replied immediately.

"There're a lot of females," Nicole said, startling me.

"Where?" I asked.

"You can't hear them?"

I listened for another few seconds, then glanced at Anna who shook her head.

"No," I said. "What are you hearing?"

"They make a... I can't describe it, but it's a low sound. That's how they communicate when they're not hunting. I think they're scared."

"What? They're scared? Of us?"

"I think so," Nicole said, finally opening her eyes and looking at me.

"You can understand them?" Rachel asked from behind us.

"Yes. Kind of," Nicole said. "Just like you can understand what Dog is feeling. Sort of, but not that obvious. I can't explain it."

"Where are they?" I asked, not giving a shit if the infected were frightened.

"Somewhere that direction," she said, pointing to the south.

I looked intently at the area her finger indicated. There was a large hangar with a few smaller buildings behind it. None of the females were visible.

"What are we doing?" Vance asked.

I glanced around, mildly surprised to see him on his feet, even if he was standing with his legs spread far apart. It was hard to resist the urge to give him a hard time about looking like a cowboy who'd been in the saddle for a long ride. Instead, I focused on the problem at hand.

Exodus

"Igor and Goose, get the girls and Vance on the plane, then go find fuel. The rest of you, form up on me."

I walked forward twenty yards, Dog sticking close. Quickly, the remainder of the team joined me, and we spread out into a defensive line between the rear of the 747 and the area where the females were hiding. A few months ago, I would have balked when Rachel, Irina and Anna joined us, rifles in their hands, but now I was happy to have the extra firepower.

Nicole had followed to stand next to me, Gonzales taking a position immediately by her side.

"Still hear them?" I asked her.

"Yes," she said after a long pause. "There's something different about these, but I don't know what it is."

"What do you mean, different?"

She was quiet for another long stretch, eyes closed as she listened intently.

"The ones we encountered in Seattle, and in the facility, were different. Angry. No, that's not it. Enraged. But these, it's..."

"Why are they not attacking? Irina asked.

"It's like they're trying to protect something," Nicole said.

"Oh, my God," Rachel breathed.

"What?" I asked when she didn't continue.

"Remember the females on the way to Mexico and on the beach?"

"Yeah," I said, not getting her point.

"They were pregnant."

Despite years of training and combat experience, every head turned away from the threat to stare at Rachel.

"Remember the ones we saw?" Rachel asked. "The pregnant ones held back. They didn't join the attack."

"Yes!" Nicole said loudly. "That could be it. That's why they're afraid. Why they're not attacking!"

"Are you fucking kidding me?" Gonzales asked. "These goddamn things are reproducing?"

"Saw it myself, Master Chief," I said. "Whole bunch of 'em, big as a beach ball. And she's right. It was the ones that weren't pregnant that were coming after us."

"We need to go clear them out," he said, eyes hard.

"No!" Nicole said, placing her hand on his arm. "They're not a threat!"

Exodus

"Maybe not now, but what about after those babies are born? What then? A mother protecting her child will be twice as dangerous as before! And what about the kids? What are we turning loose on the world if we don't kill them all?"

Nicole pulled her hand back, a look of horror on her face. She stared at Gonzales, then turned and started to walk towards the 747. After only a few steps she spun and sprinted through our line, directly towards the hangar.

46

Captain West walked into the conference room, accompanied by a tall, rangy man. He was wearing a Navy Commander's uniform, a SEAL trident gleaming under the bright lights. He quickly set about connecting a compact laptop to a ceiling mounted projector. Several senior Navy and Marine officers occupied the seats around the table, waiting for the briefing to begin. It wasn't long before Admiral Packard breezed into the room, waving everyone to stay in their seats before they even had a chance to fully stand.

"Commander, thank you for joining us," he said to the SEAL officer as he dropped into a chair at the head of the table. "Let's not waste time. Begin when you're ready."

"Thank you, sir," the SEAL said.

He tapped a key on the laptop and two, side-by-side images appeared on the large screen at the front of the room. On the left, a satellite image of a sprawling, primitive appearing prison camp spread across snowy tundra. To the right, another surveillance photo of a tall, luxury apartment building. Green grass and palm trees surrounded the ground level entrance.

"Sirs," he began. "These are our two targets. On the left is Detention Camp 7 in Siberia, and the other is the personal residence of President Barinov in Sydney.

Exodus

Both present unique challenges to a successful operation and I will briefly detail those to start, with your permission, sir."

He was looking directly at Admiral Packard as he said the last, earning a nod of approval. Clearing his throat, he continued.

"Detention Camp 7 is located one hundred and forty miles northeast of the Russian city of Irkutsk, two thousand five hundred miles from the East China Sea. It is comprised of ninety-one prisoner barracks, seventeen guard barracks and nine administrative buildings. There are also two large factories, staffed by the inmates, that produce winter clothing. The camp is a self-sustaining facility with its own power generation. Water is supplied by a series of subterranean pipes that draw from the nearby Angara river. Food is produced in the summer by forced prisoner labor in quantities sufficient to be canned or dried and stored for the winter.

"There is only one road in or out, and it is impassable much of the year due to the weather. During the narrow window when trucks can make the journey, raw materials are transported in, and finished goods are brought out. A single, improved runway serves the needs of the camp, which are few as the guards and administrative staff are full-time residents. There are no regularly scheduled flights and only a small, single-engine plane on site for the use of the camp commander. The camp is exclusively for the incarceration and punishment of political prisoners, with an estimated current population of fifty-five hundred inmates."

Packard's eyebrows shot up, and he interrupted the SEAL.

"Fifty-five hundred prisoners, Commander? Did I hear you correctly?"

"Yes, sir. That is correct."

The Admiral was quiet for a moment before nodding for the briefing to continue.

"Sir, you have identified the biggest challenge we are facing with the operation to extract Admiral Shevchenko. We have no idea where he is amongst the inmate population."

"Sir," Captain West interrupted. "I have provided the most recent photo we have of Admiral Shevchenko to Chief Simmons, and she has initiated the facial recognition program via the NSA satellites, but she is not optimistic we will be successful in identifying and locating the target."

"Why not?" Packard asked.

"It is winter in Siberia, sir. The prisoners are only outside to report for a shift at one of the factories or to go to the mess hall for their daily meal. And, when they are visible to the satellite, they are typically wearing hats and protective coverings on their faces."

Exodus

"So, Commander, what you're telling me is that if you go into the camp, you'll have to physically inspect every prisoner until you locate the target?" The Admiral asked.

"Correct, sir. And, even then, we would be working off a photo that is several years old. A photo of a younger, healthier man. I have concerns about our ability to even identify the target after months in these conditions.

"Additionally, there are nearly five hundred guards garrisoned at the camp. Apparently poorly trained and quite sloppy with their duties, but they can afford to be. The surrounding wilderness ensures that even if a prisoner were to escape, they would not survive long enough to reach civilization.

"Sir, as well trained as my men are, we cannot expect to succeed under these circumstances. If we can confidently locate the target, that is a different story, but I have not touched on the logistics of raiding a location this deep within Russian territory."

"Commander, are you saying it can't be done?" The Admiral asked, eyes boring into the SEAL officer.

"Sir, I'm saying that based on the current circumstances, we would almost certainly lose every man we send in."

"And, tip our hand to the Russians, sir," Captain West interjected quickly.

Dirk Patton

The Admiral sat quietly, staring at the two men. Finally, a Marine General from the opposite end of the table spoke up.

"Assuming we cannot locate the target with facial recognition, Commander, do you have an alternative proposal?"

"Yes, sir. I do. A small team infiltrates the camp and integrates with the inmates. I do not believe the guards will notice an additional few prisoners, especially considering the size of the population and the apparent lack of interaction between the two groups.

"Once embedded, the team will locate the target. If circumstances allow, they will escape to the surrounding forest and signal for extraction. If they are unable to escape, as long as we know a location and are confident in target identification, we can go in and get him and be back out before the guards are aware of our presence. If we do our job right, they might not even miss the prisoner we bring with us."

"What do you need for that?" The Marine asked.

"Native Russian speakers, so they can blend in. It may take some time for them to find the target. Secondly, it would be very beneficial if we had more current photos or a method to positively identify we're bringing out the right man."

Exodus

"I don't understand. The right man? Why is that a concern?"

"Sir, many of these inmates have been at the camp for over a decade. They are almost assuredly desperate and would leap at any opportunity for escape. I fully expect that there would be many of them who would claim to be the man we're looking for, simply so we'd bring them with us. We cannot make that mistake. I've looked into the possibility of some sort of DNA test as ultimate confirmation, but there's nothing we can use in the field, and we do not have the target's fingerprints on file."

"Commander," Admiral Packard said, forestalling another question from the Marine General. "What if I can get you a native Russian speaker that is personally acquainted with the target. Would that speed up the process?"

The SEAL looked at the Admiral in surprise.

"Yes, sir! That would be optimal."

"And if that person is a woman? Are there women in this camp?"

"This is a male only camp, sir. A woman would present unique challenges, and be at much greater risk than a man, but if she could positively identify the target, without question, it would be worth it."

Packard nodded, shooting a glance at Captain West.

"We don't have her yet," the Admiral said. "But, at last report, she's boarding a plane and should be here in a few hours."

The SEAL stared curiously, wanting to ask questions, but knew this was something the Admiral wasn't ready to talk about.

"We'll revisit this operation tomorrow," Packard said. "Now, please move on to Barinov."

"Yes, sir. President Barinov is currently in residence in the penthouse of the building pictured on the right. It is located overlooking Sydney Harbor in Australia. The neighborhood is on a narrow spit, called Potts Point, that thrusts north into the harbor. Russian Spetsnaz have created multiple concentric rings of security at ground level, and the only land access is guarded by Australian troops.

"A pair of Russian guided missile boats are stationed in the harbor, providing air defense. Three frigates and a cruiser are guarding the mouth of the harbor, and we believe there is an Akula class sub patrolling offshore. The security is alert and extremely competent."

"I'm not liking the sound of this, Commander," the Admiral growled. "Are you leading up to telling me this can't be done?"

"No, sir. I'm not. However, I'm informing you that this is a hardened target within the city of an ally.

Exodus

Reaching the target undetected will be nearly impossible at best. And therein lies my concern. In your tasking order, you stated that the target has the capability to release chemical weapons and he must be neutralized before he can do so. Sir, I cannot promise that.

"With the protection that is in place, it is extremely unlikely that my men and I will be able to reach the target undetected. I am confident, that with the proper support, we can achieve part of our mission and terminate Barinov. However, doing so without having to engage the target's security, and thereby alerting him to our presence, is very doubtful. It is also highly probable that there will be significant collateral damage, almost certainly involving Australian citizens."

"What about other locations?" The Marine General asked. "Does he go out for dinner? A mistress? Anything?"

"No, sir. At least, not since we've been watching, and we've also pulled archived surveillance footage. The only time he's left the penthouse was when he executed our men."

The room fell silent for several moments.

"But, there is one potential crack in their security," the Commander continued. "There is a daily delivery to the building. Foodstuffs. Alcohol. Necessities. These are provided by a local, Australian company. In addition, a cleaning company has been hired. They arrive daily at 0900 and depart at 1400. There are also frequent visits in the evenings by various local women."

"Women?"

"Escorts, sir. Very high end. It is unclear if they are for Barinov personally. The lower floors of the building are occupied by several senior Russian officers, and we have no way of knowing who the women are seeing. But, they are always accompanied to and from the building by the local police. With the Australians' cooperation, we could insert agents into any of these."

A buzz started up around the room as the assembled officers recognized the opportunity to get someone inside with a weapon. Someone who could potentially get close to Barinov and pull the trigger before he realized he was in danger.

"The PM will never go along with this," the Marine General said loud enough to cut through the conversations and silence them.

"You are correct," Admiral Packard said. "In fact, I do believe he would run straight to Barinov and reveal our plans. I've been reading reports about discontent within the ranks of their military and police. Perhaps we can start a little lower down the chain of command and find someone who resents the Prime Minister for having rolled over for the Russians."

Exodus

"Sir," Captain West spoke up. "I've had similar thoughts and began making inquiries amongst our men. SEALs, Recon Marines, Rangers... none of them know anyone within the Australian military. For the moment, we don't have a place to start."

"It sounds like we'd damn well better find one, wouldn't you agree, Captain?"

47

When Nicole raced past, Gonzales shouted and charged after her. With a curse, I yelled for everyone to stay put and took off as well. I'd had the idea that together we could catch and subdue Nicole, but had forgotten what the partial infection had done to her body. She was fast, quickly outdistancing us.

I managed to keep pace with the Master Chief, but all we could do was watch the lead Nicole had on us quickly expand. Dog trotted at my side, and I briefly considered sending him ahead to stop her but was afraid that in her emotional state she might try to fight. If she did, I wasn't at all confident that he wouldn't injure her, or worse. Gonzales and I were both slowing, unable to maintain a long-distance sprint, when Nicole disappeared through a man door into the hangar.

More than a minute later, we pounded up to the outside, and I lunged forward, body checking the Master Chief to the side when it was apparent he intended to charge through the door without stopping. He stumbled, losing more speed, then whirled on me. The panic on his face morphed to anger when I placed myself between him and the door.

"Stay the fuck out of this," he hissed, taking a step forward.

I stood my ground, glancing between the dark opening and his approaching bulk.

Exodus

"Stand down, Master Chief! That's an order!" I barked.

He wasn't in the mood to listen and surged to the side, trying to go around me. I ducked as he tried to stiff-arm me in the face, slipped inside and locked the extended limb into a hold and twirled him away from the hangar. Dog growled, gathering himself to join the tussle, and I snapped at him to stay as I advanced to meet Gonzales.

"Master Chief," I said, holding both hands up in a placating gesture. "You've got to stop! Nicole will be fine. You know they won't hurt her!"

"Get out of my way, sir," he said, lowering his head and preparing to charge.

"Get the hell away from here!" We both froze at the sound of Nicole's voice from inside the open door. "Now!"

A gamut of emotions played across Gonzales's face, but he relaxed slightly, no longer intending to run me over. I glanced over my shoulder, but couldn't see into the hangar.

"Goddamn it, now!" Nicole whispered.

Seeing the Master Chief surrender, I rushed forward, grabbed his arm and hurried across the tarmac. Dog stayed close to me, on the opposite side of my body. Quickly covering a hundred yards, we came to a stop and turned to face the hangar.

"She'll be fine, Master Chief," I said gently.

He nodded without saying anything, eyes fixed on the dark doorway. We stood there, waiting for something to happen. The sound of a vehicle engine caught my attention, and I looked around to see a fuel truck pulling to a stop beneath the 747's starboard wing, Igor and Goose jumping out of the cab and unreeling a thick hose.

"What's she doing?" Gonzales asked, the stress obvious in his voice.

"I don't know," I answered, even though he wasn't asking me. "Whatever it is, you've got to trust her. And you've got to listen to her. She's smarter than we are."

He absently nodded, his eyes never leaving the hangar door.

"Sorry about earlier, sir," he said after another couple of minutes. "I'll willingly accept any punishment you feel is appropriate."

"Punishment for what, Master Chief? For trying to protect the woman you love? Don't know how they do things in the Navy, but as far as I'm concerned, nothing happened. Just keep your shit together."

"Yes, sir."

Exodus

He took a step forward when Nicole walked out of the door. She gestured for us to stay where we were and quickly strode towards us.

"Are you OK?" He asked when she reached us.

"I'm fine," she said, shaking her head. "And you'd better learn to listen to me!"

"What's going on in there?" I asked before they got caught up in a discussion about their relationship.

"There are about two hundred females in the hangar," Nicole said, causing me to look over her shoulder and grip my rifle tighter. "Relax. They aren't going to be attacking today. Many of them have given birth in the past day or two, and all the rest are either in labor, or about to start."

All I could do was stare at her, my mouth hanging open as I tried to figure out the impact of what she was telling me.

"How are the babies?"

Surprised, I turned to find Rachel standing behind me. Nicole looked at her and sighed.

"Different," she said in a low voice. "Same red eyes. And they're not crying. Not making a sound. They seem... very aware of the world around them. Not at all like a normal newborn."

"And the mothers are caring for them?" Rachel asked.

"Yes." Nicole nodded. "That's why they're scared of us and weren't showing themselves."

"Male and female babies?" I asked, still stunned.

"More girls than boys, but yes, there are males."

"Holy Mother of God," Gonzales said, making the sign of the cross.

"This is probably happening everywhere," Rachel said after a long silence.

No one had a response to that.

"We should just go. Leave them in peace."

Nicole said the last while staring into Gonzales's eyes. He looked at her for a long time, then slowly nodded. She turned to look at me with the same intensity. I nodded, not entirely sure I was making the right decision. But, what good would it do? It's not like I could stop the next generation of infected by slaughtering a single group of mothers and newborns. Besides, no matter what they were, I couldn't stomach the idea of killing them, even though someday I might have to fight the grown children.

"Let's get the fuck out of here," I said, slowly turning.

Exodus

Rachel took my hand and we headed for the plane, Dog walking at our side. Nicole and Gonzales fell in behind us, his arm around her shoulders. To say we were all shaken to the core would be an understatement.

"Hey, Dog Face!" Vance's voice on the radio.

"Flyboy, I'm gonna kick you in the balls if you don't knock it off," I grumbled.

"Better hold off on that. We've got bigger problems. You'd better get to the plane but play it cool. We're being watched."

"Copy," I said, resisting the urge to start looking over my shoulder.

I pressed us into a fast walk, my back itching as we crossed the acres of wide open tarmac. Passing through the line of defenders, I met their worried faces and shrugged my shoulders.

"Master Chief, stay out here until we know what's going on," I said.

"Yes, sir," he answered, joining the line.

Igor and Goose had the fuel truck connected to the 747, the pump loud as it delivered its payload into the wing. I was glad to see that someone had found a set of aluminum air stairs and pushed them up to one of the open doors. Any of us on the ground could have climbed a rope, except for Dog, and he's one big lump when you've gotta throw him on your back.

He and Rachel followed me up the stairs and into the cabin. My nose wrinkled as I passed through the open door. The girls were clustered in a group near the first-class cabin, staying well away from several rows that were soaked in blood and other bodily fluids. Pushing past them, I stepped into the cockpit and leaned over Vance.

"What's wrong?" I asked, pausing in surprise when I saw him speaking into a headset.

"Stand by," he said before turning to look at me. "Plane's got sat comms integrated. Thought I'd give Pearl Harbor a call and see where the Russians are, but we've got bigger problems. Did you notice that private aviation terminal about half a mile to the west?"

"Not really," I answered. "Why?"

"Pearl's got us on satellite right now, and they're looking at half a dozen guys on the roof. And, one of them has what appears to be a Stinger. I fire these big engines up, there will be enough heat for it to achieve target lock and we're toast."

Exodus

48

"Who you talking to?" I asked.

"They bounced me around until I wound up with a Chief Petty Officer named Simmons. She sounds like she might be pretty hot, too."

Shaking my head and rolling my eyes, I held my hand out. With a humph, Vance placed an extra headset into my waiting hand. Quickly pulling it on, I swiveled the boom mic in front of my mouth.

"Jessica?" I asked.

"Sir! Very good to hear your voice. The Admiral is getting anxious for you to arrive."

"Me, too," I said. "Now, tell me what you see on that rooftop."

"Sir, you've got six men, all armed with rifles. There is also a device that I'm almost certain is a Stinger missile."

"Have you had an expert take a look?" I asked, hoping beyond hope she just didn't know what she was seeing.

"Not yet, sir. But, I put a call out, and there's a Marine on the way. He should know for sure, right?

"Yeah, he should. Good thinking. OK, tell me what these guys are up to. Were you watching us before Commander Vance called?"

"Yes, sir. I was. They were there when you arrived. Unfortunately, I can't tell you what they were doing. I tracked you from Groom Lake, and when I realized you were bypassing Nellis and going to McCarran Airport, I did a thermal scan. That's when I first saw them.

"They've got two Air Force Hummers parked behind the building they are on. That's where they were, in the vehicles, when I realized they were there. They all jumped out and ran inside before coming onto the roof, so there must be interior access. The one with the Stinger appeared to be tracking your helicopters with it as you landed. Once you were on the ground, he set it aside, and they've been watching through binoculars the whole time you've been there."

"One shot with a Stinger." Vance had been listening on the other headset. "They're saving it, waiting to get us all in one aircraft. Efficient bastards."

"Any change, Jessica?" I asked. "Does it look like they're doing anything other than just watching?"

"Not at the moment, sir."

"OK, stand by," I said, muting the connection and turning to Vance. "They don't know we know they're there. Can you take them out with the Cobra?"

Exodus

"Sure that's a good idea?" Anna asked from behind me. I hadn't realized she followed me into the plane. "If they get nervous when the helicopter takes off and shoot it down, we're stuck here without a pilot."

"Shucks, ma'am. You do care!" Vance said, wiggling his eyebrows at her.

"Maybe that wouldn't be so bad," I said, slapping his head with the back of my hand. "But, you're right. We can't risk him. Going to have to do this the old-fashioned way."

I unmuted the connection.

"Jessica," I said.

"Here, sir. I've got Master Gunnery Sergeant Avril standing next to me, and he's certain we're looking at a Stinger."

"Somehow, I never get good news from the Jar Heads," I said.

"Uh, he's on the line, sir," Jessica said, sounding embarrassed.

I couldn't help but grin.

"Master Gunny, is there any good news?" I asked.

"Well, sir, the Tangos are just sittin' there," the Marine drawled in a voice that was pure Mississippi. "Don't look like they's in any kinda big hurry. Probably waitin' for you to start those engines so they can shoot a missile up yo' ass."

"Yeah, that's what my pilot thinks, too. See any way I can approach that building without being seen?"

"Well... hold on, sir."

I listened as he directed Jessica on where to pan the view. It didn't take long.

"Buildin's free standin', with nothin' else 'round it. Open tarmac to the east and south, parkin' lot to the west and north. Two Humvees on the side opposite from ya. Hard to tell, but pretty sure they's empty. Good news is the chuckleheads is all clustered together on the east side of the roof, watchin' you. If you can get to the west side of the buildin', you got a clean shot at gettin' inside 'thout bein' seen. Hang on, I'm lookin' to see the best way to get there."

I waited impatiently, but it was less than thirty seconds before he was back on.

"Best bet is that big hangar to the south. It's open all the way, an' they'll see you goin' there for sure, but if you don' make a big deal out of it, they might not get too nervous. Git there and come out the back side. There's a couple smaller buildin's that'll screen you from 'em an' you can circle and stay in cover. From there, four hun'red yards open groun' to the blind side of the buildin' they's on. If they stay put where they are, they won' see you comin'. So, maybe somethin' to keep 'em interested while you're approachin'."

Just great. The hangar he was talking about was the one with all the female infected inside. I recalled enough of the area to know the bad guys would have a direct view of the front of it, and if I tried to slip around the side, they'd see what I was doing and might get nervous. I relayed what I was thinking to the Master Gunny, and he quickly confirmed that I remembered correctly.

"What about you?" Vance asked, looking at Anna. "You handled that Chinook pretty well."

"Not going to risk losing her, either," I said firmly.

"Look," Vance said, sighing. "They've already shown that they're waiting to get all of us with one shot. So, have her take it up and fly in the opposite direction. That shouldn't make them too nervous. She can fly around in the distance like she's looking for something. They'll be busy watching and wondering what the hell she's doing and give you a chance to take the bastards out."

I thought about that for a minute before shaking my head. I still didn't like the idea of risking Anna's life. I'd find another way.

"Thanks, Master Gunny," I said into the headset. "Got it from here."

"No problem, sir. Us Jar Heads are always happy to help out the Army whenever you get in over yo' head!"

Shaking my head, I took the headset off and dropped it onto the co-pilot's seat.

"What are you going to do?" Rachel asked.

"Making it up as I go," I said, squeezing past her and heading for the tarmac.

On the ground, I casually walked over to where Igor and Goose were monitoring the flow of fuel into the 747. I had to step close and shout to be heard over the noisy pump.

"How much longer?"

"Pilot said to go until it wouldn't take any more," Goose said, shrugging. "Hoping this one truck is enough. This plane's one big bitch."

"Where'd you find the fuel?" I asked.

"Back of hangar," Igor said, pointing to the north.

I was pleased when he indicated an area that would be shielded from the guys with the Stinger.

"Were there more trucks?" I asked, an idea taking shape.

"Three more," Goose said. "Why?"

Exodus

"Haul ass over there." I nodded in the direction he'd indicated. "Get one of them a safe distance away from the others and blow the fucking thing up."

He stared at me like I was crazy.

"Just blow it up? What the hell for?"

"Because I need a distraction," I said. "Got some bad guys with a Stinger I've got to take care of before we take off."

"I go," Igor said immediately. "He not starts truck."

Goose glanced at him, then looked back at me and nodded his head.

"He's right. No keys. They gotta be hotwired."

"Go," I said to Igor.

He didn't hesitate to turn and run for the hangar.

"So, he's not such a bad guy," Goose said as we watched the big Spetsnaz soldier sprint across the tarmac.

"Be glad he's on our side," I said, turning and trotting towards the defensive line.

"Hey, Major," Vance called over the radio. "Pearl says those guys look like they're getting antsy."

Dirk Patton

"What are they doing?" I asked as I ran.

"One of them went back inside, and another is moving around, checking their blind sides."

Shit! I'd hoped these guys were going to stay still and let me sneak up and ruin their day. I guess someone in the group was smarter than I'd thought.

"Thanks. Tell them to keep watching, and I'll check in when I get close."

By this time, I'd reached the line and came to a stop next to Nitro. Rachel and Dog had followed me, but I didn't see Anna. I gave the other operators a one-minute synopsis of what was going on and what I intended to do. All of them wanted to come with me.

"No," I said. "If it's just me, they'll be curious, but won't be worried. But, if all of a sudden a whole squad starts heading in that direction, they're going to get their knickers in a twist and try to figure out what we're up to."

"Then I should go," Nitro said. "Sorry boss, but you're not a hundred percent. One of those fuckers gets on your left, you're in trouble."

My immediate reaction was to flatly reject him. He stared at me, his jaw set as he waited for my objection. I opened my mouth, then paused when I admitted to myself that he was right. My ego wasn't as important as getting these people out of here safely. Swallowing my wounded pride, I nodded.

Exodus

"So what's the best way to get there without being..."

We all spun in surprise at the sound of an engine starting. I looked at the 747, but Goose was still calmly monitoring the flow of fuel into the plane.

"What the hell is she doing?" Nitro asked, taking a few steps in the direction of the Super Cobra.

The rotor was slowly turning as the turbine roared, and I could make out Anna through the windscreen as she donned a flight helmet. I reached up and tapped the radio earpiece to transmit.

"Anna, what the fuck are you doing?" I shouted. "Shut down, now! We've got a plan!"

"My responsibility," she answered as the rotor sped up. "I'll take care of it."

"Ma'am, don't do this!" Nitro called. "You can't take on a Stinger!"

"They didn't shoot us down when we arrived," she answered. "They aren't going to shoot me if I don't give them a reason, and by then it will be too late."

"Anna, you don't need to do this," I said.

"Yes, I do," she said. "If I hadn't given up control to them, none of this would have happened. Too many people are hurt or dead because I didn't stand against them when I had the chance. Enough's enough! Time to do what I should have done weeks ago."

The Supra Cobra's engine roared as it lifted off the tarmac. Skids barely in the air, the big helicopter spun around and with a nose down attitude raced away, following the runway.

49

"Igor, blow the goddamn truck!"

I shouted into the radio as I broke into a sprint towards the hangar with the females. Dog ran with me, and a moment later I realized Nitro and Rachel were following.

"This is going to make them nervous," Nitro said from next to me.

"And a Super Cobra taking off isn't? That damn stupid woman is going to get herself killed!"

Before we were halfway to the hangar, a thunderous explosion rocked the night from behind, lighting up the entire area. I didn't need to turn around to know that there would be a massive fireball boiling into the dark sky. The sudden illumination revealed the Cobra as it screamed towards the enemy position, mere feet above the tarmac.

Someone on the roof finally realized that the jig was up and began firing at us. Several bullets struck in front of me, blasting chunks of asphalt into the air. The fucker was leading us by too much, but that only meant he was about to adjust aim.

"Stop!" I screamed, skidding to a halt.

Nitro knew the drill and pulled up instantly, but Rachel nearly ran me over, sending me stumbling several steps forward. But, it worked. A heartbeat later, several rounds tore into the tarmac where we would have been if we'd maintained our pace.

"Run!" I shouted again, surging forward.

Dog trotted slightly to the front, looking over his shoulder to see if I was playing some sort of game. In a way, I was, but if I lost this one, it would be my last.

"Suppressive fire on that goddamn roof!" I yelled to the team members who had stayed behind.

Everyone had a sound suppressed rifle and I couldn't hear their shots, but they must have opened up because the incoming fire suddenly ceased. I didn't think there was a chance in hell they'd actually be able to target and hit the bad guys at the range they were engaging from, but bullets pinging off your cover have a way of making you keep your head down. At the moment, that's as much as I could ask for.

Ahead, the Cobra streaked around the back of a hangar, turning to line up its weapons. It suddenly flared, cutting speed to a hover as it popped up for a *look down* shot on their position. There was a ripple of flashes from one of the cylindrical rocket pods as Anna fired. But, before the ordnance could reach its destination, there was a flare from the rocket motor of a missile igniting only a few yards above the roof of the hangar.

Exodus

The weapons fired by the helicopter impacted a fraction of a second later, the structure erupting as multiple warheads detonated. Anna, aware of the inbound threat, attempted to evade, but the Stinger slammed into the Super Cobra. Its seeker head had locked onto the heat of the aircraft and struck only a foot behind the dual exhaust ports which were located above the tail boom.

For a second, the helo disappeared in a ball of fire and smoke before suddenly emerging back into view. It was no longer able to stay in the air, tilting dramatically as half the tail section fell away. The main rotor was still turning, and that threw the crippled machine into a spin as it dropped from the sky. I lost sight of it as it plunged towards the tarmac.

With the threat of the enemy on the roof of the destroyed hangar eliminated, I changed directions and charged directly for the crash site. We needed to get there quickly as there was always a possibility that Anna had survived, but the helo had been at least a mile away when it went down.

After a hundred yards of sprinting, all of us slowed. Well, all of us except Dog. He was racing ahead, grudgingly pulling up and waiting when I called him. I didn't know what might be on the far side of the hangar and didn't want him charging in by himself.

I tried to push harder but didn't have it in me. Apparently Nitro did, as he began to pull away. A horn beeped from behind and I nearly stumbled in surprise.

Glancing over my shoulder, I saw the fuel truck with Goose behind the wheel. Johnson, Bunny and Monk were clinging to a ladder-type structure on top of the tank that ran the length of the vehicle.

He slowed, and I shoved Rachel into the cab, sending Dog after her before leaping onto the passenger side running board. Surging ahead, he slowed again to allow Nitro to step up on the driver's side, then accelerated hard. With a moment to not have to concentrate on running, I looked back at the 747.

"Vance, what's your fuel state?"

"We're topped off and good to go," he answered immediately.

I acknowledged his answer, gripping the door tighter as Goose steered around the destroyed hangar. Looking through the cab, I could see the distress on Nitro's face as he clung to the opposite side of the truck. Rachel had her arms around Dog's neck, hugging him tightly.

Clearing the debris field created by the Cobra's rockets, we turned, and I got my first look at the crashed helo. The main part of the fuselage was on its side, belly facing us. The severed tail section lay a couple of hundred yards away. The Stinger had ruptured the fuel tank and spilled AvGas was feeding the flames that were spreading towards the front of the aircraft where the cockpit was located.

Exodus

Goose hit the brakes when we were still several hundred yards from the crash. I was glad he did since we were riding on a rolling bomb if it got too close to the flames. Nitro was off the running board and charging forward before we came to a complete stop, and I dropped to the tarmac and followed. We'd only gone a few steps when the fire found its way into the compromised tank and the Super Cobra vanished in a ball of searing flame. Nitro and I were both blown backward by the shockwave of superheated air, throwing our arms up and turning away to shield our faces.

"Goddamn it," Nitro said as we slowly climbed to our feet. "What the fuck was she thinking?"

We simply stood and stared at the flames.

"You heard her," I said gently. "The guilt must have been eating at her for a while."

"She didn't have a damn thing to feel guilty about! None of this was her fault!"

I nodded slowly, unsure what to say to comfort my friend.

"Major, you'd better get your ass in gear," Vance called. "Pearl just spotted a shitload of infected coming our way."

"Copy," I said, turning to Nitro. "We gotta go. Infected coming. Probably drawn to the explosions."

He didn't respond or even act like he'd heard me.

"Nitro." I reached out and put my hand on his shoulder. "We have to move, or her sacrifice will be wasted. Let's go!"

Slowly he gathered himself, shook his head, then turned to follow me back to the fuel truck. Bunny was still on the roof, keeping watch, Johnson and Monk on either side. Rachel and Dog had stayed in the cab.

"Mount up," I shouted as we trotted up.

"We heard," Johnson said, jumping onto the cab before swinging up to the top of the tank.

"How much time do we have?" I asked Vance once everyone was aboard and we were heading back to the plane.

"Not much."

I could hear the whine of engines starting in the background.

"This thing go any faster?" I shouted at Goose.

"Not a fucking sports car, sir," he yelled back. "Pedal's on the floor."

We rounded the rubble of the hangar, Goose giving it a wide berth so we didn't blow out a tire on the shards of metal scattered across the tarmac. Coming back into the open, I was glad to see the navigation lights on the 747 were flashing. The landing lights brilliantly illuminated the open runway to the aircraft's front.

Someone was standing next to the tractor that provided motivation for the air stairs, and as we drew closer, I recognized it was Igor. He jumped behind the wheel, ready to move them away from the plane the instant we were aboard. Goose wheeled up close to them dropping us off before pulling the fuel truck a safe distance away. I sent everyone up the stairs, following and stepping through the door.

Igor drove the stairs to where the tanker was parked, jumping out and following Goose to the plane. He'd already removed all the deflated emergency slides and hung a climbing rope from the main cabin door.

"We gotta go!" Vance shouted from the cockpit.

I rushed forward and looked through the windscreen. Just rounding the corner of the terminal, and faintly visible at the limit of the landing lights, was the leading edge of the infected. Females. Charging fast, and *shitload* didn't do a good job of describing how many of them there were.

Dashing to the door, I leaned out and saw Goose a third of the way up the rope, Igor waiting on the ground for him to finish the climb. I shouted at them, Goose putting on a burst of speed and Igor taking a second to look in the direction I was pointing. He must have seen the infected, and the sight spurred him to action. Leaping, he grabbed the rope only a few feet below Goose's boots and began scaling the line, hand over hand.

"Anchor me!" I shouted.

Almost instantly, Nitro's big hand locked onto the back of my belt. Leaning out the open door, I extended my arm and Goose grabbed my wrist as I clamped down on his and hauled him up into the cabin. He tumbled past, jumping to his feet and leaning out, urging Igor to climb faster.

"We're out of time!" Vance shouted.

"Wait!" I answered.

"They're here!" Rachel screamed from somewhere behind me.

"Go!" I bellowed over my shoulder, then nearly lost my balance as the 747's huge engines throttled up and the plane began pivoting to come into takeoff alignment.

Looking down, I caught my breath when I saw Igor swinging like a pendulum, legs far to the side. He was only halfway up the rope, and the momentum of the aircraft in motion was preventing him from being able to do anything other than hold on for dear life. The big Russian looked up, then I lost sight of him for a second as he swung beneath the belly of the plane. When he reappeared, he traveled through a parabola, his boots no more than ten yards from the intake of the closest engine.

"Fuck this!"

I lost sight of Goose but didn't have time to worry about him. The rope Igor dangled from was in my hands, and I began trying to pull him up. But, between his more than two hundred pounds and the force of being swung around at the end of it, I couldn't gain so much as an inch.

There was a flash of motion, and I was bulled aside as Goose rushed forward and dropped out the door. I stared in shock, then saw the additional rope trailing out into the night. Leaning farther out, I tried to see him, and Igor, but at that moment the plane straightened out and was suddenly picking up speed.

"Vance, slow down!" I screamed, now on all fours and sticking my head out into the open.

Goose had tied a rope to the base of a row of seats, then around his waist before going out. Now, he twisted at the end of it, trying to get a loop secured around Igor. Every motion of the plane sent them twirling away from each other, then the engines throttled back and we slowed to a crawl as Vance reacted to my shout.

In seeming slow motion, Goose reached the end of an arc, then swung back towards the center. But so did Igor, and the two men slammed into each other.

The impact was hard enough for me to hear, even over the roar of the idling jet engines. Igor lost his grip, arms windmilling as he fell to the tarmac.

50

"Vance! Stop the goddamn plane!" I shouted, leaning even farther out to see where Igor had landed.

"They're almost on us! If they get in front of the engines, we're fucked!" He yelled back.

"NOW, GODDAMN IT!" I roared.

A second later, the brakes groaned and we came to a stop. Goose swung back and forth, suspended at the end of the rope. With Nitro holding me, I thrust most of my upper body through the door and ducked my head, trying to see Igor. After a couple of seconds, I spotted his legs, and he wasn't moving.

The screams of attacking females reached my ears an instant before I saw the first one. They raced in, gathering around Igor and leaping for Goose's dangling legs, sending him in a panicked scramble up the rope. Pulling back into the cabin, I twisted my rifle around and reached for the rope Igor had been climbing, intending to go down and fight my way through.

"No!" Nitro cried in my ear when he saw what I was trying to do.

Ignoring him, I bent and grabbed the rope, but he wrapped his arms around me and pulled me away from the door as a body flashed past on its way to the tarmac below. Twisting around, I grabbed Nitro's wrist and levered it to the side, then slipped away and lunged for the door. Together, he and Johnson tackled me to the floor, and I heard Rachel yelling for Dog to stay.

Nitro had his not inconsiderable body weight on my back, my arms pinned beneath me, and Johnson was sitting on my legs. I thrashed, but couldn't free myself from them. Shuddering in anger, I screamed my frustration. A moment later, Goose's face appeared as he climbed up. He scrambled into the cabin and turned to look down at the ground.

"Who the fuck went out?" I shouted.

Rachel leaned down next to my face.

"You need to stop," she said, calmly. "That was Nicole. We've seen what she can do. Now, quit fighting. We're already in a sea of infected. There's nothing you can do."

Slowly, the energy drained out of me, and I stopped resisting Nitro and Johnson.

"Quiet," Rachel mumbled in my ear. "Don't stir them up."

"Got your shit together if I let you up?" Nitro asked in a low mutter.

I nodded my head and almost instantly his crushing weight was gone off my back. Johnson untangled from my legs, and I squirmed forward to get a view of what was happening outside.

The breath caught in my throat when I looked down at a solid mass of females. They were crowded in so tightly the ground was completely invisible. But, they were just standing there, all of them intently watching something I couldn't see. The engines were still running, and I didn't like how close some of them were to the voluminous intakes. Raising up on an elbow, I turned to see Nitro ready to grab me if I did anything stupid.

"Tell Vance to kill the engines," I said quietly.

He frowned and raised a questioning eyebrow.

"There are females standing directly in front of the intakes. If even one gets sucked in, we're not going anywhere."

He nodded and moved quickly to the cockpit. Apparently, it took some convincing as nearly a minute passed before the engines spooled down and went silent.

Absent the whining roar, I could hear an odd humming sound. Actually, it sounded more like a song than anything. There was a lilting quality, and in a strange way, it was almost soothing. I looked to the side as Rachel pushed in between me and Goose. The three of us sat there, mesmerized.

"What the hell is that?" Nitro asked from behind.

I simply shook my head.

The song continued for several minutes, suddenly stopping. When it did, the females beneath us moved. Slowly, they began shuffling to the side, the tarmac becoming visible once again. As they pressed back, those who were farther out shifted to make room.

Once a wide path was open, they all came to a stop and stood stock still. Nicole appeared a few seconds later, leading an unsteady Igor. His arm was draped over her shoulders, and I wasn't sure he'd have been on his feet if not for her. Bite marks were visible on his exposed skin, blood running freely. His shirt was rent open, revealing damage to his torso caused by slashing nails.

Nicole brought him to a point directly beneath the door and, moving cautiously, tied a loop in the end of the rope that dangled to the ground and slipped it over his head. Once it was below his shoulders, she worked it under his arms and cinched it tight. Without looking up or saying a word, she steadied him with one hand while twirling a finger on the other.

"Pull!" I said as quietly as I could.

Grabbing the rope, I pulled it tight then began heaving on it as Nitro and others lent their strength. When Igor appeared at the sill, Rachel and Goose grabbed him and brought him aboard as gently as they could. The team immediately lifted him up and carried him farther into the cabin with Rachel staying at his side. Dog whined softly, then jumped off his seat to follow Igor.

Nitro and I eased up to the door, looking around when Gonzales put his hands on our shoulders. The three of us looked down at Nicole, who was standing in the middle of the throng of females. She slowly turned a circle, looking at them, then the song started up again, and I realized it was her.

For nearly a minute she sang to them, tones only, no words, then raised her arm. As her hand came level with the ground, the song ended. For several seconds, nothing happened, then as one, the females turned in the direction she'd pointed. Slowly at first, then, like a damn breaking, they began running. Nicole remained where she was, unmoving, like a boulder in a stream.

There were no screams as the infected ran. No sound at all, other than the slap of thousands of feet on the tarmac. Despite the speed of the females, it was several minutes before the last one disappeared. Nicole heaved a sigh and looked up, smiling when she saw the Master Chief.

I kicked the line out of the door, and it slapped onto the asphalt by her feet. She reached out and grabbed it, climbing up faster than I've ever seen anyone scale a rope. Gonzales reached out and bodily lifted her into the cabin, crushing her against him in relief.

"We can leave now," she said when he finally put her down. "The runway is clear."

For a few seconds, all I could do was stare at her. She met my eye, and I could see the exhaustion on her face. I turned and shouted for Vance to get us in the air.

Exodus

51

We took off at a steeper angle than the commercial aircraft had probably ever achieved, but that's what you get with a military pilot. There was no gentle glide through ten thousand feet, followed by a slow ascent to cruising altitude. Vance kept the power on, finally leveling out after banking sharply. I undid my seatbelt, moved Dog off my feet and made my way forward to the flight deck.

"Didn't know a 747 could climb like that," I said.

"Me either," he answered with a grin.

"Heading south to go around the Russians?"

"East, first," he said, reaching out and tapping an electronic navigation screen. "This thing's about the size of a World War II destroyer, and as stealthy as your grandpa after eating chili. No way they don't already have us on radar, so I'm heading away, hoping they don't decide to come after us."

"And, if they do?"

"Well, as far as I know, they weren't patrolling inland. Just hugging the coastline. They're apparently there to prevent any aircraft from Hawaii making it to the mainland. If that's the case, we're starting out with a several hundred-mile buffer, and going farther away every second."

"Could they catch us if they wanted to?"

"Maybe," he said, shrugging. "A tail chase is a bitch, even if you're after a much slower aircraft. I had time to look through a manual while you were fucking around at the airport. Cruise speed for this baby is about five hundred and seventy miles an hour, but I'm pushing it to the limit right now, and we're at just under seven hundred miles an hour. That means to catch us, they'd have to go supersonic, which guzzles fuel, and means they'd have to have an aerial tanker to fill up along the way. I'm pretty sure they don't, so my best guess answer is no. They can't intercept."

I breathed a sigh of relief. I'd been more worried about being forced or shot down than I'd let on.

"Good. So, what's your plan?"

"Go a few hundred miles east. That should get us well beyond the range of any radar they've got up, even airborne. At that point, we turn south and stay over Mexico until we reach Guadalajara, which is south of the southern tip of Baja, then due west to Hawaii. Going to take a while, so you might as well get some sleep."

"If that's the way to go, what were you doing over the Sea of Cortez when you got shot down? Why weren't you farther south to avoid them?" I asked, ignoring his suggestion.

Exodus

"They hadn't started patrolling the Baja peninsula when I came through. Got caught by surprise on my way home."

"Where had you been, by the way?"

"Checking some oil rig off the Texas coast. Don't know why. I'm just a stick jockey."

"Checking it for what?" I asked.

"Seeing if it was still operational."

"Why? Is the Admiral thinking we need to start getting oil from the Gulf?"

"No, don't think this is a real platform. When I buzzed it, I got lit up by antiaircraft tracking radar and contacted on the guard channel. If it was really pumping oil... well, anyway, I talked to them for a couple of minutes to verify they were alive and well, then had to scoot for home.

"Guessing it's some sort of secret project disguised as an oil rig. Maybe a weapons or surveillance platform. Who knows? All I was supposed to do was see if there was anyone still alive."

There was a soft beeping sound from the incredibly complicated control panel and he held up a finger for me to wait. Pressing a button, he spoke to someone for a few seconds before signing off. With a smile, he turned the yoke, banking the big plane until the navigation screen showed us traveling south.

"That was Pearl," he explained. "The Russians reacted when we took off but gave up after only a hundred miles. They're going to keep an eye on things and give me a heads up if the Ivans try to intercept as we head south."

I looked out the windscreen, but there was nothing visible other than the night sky.

"OK," I said. "Let me know if anything changes."

I turned to leave, stopping when he called my name.

"Think you could send Rachel up here? The last shot is wearing off."

"I'll let her know," I said. "By the way, that was a hell of a thing you did, protecting those girls like that."

"My momma didn't raise a fool," he chuckled. "Give up women? Are you kidding? Gotta protect my turf!"

I grinned and walked out of the cockpit, stopping where Rachel was sitting with Dog and Irina. Igor, asleep or unconscious, was stretched out on a business class seat that had been folded down into a bed.

"How is he?" I asked.

"Incredibly, nothing's broken," Rachel said. "He has a serious concussion and a lot of soft tissue damage from the infected, but he'll be OK. As long as he has time to heal."

"Tough fucker," I mumbled, watching as Irina gently stroked his forehead. "By the way, Vance needs another shot."

Rachel nodded and stood, picking up her pack.

"Are we safe?" She asked.

"Seems so," I said. "We should be in Hawaii in a few hours."

"No infected there, right? And no one trying to kill us?" Rachel looked at me expectantly.

"No," I said, shaking my head.

I started to smile, then Rachel's question reminded me of Nicole. What the hell was going to happen to her when we arrived? The Admiral had already told me, in no uncertain terms, that he wouldn't allow any infected into the islands. And while Nicole might not technically be an infected, she was close enough to set off alarm bells the instant someone saw her eyes.

"What's wrong?" Irina asked, seeing the expression on my face.

I sighed and explained my thoughts.

"They can't turn her away!" Rachel protested.

Irina nodded in agreement.

"I'm not worried about that," I said. "I'm worried they're going to lock her away in an isolation chamber."

"You can't let that happen!" Rachel said.

"I can't stop it if that's what the Admiral decides to do," I said. "I'm not in charge once we get there, and I can't just do whatever I think is best. We're going back to the real world. There will be laws and rules we have to follow, whether we like them or not."

Rachel stood there glaring at me. After several uncomfortable seconds, she turned and headed for the flight deck to attend to Vance. I watched her walk away, then followed quickly to retrieve something I'd noticed in the cockpit. When I came back, I had to stop and pet Dog before he'd let me continue down the aisle. I rubbed his muzzle, ruffled his ears and looked at Irina as she continued to fawn over Igor.

"He's in love with you," I said, glad Igor wasn't awake to hear me spill his secret.

"I wish he'd tell me."

"Is it mutual?" I asked, mildly surprised by her response.

"Yes," she smiled. "It always has been. But, I was an officer, and it wasn't possible. Then, everything we've been through, and Martinez, and…"

"Look," I said when it was obvious she wasn't going to finish her thought. "If there's one thing I've learned, it's that the person you love could be gone in an instant. Don't waste time. Tell him how you feel."

"I could say the same to you," Irina said, tilting her head in the direction Rachel had gone.

"That's different," I said.

"Only because you're letting it be," she said. "You're right. There's no time to waste, so quit wasting it."

We looked at each other for a few moments, then I smiled and turned to go find Nicole. She was seated with Gonzales, her head on his shoulder, eyes closed. He was awake and watched me approach.

"She OK?" I asked quietly, not wanting to wake her.

"She's fine," Nicole answered before the Master Chief could speak.

She opened her eyes, reminding me of how shocking she would appear to the people in Hawaii.

"What the hell happened back there?" I asked.

"I don't really know," she said. "I don't know how I know to sing like that. I just do."

"That was amazing," I said. "You saved Igor's life. All our lives."

Nicole sat up and shrugged, looking down at her lap where she held Gonzales's big hand with both of hers.

"They weren't there to attack us, at least not like we're used to," she said.

"What do you mean?"

"When Igor blew up the fuel truck, then the shooting started and all the rockets from the helicopter, well, it terrified the mothers that were in the hangar. You couldn't hear them?"

"No," I said. "I couldn't hear anything other than the fighting."

"The other females did," she said. "And they answered. Came running to protect the others."

"Are you sure?" I asked, stunned at the thought of that level of community among the infected.

"Yes," Nicole said, nodding. "I felt the impulse, too. But, I understood that we weren't there to harm them."

I stared at her, unsure what to say next. Before things got awkward, I changed subjects.

"So, we may have a problem when we land in Hawaii."

Exodus

"Because I'm infected," Nicole said calmly. "The same reason I wasn't allowed to evacuate when the Rangers left."

I nodded, holding my hand up as Gonzales sat forward, eyes flashing in anger.

"Master Chief, we're about to be back in the real world. Keep your wits about you," I said, then turned to Nicole. "And I promise I will do everything I can to protect you. But a little insurance might not be a bad thing."

I reached into my pocket and held up a pair of aviator style sunglasses with mirrored lenses. They'd been laying on a small shelf next to a folding jump seat in the cockpit. Nicole looked at them for a second. With a smile, she took them from my hand and slipped them on. Her red eyes were completely hidden.

"Just keep a low profile when we arrive," I said.

Gonzales was looking at her, grinning from ear to ear.

"Thank you, sir," he said. "I promise. No more Army jokes!"

"That's OK, Master Chief," I said, smiling back at him. "I know it's hard for a squid to remember big words."

52

We had to go a couple of hundred miles farther south than Guadalajara before turning west for the final leg of our flight. Russian fighters were patrolling steadily, but for some reason didn't seem that interested in attempting an intercept. That was probably just as well because we picked up an escort of two dozen F-18s while still over Mexico.

They'd hauled ass out of Pearl Harbor when we took off from Las Vegas, bringing their own flying gas station with them. Personally, I was more than thrilled to have them formed up on each wing. I'd had about enough of being shot at for a while.

"Whatcha doin', boss?"

I looked up from the notepad I was scribbling on to see Nitro lower his bulk into the seat next to mine.

"Writing up a couple of recommendations for the Admiral to review," I said, scrawling my signature across the bottom of one of the pages. "By the way, any idea what the Navy awards that's equivalent to our Distinguished Service Cross?"

"No clue," he said, shrugging his shoulders and raising his voice. "Hey? Any of you squids know what's equivalent to a DSC in the Army?"

Exodus

"Yeah, it's called a tampon," Goose answered, earning a thrown boot to the head from Bunny who was a former Army Ranger.

"Navy Cross," Monk said.

"Who you nominating?" Nitro asked, glaring at Goose and Bunny to prevent things from getting out of hand.

"Vance," I said, earning a nod of agreement.

"He deserves it. Any man that'll keep his mouth shut to protect some civilians, all while getting his nut sack split open, is OK in my book."

I nodded, filling in the blank space I'd left at the beginning of the letter now that I knew what to call the medal.

"Who else?" Nitro asked.

"What?"

"You said a couple of nominations. That means two."

"Goddamn, Nitro. When did you learn to count?" I asked.

He glared at me for a moment, then flexed his massive arms as he shook his head.

"Here," I said, holding out the pad. "Read this."

The nomination wasn't long, in fact, less than a page. Nitro read it quickly, going very still, then reread it much slower. He handed it to me and tilted his head back onto the seat.

"That's good," he said. "Thanks for only talking about what she did at the end."

"Was it really her fault?" I asked, signing the nomination for Anna to receive a posthumous Distinguished Service Cross.

"No, but she thought it was," Nitro said.

"Why?"

"Because she wouldn't let us deal with the bullshit when it started. Thought she could reason with William, the militia leader. Only there wasn't no reasoning with that motherfucker."

"Could've taken matters into your own hands," I said softly.

"Thought about it," Nitro said. "Only thing that stopped me was worrying what would happen to her if things went bad for us."

"I didn't mean anything by that," I said, realizing how my comment must have sounded.

"Known and fought with you too long," Nitro sighed. "Knew what you meant."

Exodus

We sat quietly for several minutes, each of us lost in our own thoughts.

"So, what now?" He asked. "Gonna settle down with Rachel and raise pineapples?"

When he mentioned her name, I automatically looked for Rachel. She was leaned over Igor, treating the wounds inflicted by the females. Some needed to be stitched up, some just cleaned and dressed. She was worried about infection and had already had Vance call ahead to Pearl Harbor to request a waiting ambulance.

I'd questioned her fear, being told that the sheer number of wounds, from both bites and slashing nails, guaranteed a bacterial infection. If left untreated, or not treated as quickly as possible, there was the very real possibility of a runaway infection that could lead to sepsis and death. But, with proper care, he'd quickly be back on his feet.

"Australia," I said, still watching Rachel work.

"What's there?"

"The man that started all of this," I said. "He and I have an appointment."

Nitro grunted, turning his head to look at me after a stretch of silence.

"Want company?" He asked.

Dirk Patton

The rising sun chased us across the Pacific Ocean. It lit the water beneath us, turning it an incredible shade of blue as we began our descent to the Honolulu International Airport, which shares runways with Hickam Field. I had moved forward to sit with Rachel, Dog crowded in between us with his chin on my boot.

"There's hardly any traffic on the roads!"

Rachel had the window seat and was looking at the ground as we approached the airport.

"Probably very little gas available to the public," I said. "Certainly not enough for anyone to be driving that doesn't have a legitimate need to be doing so."

Igor, across the aisle, groaned, drawing our attention. He lifted his head and looked around, not understanding where he was. Irina quickly leaned forward and spoke softly in his ear, then placed a lingering kiss on his cheek as she took his hand. She glanced in my direction, then returned her attention to Igor.

"What the hell's going on there?" Rachel whispered in my ear.

I took her hand and ignored the question.

"I'm going to Australia as soon as I can," I said. "I expect the Admiral will object if he finds out what I'm planning."

Exodus

"Didn't you give me a speech about this being the real world and there are rules we have to follow?" I turned and looked at her, not having a good response. "Isn't it time to stop fighting? Hasn't there been enough death? Anyway, you need surgery to remove that bullet fragment. The longer you wait, the greater the possibility that the damage can't be repaired. You could lose your eye permanently."

I thought about what she said, and truth be told, I was sorely tempted. Finding a little shack on an isolated beach for us, and Dog, sounded damn good. Besides, Barinov was an old man. What would I really achieve by killing him? Was robbing him of three or four years to satisfy my desire for revenge worth continuing to risk my life? Was that what Katie would want, or would she tell me to find whatever happiness I could in what was left of the world?

"I'll think about it," I said as the landing gear thumped onto the runway.

"Look at that!"

I glanced around when Nitro spoke. He had his face pressed to a window, and I turned and leaned across Rachel to see outside the aircraft.

The runway was lined with people. People in uniform. Hundreds, no, thousands of them. Packed in, shoulder to shoulder and three or four deep. It seemed as if every other person was holding an American flag, the red, white and blue gleaming in the early morning sun.

"What the hell?" I breathed, in shock at the turnout. "Who are they here for?"

I looked across the cabin, seeing the same thing on the opposite side of the runway. The plane was slowing, Vance not using the thrust reversers in deference to the crowds standing at the edge of the tarmac. Dog sat up and sneezed, and I took advantage of the moment to step into the cockpit.

The display was even more impressive from the front where I could see the extra-long stretch of asphalt extending into the distance. For as far as it went, flags waved, and people seemed to be cheering.

"Guess all the ladies of Oahu heard I was coming back," Vance said.

"See a lot of husbands out there. You might want to stay on the plane," I said, earning a chuckle from the pilot.

A few hundred yards ahead a large group stood to the side, clustered around several Humvees. Next to them was a set of truck mounted air stairs and an ambulance with flashing roof lights. A man in an Air Force uniform was standing in the center of the runway, wearing a pair of bright orange gloves that extended to his elbows. Vance slowed us to taxi speed, then followed his directions until we were brought to a full stop. He cut the engines, and they spooled down with a whine that descended the scale to a low groan before going silent.

Quickly, there was a pounding on the cabin door, and Nitro popped it open. Fresh sea air flooded into the plane, flushing out the funk of fighting men who haven't had a shower in far too long. Two Air Force enlisted stood on the air stairs, looking in curiously as the door swung fully open.

"Wounded first," I said.

"How many, sir?" The senior of the two asked.

"Two," I said. "Get litters."

He turned away and raised a radio to his mouth to relay the request.

"Fuck that," Vance said. "I can walk."

"No, you don't!" Rachel had come up behind me. "The more you walk, the more stress you put on your... injury. Just lay back and do what I tell you."

Vance looked at her and grinned.

"You don't know how long I've been waiting for you to say that, sweetie!"

"Call me sweetie again, and I'll finish the job they started," Rachel said, smiling at him.

"Long as you're gentle," Vance said.

Thankfully, two pairs of Air Force corpsman arrived at that moment with the requested litters. Irina hovered as Goose and I carefully loaded Igor and tightened the straps. Two of the medics stepped forward to carry him, but Goose shooed them away. He and Johnson lifted the big Russian and carefully made their way through the open door and onto the stairs, Irina close behind.

"OK, your turn," I said to Vance.

Nitro and I squeezed into the cockpit and gently lifted him out of the pilot's seat, carrying him back to the cabin where we loaded him onto the second litter. I didn't fail to notice several grunts of pain as we moved him, nor the greasy sheen of sweat that coated his face.

"No," he said when we started to pick up the litter. "Pilot always goes last."

I looked at him for a beat, shaking my head, then turned and told Bunny and Monk to get all the girls off the plane. Gonzales placed Nicole amongst them, her shades firmly in place, then brought up the rear of the group. Rachel squeezed my arm and followed them out.

"Thank you," Vance said when all that was left were me, Dog and Nitro.

"Don't thank me yet," I said as we squatted and lifted him between us. "Can't see too well with only one eye. Might trip and drop you on the way down."

Exodus

Nitro took the lead, carrying the end of the litter with Vance's feet. I had his head and, despite, or perhaps because of my little joke, I moved carefully. Dog stayed a step behind, nails clicking loudly on the aluminum treads of the air stairs. At ground level, we deposited Vance onto a gurney and the corpsman whisked him to the waiting ambulance.

Turning, I came to attention and brought up a salute as Admiral Packard stepped forward. He returned it with a smile then extended his hand. As I shook it, I noticed Colonels Blanchard and Pointere standing to his rear, and several other familiar faces behind them. A hulking Marine in full battle rattle stood close to the Admiral's side, eyeing the weapons on my body, as well as Dog.

"Major, it is a pleasure to finally meet you in person," the Admiral said.

"Thank you, sir," I said. "And thank you for everything you've done."

"Don't thank me yet," he said. "We need to have a conversation. Do you need to go to medical for that eye?"

"No, sir," I said. "I'm good to go."

"No, he's not!"

The Admiral looked over my shoulder and I sighed when Rachel interrupted.

"Maybe I should see a doctor, sir," I said in resignation.

Packard smiled again and nodded.

"Find me as soon as you've done that, Major. And, welcome to Pearl Harbor!"

"Yes, sir, I will. Thank you, sir."

We exchanged salutes again, then the Admiral turned and swept through the assembled crowd, half a dozen Marines forming a tight bubble around him and clearing people out of the way. Blanchard and Pointere stepped forward, each shaking my hand and telling me how glad they were to see me.

"What's all this?" I asked Colonel Blanchard, waving at the crowd that was pressing in, seemingly wanting a closer look at me.

"You're quite the celebrity," he grinned. "Seems word about you has gotten out. Everything you've done, but especially how you surrendered to the Russians to save Hawaii."

I didn't know what to say, just stood there looking around, overwhelmed by the sheer size of the crowd.

"I'll let you adjust to it," Blanchard said, shaking my hand again before turning away.

Exodus

As soon as he was gone, Chico and Drago hurried forward, each of them feeling the need to wrap me up in a hug. I hid my dislike for this type of greeting from another man and exchanged a few words with each, promising to let them buy me a beer at the first opportunity. When they stepped aside, a short, blonde girl wearing a Chief Petty Officer's uniform came to attention and saluted me.

"Hello, sir," Jessica said when I returned the greeting.

Unconcerned about military decorum, I stepped forward and surprised her when I folded her into my arms and lifted her feet off the ground. I held her for a few seconds before gently putting her back on the asphalt. Laughter and a few cheers erupted from the surrounding crowd, many wearing enlisted rank, but more than a few officers also pressing in.

"I can't ever repay you, Chief!" I said, trying not to grin at the blush on her face.

"I can say the same, sir," she said, a huge smile on her face.

Dog, curious about someone I was obviously so fond of, pushed in and bumped his head against her hip. If I'd had any doubt that she was a good person, it would have vanished when she dropped to a knee to rub his neck.

53

William Atherton drank deeply from the bottle of water, sighing as he drained the last drop. It had been an arduous journey, returning to the bunker from Las Vegas. It was only dumb luck that he hadn't been on the roof of the hangar when the bitch had fired the volley of rockets that had killed his men. Having grown tired of watching the group that was fueling the 747, he'd gone out into the desert for some privacy so he could reflect on what he wanted to do next.

He'd been standing there, lost in thought, when the Super Cobra had come screaming in and attacked. In horror, he'd watched as the rockets roared out of its weapon's pod, then a gasp escaped his lips when the Stinger missile reached out and slammed into the helicopter.

It had staggered in the air, the tail boom shearing off a moment before it crashed to the ground, less than fifty yards from where he was standing. Frozen in place by the sudden turn of events, he'd been shocked when the armored canopy over the cockpit began to move. The pilot was still alive!

Without a plan, he raced forward and looked through the spiderwebbed glass, stunned when the General looked back at him. Tearing the canopy open, he reached in and dragged her bleeding body onto the tarmac. Looking up, he saw the utter devastation she'd wrought on his men and began to reach for his pistol, intending to shoot her in the head.

Flames sprang up among the wreckage, feeding on a ruptured fuel tank and staying his hand. Not knowing what he'd do with her, he leaned down and struck her on the side of the head. The blow was too much for her already injured skull, and she lapsed into unconsciousness.

Picking her up, he slung her over his shoulders and ran for the stretch of desert that bordered the runway. He'd hidden behind a runway marker as the other people arrived, but they'd remained at a distance because of the burning helicopter. After it had exploded into an inferno, they'd boarded their vehicle and raced away. Remaining hidden, he'd begun to think they'd encountered a problem when the 747 finally roared into the night and climbed away from the Nevada desert.

Gathering the General into his arms, he carried her inert form to the parked Humvees he and his men had arrived in. One of them was completely buried in debris, but with a little effort he cleared the other and tossed her into the back. He had drawn a large group of infected, but was able to climb behind the wheel and race away before they reached him.

Finally arriving at the bunker that had saved him and his people from the attacks and ensuing infection, he was dismayed to find only three of his followers. They had somehow survived the assault on the Air Force facility at Groom Lake. Now, they were securely locked inside, safe from the horrors that prowled the world above.

William turned at the rustle of fabric from the far side of the room. Anna lay on a hospital gurney, securely strapped down. She was regaining consciousness, slowly turning her head from side to side. Striding across the room, he loomed over her, staring at her face. When her eyes finally opened, they were unfocused, but he could tell she was aware of his presence.

"Hello, bitch," he said.

Printed in Great Britain
by Amazon